ase of Exploding Mangoes

A Case of Exploding Mangoes

Mohammed Hanif

W F HOWES LTD

This large print edition published in 2008 by
W F Howes Ltd
Unit 4, Rearsby Business Park, Gaddesby Lane,
Rearsby, Leicester LE7 4YH

1 3 5 7 9 10 8 6 4 2

First published in the United Kingdom in 2008
by Jonathan Cape

A CIP catalogue record for this book is available
from the British Library

ISBN 978 1 40742 994 6

Typeset by Palimpsest Book Production Limited,
Grangemouth, Stirlingshire
Printed and bound in Great Britain
by MPG Books Ltd, Bodmin, Cornwall

FSC
Mixed Sources
Product group from well-managed
forests and other controlled sources
Cert no. SGS-COC-2953
www.fsc.org
© 1996 Forest Stewardship Council

For Fatima, Razia, Nimra
& Channan

PROLOGUE

You might have seen me on TV after the crash. The clip is short and everything in it is sun-bleached and slightly faded. It was pulled after the first two bulletins because it seemed to be having an adverse impact on the morale of the country's armed forces. You can't see it in the clip but we are walking towards Pak One, which is parked behind the cameraman's back, in the middle of the runway. The aeroplane is still connected to an auxiliary fuel pump, and surrounded by a group of alert commandos in camouflaged uniforms. With its dull grey fuselage barely off the ground, the plane looks like a beached whale contemplating how to drag itself back to the sea, its snout drooping with the enormity of the task ahead.

The runway is in the middle of Bahawalpur Desert, six hundred miles away from the Arabian Sea. There is nothing between the sun's white fury and the endless expanse of shimmering sand except a dozen men in khaki uniforms walking towards the plane.

For a brief moment you can see General Zia's face in the clip, the last recorded memory of a much photographed man. The middle parting in his hair glints under the sun, his unnaturally white teeth flash, his moustache does its customary little dance for the camera, but as the camera pulls out you can tell that he is not smiling. If you watch closely you can probably tell that he is in some discomfort. He is walking the walk of a constipated man.

The man walking on his right is the US Ambassador to Pakistan, Arnold Raphel, whose shiny bald head and carefully groomed moustache give him the air of a respectable homosexual businessman from small-town America. He can be seen flicking an invisible speck of sand from the lapel of his navy-blue blazer. His smart casual look hides a superior diplomatic mind; he is a composer of sharp, incisive memos and has the ability to remain polite in the most hostile exchanges. On General Zia's left, his former spymaster and the head of Inter Services Intelligence General Akhtar seems weighed down by half a dozen medals on his chest and drags his feet as if he is the only man in the group who knows that they shouldn't be boarding this plane. His lips are pinched and, even when the sun has boiled everything into submission and drained all colour out of the surroundings, you can see that his normally pale skin has turned a wet yellow. His obituary in the next day's newspapers would describe him as the Silent Soldier and one of the ten men standing between the Free World and the Red Army.

As they approach the red carpet that leads to the

Pak One stairway you can see me step forward. You can tell immediately that I am the only one in the frame smiling, but when I salute and start walking towards the aeroplane, my smile vanishes. I know I am saluting a bunch of dead men. But if you are in uniform, you salute. That's all there is to it.

Later, forensic experts from Lockheed will put the pieces of crashed plane together and simulate scenarios, trying to unlock the mystery of how a superfit C130 came tumbling down from the skies only four minutes after take-off. Astrologists will pull out files with their predictions for August 1988, and blame Jupiter for the crash that killed Pakistan's top army brass as well as the US Ambassador. Leftist intellectuals will toast the end of a cruel dictatorship and evoke historic dialectics in such matters.

But this afternoon, history is taking a long siesta, as it usually does between the end of one war and the beginning of another. More than a hundred thousand Soviet soldiers are preparing to retreat from Afghanistan after being reduced to eating toast smeared with military-issue boot polish, and these men we see in the TV clip are the undisputed victors. They are preparing for peace and, being the cautious men they are, they have come to Bahawalpur to shop for tanks while waiting for the end of the cold war. They have done their day's work and are taking the plane back home. With their stomachs full, they are running out of small talk; there is the impatience of polite people who do not want to offend each other. It's only later that people would say, *Look at that clip, look at their tired, reluctant walk, anybody can tell that they were being shepherded to that plane by the invisible hand of death.*

The generals' families will get full compensation and receive flag-draped coffins with strict instructions not to open them. The pilots' families will be picked up and thrown into cells with blood-splattered ceilings for a few days and then let go. The US Ambassador's body will be taken back to Arlington Cemetery and his tombstone would be adorned with a half-elegant cliché. There will be no autopsies, the leads will run dry, investigations will be blocked, there will be cover-ups to cover cover-ups. Third World dictators are always blowing up in strange circumstances but if the brightest star in the US diplomatic service (and that's what was said about Arnold Raphel at the funeral service in Arlington Cemetery) goes down with eight Pakistani generals, somebody would be expected to kick ass. *Vanity Fair* will commission an investigative piece, the *New York Times* will write two editorials, sons of the deceased will file petitions to the court and then settle for lucrative cabinet posts. It would be said that this was the biggest cover-up in aviation history since the last biggest cover-up.

The only witness to that televised walk, the only one to have walked that walk, would be completely ignored.

Because if you missed that clip, you probably missed me. Like history itself. I was the one who got away.

What they found in the wreckage of the plane were not bodies, not serene-faced martyrs, as the army claimed, not the slightly damaged, disfigured men not photogenic enough to be shown to the TV cameras or to their families. *Remains*. They found *remains*. Bits of flesh splattered on the broken aeroplane parts, charred bones sticking to mangled metal, severed limbs and faces melted into blobs of pink meat. Nobody can ever say that the coffin that was buried in Arlington Cemetery didn't carry bits of General Zia's remains and what lies buried in Shah Faisal mosque in Islamabad are not some of the remains of the State Department's brightest star. The only thing that can be said with certainty is that my remains weren't in either of those coffins.

Yes, sir, I was the one who got away.

The name Shigri didn't figure in the terms of reference, the investigators from the FBI ignored me and I never had to sit under a naked bulb and explain the circumstances that led to me being present at the scene of the incident. I didn't even figure in the stories concocted to cover up the truth. Even the conspiracy theories which saw an unidentified flying object colliding with the presidential plane, or deranged eyewitnesses who saw a surface-to-air missile being fired from a lone donkey's back didn't bother to spin any yarns about the boy in uniform with one hand on the

5

scabbard of his sword, stepping forward, saluting, then smiling and walking away. I was the only one who boarded that plane and survived.

Even got a lift back home.

If you did see the clip you might have wondered what this boy with mountain features is doing in the desert, why he is surrounded by four-star generals, why he is smiling. It's because I have had my punishment. As Obaid would have said, there is poetry in committing a crime after you have served your sentence. I do not have much interest in poetry but punishment before a crime does have a certain sing-song quality to it. The guilty commit the crime, the innocent are punished. That's the world we live in.

My punishment had started exactly two months and seventeen days before the crash when I woke up at reveille and without opening my eyes reached out to pull back Obaid's blanket, a habit picked up from four years of sharing the same room with him. It was the only way to wake him up. My hand caressed an empty bed. I rubbed my eyes. The bed was freshly made, a starched white sheet tucked over a grey wool blanket, like a Hindu widow in mourning. Obaid was gone and the buggers would obviously suspect me.

You can blame our men in uniform for anything, but you can never blame them for being imaginative.

FORM PD 4059
Record of Absentees without Leave or
Disappearances without Justifiable Causes

Appendix 1
Statement by Junior Under Officer Ali Shigri,
Pak No. 898245

Subject: Investigation into the circumstances in
which Cadet Obaid-ul-llah went AWOL

Location where statement was recorded: Cell No. 2,
Main Guardroom, Cadets' Mess, PAF Academy

I, Junior Under Officer Ali Shigri, son of the late
Colonel Quli Shigri, do hereby solemnly affirm and
declare that, at the reveille on the morning of 31
May 1988, I was the duty officer. I arrived at 0630
hours sharp to inspect Fury Squadron. As I was
inspecting the second row, I realised that the sash
on my sword belt was loose. I tried to tighten it.
The sash came off in my hand. I ran towards my
barracks to get a replacement and shouted at Cadet
Atiq to take charge. I ordered the squadron to mark
time. I could not find my spare sash in my own
cupboard; I noticed that Cadet Obaid's cupboard

7

was open. His sash was lying where it is supposed to be, on the first shelf, right-hand corner, behind his golden-braided peaked cap. Because I was in a hurry I didn't notice anything unlawful in the cupboard. I did, however, notice that the poem on the inside of the door of his cupboard was missing. I do not have much interest in poetry but since Obaid was my dorm mate I knew that every month he liked to post a new poem in his cupboard but always removed it before the weekly cupboard inspection. Since the Academy's Standard Operating Procedures do not touch upon the subject of posting poetry in dorm cupboards I had not reported this matter earlier. I arrived back at 0643 to find that the entire squadron was in Indian position. I immediately told them to stand up and come to attention and reminded Cadet Atiq that the Indian position was unlawful as a punishment and as an acting squadron commander he should have known the rules. Later, I recommended Cadet Atiq for a red strip, copy of which can be provided as an appendix to this appendix.

I didn't have the time for a roll call at this point as we had only seventeen minutes left before it was time to report to the parade ground. Instead of marching Fury Squadron to the mess hall, I ordered them to move on the double. Although I was wearing my sword for that day's silent drill practice and was not supposed to move on the double, I ran with the last file, holding the scabbard six inches from my body. Second Officer in Command saw us from his Yamaha and slowed down when passing us. I ordered the squadron to salute but 2nd OIC did not return my salute and made a joke about my sword and two legs. The joke cannot be reproduced in this statement but I mention this fact because some doubts were raised in the interrogation about whether I accompanied the squadron at all.

I gave Fury Squadron four minutes for breakfast and I myself waited on the steps leading to the dining hall. During this time I stood at ease and in my head went through the commands for the day's drill. This is an exercise that Drill Instructor on Secondment, Lieutenant Bannon, has taught me. Although there are no verbal commands in the silent drill, the commander's inner voice must remain at strength 5. It should obviously not be audible to the person standing next to him. I was still practising my silent cadence when the squadron began to assemble outside the dining hall. I carried out a quick inspection of the squadron and caught one first-termer with a slice of French toast in his uniform shirt pocket. I stuffed the toast into his mouth and ordered him to start front-rolling and keep pace with the squadron as I marched them to the parade square.

I handed over command to the Sergeant of the Day, who marched the boys to the armoury to get their rifles. It was only after the Quran recitation and the national anthem were over, and the Silent Drill Squad was dividing into two formations, that the Sergeant of the Day came to ask me why

Cadet Obaid had not reported for duty. He was supposed to be the file leader for that day's drill rehearsal. I was surprised because I had thought all along that he was in the squadron that I had just handed over to the Sergeant.

'Is he on sick parade?' he asked me.

'No, Sergeant,' I said. 'Or if he is I don't know about it.'

'And who is supposed to know?'

I shrugged my shoulders, and before the Sergeant could say anything Lieutenant Bannon announced that silent zone was in effect. I must put it on record that most of our Academy drill sergeants do not appreciate the efforts of Lieutenant Bannon in trying to establish our own Silent Drill Squad. They resent his drill techniques. They do not understand that there is nothing that impresses civilians more than a silent drill display, and we have much to learn from Lieutenant Bannon's experience as the Chief Drill Instructor at Fort Bragg.

After the drill I went to the sickbay to check if Cadet Obaid had reported sick. I didn't find him there. As I was coming out of the sickbay I saw the first-termer from my squadron sitting in the waiting area with bits of vomited toast on his uniform shirt's front. He stood up to salute me, I told him to keep sitting and stop disgracing himself further.

As the Character Building Lecture had already started, instead of going to the classroom, I returned to my dorm. I asked our washerman Uncle Starchy to fix my belt, and I rested for a while on my bed. I also searched Obaid's bed, his side table and his cupboard to find any clues as to where he might be. I did not notice anything untoward in these areas. Cadet Obaid has been winning the Inter Squadron Cupboard Competition since his first term at the Academy and everything was arranged according to the dorm cupboard manual.

I attended all the rest of the classes that day. I was marked present in those classes. In Regional Studies we were taught about Tajikstan and the resurgence of Islam. In Islamic Studies we were ordered to do self-study because our teacher Maulana Hidayatullah was angry with us because when he entered the class some cadets were singing a dirty variation on a folk wedding song.

It was during the afternoon drill rehearsal that I got my summons from the 2nd OIC's office. I was asked to report on the double and I reported there in uniform.

The 2nd OIC asked me why I had not marked Cadet Obaid absent in the morning inspection when he wasn't there.

I told him that I had not taken the roll call.

He asked me if I knew where he was.

I said I didn't know.

He asked me where I had disappeared to between the sickbay and the Character Building Lecture.

I told him the truth.

He asked me to report to the guardroom.

When I arrived at the guardroom, the guardroom duty cadet told me to wait in the cell.

When I asked him whether I was under detention he laughed and made a joke about the cell mattress having too many holes. The joke cannot be reproduced in this statement.

Half an hour later 2nd OIC arrived and informed me that I was under close arrest and he wanted to ask me some questions about the disappearance of Cadet Obaid. He told me that if I didn't tell him the truth he'd hand me over to Inter Services Intelligence and they would hang me by my testicles.

I assured him of my full cooperation. 2nd OIC questioned me for one hour and forty minutes about Obaid's activities, my friendship with him and whether I had noticed anything strange in his behaviour in what he described as 'the days leading up to his disappearance'.

I told him all I knew. He went out of the cell at the end of the question–answer session and came back five minutes later with some sheets of paper and a pen and asked me to write everything that had happened in the morning and describe in detail where and when I had last seen Cadet Obaid.

Before leaving the cell he asked me if I had any questions. I asked him whether I'd be able to attend the silent drill rehearsal as we were preparing for the President's annual inspection. I requested 2nd OIC to inform Lieutenant Bannon that I could continue to work on my silent cadence in the cell. 2nd OIC made a joke about two marines and a bar of soap in a Fort Bragg bathroom. I didn't think I was supposed to laugh and I didn't.

I hereby declare that I saw Cadet Obaid last when he was lying in his bed reading a book of poetry in English the night before his disappearance. The book had a red cover and what looked like a lengthened shadow of a man. I don't remember the name of the book. After lights out I heard him sing an old Indian song in a low voice. I asked him to shut up. The last thing I remember before going to sleep is that he was still humming the same song.

I did not see him in the morning and I have described my day's activities accurately in this statement in the presence of the undersigned.

In closing I would like to state that in the days leading up to Cadet Obaid absenting himself without any plausible cause, I did not notice anything unusual about his conduct. Only three days before going AWOL he had received his fourth green strip for taking active part in After Dinner Literary Activities (ADLA). He had made plans to take me out at the weekend for ice cream and to watch Where Eagles Dare. If he had any plans about absenting himself without any justifiable cause he never shared them with me or anyone else as far as I know.

I also wish to humbly request that my close arrest is uncalled for and if I cannot be allowed to return to my dorm I should be allowed to keep the

command of my Silent Drill Squad because
tomorrow's battles are won in today's practice.

Statement signed and witnessed by:
Squadron Leader Karimullah, 2nd OIC,
PAF Academy

LIFE IS IN ALLAH'S HANDS BUT . . .

CHAPTER 1

There is something about these bloody squadron leaders that makes them think that if they lock you up in a cell, put their stinking mouth to your ear and shout something about your mother they can find all the answers. They are generally a sad lot, these leaders without any squadrons to lead. It's their own lack of leadership qualities that stops them mid-career, nowhere for them to go except from one training institute to another, permanent seconds in command to one commander or the other. You can tell them from their belts, loose and low, straining under the weight of their paunches. Or from their berets, so carefully positioned to hide that shiny bald patch. Schemes for part-time MBAs and a new life are trying hard to keep pace with missed promotions and pension plans.

Look at the arrangement of fruit salad on my tormentor's chest above the left pocket of his uniform shirt and you can read his whole biography. A faded paratrooper's badge is the only thing that he had to leave his barracks to earn. The medals in the first row just came and pinned themselves to his chest. He got them because he was there. The 40th Independence Day medal. The Squadron Anniversary medal. Today-I-did-not-jerk-off medal. Then the second row, fruits of his own hard labour and leadership. One for organising a squash tournament, another for the great battle that was tree-plantation week. The leader with his mouth to my ear and my mother on his mind has had a freebie to Mecca and is wearing a haj medal too.

As Obaid used to say, 'God's glory. God's glory. For every monkey there is a houri.'

2nd OIC is wasting more of his already wasted life trying to break me down with his bad breath and his incessant shouting. Doesn't he know that I actually invented some of the bullshit that he is pouring into my ear? Hasn't he heard about the Shigri treatment? Doesn't he know that I used to get invited to other squadrons in the middle of the night to make the new arrivals cry with my three-minute routine about their mothers? Does he really think that fuck-your-fucking mother, even when delivered at strength 5, still has any meaning when you are weeks away from the President's annual inspection and becoming a commissioned officer?

The theory used to be damn simple: any good soldier learns to shut out the noise and de-link such expressions from their apparent meaning. I mean, when they say that thing about your mother, they have absolutely no intention – and

I am certain no desire either – to do what they say they want to do with your mother. They say it because it comes out rapid-fire and sounds cool and requires absolutely no imagination. The last syllable of 'mother' reverberates in your head for a while as it is delivered with their lips glued to your ear. And that is just about that. They have not even *seen* your poor mother.

Anybody who breaks down at the sheer volume of this should stay in his little village and tend his father's goats or should study biology and become a doctor and then they can have all the bloody peace and quiet they want. Because as a soldier, noise is the first thing you learn to defend yourself against, and as an officer noise is the first weapon of attack you learn to use.

Unless you are in the Silent Drill Squad.

Look at the parade square during the morning drill and see who commands it. Who rules? There are more than one thousand of us, picked from a population of one hundred and thirty million, put through psychological and physical tests so strenuous that only one in a hundred applicants makes it, and when this cream of our nation, as we are constantly reminded we are, arrives here, who leads them? The one with the loudest voice, the one with the clearest throat, the one whose chest can expand to produce a command that stuns the morning crows and makes the most stubborn of cadets raise their knees to waist level and bring the world to a standstill as their heels land on the concrete.

Or at least that is what I believed before Lieutenant Bannon arrived with his theories about inner cadence, silent commands, and subsonic drill techniques. 'A drill with commands is just that – a drill,' Bannon is fond of saying. 'A drill without commands is an art. When you deliver a command at the top of your voice, only the boys in your squadron listen. But when your inner cadence whispers, the gods take notice.'

Not that Bannon believes in any god.

I wonder whether he'll visit me here. I wonder whether they will let him into this cell.

2nd OIC is exhausted from his business with my mother and I can see an appeal to my better sense on its way. I clench my stomach muscles against the impending 'cream of the nation' speech. I don't want to throw up. The cell is small and I have no idea how long I am going to be here.

'You are the cream of our nation,' he says shaking his head. 'You have been the pride of our Academy. I have just recommended you for the sword of honour. You are going to receive it from the President of Pakistan. You have two choices: graduate with honour in four weeks or go out front-rolling to the sound of drums. Tomorrow. Clap. Clap. Tony Singh style.' He brings his hands together twice, like those Indian film extras in a qawwali chorus.

They did that to Tony Singh. Drummed the poor bugger out. I never figured out what the hell Tony

Singh was doing in the air force of the Islamic Republic anyway. Before meeting Tony Singh (or Sir Tony as we had to call him since he was six courses senior to us), the only Tony I knew was our neighbour's dog and the only Singh I had seen was in my history textbook, a one-eyed maharaja who ruled Punjab a couple of centuries ago. I thought the Partition took care of all the Tonys and the Singhs, but apparently some didn't get the message.

Tony Singh didn't get the message even when they found a transistor radio in his dorm and charged him with spying. *Top of the Pops* was Sir Tony's defence. They reduced the charge to un-officer-like behaviour and drummed him out anyway.

A lone drummer – a corporal who, after carrying the biggest drum in the Academy band all his life, had begun to look like one – led the way; keeping a thud, thud, thud-a-dud marching beat. More than one thousand of us lined both sides of Eagles Avenue that leads from the guardroom to the main gate.

At ease, came the command.

Tony Singh emerged from the guardroom, having spent a couple of nights in this very cell. His head was shaved, but he still wore his uniform. He stood tall and refused to look down or sideways.

Clap, came the command.

We started slowly. 2nd OIC removed Sir Tony's belt and the ranks from his shoulder flaps and then he took a step forward and whispered something into Sir Tony's ear. Sir Tony went down on

21

his knees, put both his hands on the road and did a front roll without touching his shaved head on the ground.

The bugger was trying to be cocky even when his ass was raised to the skies.

His journey was painfully slow. The drumbeat became unbearable after a while. Some cadets clapped more enthusiastically than others.

I glanced sideways and saw Obaid trying hard to control his tears.

'Sir, I swear to God I have no knowledge of Cadet Obaid's whereabouts,' I say, trying to tread the elusive line between grovelling and spitting in his face.

2nd OIC wants to get home. An evening of domestic cruelty and *Baywatch* beckons him. He waves my statement in front of me. 'You have one night to think this through. Tomorrow it goes to the Commandant and the only thing he hates more than his men disappearing is their clever-dick collaborators. He is looking forward to the President's visit. We are all looking forward to the visit. Don't fuck it up.'

He turns to go. My upper body slumps. He puts one hand on the door handle and turns; my upper body comes back to attention. 'I saw your father once, and he was a soldier's bloody soldier. Look at yourself.' A leery grin appears on his lips. 'You mountain boys get lucky because you have no hair on your face.'

I salute him, using all my silent drill practice to contain the inner cadence, which is saying, 'Fuck your mother too.'

I wonder for a moment what Obaid would do in this cell. The first thing that would have bothered him is the smell 2nd OIC has left behind. This burnt onions, home-made yogurt gone bad smell. The smell of suspicion, the smell of things not quite having gone according to plan. Because our Obaid, our Baby O, believes that there is nothing in the world that a splash of Poison on your wrist and an old melody can't take care of.

He is innocent in a way that lonesome canaries are innocent, flitting from one branch to another, the tender flutter of their wings and a few millilitres of blood keeping them airborne against the gravity of this world that wants to pull everyone down to its rotting surface.

What chance would Obaid have with this 2nd OIC? Baby O, the whisperer of ancient couplets, the singer of golden oldies. How did he make it through the selection process? How did he manage to pass the Officer-Like Qualities Test? How did he lead his fellow candidates through the mock jungle survival scenarios? How did he bluff his way through the psychological profiles?

All they needed to do was pull down his pants and see his silk briefs with the little embroidered hearts on the waistband.

Where are you, Baby O?

★   ★   ★

Lieutenant Bannon saw us for the first time at the annual variety show doing our Dove and Hawk dance. This was before the Commandant replaced these variety shows with Quran Study Circles and After Dinner Literary Activities. As third-termers we had to do all the shitty fancy-dress numbers and seniors got to lip-sync to George Michael songs. We were miming to a very macho, revolutionary poem. I, the imperialist Eagle, swooped down on Obaid's Third World Dove; he fought back, and for the finale sat on my chest drawing blood from my neck with his cardboard beak.

Bannon came to meet us backstage as we were shedding our ridiculous feathers. 'Hooah, you zoomies should be in Hollywood!' His handshake was exaggerated and firm. 'Good show. Good show.' He turned towards Obaid, who was cleaning the brown boot polish from his cheeks with a hankie. 'You're just a kid without that warpaint,' Bannon said. 'What's your name?'

In the background, Sir Tony's 'Careless Whisper' was so out of tune that the speakers screeched in protest.

Under his crimson beret, Bannon's face was beaten leather, his eyes shallow green pools that had not seen a drop of rain in years.

'Obaid. Obaid-ul-llah.'

'What does it mean?'

'Allah's servant,' said Obaid, sounding unsure, as if he should explain that he didn't choose this name for himself.

'What does your name mean, Lieutenant Bannon?' I came to Obaid's rescue.

'It's just a name,' he said. 'Nobody calls me Lieutenant. It's Loot Bannon for you stage mamas.' He clicked his heels together and turned back to Obaid. We both came to attention. He directed his over-the-top, two-fingered salute at Obaid and said the words which in that moment seemed like just another case of weird US military-speak but would later become the stuff of dining-hall gossip.

'See you at the square, Baby O.'

I felt jealous, not because of the intimacy it implied, but because I wished I had come up with this nickname for Obaid.

I make a mental note of the things they could find in the dorm to throw at me:

1. One-quarter of a quarter-bottle of Murree rum
2. A group photo of first-termers in their underwear (white and December-wet underwear actually).
3. A video of *Love on a Horse*.
4. Bannon's dog-tags, still listed as missing on the guardroom's Lost and Found noticeboard.

If my Shigri blood wasn't so completely void of any literary malaise, I would have listed poetry as

Exhibit 5, but who the fuck really thinks about poetry when locked up in a cell unless you are a communist or a poet?

There is a letter-box slit in the door of the cell, as if people are going to send me letters. *Dear Ali Shigri, I hope you are in the best of health and enjoying your time in . . .*

I am on my knees, my eyes level with the letter-box slit. I know Obaid would have lifted the flap on the slit and would have sat here looking at the parade of khaki-clad butts, and amused himself by guessing which one belonged to whom. Our Baby O could do a detailed personality analysis just by looking at where and how tightly people wore their belts.

I don't want to lift the flap and find someone looking at me looking at them. The word is probably already out. That butcher Shigri is where he deserves to be, throw away the key.

The flap lifts itself, and the first-termer shitface announces my dinner. 'Buzz off,' I say, regretting it immediately. Empty stomach means bad dreams.

In my dream, there is a Hercules C130, covered with bright flowers like you see on those hippie cars. The plane's propellers are pure white and move in slow motion, spouting jets of jasmine flowers. Baby O stands on the tip of the right wing just behind the propeller, wearing a black silk robe and his ceremonial peaked cap. I stand on the tip of the left wing in full uniform. Baby O is shouting something above the din of the aircraft. I can't really make out any words but his gestures tell me that he is asking me to come to him. As I take the first step towards Baby O, the C130 tilts and goes into a thirty-degree left turn, and suddenly we are sliding along the wings, heading for oblivion. I wake up with one of those screams that echoes through your body but gets stuck in your throat.

In the morning they throw poetry at me. Rilke, for those interested in poetry.

The Officer in Command of our Academy, or the Commandant as he likes to call himself, is a man of sophisticated tastes. Well-groomed hair, uniform privately tailored, Staff and Command College medals polished to perfection. Shoulder flaps full. OK, the crescent and crossed swords of a two-star general haven't arrived, but this guy is having a good time waiting for all of that.

Some crumpled sheets of paper stuffed in the obligatory gash in my mattress are what they find. *Clues*, they think.

I don't read poetry and used to refuse to even pretend to read the strange poetry books that Obaid kept giving me. I always made the excuse that I can only appreciate poetry in Urdu, so he went ahead and translated this German guy's poems into Urdu for my birthday, wrote them in rhyming Urdu since I had also taken a stand against poetry that didn't rhyme. He translated five poems in his beautiful calligrapher's handwriting, all little curves and elegant dashes, and pasted them on the inside of my cupboard.

In the clean-up operation that I carried out the morning of his disappearance, I stuffed them into the mattress, hoping that 2nd OIC would not go that far in his search for the truth.

I have thought of most things and have ready answers, but this one genuinely baffles me. What are they going to charge me with? Rendering foreign poetry into the national language? Abuse of official stationery?

I decide to be straight about it.

The Commandant finds it funny.

'Nice poem,' he says straightening the crumpled paper. 'Instead of the morning drill, we should start daily poetry recitals.'

He turns to 2nd OIC. 'Where did you find it?'

'In his mattress, sir,' 2nd OIC says, feeling pleased with himself, having gone way beyond the call of his bloody duty.

Rilke is crumpled again and the Commandant fixes 2nd OIC with a look that only officers with inherited general-genes are capable of.

'I thought we took care of that problem?'

Serves you right, asshole, my inner cadence booms.

The Commandant has his finger on the pulse of the nation, always adjusting his sails to the winds blowing from the Army House. Expressions like *Almighty Allah* and *Always keep your horses ready because the Russian infidels are coming* have been cropping up in his Orders of the Day lately, but he has not given up on his very secular mission of getting rid of foam mattresses with holes.

'You know why we were a better breed of officers? Not because of Sandhurst-trained instructors. No. Because we slept on thin cotton mattresses, under coarse woollen blankets that felt like a donkey's ass.'

I look beyond his head and survey the presidential inspection photos on the wall, the big shiny trophies caged in a glass cupboard, and try to find Daddy.

Yes, that nine-inch bronze man with pistol is mine. Best Short Range Shooting Shigri Memorial Trophy, named after Colonel Quli Shigri, won by Under Officer Ali Shigri.

I don't want to think right now about Colonel Shigri or the ceiling fan or the bed sheet that connected them. Thinking about Dad and the ceiling fan and the bed sheet always makes me either very angry or very sad. Not the right place for either of these emotions.

'And now look at them,' the Commandant turns towards me. My arms lock themselves to my sides, my neck subtly shifts itself into a position so that I can keep staring at the bronze man.

'Spare me,' I think, 'I didn't invent the bloody technology that makes foam mattresses.'

'And these pansies . . .' Nice new word, I tell myself. This is how he maintains his authority. By coming up with new expressions that you don't really understand but know what they mean for you.

'These pansies sleep on nine-inch thick mattresses under silky bloody duvets and every one of them thinks that he is a Mughal bloody princess on her honeymoon.' He hands over the crumpled Rilke to 2nd OIC, a sign that the interrogation can proceed.

'Is this yours?' 2nd OIC asks, waving the poems in my face. I try to remember something from the poems but get stuck on a half-remembered line about a tree growing out of an ear, which is weird enough in English but sounds completely crazy in rhyming Urdu. I wonder what the bugger was writing in German.

'No, but I know the handwriting,' I say.

'We know the handwriting too,' he says triumphantly. 'What is it doing in your mattress?'

I wish they had found the bottle of rum or the video. Some things are self-explanatory.

I stick with the truth.

'It was a birthday present from Cadet Obaid,' I say. 2nd OIC hands the poems back to the Commandant, as if he has just rested his case whatever the case is.

'I have seen all kinds of buggers in this business,' the Commandant starts slowly. 'But one pansy giving poetry to another pansy, then the other pansy stuffing it in the hole in his mattress is a perversion beyond me.'

I want to tell him how quickly a new word can lose its charm with overuse, but he is not finished yet.

'He thinks he is too smart an ass for us.' He addresses 2nd OIC who is clearly enjoying himself. 'Get ISI to have a word with him.'

I know he is still not finished.

'And listen, boy, you might be a clever dick and you might read all the pansy poetry in the whole world but there is one thing you can't beat. Experience. How is this for poetry? When I started wearing this uniform . . .'

I have a last look at the bronze man with the pistol. Colonel Shigri's bulging eyes stare at me. Not the right place, I tell myself.

The Commandant senses my momentary absent-mindedness and repeats himself. 'When I started wearing this uniform, you were still in liquid form.'

2nd OIC marches me out of the Commandant's office. On my way back I try to avoid the salutes offered by cadets marching past me. I try to pretend I am having a leisurely stroll with 2nd OIC, which will end in my dorm rather than the cell.

All I can think about is the ISI.

It has to be an empty threat. They cannot call in the Inter bloody Services bloody Intelligence just because a cadet has gone AWOL. ISI deals with national security and spies. And who the fuck needs spies these days anyway? The US of A has got satellites with cameras so powerful they can count the exact number of hairs on your bum. Bannon showed us a picture of this satellite and claimed that he had seen bum pictures taken from space but couldn't show them to us because they were classified.

ISI also does drugs but we have never done drugs. OK, we smoked hash once, but in the mountains I come from, hashish is like a spice in the kitchen, for headaches and stuff. Obaid got some from our washerman Uncle Starchy and we smoked one moonlit night in the middle of the parade square. Obaid had a singing fit and I practically had to gag him before bringing him back to our dorm.

I need to get an SOS to Bannon.

Shit on a shingle. Shit on a shingle.

CHAPTER 2

Before morning prayers on 15 June 1988, General Mohammed Zia ul-Haq's index finger hesitated on verse 21:87 while reading the Quran, and he spent the rest of his short life dreaming about the innards of a whale. The verse also triggered a security alert that confined General Zia to his official residence, the Army House. Two months and two days later, he left the Army House for the first time and was killed in an aeroplane crash. The nation rejoiced and never found out that General Zia's journey towards death had started with the slight confusion he experienced over the translation of a verse on that fateful day.

In Marmaduke Pickthall's English translation of the Quran, verse 21:87 reads like this:

And remember Zun-nus, when he departed in wrath: he imagined that We had no power over him! But he cried through the depths of darkness, 'There is no god but thou: glory to thee: I was indeed wrong!'

When General Zia's finger reached the words *I was indeed wrong*, it stopped. He retraced the line with his finger, going over the same words again and again with the hope of teasing out its true implication. This was not what he remembered from his earlier readings of the verse.

In Arabic it says:

لآ إِلَـٰهَ إِلَّآ أَنتَ سُبْحَـٰنَكَ إِنِّى كُنتُ مِنَ ٱلظَّـٰلِمِينَ

Which should translate as:
And I am one of those who oppressed their own souls.

But in this version it said:
I was wrong.

The General knew the story of Jonah well. The fact that Jonah was Zun-nus here did not confuse him. He knew Jonah and Zun-nus were one and the same, a frustrated prophet who walked out on his clan, ended up in a whale's belly, then chanted this verse over and over again till the whale spat him back out, alive and well.

General Zia had taken to reading the English translation of the Quran before his morning prayers because it helped him prepare for his acceptance speech at the Nobel Prize presentation ceremony. For the first time in the history of the prize, he would insist on a recitation from the Quran before his acceptance speech. The prize hadn't been announced yet, but he was hopeful and he was looking for a suitable passage to quote.

Jonah's prayer was not going to be in the speech, but the discrepancy between what General Zia remembered and what he had before him now on the page still bothered him. Absent-mindedly, he shifted his weight and scratched his left buttock on the prayer mat, his index finger still going back and forth over the troublesome verse. The prayer mat was a four feet by two antique carpet from Bukhara, embellished with gold thread, and adorned, on the right-hand corner, with a solid gold compass which permanently pointed towards Khana Kaaba in Mecca.

Presenting it to the General, the second Crown Prince of Saudi Arabia, Prince Naif, had joked, 'This will point you towards Mecca even if you are in space.'

And General Zia had replied with humour characteristic of their relationship, 'And if wishes were Aladdin's carpets, sinners like me would always be flying to Mecca.'

General Zia thought maybe he should deliver his speech in Urdu or polish up his Arabic and surprise his Saudi friends. On his visits to the UN he had met these highly paid women in suits, who translated into all these languages as you spoke. Surely the Swedes could afford them. Then he thought of his good friend Ronald Reagan fidgeting with his headphones, getting restless, and decided to stick to English. Better to look at another translation, he told himself. He got up from the prayer mat, wrapping his Chinese silk nightgown around the bulge of his belly. 'The only civilian part of my body and hence out of control,' he was fond of saying.

Before he moved here, the marble-floored room

with mahogany-panelled walls contained books on military history and his predecessors' portraits. He had all the books and pictures removed to the guest-room annexe and changed it into a prayer room. Army House, which now also served as the Chief Martial Law Administrator's office, was a colonial bungalow, with fourteen bedrooms, eighteen acres of lawns and a small mosque. It reminded him of old black-and-white films, of benevolent rulers who were close to their people. The new President House was ready. He entertained foreign dignitaries and local mullahs there a couple of days a week but was reluctant to move in. He felt lost in the President House's palatial corridors and had instructed his Chief Staff Officer to tell the First Lady that it was still a work in progress.

'The bathrooms are not finished yet and there are some security concerns,' he said whenever she pestered him about the house move. The new President House reminded him of Prince Naif's palace, and although he loved and respected Prince Naif like a brother, what was good for the Crown Prince of the oil-rich desert kingdom was not necessarily suitable for the humble ruler of this poor nation of one hundred and thirty million people.

He was not sure about that number, but it was a neat figure and he would stick to it till he could get around to ordering a new census.

He wrapped the Pickthall translation in a green velvet cover and put it back on the shelf with other copies, commentaries and interpretations of the holy book. He wondered whether he should change into his uniform before going for his morning prayers. Inter Services Intelligence Chief was due to see him at 0630, the prayers would finish at 0615 and he wanted to spend some time talking to the imam of the Army House mosque.

Between making a decision and implementing it, General Zia sometimes liked to seek divine opinion. And although changing into uniform before or after morning prayers wasn't likely to affect the destiny of his one hundred and thirty million subjects, he picked up another volume of the Quran from the shelf anyway, closed his eyes, opened the book at random and moved his finger on the pages in front of him with his eyes shut. He wished himself and his country a safe day, opened his eyes and found his finger pointing at:

لَا إِلَـٰهَ إِلَّا أَنتَ سُبْحَـٰنَكَ إِنِّى كُنتُ مِنَ ٱلظَّـٰلِمِينَ

The pre-dawn routine that gave Army House a head start over its subjects had already begun outside his study. The commandos on the night shift were flicking back the safety catches on their Kalashnikovs and stretching their limbs; a team of gardeners was being body-searched at the main guardroom; General Zia's personal batman was pinning seven identical sets of medals to seven different uniforms; the first of the hundreds of house sparrows hiding behind floodlights and ack-ack guns that provided the Army House with security cover was chirping away in an attempt to start the morning conversation.

General Zia sighed, pressed the Quran against both his eyes, kissed its spine and replaced it on the shelf. He hugged himself to control the shivers running through his body. The same verse from two different volumes, so early in the morning. That had never happened before.

Starting with the night of the coup, he had always consulted the book for guidance and always found the answers he was looking for. Eleven years ago, moments before ordering his troops to carry out Operation Fairplay that removed Prime Minister Bhutto and installed him as the head of the country, he had opened the Quran and found *He it is who hath made you regents in the earth.*

Then two years later, between fending off world leaders' pleas to not to hang Bhutto and signing his death warrant, Zia had opened up the holy book and found this: *And the guilty behold the fire and know that they are about to fall therein, and they find no way of escape thence.*

He had read enough Muadudi to know that the Quran wasn't a book of omens, to be used in worldly affairs, but like a child taking a peek at his surprise birthday presents, General Zia couldn't resist the temptation.

What is a lone man standing at the crossroads of history to do?

After eleven years he was feeling a creeping habit

setting in. For he had started consulting the holy book daily as if it was not the word of God but his daily horoscope on the back page of the *Pakistan Times*. This morning he felt like an addict who looks himself in the mirror after a long time and doesn't recognise what he sees. He felt a strong urge to have another go. He picked up another volume of the Quran, but with trembling hands put it back on the shelf without opening it. He realised he needed help; he needed to speak to the imam at the Army House mosque.

Walking along the corridor that led to the mosque, he passed his bedroom. He opened the door gently and took a peek. The table lamp was on and his wife was sleeping with her ample back towards him. Every time he saw her like this he remembered what Prince Naif had told him about why Bedouins had such huge organs. According to the Prince they had evolved in response to the huge derrières of their women.

'Evolution happens very fast in the desert,' General Zia had joked.

His wife stirred in her sleep, the huge mounds that were her buttocks quivered and the General shut the door gently and went to his own room which doubled as his late-night office as well as a walk-in cupboard. He had decided to change before prayers. He didn't want to keep the ISI Chief waiting.

His room was sparsely furnished, a standard wooden army-issue double bed, a stack of morning newspapers on one bedside table, on the other a glass of milk covered with an embroidered napkin.

The glass of milk was one of those domestic routines that had changed its meaning during the thirty-four years of his marriage. As a newly-wed captain his wife put it on his side table as an innocent domestic aphrodisiac. When, as a major, he experimented with whisky to impress his superiors, it became a cure for his hangovers. Through his days as a colonel and brigadier it took care of his ulcers caused by promotion anxiety. Now it was a mere talisman. The First Lady recited some verses, blew on the milk and plonked it on his side table knowing fully well that he wouldn't drink it. 'For your long life,' she would say. 'To foil the conspiracies of your enemies.' He hadn't touched it for years but he didn't have the heart to tell her to stop. Who could argue with women? If three Special Services Group platoons surrounding his residence, a battery of anti-aircraft guns, and six different-coloured phones representing six different hotlines arranged on a table in his bedroom couldn't save him, how was a glass of milk going to protect him against the conspiracies that the First Lady kept dreaming about? But who could argue with a First Lady who was always complaining of cramped housing and nothing good on the national television?

He looked at his watch and realised that if he started changing into his uniform he would be late for his prayers. Not that it mattered, because the imam would wait for him to turn up before starting the prayer, but Jonah's verse had induced palpitations in his heart and he felt that he would be able to find peace in the mosque.

As he stepped out of the side door of the Army House that led to the mosque, two commandos standing in the shadows saluted. General Zia, absorbed in muttering the verse that he always recited before stepping out in the morning, was startled by the thud of the boots landing on the concrete. He stumbled at the doorstep and took a step backward. He stepped out again and instead of returning the salute nodded at them. He tried to recite the verse again but his mind seemed to have returned to Jonah's incessant pleas.

The imam started the prayers as soon as General Zia took his place behind him. The Chief of the Inter Services Intelligence, General Akhtar, stood on his left, his movements a fraction of a second slower than General Zia's, as if, even when prostrating himself before Allah, General Akhtar wanted his cue to come from his boss. For General Zia, it was reassuring to have someone as his eyes and ears who prayed with him. He knew he had a brother in faith, and also that the brother was here with him and not somewhere else nurturing some dark ambition.

Like most people who pray five times a day, General Zia was finding it difficult to concentrate on the actual prayer. His lips muttered the right verses, his hand went up to his ears, his knees bent to the imam's call and his forehead touched the ground with practised efficiency, but his mind was stuck with Jonah, inside the whale. There were gushing noises and giant bubbles and Jonah's flailing arms in the darkness. He swallowed hard and felt a swarm of little fish nibbling their way towards his heart. He retched and gulped for air as the whale plunged deeper into the sea. General Zia skidded through a sea of slime before coming to rest against a thick wall of warm flesh. So absorbed was he in the innards of the whale that it took him some time to realise what the imam was saying.

General Zia had been the army chief for only sixteen months when he launched the coup and installed himself as the Chief Martial Law Administrator. He wasn't sure how much the eight generals who formed his council trusted him or – more important – respected him. They all saluted him, called him Chief even in their private conversations according to the telephone transcripts that General Zia had seen, and carried out his orders. But could he really trust this clean-shaven, whisky-swilling, elitist bunch? Given his mistrust of anyone with more than two stars on their shoulders, it was understandable that in the first Corp Commanders' meeting after the night of the coup, General Zia was a bit shaky, not sure what these generals wanted from him, not sure what they wanted him to do with this country. They had carried out the coup as if they were reporting for a drill inspection, but General Zia knew that he couldn't take their loyalty for granted. He would have to kill the cat at the very beginning.

General Zia had married when he was a captain in the armoured division. He was also a virgin. One of his maternal uncles took him into a corner on his wedding night and whispered an old Persian proverb in his ear: 'Kill the cat on the first day.' Uncle squeezed his shoulder, laughed a vulgar laugh and pushed him into the room where the future First Lady waited on a bed, a bundle of red silk. Zia didn't know any Persian and found no cat to kill that night.

'Would you like to change into something more comfortable?' General Zia had asked, twirling the embroidered hem of her red silk shirt. 'This is comfortable enough,' she had answered, snatching the hem away from his hands. She turned her back to him and went to sleep.

The fumbling failure of that first night, he knew, had resulted in a marriage in which his authority was never fully established. Twenty-three years later, the morning after his midnight coup, he knew the meaning of the proverb. He intended to kill the cat, bury it and hoist his flag over its grave. He just wasn't quite sure how he would go about it. Allah will help me, he thought, before entering the conference room.

43

In the first meeting after General Zia's coup, eight generals, including the heads of the navy and the air force, sat around a table in the conference room of General Headquarters. Keeping in mind the historic nature of the session, the orderlies had sprayed rose-scented air freshener generously and the room smelled like a freshly sealed coffin. The Adjutant General, General Beg – a two-star general given to unpredictable fits of sneezing – sat in a corner with a white handkerchief over his nose, ready to record every word that was uttered in the conference. A copy of the agenda lay before each of them in a green leather folder embossed with golden crossed swords cradling a thin, new moon. General Zia noticed that although all eight of them stood up and saluted, they all sat down without waiting for him to take his chair first. They shifted in their seats and before he could declare the meeting open the Naval Chief said, 'I want to bring it on the record that I was informed about the coup when it was already under way . . .'

The Adjutant General's suppressed sneeze distracted everyone for a moment and General Zia found the opening he badly needed. He fixed the Naval Chief with a benevolent stare and spoke in a pleading voice. 'Of course we'll hear your protest and of course we'll need your guidance in what we have set out to do. But since we are all meeting for the first time after we were able to save our country without spilling a single drop of blood, should we not start the meeting with a recitation from the Quran? May Allah guide us in all our endeavours.'

They shifted in their seats, not knowing how to deal with this. They were all Muslims and they all knew that the Chief had a religious bent. Some of them even called him 'the mullah' when talking on secure telephone lines. But a meeting was a meeting and mixing religion with the business of running the country was a concept not comprehensible to them. A quarter of a century of military training had prepared them for many tasks; they could make toasts in five different languages, they could march in step and hold joint military exercises with the best armies in the world. If they chose to shed their uniforms they could take up diplomatic careers or run universities. But all their staff-and-command courses and all their survival skills were not enough. They didn't know how to say no to an offer of a recitation from the Quran from their own Chief. They shifted some more in their seats. They breathed in some more rose-scented air.

General Zia took out a slim, magenta-coloured copy of the Quran from his folder, put on his reading glasses and started to recite. All the commanders looked down respectfully and listened in silence; some put their hands in their laps, wondering whether the time had come for them to face the consequences of their godless ways.

The recitation didn't last more than three

minutes. General Zia's voice was croaky but something about reading the Quran aloud makes even the most toneless voice sound bearable. He finished the recitation and handed the Quran to the General on his left.

'Since General Akhtar speaks very good English, I'll ask him to read out the translation for those of us who don't understand Arabic.'

Utter nonsense, the Naval Chief thought. None of us understands Arabic.

General Akhtar started reading haltingly: '"I begin in the name of God, the holiest, the most merciful."' General Zia stared at him without blinking as the translation was read out. As soon as he finished General Zia grabbed the copy from him and held it up to his generals.

'What do you think it says here in this part that I just recited?' There was a moment's silence. General Beg snivelled behind his handkerchief. 'Come on, speak up.' General Zia raised his voice. Then he obeyed his own command: 'In Arabic it says "In the name of Allah". It doesn't say in the name of God, it doesn't say in the name of gods, it doesn't say in the name of some nameless deity. It says: "In the name of Allah".' He left a dramatic pause. 'Let me remind my brothers here that the very first thing that a non-Muslim has to say to become a Muslim, the very first article of faith that every believer has to profess is: There is no God but . . .' He paused again and looked around the table expecting them to complete the first *kalima*. No one spoke up. He repeated. 'There is no God BUT . . .'

'Allah,' they all murmured, like schoolchildren unsure if they were being asked a trick question.

'Yes.' General Zia brought down his fist on the table. 'My dear generals, let's get one thing clear before we hear your protests and your suggestions: There is no God but Allah. And since Allah Himself says there is no God, let's abolish the word. Let's stop pretending God *is* Allah. It's a Western construct, an easy way to confuse who is the creator and who the destroyer. We respect all religions, especially the religions of Christianity and Judaism. But do we want to become like them? Christians call Jesus the son of God. Are we to understand that some god came down while Mary was fast asleep and . . .' Here he made a circle with the thumb and forefinger of his left hand and poked at it with the middle finger of his right hand. 'Jews are pretty close to calling Moses their God. You might think that it's all the same to our people, God, Allah, same difference?' He mimicked the clipped English accent many of his generals preferred. 'But who should be telling them that we believe in Allah and not in any other god? Didn't Allah choose us to clear up this confusion?' Then as an afterthought he appealed to the patriotism of his fellow generals. 'Even Hindus call their six-armed monsters their gods. Isn't that a reason enough to stay away from this word? And if any of you have any concerns that people will not appreciate the difference between God and Allah, I suggest we leave it to Allah.'

The complete silence that followed his short speech satisfied General Zia.

'Can we now hear the Naval Chief's protest?'

The Naval Chief, still reeling from the lecture about God's nomenclature, suddenly felt very small. He was worrying about a breach in protocol when the whole nation was calling God by all sorts of wrong names.

The generals who had called Zia a mullah behind his back felt ashamed at having under-estimated him: not only was he a mullah, he was a mullah whose understanding of religion didn't go beyond parroting what he had heard from the next mullah. A mullah without a beard, a mullah in a four-star general's uniform, a mullah with the instincts of a corrupt tax inspector.

The others sat stunned around the table, still trying to comprehend what they had just heard. If General Zia could have read their minds this is what he would have read:

What did they teach him at Sandhurst?

A country that thinks it was created by God has finally found what it deserves: a blabbering idiot who thinks he has been chosen by Allah to clear his name.

He really makes sense. How come I didn't think of it before?

Who is he going to appoint as his deputy?

Am I in an army commanders' meeting or a village mosque?

I am going to prohibit the word God at home.

Who would have thought there was a theocratic genius in that uniform?

Can we get on with the agenda? We have just toppled an elected bloody government, how the hell are we going to run this country? Is Allah going to come down and patrol the bloody streets?

The only person who voiced his thoughts was General Akhtar, a former middleweight boxer, a clean-shaven man of tribal origin who was packed with so much soldierly dignity that he could have been born in any country on any of the five continents and he still would have become a general. His ability to carry himself with martial grace and his talent for sucking up to his superiors was so legendary that according to a joke popular in the trenches, he could wipe out a whole enemy unit by kissing their asses.

The other generals stopped thinking and moved forward in their chairs to listen to General Akhtar. 'By Allah's grace you have brought this country back from the edge of destruction, by Allah's mercy you have saved this country when the politicians were about to push it over the edge of a precipice. I want to thank –' He stopped himself as he was about to thank God. He folded his boxer's hands respectfully on the green folder. 'I want to thank Allah and our visionary Chief of Staff to whom Allah has given the wisdom to take the right decision at the right time.' He looked around the table before continuing. 'I also want to thank our very professional commanders sitting around this table who carried out the coup on the orders of our Chief in such an orderly manner that not a single bullet had to be fired, not a single drop of blood had to be shed.'

The power balance in the room suddenly shifted and the eight men, despite their different levels of affiliation to religion, diverse tastes in whisky and women, and various English accents, reached the same conclusion: General Akhtar had beaten them to it. They should have spoken these words. The rose-scented air in the meeting room suddenly felt stale. General Beg wiped his nose and put his handkerchief back in his pocket.

The conference moved on to the agenda, to the urgent matter of securing the country's borders, finding legal cover for the coup and enlisting politicians who could be trusted to support the military regime. General Zia hinted at the nice things to come: 'I need governors for the provinces, I need ministers to run the ministries. Who can I count on except the professionals gathered around this table?'

They got up and left the room reassured, but none forgot their Chief's message. In the next eleven years, many of these generals would retire. Some would go on to govern provinces, others would be replaced by their juniors. Two things that weren't even on the agenda survived every upheaval that followed. General Akhtar remained a general until the time he died, and all God's names were slowly deleted from the national memory as if a wind had swept the land and blown them away. Innocuous, intimate names: Persian *Khuda* which had always been handy for ghazal poets as it rhymed with most of the operative verbs; *Rab*, which poor people invoked in their hour of distress; *Maula*, which Sufis shouted in their hashish sessions. Allah had given Himself ninety-nine names. His people had improvised many more. But all these names slowly started to disappear: from official stationery, from Friday sermons, from newspaper editorials, from mothers' prayers, from greeting cards, from official memos, from the lips of television quiz-show hosts, from children's story books, from lovers' songs, from court orders, from telephone operators' greetings, from habeas corpus applications, from inter-school debating competitions, from road inauguration speeches, from memorial services, from cricket players' curses; even from beggars' begging pleas.

In the name of God, God was exiled from the land and replaced by the one and only Allah who, General Zia convinced himself, spoke only through him. But today, eleven years later, Allah was sending him signs that all pointed to a place so dark, so final, that General Zia wished he could muster up some doubts about the Book. He knew if you didn't have Jonah's optimism, the belly of the whale was your final resting place.

As the imam started reciting the after-prayer prayer, it took General Zia a moment to realise that he was being subjected to Jonah's story yet another time. It took him another moment to realise that the imam had never before recited this verse at morning prayers. He broke into violent sobs. The other worshippers continued with their prayers; they were used to General Zia crying during his prayers. They were never sure if it was due to the intensity of his devotion, the matters of state that occupied his mind or another tongue-lashing from the First Lady. Everyone pretended to ignore the presidential tears. General Zia turned his face to the left, turned his face to the right, blessed the entire world and grabbed General Akhtar's hand. He began to speak but choked on his own words. General Akhtar squeezed General Zia's hand and patted his back to calm him down. The words finally came out: 'Can you please raise my security level?' General Akhtar nodded enthusiastically and squeezed his hand again with a boxer's grip. General Zia snivelled, his left eye shed a tear, his right eye looked suspiciously towards the imam. 'Raise it to level red please.'

CHAPTER 3

'I don't want inter Services Intelligence poking their nose in my business,' 2nd OIC mutters as he walks me back from the Commandant's office to my cell. I want to say, 'Amen, sir. Amen.' But one look at him and I decide to keep my mouth shut. He seems to be in an introspective mood. Every visit to the Commandant's office saps the 2nd OIC of his leftover ambition. For a moment I pity him. I pity his crouched walk. I want to pat his belly straining against his uniform's shirt buttons. I want to repair the worn-out heels of his shoes.

We have been studying *The Art of War* in our War Studies class and fragments of Sun Tzu are still fresh in my mind. Didn't he say that if the enemy leaves a door open, don't hesitate, rush in?

'Sir, I agree with you, it will be a disgrace for the Academy if the ISI has to be called in,' I say, sounding very concerned.

'And who the hell is responsible for this disgrace? Who is not cooperating with the inquiry?' He waves his investigation file in my face.

'I swear to God, sir –' I say and shut up because

he looks into my eyes, takes a turn and instead of marching me back to the cell, starts walking towards the mosque.

Falcons Road, which leads to the mosque, is melting under my boots. My fellow cadets are either in their Character Building Class or strapped to their seats in cockpit simulators, practising emergency landings. And here I am, being frogmarched to Allah's house. It's not even time for prayer. And 2nd OIC, I know, is not the praying type. I am not godly either, but since the Commandant declared all five daily prayers compulsory and started a roll call, I have paid Him a few visits.

Obaid turned very pious for a few days, even got me a book from the library called *Health, Wealth and Wisdom Through Prayer*. He spent more and more of his time off in the mosque. His devotion ended the day a duty cadet caught him doing yoga between the prayers. One moment he was sitting there in lotus position, his thumbs and forefingers resting on his knees, trying to unlock his kundalini, and the next moment he was being charged with performing Hindu worship in a mosque. He was only let off when I threatened the duty cadet that he'd never again be invited to our video nights.

I can't think of anything 2nd OIC can find in the mosque to add to his file.

Unless Allah has volunteered to stand witness against me.

The mosque is made from a series of old barracks converted into a low-ceilinged prayer hall with a plywood minaret stuck on top, a temporary arrangement, as the architectural model for Allah's new abode is encased in a glass box next to the entrance to the mosque. It has a green dome with golden stripes and four minarets and little plastic figures worshipping in the compound. We stop at the mosque's gate. 2nd OIC sits down to take his shoes off. I remain standing, not sure what is expected of me.

'You are coming in with me, Under Officer,' he says.

'My clothes are not clean, sir.' I trot out the same half-truth that I have used for months to avoid compulsory prayers.

'Don't worry, we just need to talk.'

My stomach pulls a negative g. Sun Tzu knew his element of surprise, but he never wrote about what it felt like to be on the receiving end of it.

The mosque is empty at this time except for a few cadets dressed in white shalwar qameez and skullcaps and absorbed in what seems like a very intense game of cards. I don't recognise their faces but I can tell from their clothes that they are the latest victims of the ongoing starch war. Our Commandant wants everyone to wear double-starched uniforms, even in June, which leads to regular outbreaks of rashes and ugly skin infections. There are always long lines of cadets at the sickbay, legs straining hard to avoid the razor-sharp creases of the trousers, hands trying to itch in impossible places. The Medical Squadron considers it a health hazard and has hit back with its own Standard Operating Procedures for Dealing with the Outbreak of an Epidemic. Anyone who gets a skin infection because of his starched uniform gets a prescription which says 'no starched uniforms'. The Commandant won't have any non-starched uniforms on active duty and he can't really allow them to stay in their dorms, so they have all been ordered to spend their day in the mosque.

'Is that a punishment or a reward?' Obaid used to ask. The only clear winner in this running feud between the medical establishment and our Commandant is God Himself. The mosque these days has more worshippers than ever before.

When our boys in white see the 2nd OIC approaching they scramble to collect their cards and coins and transform themselves from a bunch of one-rupee rummy-rascals to devout young men. 2nd OIC gives them an appreciative look as if merely by pretending to pray they have absolved themselves in his and Allah's eyes. I don't get it even when he picks up a copy of the Quran from the book racks along the wall in the main prayer hall, hands it over to me and stands there staring. I wait for his next command.

'Now put your right hand on it and tell me that you don't know why Obaid went AWOL. Tell me you have no knowledge of his whereabouts.'

If I wasn't in the mosque I could have told him where to go.

'I can't swear, sir, not on the Quran,' I say.

'So you do know about this,' he says. 'By refusing to swear you are admitting your guilt? Look, it's just you and me and our Allah.' He puts his own right hand on the Quran. 'Tell me the truth and I swear on the holy Quran I'll get you out of this mess.'

'My father made me promise never to swear on the Quran, even if I was telling the truth. In fact, specially if I was telling the truth,' I say in a weary voice, my fingers numb around the velvet cover on the Quran.

'Your father never said a prayer in his life,' he says.

'You are right, sir, but he was a very spiritual man. He respected the sacred Quran and never involved it in worldly affairs,' I say, wondering how Colonel Shigri would have liked being described as a spiritual man.

The Colonel did go through a hectic spiritual phase during which he terminated his whisky sessions at midnight and spent the rest of his nights reciting the Quran. And he *did* tell me never to swear on the holy book. But his spiritual journey didn't last long enough for anyone to know whether it was, in his own words, 'a change or *for* a change'. His copy of the Quran was lying open on his study desk the morning he was found hanging from the ceiling fan by his own bed sheet.

Ceiling fan.

Bed sheet.

His eyes popping out of their sockets.

The Colonel weighed a bloody ton. Where were the laws of physics?

'Some people insist on digging their own grave.' 2nd OIC snatches the Quran from my hand and puts it back on the shelf.

'Sir, I really don't know, but that doesn't mean I can't help you find out,' I say, trying desperately to inject my own element of surprise into the proceedings.

'Don't f—,' he starts to say, but realises that he is in the mosque.

'Get out and fall in outside the mosque,' he shouts at the starch victims.

'I don't know why the Commandant wants to involve ISI in this,' I say. 'Because, sir, you know that Obaid is my friend and I want to find out as much as you do where he went and why,' I say, trampling over everything Sun Tzu has taught us trainee warriors.

'Shut your trap,' he barks. 'I am not interested in your sentiments.'

He goes out and has a go at the cadets in white.

'You are turning God's house into a bloody gambling den . . .'

One good thing about visiting the mosque is that sometimes it can calm even sinners like me. It is in His hands now, Colonel Shigri used to say in his spiritual phase.

Second night in the cell and I am already feeling

58

at home. Dinner is served. I slip the first-termer a five-rupee note and busy myself with chicken curry, rice and cucumber salad. By the time I finish, the duty cadet is back with a bottle of Coke and two Gold Leaf cigarettes. I finish the bottle in two long gulps and light a Gold Leaf, saving the other one for later.

'You got any magazines?' I ask the duty cadet.

He disappears and returns with a year-old copy of *Reader's Digest*. I was hoping he'd bring something less intellectual. But then prisoners can't choose their own entertainment. The duty cadet leaves with the dinner tray, forgetting to take the matchbox from me.

One day this asshole is going to be court-martialled.

Stubbing out the Gold Leaf, I take off my shoes and belt and shirt and settle in for the night. I read 'Humour in Uniform' first. Nothing very funny. The only female pictures are in a black-and-white photo feature about Nancy and Ronald Reagan entitled 'When They Were Young'. Even at twenty-eight she had the face of an old cat's arse. The Academy censors have done a good job of obliterating her non-existent breasts with a black marker. Even in times as desperate as these I skip the photos and start reading the condensed version of *Escape from Colditz*.

I leave it halfway through and compare my situation with Lieutenant Anthony Rolt's. It's obvious to me that I am worse off. Even if I do make a hang-glider out of this foam mattress and some matchsticks, where the hell am I going to jump from?

I flick the pages in a last attempt to find inspiration. In 'Life is Like That' there is a five-line anecdote about someone called Sherry Sullivan who washed her car wearing an overall and her neighbour mistook her for her husband. The name does something and my armies are suddenly on the march. I avoid the hole in the mattress. These holes are like highway whores, filthy and tired.

My encounter with Sherry Sullivan ends in such violent throes of passion that the second Gold Leaf is forgotten and I enter a sleep so blissful that in my technicolour dreams the 2nd OIC is shining my boots and the Commandant is polishing my sword with the tip of his tongue. Captain Rolt's hang-glider lands safely in Trafalgar Square.

The morning is even more glorious. I am woken by a waft of Old Spice. Loot Bannon is standing at the door. 'Wakey-wakey, dear inmate.'

There are about one thousand and fifty things that I need to ask him. But he is in too cheerful a mood.

'Nice pad you got here,' he says.

'It's not as bad as it looks,' I say. 'You found yourself a new Silent Drill Commander?' My attempt at sarcasm is ignored. I light up my second Gold Leaf.

'I see your supply lines are secure.' His turn to be witty.

'Did Obaid tell you anything?' I ask. My matter-of-fact voice surprises me. Gold Leaf on an empty stomach always turns me into a detached thinker.

I know what they call me and Obaid behind our backs.

Fort Bragg bitches.

Just because we are chummy with Bannon. Although Bannon is merely a drill instructor from Fort Bragg – only a lowly lieutenant – in the Academy's food chain he is somewhere between a shark and a spotted leopard.

'Baby O is on the lam,' he says as if it's breaking bloody news.

I take a last long puff from the cigarette, inhale a smouldering filter and break into a cough.

'I'm meeting El Comandante for my routine this afternoon. I should have some top info for you by then.' He is suddenly his distant Yankee self.

'And by the way, the Commandant wants you to carry on the good work with the Silent Drill Squad,' he says.

In my relief I decide to stick to philosophy.

'You know what Sun Tzu said? Wait your enemy out and you have won half the battle.'

'Did that old Chink really say that?'

'If he had spent a night in this cell jerking off to *Reader's Digest* he would have reached the same conclusion.'

As I come down the stairs from the guardroom, surveying the world like only a paroled prisoner can, I confront the limits of my freedom. A middle-aged military police chap carrying an ancient Enfield 303 rifle is waiting for me.

'I have orders to keep you under close guard,' he says. I should have expected it; they are not going to let me roam freely. The only surprise is that Bannon conveniently forgot to tell me about this arrangement. Bannon's memory has more holes than an overused short-range shooting target.

Let's see how fast my guard can run.

There is enough time to get to the parade square. I can probably funeral-march to my dorm, have a leisurely bath and still make it in time for the parade, but I feel a sudden burst of energy and start moving at the double, my guard and his 303 rifle trying hard to keep pace with me. The morning breeze welcomes me and I am suddenly flying. The distance between me and my guard keeps increasing. A formation of new recruits passes me and they greet me at strength 5, with the enthusiasm of those starting a new life. 'Buck up, boys. The country needs you,' I shout back.

I whistle at a pair of crows kissing on the telephone pole. Our old washerman carrying our laundry on his donkey cart is startled out of his slumber by my loud greeting: 'Good morning, Uncle Starchy, go easy on the white stuff.'

In my squadron, the boys are already lined up for the morning dress inspection. Eighty-six yawning faces are spooked to see me running so early in the morning. They come to attention like the creaking wheels of a plane forgotten on the tarmac for too long.

I stand in front of the formation and start jumping on the spot.

'Come on. Wake up,' I shout. 'I disappear for a day and you turn into sissies. Where is the Fury Squadron spirit?'

Without any further command they join me, at first reluctantly, and then catching my rhythm they all start running on the spot. I go through the rows, keeping my hand level with their chests, and soon everyone is bringing their knees to touch my hand.

They are happy to have me back.

As if the buggers have a choice.

The police guard stands in a corner, still breathless from running and quite baffled at this enthusiastic reception for his prisoner.

'Right turn. Quick march,' I order. 'See you on the square, boys.'

I run towards my dorm not looking back at the police guard. I want to see if he is as meek as he looks. What exactly does he want to guard me from anyway?

He follows me. The bugger follows me all the way into the room and stands close to the door, quite alert by now. I open my cupboard and glance towards Obaid's bed from the corner of my eye. A crisp white sheet is folded over a grey blanket. It looks like a Hindu widow in mourning. I take a deep breath and survey my cupboard. Here's all my life folded up, in neat little piles: uniform shirts on the left, trousers on the right, my Under Officer's golden epaulettes at a right angle to the peaked cap, toothbrush in line with toothpaste tube and shaving cream balanced on its cap and parallel to shaving brush; all the exhibits of my everyday life are displayed according to the standard cupboard manual. I open the drawer to check what I already know. They have been through it. I glance at the sword hanging on the inside of the cupboard door. A green silk thread from its tasselled hilt is casually tied around the top of the scabbard; exactly the way I left it. I think about going towards Obaid's bed. My guard looks at the bed too. I start to undress.

My hands move down the front of my shirt, opening the buttons while I quickly go through my options. I throw my shirt over my shoulder without looking back and pull the vest out of my trousers. The guard shuffles his feet, his fingers fidget around the ancient muzzle of his rifle. The bugger has no plans to move. Turning to him I yank down the zip on my fly, then move towards him with my fingers pulling down the waistband on my underwear.

'Uncle 303, you really want to see?'

He beats an embarrassed retreat out of the room, walking backwards.

I bolt the door and lunge towards Obaid's bed. No point looking in the side table. They have taken everything. I turn the mattress around. They have obviously not thought that there can be other places in the mattress besides the obligatory hole. There is a zip on the side, I open it, slip my hand in. My fingers go back and forth, exploring the dead spongy surface of the foam mattress. I find an opening and slip my hand into the foam tunnel. My fingers touch a smooth piece of silk cloth and I pull it out.

Obaid's hankie, rose-patterned. It smells of Poison and Obaid and there is a five-digit number on it. Obaid's handwriting, all elegant dashes and curves.

As if they are going to let me near a phone. The only phone from where you can dial outside the Academy is in the sickbay. And my guard is knocking impatiently on the door.

Obaid had arrived two days after our training had commenced and always maintained that air of someone who is just a step behind in life. When I first saw him he was wearing fake Levi's, a very shiny pair of oxford shoes and a black silk shirt with a logo on its pocket that read 'Avanti'. His blow-dried, jet-black hair covered his ears. And if his city-boy civilian dress wasn't enough to make him stand out amid a formation of khaki-clad jarheads, he was also wearing a rose-patterned handkerchief carefully folded and tucked under his collar. He removed the hankie from time to time to absorb the invisible droplets of sweat from his forehead. He stood with all his weight on one leg, right thumb tucked in his jeans pocket, left arm hanging aimlessly, ass cocked, and stared into the distance over the trees, as if expecting to see an aircraft taking off.

He should have kept his eyes on the door, from where soon-to-be-drummed-out Sir Tony emerged for our dress inspection. His starched khaki shirt was unbuttoned to his navel, his hands fumbling with the buckle of his belt. As he approached I thought he was buckling it, but he yanked it out and shouted, 'ATTENTION.' I put my heels together, puffed my chest out, pulled my shoulders back, locked my arms at my sides and glanced towards Obaid. He shifted his weight onto his right foot and tucked his left thumb into his jeans pocket too, as if posing for a Levi's ad. Sir Tony was the kind of sir who believed that authority was all about half-finished sentences and chewed-up words.

'Shun, bastards, shun,' he barked, charging at the squadron.

My spine stiffened even more. His belt whiplashed in front of my eyes, making me blink. I heard it strike Obaid's cocked ass. So unexpected was the attack that Obaid could only whimper. His knees buckled and he fell on the ground, one hand taking the fall, the other trying feebly to protect his behind from further assault. It didn't come.

Sir Tony gave him a full dress inspection. The rose-patterned hankie was the first item of clothing

66

to come off. Sir Tony rolled it around his finger and smelled it. 'Fake fucking Poison,' he said, showing off his knowledge of the perfume trade. Sir Tony shoved the hankie in Obaid's mouth, extended his right leg and waved his shoe in Obaid's face. Obaid understood the meaning of this gesture, but obviously the symbolism was lost on him. He went down on his knees, took the hankie out of his mouth and tried to wipe Sir Tony's right shoe, which was now level with his nose. Sir Tony stood with his hands on his hips looking around at the rest of us. We had already been at the mercy of his whims for two days and we knew that anyone who tried to glance towards him would be the next victim, so we stood and stared, stared and stood. Sir Tony gave him a slight kick in the chin and Obaid got the message. He put the hankie back in his mouth and started polishing the shoe, his face making little circles around the toe.

Both shoes polished to his satisfaction, Sir Tony busied himself with the rest of Obaid's outfit. He spent a considerable time struggling to tear the pocket with the Avanti logo from Obaid's shirt. It was silk; it wouldn't come off. He ripped off all the buttons and removed the shirt. Obaid wasn't wearing anything under it. Obaid hesitated when Sir Tony pointed towards his trousers but Sir Tony started fidgeting with his belt buckle and within seconds Obaid was standing there in only his briefs and white socks and shiny oxford shoes, the rose-patterned hankie still in his mouth. Sir Tony pulled the hankie out of his mouth and with a certain tenderness tied it around Obaid's neck. Obaid was at attention now, trembling slightly, but he stood straight and stiff, his arms locked to his sides.

'Take charge.' Sir Tony patted Obaid's cheek and walked off, tightening his belt. We fell in behind him and Obaid marched us back to our dorm. It was only when he was in front of us, naked except for his briefs and oxfords, leading us into our dorm for his first night in the squadron, that I noticed that his briefs were also silk, too small and too tight, with little embroidered hearts on the waistband.

'Nice jeans,' I whispered from my bed after the lights-out bell on his first night in the dorm. Obaid was in the bed next to mine, his blanket was aglow as a tiny torch moved under it. I couldn't decide if he was reading a book or inspecting his privates for any damage.

'My father makes them.' He switched off the torch and removed the blanket from his head. The way he uttered *my father* told me that he didn't like him much.

'Your father owns Levi's?'

'No, he just owns a factory. Exports. Hong Kong. Bangkok.'

'Must make a lot of money. Why didn't you go into the family business?'

'I wanted to follow my dreams.'

Hell. Not one of those crazy civilians looking for martyrdom in all the wrong places?

'What dreams? Licking other people's boots?'

'I want to fly.'

The boy had obviously spent too much time around his father's warehouses spellchecking fake labels. I stayed silent for a while. Someone in the neighbouring dorm was sobbing, probably not getting used to all the F-words being poured into his ear about his mother whom he was definitely still missing.

Me? Spent my sixth birthday in a dorm like this one. Never had that problem.

'What does your dad do?' He turned his torch on and pointed it at me.

'Turn that thing off. You'll get us into trouble,' I said. 'He was in the army.'

'Retired?'

'No. He died.'

Obaid sat up in his bed and clutched his blanket to his chest.

'I'm sorry. What happened?'

'He was on a mission. Classified.'

Obaid was silent for a moment.

'Your father was a *shaheed* then. It's an honour to be your roommate.'

I wondered whether I would prefer to have a father who was alive and manufacturing fake American brands or a legend hanging from a ceiling fan.

'And did you really dream about joining the armed forces?'

'No. Books. I like reading.'

'Does your father make books too?'

'No. He hates books. But it's my hobby.'

The sobbing in the next dorm settled into a low whimper.

'Do you have a hobby?'

'I didn't join the armed forces to collect stamps,' I said, pulling the blanket over my head.

I unlace my boots, roll off my socks, take a starched pair of khaki cotton trousers and a shirt from the hanger. My trousers stick to themselves like two pieces of cardboard glued together and make tearing sounds as my legs part them. I tuck my stiff shirt in with one hand and open the door with the other.

'Congratulations, Uncle 303, your prisoner hasn't escaped.'

I look in the mirror. Three days without a shave and there are just a few scattered hairs on my chin. Like cactus thorns, Obaid used to say, sparse but prickly.

I take the razor from the drawer. A few dry strokes get rid of the thorns.

I never saw a hair on Colonel Shigri's face. He was freshly shaved when they took him down from the ceiling fan.

I can see in the mirror that my guard, standing behind me, is smiling.

★　★　★

My Silent Drill Squad comes to attention as I arrive in the parade square. Bannon is not there. I can tell he is in his cool-dude phase, which normally entails lighting up a joint with his first cup of Nescafé Instant. I don't have to wait for him. My boys are standing in three rows, eighteen of them, their right hands resting on the muzzles of their G3 rifles, bayonets naked and pointing towards the sky.

I start the dress inspection, a leisurely slow march, my left hand on the sword hilt, my distorted face reflected in the toes of their shoes. They are eighteen of the best: a smudged shoe or a crooked crease or a loose belt is not expected from this bunch, but you can't really complete the inspection without picking on someone. As I approach the second to last person in the third row I mark my victim. I draw the sword with my right hand, turn round and before the guy can blink put the tip just above his belt, on his tummy, which had relaxed after my approving nod. The tummy is sucked in. Not just by the boy at the tip of my sword – but there is an inaudible sucking-in of tummies all around; spines, already straight, stretch to their full potential. My sword makes an arch in the air, the tip finds the mouth of its scabbard and is pushed into its velvet interior. I start my march as the sword's hilt clicks with the top of the scabbard. Not a word is exchanged. My eyes go on roving along the lines of still, stern faces and unblinking eyes.

71

Good boys, they are.

We can begin.

All the bullshit about the sound of silence is just that, bullshit. Silence is silence and our Silent Drill Squad has learned that by now. We have done this for one hundred and ten days, seven days a week. The ones with malfunctioning internal clocks, those in the habit of glancing sideways to get their cues, those counting silently to coordinate their manoeuvres and those twiddling their toes in their shoes to keep their blood circulation going, have all been eliminated.

Here, my wish is their command.

Bannon, who has appeared quietly during my inspection, comes to attention with an exaggerated bang of his boot on the concrete, a sign for me to start. I ignore the red ropes unfurling under his drooping eyelids, execute an about-turn and draw my sword; holding it in front of my chest, I bring the hilt level with my lips. Salute performed and accepted in silence, I turn back and march four steps towards the silent squad. As my heel lands at the fourth step, the squad comes to attention in unison.

Perfect start.

My sword goes back into the scabbard and as the hilt clicks into place there is a swish in the air. The rifles leave their left hands with bayonets up in the air, complete a circle above their heads and land safely in their right. Then both hands grip the rifles, hold them in front of their chests and bang the magazines thrice. My rifle orchestra plays for five minutes, rifles swoon and circle in the air. Their hands clapping the magazines are perfectly timed. Ten pounds of metal and wood moulds itself to my silent commands.

My inner cadence rules.

The squad divides itself into two, both flights march ten steps in opposite directions, come to a halt, turn back and, with easy elegance, dissolve into a single row.

Time to show the buggers how it's done.

I stand three feet from the file leader. We are eyeball to eyeball. A single blink or a sideways glance can be fatal. The file leader brings his rifle to chest level and throws it at me. The rifle makes a semi-arch and my practised right hand receives it. One. Two. Three. My right hand throws it spiralling over my head and it lands in my left. For the next sixty seconds it leaps and dances over my head and around my shoulders. For onlookers, the G3 rifle is a blurred swirl of metal and wood, at one with me before it does a triple loop and lands in the file leader's hand.

For the finale, the squad lines up in two rows again and I start my slow march down the middle, sword held straight in front of my chest. Every step I take is a command for both files to throw their rifle to the guy standing opposite them. It's like walking through a calibrated assault of flying swords. Throw. Catch. You miss a beat and your bayonet can lodge itself in your partner's eye. I am walking between a twenty-metre spiral of rifles circling in the air. It looks spectacular but is easy to achieve with three months of practice.

As I approach the last pair, I give a sideways glance to the guy on my right, just a deflection of my eyeballs. His hand trembles as he receives the rifle that has just swished past my nose. His right hand is a nanosecond late in his throw, the rifle makes a half-circle in the air and its butt comes at my temple.

Perfect.

Blackout.

If the bastard had delayed it another beat, it would have been the bayonet instead of the butt.

The medical orderlies take off my shoes, remove the sword and loosen my belt. The ambulance is silent. Someone slips an oxygen mask on my face. I give in to the stretcher's comfort and breathe deeply. I wish I could afford the luxury of passing out but my condition needs to stabilise quickly. I don't want the overefficient buggers to open my skull.

As my back rests on the white sheets in the sickbay's special care room, an orderly slips a needle into my arm. A curtain is drawn. The phone is on the other side of the curtain. I feel calm, too calm even to take a reassuring look at it.

I wake up groggy and immediately know they put a sedative in the drip.

Bannon is sitting on a stool at my bedside.

'It's not about Obaid,' he says. 'There's a plane missing. A whole goddam machine, gone.'

I hope it's a sedative-induced hallucination, but Bannon's hand is on my shoulder and he is the only person in the Academy who calls an aircraft a plane.

'An MF17 is missing and they think Obaid took it.'

'What do you think?' I ask him, feeling stupid and sleepy at the same time.

Baby O flew away with a whole aircraft?

Emergency procedures for Mushshak, MF17, two-seater, dual-control, propeller aircraft, powered by two hundred horsepower Saab engine:

Engine on fire:
Cut the throttle.
Go into a thirty-degree descent.
Trim the ailerons.
Look for a field to land in.
If the fire continues:
Release the catch on safety belt.
Eject the canopy.
Keep your head down.
Climb onto the right wing.
Jump.

'Why the right wing?' I had raised my hand in the Emergency Procedures class.

So that you die quicker, came the reply.

There are no parachutes on MF17s.

'The plane is still missing,' says Bannon.

'Who the fuck cares about the plane? It can't

be in the air forty-eight hours after it took off. You put the bloody idea in his head in the first place. Now don't just sit there, do something,' I shout at him and realise my voice is choked. Must be the sedatives, I tell myself.

'It disappeared off the radar, ten minutes after take-off,' Bannon says in a low whisper.

'Did they scramble the fighters?'

'No, they thought it was a routine training flight,' he says. 'Obaid used your call sign.'

CHAPTER 4

Geneneral Zia ul-Haq was rehearsing his special address to the nation in front of a TV camera when the chief of his security, Brigadier TM, entered the room. Brigadier TM's salute, regardless of the time of the day or the importance of the occasion, was a spectacle to behold. As his foot landed on the thick carpet, the quality of his respect reverberated through the velvet curtains of the Army House's living room and once again General Zia missed his cue to stop reading from his written speech and be spontaneous. This was the point where he was supposed to push aside the stack of papers in front of him with his left hand, remove his reading glasses with his right hand, look straight into the camera and say: 'My dear countrymen, now I want to say something from the heart . . .' But his right and left hands didn't seem to be talking to each other. All morning long he had either removed his glasses while still reading or pushed the written speech aside and stared silently into the camera with his glasses still on. General Zia looked at his Information Minister, who watched the speech on a TV monitor with his hands folded at his crotch, nodding enthusiastically at every sentence and every pause. The Information Minister asked the TV crew to leave the room.

Brigadier TM stood still beside the door, his eyes scanning the camera and the monitor the TV crew had left behind. Something in the room was different: the air was heavier, the colours were not as he remembered them from yesterday. 'It is a very forceful speech, sir,' said the Information Minister, trying to ignore General Zia's hostile stare. With General Zia's decision to confine himself to the Army House after the imposition of Code Red, his Information Minister was suddenly left with nothing to issue as the head-line for the evening television news. After two days of recycled footage, he had suggested that General Zia record a special address to the nation.

'This speech is dead. No emotions,' General Zia said. 'People will not only think that I am a pris-oner in my own Army House, but that I am also suffering from some kind of dementia.'

The Information Minister nodded enthusiastic-ally as if that had been his plan all along.

'And that part about the great threats facing our great nation sounds too poetic. Name those threats; make them more – make them more threatening. The paragraph that says *I will not move into the President House because it has blood in its foundations* doesn't make sense. Whose blood? Say something about blood-sucking politicians.

Say something about poor people. You do know there are poor people in this country? I am sure you don't want to become one of them.'

The Information Minister picked up the speech and left the room, without being offered a hand to shake and with nothing to tell the nation in the evening-news bulletin.

'Sit down, son.' General Zia turned towards Brigadier TM and sighed. 'You are the only man in this country I can still trust.'

As Brigadier TM sat on the edge of the sofa he immediately realised that the seat under him was also unfamiliar, deeper and softer.

General Zia's overall security was the responsibility of General Akhtar and his Inter Services Intelligence, but the man picked to ensure his personal safety was Brigadier TM, a barrel of a man, actually a barrel-full-of-suspicions of a man who had been Zia's shadow for the past six years. His team of armed commandos formed a ring around General Zia's office and living area and then concentric circles around that ring in a two-mile radius. For a further three miles the job of maintaining security fell to ordinary army soldiers. Outside this circle stood the civilian police, but nobody expected them to do much except stop traffic and baton-charge any enthusiasts trying to get a glimpse of General Zia's convoy. This five-mile circle was ready to move at very short notice, keeping General Zia in the centre, but ever since he'd cancelled all public engagements that might take him out of the Army House, Brigadier TM's focus of suspicion had become the Army House itself.

When General Zia saw him for the first time TM was a major and a speck in the sky, leading a formation of paratroopers jumping out of a Hercules C130 at the National Day Parade. The speck bloomed into a green-and-white parachute and TM, manoeuvring his parachute's cord-controls, landed in the one-metre circle marked with white chalk right in front of the dais from which General Zia was inspecting the parade. Commissioned in the military at a time when para-chutes were still an exotic entity, General Zia was fascinated by TM's precision landing. He stepped down from the dais, hugged TM and told him to stick around for the post-parade party. TM was at his back when General Zia went along the reception line of ambassadors and other foreign dignitaries. Then General Zia stepped outside the VIP area and went 'mingling with the milling crowds' on the Information Minister's suggestion. The minister had already dictated the headline to state television and was now obliged to make it happen. The crowd with which Zia mingled comprised an all-male congregation of primary-school teachers, court clerks, office peons and government bureaucrats' domestic staff, ordered here by their bosses. Many in the crowd were soldiers in civvies bussed in from the neighbouring cantonment. With TM at his side, General Zia felt that the crowd suddenly became more disciplined. TM's towering, bulky presence made Zia forget his old habit of looking around, scanning the crowd for anyone who might fling a stone or hurl abuse at him. Brigadier TM navigated the crowd effortlessly, his elbows working like the oars of a skilled rower as if the milling crowd was nothing but dead water in a still lake.

'Your jump was perfect. You do that thing beautifully,' General Zia said, making a shapeless flower with his hands in the air. They were in the General's car going back to the Army House after the post-parade ceremonies. 'What if that thing doesn't open after you jump?'

'Life is in Allah's hands,' TM said, sitting at the edge of the car seat, 'but I pack my own parachute.' General Zia nodded his head in appreciation, expecting to hear more. TM was a man of few words but the silence made him uncomfortable and he volunteered some more information. 'I have written a slogan outside our parachute packing cabin: "*Life-packing in Progress*".' This was TM's first and last literary flourish; his body was more articulate. TM's body was a tree trunk, permanently stuck in jungle camouflage uniform. His small head was always covered with a crimson beret, cocked over his left ear. His small brown eyes constantly searched for invisible enemies. Even at official receptions, where the rest of the military wore their ceremonial uniforms with golden braids, there was one man behind General Zia in his drab battle fatigues, his eyes darting from a VIP's face to a waiter to a lady with her hand in her bag. During his six years as General Zia's Chief of Security, not only had he kept General Zia safe against all visible and invisible enemies, but also conducted him through so many milling crowds that General Zia had started to think of himself as a man of the people.

Now that General Zia had raised his security threat level to red without consulting the Brigadier, he wanted a proper assessment of the situation. Brigadier TM shifted on the edge of the sofa. He was not used to having a conversation with General Zia while sitting down. He tried hard to sit still and concentrate but his eyes kept scanning the presidential crests on the burgundy velvet curtains and the matching Persian rug. Suddenly all the air went out of his lungs and his shoulders collapsed in disbelief. The curtains and the carpets were new. How did all this stuff get here without his knowledge?

'Who wants to kill me?' General Zia asked in a neutral tone, as if enquiring about the lawn-mowing arrangements. Brigadier TM caressed the brocade sofa cover with the tips of his fingers and wondered how someone had managed to change it without his security clearance.

The Brigadier was the only man in General Zia's military staff with round-the-clock access to his working as well as family quarters. He was also the only man in his inner circle who didn't join Zia for his five daily prayers, a privilege so exceptional that it baffled the others. Anyone who happened to be around General Zia at prayer time was expected to join him, no matter where they were, be it his official plane or the National Command's bunker. General Zia would look at his watch and everyone, including the peons and politicians who didn't even know when to stand up or bow during the prayers, would line up with him as if their piety had been waiting for this very moment to be realised. During these prayers, Brigadier TM stood with his back to the congregation, keeping a close eye on all possible access points. In the beginning it weighed on General Zia's conscience, and he asked TM how he felt about not being able to join him for prayers.

'Duty is worship, sir,' he said. 'If I was in a war I would not be expected to leave my gun and pray.' Subsequently, General Zia always remembered to add a few words for TM, reminding Allah that the Brigadier couldn't offer his prayers because he was on duty.

Brigadier TM's eyes darted around the room, feeling irritated with the new textures, the different colours. TM knew that security wasn't just about throwing yourself in front of an assassin's bullet or pulling out the fingernails of a potential conspirator; it was more about anticipating the subtle shifts in everyday life patterns. 'General Akhtar has all the files, sir. Separate files on all the suspects. And on all possible scenarios,' he said distractedly. His eyes were scanning the wall where a portrait of the Founder of the Nation had appeared, a portrait that he had never seen before.

'Those files lie. I am asking *you*, not General Akhtar. You are my shadow, you should know. You see everyone who comes to meet me; you know every nook and corner in this house. It's your job to protect me. As your Commander-in-Chief, I demand to know: who are you protecting me from? Who is trying to kill me?' General Zia's voice rose, his crossed eyes got entangled with each other, two globs of spit escaped his lips, one lodged itself in the General's moustache and the other was absorbed in the vine and flowers of the Persian rug under his feet.

Brigadier TM was not used to being addressed in this tone. He had always known that General Zia felt threatened by his physical presence when they were by themselves and only felt comfortable when they had company. Brigadier TM was trained in these matters and he immediately knew that this raised voice, this demanding tone, was actually the voice of fear. Brigadier TM had a lot of experience in smelling fear. When you asked them the last question, when they discovered that the time for explanations was over, when they realised that the interrogation had ended and there would be no court trial. It was only then that they raised their voices, they shouted, they pretended they were not scared. But you could smell it just as you can smell it in goats before the slaughter; a bleat on their lips and piss between their legs, like men shouting when you strode into their room and shut the door behind you.

'Everyone,' he said.

General Zia stood up from his sofa in alarm. 'What do you mean, Brigadier Tahir Mehdi? Who?' he shouted, and this time his spit was a shower in TM's face. When General Zia didn't call you *my brother, my son, respected sister* and addressed you by your name he was in a bad mood. When he addressed you with your name and rank you had probably already lost that rank. Brigadier TM had no fear of being fired. He would happily go back to training his boys and doing precision para jumps. General Zia knew about this because, in a rare moment, TM had confessed to General Zia that there were only a few bones left in his body that he hadn't broken in the pursuit of his passion. He had seemed very proud.

'I suspect everyone. Even my own boys.'

'Your commandos? They are here twenty-four hours a day.'

'I send them back to their units every six weeks and get new ones. You might have noticed. There is no point trusting anyone, sir. Indira Gandhi, what happened?'

A shudder ran through General Zia. Indira had been gunned down by her own military body-guards while taking a stroll in her own garden. General Zia had to go to India to attend her funeral, where he saw at first hand the abomination that was the Hindu religion. They built a pyre of wood, poured some melted butter over it and then Indira Gandhi's own son lit the flame. General Zia had stood there watching as Indira's body, draped in a white cotton sari, caught fire. At one point it seemed she was going to get up and run away but then her skull exploded. The General thanked Allah for giving them Pakistan so their children didn't have to witness this hell on earth every day.

'How do you choose these boys? Why six weeks? Why can't they get any ideas before six weeks?'

'Because of their families; we take care of them for six weeks. I also run background checks. No homos. Communists. No news junkies. They wouldn't be around you.'

'You mean they can get ideas by reading newspapers? Have you seen our newspapers? I think you need to revise your guidelines.'

'Any man who has the ability to read a newspaper cannot have the will to throw himself between you and your assassin's bullet,' said Brigadier TM. He was still trying to solve the sofa-curtain-carpet-portrait mystery.

Brigadier TM's boys were recruited from remote villages and trained so strenuously that by the time they finished their training – if they finished at all, as more than two-thirds begged to be returned to their villages – they had a vacant look on their faces. Unquestioning obedience was drilled into them by making them dig holes in the earth all day only to fill other holes the following day. They were kept away from civilians for so long that they considered anyone in civvies a legitimate target. General Zia spread his hands in exasperation and waited for TM to say something more.

'These are my procedures,' Brigadier TM said, getting up, 'and they seem to have worked so far. If you'll allow me, we can bring back the K-9 Platoon.'

General Zia noticed with satisfaction that he hadn't used the word 'guard dogs'.

'Why do we need those filthy dogs? Are they better than your commandos?'

Brigadier TM put his hands behind his back, looked above Zia's head and gave the longest speech of his career. 'We have got air cover. We cover all the access points to the Army House. We monitor all movements within a five-mile radius. But what if someone outside that radius is digging a tunnel right now, long and deep, which leads up to your bedroom? We have got no underground cover.'

'I have cancelled all my public engagements,' said General Zia. 'I won't go to the President's House even for state functions.'

And suddenly Brigadier TM felt like a civilian. Too slow to understand the obvious, to see what stared him in the face. The carpets, the curtains and the sofas were from the newly built President's House. He still couldn't figure out where he had seen the portrait.

'I am not leaving the Army House until you find out who it is. Go through General Akhtar's files. Major Kiyani has got a suspect, talk to him.'

'I need a day off, sir,' Brigadier TM said, coming to attention.

General Zia had to muster all his self-control to remain calm. Here he was, worrying about all these threats to his life, and his Security Chief wanted to get away for some rest and recreation.

'I am leading the para jump at the National Day Parade, sir,' Brigadier TM explained.

'I was thinking of cancelling the parade,' General Zia said. 'But General Akhtar keeps insisting we can't have a National Day without the National Day Parade, so I am thinking of cutting down on the ceremonies. We won't have the post-parade mingling with the people. But you can do your jumps if you want. I am not going to the Academy either. They were planning some kind of silent drill display. Do you know what that is?'

Brigadier TM shrugged his shoulders and his eyes scanned the room one last time.

Before leaving the room Brigadier TM didn't forget to point out the security breach. 'Sir, if you want anything transported from President's House, do let me know and I'll arrange the security clearance.'

General Zia, still thinking about the tunnel under his bedroom, threw his hands in the air and said, 'The First Lady. I don't know what that woman wants. You try talking to her.'

CHAPTER 5

Istay still in the bed, eyes shut as I listen. Someone is moaning in the adjoining room. I can hear the faint sound of the Academy band practising a slow march. Every sound is filtered, muted; the light seems to be fading away. This is just like the afternoons I remember at our house on Shigri Hill, where a bright puddle of light on a mountain peak tricks you into believing that there is still a lot of daylight left. One moment the sun is a juicy orange dangling low on the horizon and the highest mountains are awash in bright sunlight. The next moment the only light is a flicker from a fire on a distant peak. Night on the mountains is a black sheet flung from the skies. The day packs up and leaves without giving anyone any notice, without any formal goodbyes.

Just like Baby O.

I try to banish the mountain dusk from my mind and focus on my current plight. There is sadness about the lost day, but there is a phone on the other side of the curtain and Obaid is not the kind of person to scrawl numbers on his favourite hankie if they don't mean anything.

I open my eyes and see the silhouette of the duty nurse bent over a newspaper on the other side of the curtain. I let out a slow moan to see if he is alert. He lifts his head from the paper, looks vaguely towards me, then gets busy with his newspaper again.

In his yogi phase Obaid claimed that if you meditated regularly you could will people to do things – small things usually. If you stare at a stranger's neck long enough he is bound to turn and look towards you. Obaid had demonstrated it a number of times. The success is random at best, and making them move from point A to B is an altogether bigger challenge. I don't have much experience, but I stare and stare, and after about half a century, the nurse gets up and leaves.

I can't be sure whether he has gone for his prayers or for an early dinner. Maybe his shift has ended. All I know is that this is my only window of opportunity.

As my limbs go into action, everything happens very fast; shirt, boots, belt, sword, cap find their place on my body like rifle parts coming together in the hands of an experienced soldier. The tone on the telephone is loud and clear and I start dialling the number urgently, as if Obaid is going to pick up the phone at the other end.

As I am dialling the last two digits my nose catches the faint smell of Dunhill. My first thought is that some cheeky bugger is smoking in the sickbay. My morale gets a boost with the thought that I can probably get a cigarette off him after I finish the phone call.

The phone is answered on the second ring. The operator, used to receiving too many calls, replies in a neutral tone; he will only decide what to do with me after he can identify my rank, and can establish my status in the scheme of things.

'*Asslam u alaikum*, Army House,' the operator says, and the shock of being connected to that place is mixed with relief that the operator seems to be a civilian. It's usually easy to impress them.

'Khan sahib,' I start. 'I'm a relative of General Zia. I know you can't put me through to him, but can you take an urgent message?'

'Your name, sir?'

'Under Officer Ali Shigri. Son of Colonel Quli Shigri. The late Colonel Shigri.' I always find this the hard part, but the name works and I suddenly feel I am being listened to. Not that he actually believes that I am related to the General, but he has obviously heard of Colonel Shigri. Who in the Army House doesn't know the late Colonel Shigri?

'Do you have a pen and paper?'

'Yes, sir.'

'Write: Colonel Quli Shigri's son called. He gives his respects. He gives his salaam. Did you get that? Salaam.'

'Yes, sir.'

'He says that he wants to pass on some very important, very urgent information about the missing plane. It's a matter . . . did you get that?'

He replies in the affirmative and I think hard about an attention-grabbing end to my message:

My only friend in the world is in danger. If you guys have him, be nice to him.

I have some top CIA info that I can't trust anyone with.

Save my ass.

'It's a matter of national security,' I say. 'He must get this directly from you.'

I smell the Dunhill smoke in the room before I hear the voice. I would recognise it from my coffin.

'Under Officer Ali?'

The fact that the voice has used my first name makes me put the phone down abruptly.

Major Kiyani of the Inter Services Intelligence is standing in the doorway, one hand leaning on the frame, the other holding the cigarette in front of his chest. He is in civvies. He is always in civvies. A cream-coloured silk shalwar qameez, neatly pressed, his gelled hair glistening under the bulb's light, a curl carefully arranged in the middle of his forehead where his burly eyebrows meet.

I have never seen him in uniform. I am not even sure whether he has one or knows how to wear one. I saw him for the first time at Dad's funeral; his cheeks were slightly sunken and his eyes seemed sincere. But then there were so many people there and I had assumed he was just another one of Dad's disciples swarming around our house, fixing things, taking care of his papers.

'I realise that it's very painful for you, but the

Colonel would have wanted this done quickly,' he had said, dabbing his eyes with a white hankie, after we deposited Dad's flag-draped coffin under his favourite apple tree on Shigri Hill.

In ten minutes he had drafted a statement on my behalf and made me sign it. The statement said that as the only male member of the family, I didn't want an autopsy, I didn't suspect foul play and I had found no suicide note.

'Call me if you ever need anything,' he had said and left without giving me a phone number. I never needed anything. Not from him.

'I see you are all dressed up and ready to go,' he says.

With people like Major Kiyani there are no identification cards, no arrest warrants, no pretence at doing something legal or for your own good. There is a cruel stillness about him. The stillness of a man who lights up in a hospital room and doesn't even look around for something to use as an ashtray.

'Where are we going?' I ask.

'Somewhere we can talk.' His cigarette makes a directionless wave in the air. 'This place is full of sick people.'

'Am I under arrest?'

'Don't be so dramatic.'

A Toyota Corolla without a number plate is parked outside, a white, early-1988 model. It is still not available on the market. The car is gleaming and spotless white, with matching starched cotton seat covers. As he starts the car I realise we are headed out, out of here, somewhere not very close, somewhere not very pleasant.

I am already missing my dorm, my Silent Drill Squad, even 2nd OIC's sad, tired jibes.

The car is very empty. Major Kiyani doesn't carry a briefcase or a file or a weapon. I look hungrily at his packet of cigarettes and gold lighter lying on the dashboard in front of him. He sits back, his hands resting lightly on the steering wheel, ignoring me. I study his pink, manicured fingers, the fingers of a man who has never had to do any real work. One look at his skin and you can tell he has been fed on a steady diet of bootleg Scotch whisky, chicken korma and an endless supply of his agency's safe-house whores. Look into his sunken cobalt-blue eyes and you can tell he is the kind of man who picks up a phone, makes a long-distance call and a bomb goes off in a crowded bazaar. He probably waits outside a house at midnight in his Corolla with its headlights switched off while his men climb the wall and rearrange the lives of some hapless civilians. Or, as I know from personal experience, he appears quietly at funerals after accidental deaths and unexplained suicides and wraps things up with a neat little statement, takes care of any loose ends, saves you the agony of autopsies and the foreign press speculating about decorated colonels swinging from ceiling fans. He is a man who runs the world with a packet of Dunhills, a gold lighter and an unregistered car.

He reaches into his glove compartment and starts rummaging for a tape.

'Asha or Lata?' he asks.

I see a palm-sized holster and the ivory handle of a grey metal pistol and suddenly feel at ease. The presence of a gun in the glove compartment justifies this journey. He can take me wherever he wants to take me.

To tell you the truth I really can't tell the difference between Lata and Asha. They are old, fat, ugly Indian sisters who both sing like they were teenage sex kittens. One probably sounds sexier than the other, I can never tell. But across the country battle lines are drawn between those who like Asha and those who like Lata. Tea or coffee? Coke or Pepsi? Maoist or Leninist? Shia or Sunni?

Obaid used to say it's all very simple. It all depends on how you are feeling and how you would rather feel. That was the most fucked-up thing I ever heard.

'Lata,' I say.

He says I have got my dad's good taste and inserts a tape into the player. It's a male folk singer singing a ghazal, something about erecting a wall in the desert so that no one can bother the wandering lovers.

'Don't worry,' he says. 'We know you are from a good family.'

CHAPTER 6

One person in Islamabad hoping to improve the quality of his life after General Zia's disappearance from public life was a newly married, balding, forty-five-year-old diplomat, a man who would not live to celebrate his forty-sixth birthday.

Arnold Raphel was washing a bunch of arugula in his kitchen, a part of the house he was not very familiar with. Like any US ambassador's kitchen, it was designed for a team of chefs, waiters and their helpers, not for the brightest star in the State Department trying to prepare a supper for two. Arnold Raphel wanted to surprise his wife Nancy, referred to as Cupcake in moments of intimacy, by giving her a Foggy Bottom evening in Islamabad. He had asked the domestic staff to take the evening off, ordered his communication room to reroute all important calls to the First Secretary's residence and shut the doors to his vast drawing rooms, dining halls and guest suites. On her return from her weekly tennis game, Nancy would find that there were just the two of them, in their own living area, no servants milling about waiting for dinner instructions. For one evening they would live the life of a newly married couple; an early supper just like they used to have in their two-bedroom condo in Washington and then spontaneous lovemaking after watching the Redskins triumph over the Green Bay Packers in a crucial NFL play-off.

The beers were chilling in the morgue-size fridge, the Hawaiian steaks marinating in white ceramic dishes. Arnold had already programmed his dish antenna to receive the game and now he was going through the kitchen shelves looking for olive oil and a pepper grinder. He was determined to create a little bit of the East Coast behind the barbed-wire-topped walls of his eighteen-bedroom ambassadorial mansion. He was trying not to think of the three different layers of security surrounding his residence, the numerous antennae and satellite dishes stuck on the roof and colour-coded telephones dotting the whole living area.

Arnold wanted to make it a memorable evening. He wasn't a domestic type of diplomat but he was acutely aware that Nancy had put her own career in the State Department on hold so that she could be with him in this blasted city. For one evening, it'd be just like the old days when after putting in long hours at their Washington office they would take turns doing meals, Nancy cooking yet another variation on lasagne and Arnold when it was his turn getting a sudden urge to order Chinese takeout. Islamabad was a whirl of conspiracies and dinner parties; there were more CIA subcontractors and cooks per household than meals in a day. Nancy had started referring to herself as Nancy begum, the housewife with no housework.

Arnold had abandoned his search for olive oil and was taking a Budweiser out of the fridge while humming the Redskins' anthem when the red phone rang. There were only three people who could call him on this phone and he couldn't pass any of them on to his First Secretary. It was most probably his boss from Washington, George no-lunch Shultz. It was lunch hour in Foggy Bottom and the Secretary of State kept his calls brief so Arnold picked up the phone without thinking, ready for a quick diplomatic update.

It was General Zia ul-Haq, the President of his host country, on the line, polite and pointless as ever: how's Nancy's health, how was she adjusting to the local weather, was she getting along with the servants, were they planning to have babies soon? Arnold went along: Nancy loved Islamabad, she had started taking Urdu lessons, she was getting used to having so many servants, she would love to call on the First Lady sometime.

'Arnie, why don't you bring her over?' When General Zia called him Arnie, he always wanted Arnold Raphel to do something beyond the call of his diplomatic duty.

'Sure, Mr President. No true diplomat should ever eat at home. Just waiting for your invitation.'

'I know that these things should be arranged in

advance, but we are having another American friend over for dinner and he would like to see you very much.'

Arnie looked at his Hawaiian steaks and panicked. Not another brainstorming session with a visiting delegation of the Pakistani Association of North American Doctors, Arnie thought. Not another wasted evening discussing models for some proposed mosque in some godforsaken New Jersey neighbourhood. Not another debate about how a minaret can be adapted so that it reflects true Islamic architectural sensibility without clashing with American aesthetic values. He was wondering how to make it clear to the General that his brief as the ambassador didn't include being used as a guinea pig for spreading Islam in North America. He was thinking about a diplomatic enough excuse, something about Nancy having a stomach bug or entertaining a group of local newspaper editors; both useless, he knew. His domestic staff had probably already reported to the General that Ambassador Sahib was planning a honeymoon at home, and the General himself would definitely know who was entertaining local editors and where.

Before Arnie could come up with something, General put an end to his dreams of a cosy domestic evening. 'Bill is coming over for dinner,' he said.

'Bill Casey?' Arnie asked, feeling very unlike the Ambassador of the United States. He wondered whether his friends in Langley were planning to put the boot in after entrusting him with the biggest assignment since Saigon. 'The only difference is you'll be managing victory rather than a defeat,' Bill had told him. The embassy was full of Bill's people anyway, from the trio of cultural, commercial and military attachés to the political officers and the communication analysts. Sometimes Arnold wondered whether his cook was also getting his recipes from Langley. He realised the need for this, as Bill always kept reminding him that the CIA was running the biggest covert operation against the Soviets from Pakistan since their last biggest covert operation against the Soviets from somewhere else. Bill kept reminding everyone that he had the Russkis by their balls in Afghanistan. Bill was always telling his old chum Ronald Reagan that it was the Wild West all over again, that the Afghans were cowboys with turbans and that they were kicking Soviet ass as it had never been kicked before.

But Arnie was the ambassador around here and he shouldn't have to find out about Bill's imminent visit from General Zia. The Director of the CIA could visit wherever he wanted and whomever he wanted, but even the Director of the CIA had to inform the ambassador who was, technically, his host. But what can you do about Bill, or as Nancy always called him, Bill get-Ronnie-on-the-line Casey?

General Zia laughed. 'Don't worry, it's just an

informal visit. When Bill gets together with Prince Naif they do crazy things, you know. They called from Jeddah an hour ago and said they felt like eating that bitter-gourd, mutton-curry combination that the First Lady made last time they were here. And I said, "My wife is your sister and you know sisters love to feed their brothers."'

'I'll receive him and bring him over,' Arnie said. He had no idea where and when Bill was arriving.

'Don't worry,' General Zia said. 'They were racing their planes from Saudi to here. The Prince won and is already here. General Akhtar is picking Bill up. His plane should be landing now. You come over and if Nancy likes bitter gourds, bring her along as well.'

The Chief of Inter Services Intelligence, General Akhtar Abdur Rehman's devotion to his duty was not the ordinary devotion of an ambitious man to his work. General Akhtar approached his work like a poet contemplating an epic in progress; conjuring up battles in his imagination, inventing and discarding subplots, balancing rhyme and reason. His work could take him in a single day from an interrogation centre to a state banquet to an unlit tarmac runway at an airport, where he would receive a guest whose arrival time he never knew. Pakistan's second most powerful man didn't mind waiting in the dark if the visitor happened to be the second most powerful man in United States of America.

The next time General Akhtar stood on an airfield, he would be in a uniform, he would not want to board the plane but would be forced to do so, out of sheer reverence for his chief. And that would be the last order he would ever obey.

General Akhtar looked into the orange-tinged Islamabad sky and wondered what was taking his guest so long.

Bill Casey's C141 Star Lifter, carrying him from Saudi Arabia, circled over the military airbase outside Islamabad. The clearance for landing had been given, but Bill was still freshening up after a two-hour nap. The interior of this plane was part hotel room, part communication bunker; a flying command centre carrying so much black metal with blinking lights that a team of three sergeants worked full time monitoring and decoding the incoming and outgoing messages. There were modular frequency jammers to override all other transmitters working in a ten-mile radius, digital deflectors to misguide any missiles lobbed at the jet, double jammers to counter-jam any other jamming equipment operating in the area. It could also fly under five different identities, switching from one call sign to another as it crossed continents. It was Duke One when it took off from Saudi Arabia. Somewhere over the Arabian Sea, it had become Texan Two.

Bill's suite on the plane was a basic budget-hotel affair, a double bed, a shower and a small television. He shaved and repacked his bag to while

102

away some time so that Prince Naif could win the race. Five years of dealing with his Saudi counter-part had taught Bill one lesson: you can take a Bedouin out of a desert, you can take him off his camel and give him the most expensive flying machine in the world, but there was no point trying to take the camel jockey out of him. If the Prince wanted to race his plane on his way to dinner, the CIA chief would oblige.

As Bill's C141 made its final approach to the runway and the pilot started communication with air traffic control, the counter-jammers went to work. Thousands of listeners tuning into *Golden Oldies* from Ceylon Radio heard their favourite songs interrupted by a chorus of bagpipes issuing from the cover pulse generators on the plane. The arrival was so secret that even the air traffic controller, used to the arrival of American military planes at odd hours, didn't know that he was communicating with a VIP flight. Giving respectful instructions to the pilot, he thought, Here comes another plane full of booze and pig meat for those American spies at the US Embassy.

The plane taxied to the furthest end of the runway and the runway lights were switched on only when it had come to a complete halt. Six identical black Mercedes limousines were parked close to the runway. Four motorcycle outriders – or pilots as they are called in the VIP Security Unit – waited on their Kawasaki 1000 motorcycles in front of the convoy, their helmet earphones on standby for instructions. General Akhtar Abdur Rehman saluted Bill Casey, a salute complete with stamping of the heel and his straight palm parallel with his right eyebrow.

'Welcome, Field Marshal,' he said. The tableau had started as a joke when Bill, in his first meeting with Akhtar, kept calling him Generalissimo. 'Well, if I am a general, you must be the field marshal, sir,' Akhtar had said and now he insisted on the role play whenever Bill visited.

'Damn, Akhtar,' Bill Casey raised a limp hand to his eyebrow. 'I'm dead tired.'

As the outriders switched their sirens on one by one, General Akhtar and Bill Casey got into the fourth limousine, a posse from CIA's Special Operations Group, wearing suits and carrying no visible arms, and a group of Pakistani commandos with their sleek little Uzis, got into the other limousines and the journey to the Army House started. It was a forty-minute drive for civilians. The VIP convoy, with all traffic and pedestrian crossings blocked, could make it in twelve minutes, but General Akhtar seemed to be in no hurry.

'Would you like a drink before dinner, sir?' he asked, with both his hands in his lap.

'Are we going straight to dinner?' Bill asked wearily.

'Prince Naif is already there, sir.'

'And my friend,' Bill mimed General Zia's moustache with the thumb and forefinger of his right hand, 'is he really having these visions?'

General Akhtar smiled a coy smile, puffed out his chest and said in a very concerned tone. 'Eleven years is a long time. He's a bit tired.'

'Tell me about it.' Bill slumped into his seat. 'Go ahead. Get me drunk.' General Zia never served alcohol at his dinners, even state dinners, not even for known alcoholics. General Akhtar Abdur Rehman considered it his duty to keep his guests in good humour, either at his office or during the drive to the Army House. He tapped the driver's seat, and without looking back, the man passed him a black canvas bag. Akhtar produced two glasses, a silver ice bucket, a bottle of Royal Salute whisky and poured Bill half a glass and himself a glass of water; he asked the driver to slow down and said, 'Cheers.'

'Cheers,' said Bill. 'Cheers to you, General. Nice country you got here.' He flicked open the curtain on the limousine window and watched the crowd gathered along the roadside, straining against the security police and waiting for this convoy to hurry up and pass so that they could get on with their lives.

'Sad, though, you can't sit down somewhere and have a goddam drink. Cheers.'

Behind the cordons set up along the road by the police for this VIP procession, people stood and waited and guessed: a teenager anxious to continue his first ride on a Honda 70, a drunk husband ferociously chewing betel nuts to get rid of the smell before he got home, a horse buckling under the weight of too many passengers on the cart, the passengers cursing the cart driver for taking this route, the cart driver feeling the pins and needles in his legs begging for their overdue opium dose, a woman covered in a black burqa – the only body part visible her left breast feeding her infant child – a boy in a car trying to hold a girl's hand on their first date, a seven-year-old selling dust-covered roasted chickpeas, an old water carrier hawking water out of a goatskin, a heroin addict eyeing his dealer stranded on the other side of the road, a mullah who would be late for the evening prayer, a gypsy woman selling bright pink baby chickens, an air force trainee officer in uniform in a Toyota Corolla being driven by a Dunhill-smoking civilian, a newspaper hawker screaming the day's headlines, Singapore Airline's crew in a van cracking jokes in three languages, a pair of home-delivery arms dealers fidgeting with their suitcases nervously, a third-year medical student planning to end his life by throwing himself on the rail tracks in anticipation of the Shalimar Express, a husband and wife on a motorbike returning from a fertility clinic, an illegal Bengali immigrant waiting to sell his kidney so that he could send money back home, a blind woman who had escaped prison in the morning and had spent all day trying to convince people that she was not a beggar, eleven teenagers dressed in white impatient to get to the field for their night cricket match, off-duty policemen waiting for free rides

106

home, a bride in a rickshaw on her way to the beauty salon, an old man thrown out of his son's home and determined to walk to his daughter's house fifty miles away, a coolie from the railway station still wearing his red uniform and in a shopping bag carrying a glittering sari he'd change into that night, an abandoned cat sniffing her way back to her owner's house, a black-turbaned truck driver singing a love song about his lover at the top of his voice, a bus full of trainee Lady Health Visitors headed for their night shift at a government hospital; as the smoke from idling engines mixed with the smog that descends on Islamabad at dusk, as their waiting hearts got to bursting point with anxiety, they all seemed to have one question on their minds: 'Which one of our many rulers is this? If his security is so important, why don't they just lock him up in the Army House?'

CHAPTER 7

I stare through the windscreen with such intensity it's as if I am the one driving the car. I can only admire how Major Kiyani doesn't believe in giving anyone the right of way on this narrow, potholed road. He maintains his speed in the face of an oncoming truck, flicks the car headlights to full beam, his fingers tap to the music on the steering wheel and at the last possible moment it's the truck that swerves and pulls off the road. Major Kiyani's Corolla seems like an extension of his powers, unblinking, unlimited and needing no justification.

A child bolts out of a golden, harvest-ready wheat-field and Major Kiyani presses the car horn and keeps it pressed for a mile.

The traffic is thin at this time of the evening, mostly trucks and night buses, an occasional tractor with a few tonnes of sugar cane on an overloaded trolley with some urchins following along, trying to pull out a sugar cane or two. We pass a bull cart crawling along the side of the road; the pair of bulls pulling it are blinded by our car's headlights; the dog walking by the cart yelps just once before ducking to avoid the speeding monster.

Slowly, very slowly, answers begin to emerge in my head, answers to the questions that Major Kiyani will inevitably throw at me. He needs to find out what I know. I need to make sure that every bit I give him widens the gap between what he knows and what he would like to know. The premise for my optimism is a philosophical notion: Major Kiyani would not be taking me away if he *knew*. I wouldn't be sitting on a starched white cover of the comfy seat of this Corolla listening to ghazals, if he knew. I would be in the back of a jeep, handcuffed and blindfolded and charge-sheeted and sentenced by now. Or maybe hanging from my own bed sheet in my own dorm.

Where is Major Kiyani from?

Inter Services Intelligence.

What does the agency do?

Investigate.

What do they investigate?

What they don't know.

Before falling off the edge of the cliff, I am sure, everyone tells himself a story which has a happy ending. This is mine.

The optimism goes straight to my bladder and I want Major Kiyani to get us to our destination, wherever it is. The road signs tell me that we are headed towards Lahore, but there are half a dozen turns in the road leading to various parts of the country and Major Kiyani probably travels in the opposite direction to where he wants to take you. We sit for a long time in a traffic jam caused by roadblocks set up by the police, as a convoy of black limousines crawls past.

'Everything I know about this profession your dad taught me,' he says, looking ahead. 'But it seems you never learned anything from him. Americans are trouble. I know your friend Bannon is behind this mad adventure.'

'Then why isn't he travelling with you instead of me?' I ask.

'You know why,' he says. 'He is an American, our guest. He shouldn't be mixed up with the likes of you. Drill is for the parade square. What he does off the square is my business.'

'Have you found the plane?' I say, careful not to mention Obaid.

He turns his face towards me; a truck comes at us; I jump in my seat and hold the dashboard. With the slightest movement of the steering wheel, he swerves the car into a service road and parks at a roadside restaurant. He opens the glove compartment, takes the gun and tucks it under his shirt.

He opens the car door then looks back at me. 'You and your friend probably think you invented buggery, but it existed long before you started wearing this uniform.'

He orders food. I order dal, he asks for chicken karahi. 'Make his special,' he tells the waiter. 'Our young man needs nourishment.' We eat in silence.

The food is too spicy for my mountain tastes. I need to go to the loo. I am not sure whether I should just get up and go or ask for his permission.

I get up, pointing towards the loo. He signals with his eyes for me to keep sitting. 'Maybe you should wait. We won't be long.'

I look at the turbaned man guarding the restaurant loo and think maybe he is right. Roadside restaurants' loos are generally filthy and I'd rather be relieving myself in an open field under a star-filled sky rather than in a room full of piss and the smell of spicy shit.

A waiter hovers around us after we finish our dinner, expecting further orders. Major signs his name in the air, the waiter brings the bill, Major scribbles something on it and gets up to leave without paying anything.

He must be a regular here, I think. He must have an account with these people.

The rest of the journey is a battle between the muscles that control my bladder and Major Kiyani's sudden fit of patriotism. I nod my head enthusiastically when he reminds me that the last time anyone tried to disappear with a plane the country broke into two. I squeeze my thighs and practically jump in my seat when he talks about my dad's illustrious career. 'You know what they said about your dad? That he was one of the ten men standing between the Soviets and the Free World.' I nod my head enthusiastically when he goes on and on about the sacrifices that invisible soldiers like him and my dad have to make for the sake of national security.

I squeeze my thighs. I want to say, 'Can I pee first and then we can save the world together?' Our car takes its final turn into a narrow road that leads to the majestically sombre gate of the Lahore Fort.

In the historic city of Lahore, the Fort is a very historic place. It was built by the same guy who built the Taj Mahal, the Mughal King Shahjahan. He was thrown into prison by his own son, a kind of forced premature retirement. I have never been to the Fort but I have seen it in a shampoo ad.

Do I look like the kind of person who needs a lesson in history at midnight? The Fort is clearly closed to tourists. I am sure the Major can get after-hours access anywhere, but shouldn't he be taking me to an interrogation centre or a safe house or wherever it is that he takes people when he wants to have a chat?

As the car approaches the gate two soldiers emerge from the shadows. The Major slides his window down and stretches his neck out but doesn't speak. The gate, probably built to accommodate an elephant procession, opens slowly and reveals an abandoned city dreamed up by a doomed king.

Parts of the Fort are dimly lit, revealing bits of its stone walls so wide that horses can gallop on them, gardens so vast and green that they disappear and appear again after you have driven for a while. The Court for the Commons and the Ladies'

Courtyard stand in their crumbling, faded glory. I wonder where the famous Palace of Mirrors is. That's where they did the shampoo advert.

The only signs of life in this deserted sprawl of useless splendour are two army trucks with their headlights on and engines idling. Major Kiyani parks the car beside these trucks. We get out of the car and start walking towards the Court for the Commons. It's dimly lit and I can't really see the source of the light. I expect spear-carrying Mughal soldiers to appear from behind the pillars to take us to the King, who, depending on his mood, would either ask us to join in his late-night debauchery or have our heads chopped off and thrown from the walls of the Fort.

Major Kiyani takes an abrupt turn and we start descending a stairway made of concrete, definitely not built by the Mughals. We enter a vast, empty hall that looks eerily like an aviation hangar. Right in the middle of the hall, sitting under what must be a thousand-watt bulb, is a subedar major who gets up and salutes Major Kiyani as we approach his metal table, which is piled high with heaps of bulging yellow folders.

Major Kiyani nods his head but doesn't speak a word. He pulls up a chair, grabs a file and starts flicking through the pages as if oblivious to my presence.

Then he remembers.

'Show Under Officer Shigri to the toilet,' he says without looking up from his file. I walk behind the

Subedar Major down a well-lit corridor lined with iron doors on both sides, with stencilled white numbers on them. There is absolute silence in the corridor, but behind the doors I can hear the muted snores of dreaming men. At the end of the corridor there is a small rusted iron door without a number. The Subedar Major produces a key, opens the lock and moves aside. I open the door and take a step inside. The door hits my back and is locked behind me. That terrible smell of the closed toilet which has not seen a drop of water for ages welcomes me, my head hits the wall, a thousand-watt bulb is switched on. So bright is the light, so overpowering the stench, that I cannot see anything for the first few moments.

It is a loo, that much is clear. There is a hole in the ground so full of indistinguishable faeces that bubbles are forming on its surface. The floor is covered with a thick slimy layer of some garish liquid. There is a water tap one foot above the ground but it has stayed dry for so long that it's rusting. There is a grey WC with a broken chain, I open it and take a peek inside. There is two inches of water at the bottom, reflecting its inner rusted orange surface.

My need to pee has disappeared forever. The stench is so strong that it's difficult to think about anything else.

I stand against the wall and close my eyes.

They have a file on me somewhere, which says Under Officer Shigri can't stand dirty bathrooms.

I have done my jungle survival course, I have learned how to hunt snakes in the desert and quench my thirst. No one ever thought of designing a course on how to survive stinking bathrooms.

I charge at the door and start banging with both my clenched fists. 'Open this bloody door. Get me out of this shithole. This place stinks.'

I bang my head on the door a couple of times and the stupidity of my actions becomes obvious to me. All the shouting takes the edge off the stench. It's still the smell of piss and shit but somehow it's become subdued. Or am I already getting used to it?

They are in no mood to interrogate me at this hour. This is going to be my abode for the night.

My back goes to the wall, I clench my toes in my boots and resolve to spend the night standing up. There is no way I am going to give these butchers the pleasure of watching me lie down in this pool of piss. There is scribbling on the wall but I can't be bothered to read it. I can make out the words General Zia and his mother and sister, my imagination can connect the dots.

The idea that this place has hosted people who were angry enough at the General to write things about his mother and sister is puzzling. I might be down on my luck but the last time I checked I was still a trainee officer in uniform and the fact that they have put me in this shithole for civilians is the ultimate insult.

★   ★   ★

Colonel Shigri had tried to talk me out of joining the armed forces.

'The officer corps is not what it used to be,' he said, pouring himself the first whisky of the evening after returning from his umpteenth trip to Afghanistan.

'People who served with me were all from good families. No, I don't mean wealthy families. I mean respectable people, good people. When you asked them where they were from, you knew their fathers and grandfathers were distinguished people. And now you've got shopkeepers' sons, milkmen's boys, people who are not good for anything else. I don't want those half-breeds fucking up my son's life.'

Daddy, you should see me now.

He knew in his heart that I was not convinced. He called me again when he was pouring his last whisky, his seventh probably. He was a three-whiskies-an-evening man but he felt unusually thirsty when he returned from his Afghan trips. There was bitterness in his voice now that I wasn't familiar with at that point but which would become permanent.

'I have three war decorations, and wounds to prove them,' he said. 'You go to any officers' mess in the country and you'll find a few people whose lives I saved. And now? Look at me. They have turned me into a pimp. I am a man who was trained to save lives, now I trade in them.'

He kept twirling his whisky glass in his fingers

116

and kept repeating the word 'pimp' over and over again.

I doze off and dream of pissing in the cold clear stream that runs by our house on Shigri Hill. I wake up with my knees trembling and the grime from the floor seeping into my toes. The left side of my trousers is soaking wet. I feel much better.

Stay on your bloody feet. Stay on your bloody feet.

That is the first thing I tell myself before taking stock of my situation. What did they do to the renegade soldiers of the Mughal Army? A swift decapitation or being scrunched under the foot of an elephant would probably be a better fate than this.

The stench has grown fetid and hangs heavy in the air. I close my eyes and try to imagine myself back on Shigri Hill. The mountain air wafts in despite the iron doors and the underground prison and the walls of the Fort. It swirls around me, bringing back the smell of earth dug by goats' hooves, the aroma of green almonds and the sound of a clear, cold stream gushing past. The silence of the mountains is punctuated by a humming sound, coming from a distance but not very far away. Somebody is singing in a painful voice. Before I can identify the voice a bucket of water is poured over my head and my face is pushed so close to a thousand-watt bulb that my lips burn. I don't know who is asking the questions. It could be Major Kiyani. It could be one of his brothers without uniform. My answers, when I can muster them, are met with further questions. This is not an interrogation. They are not interested in my answers. The buggers are only interested in sex.

Did Lieutenant Bannon and Obaid have a sexual relationship?

They were very close. But I don't know. I don't think so.

Did you and Obaid have a sexual relationship?

Fuck you. No. We were friends.

Did you fuck him?

I can hear you. The answer is no, no, no.

He wasn't in his bed the night before he disappeared. Do you know where he was?

The only person he could have been with is Bannon. They went on walks sometimes.

Is that why you marked him present in the Fury Squadron roll call?

I assumed he would come straight to the parade square. He did that occasionally.

Did Obaid have any suicidal tendencies? Did he ever talk about taking his own life?

I imagine a two-seater aeroplane going down on all its three axes and the hot white glare of the bulb begins to fade away.

He read poetry. He sang songs about dying but he never actually talked about dying. Not to me. Not in any suicidal way.

CHAPTER 8

The large reception room in the Army House was reserved for receiving visiting foreign dignitaries from the USA and Saudi Arabia, the VVIPs. After winning his air dash from Saudi Arabia to Islamabad, Prince Naif was seated on a velvet sofa, smoking Marlboro Reds and boasting about the sound barrier that his F16 broke on his way to dinner. 'Our brother Bill is probably still flying over the Arabian Sea.' Laughing, the Prince raised both arms and mimed the flight of a tired bird.

'Allah's glory,' said General Zia. 'It's all His blessing. I went on a ride in one of ours and my old bones were aching for days. You, by the grace of Allah, are still a young man.'

General Zia kept looking out of the corner of his eyes at Dr Sarwari, who had accompanied Prince Naif at his request but seemed to have been forgotten in Prince Naif's victory celebrations. General Zia wanted to have a word with the royal doctor about his condition.

General Zia's condition, although he himself preferred to call it an itsy-bitsy itch, had been messing up his prayer routine. He had always been very proud of the fact that he was the kind of Muslim who could do his ablutions for his morning prayers and say his late-night prayers with the same ablutions. All the things that break an ablution had been eliminated from his daily routine; garlic, lentils, women who didn't cover their heads properly. But since he had confined himself to the Army House this itch had started.

He had called his staff surgeon first, had told him about the tiny drops of blood he had found on the seat of his pants, but couldn't bring himself to talk about the itch.

'Do you get burning, itching in your rectal passage?' the staff surgeon had asked.

'No,' he had said abruptly.

'Sir, internal bleeding can be dangerous but yours seems like a case of worms, tapeworms. If you let me know when you can come to the Combined Military Hospital I'll arrange for a full check-up.'

General Zia had mumbled something about Code Red and dismissed the doctor. Although the staff surgeon was security cleared Zia didn't want him to go around sending his tests to other labs or even consulting his doctor colleagues. His own daughter had just graduated from a medical school but he could hardly talk to her about something like this.

Then Prince Naif called and General Zia remembered that Prince Naif always travelled with his personal physician, the only person in his entourage who wore suits and carried a black leather bag, and the only one who stayed silent, neither cracked a joke nor laughed at the Prince's non-stop comedy act.

'I don't share my doctor with anyone,' Prince Naif said in mock seriousness when General Zia finally asked his permission to have a private consultation with his physician. 'He has seen more of me than any of my wives. But anything for you, my brother, anything. Even my secret weapon.' He gestured towards the doctor, who sat pretending they were talking about someone else.

'It's just a private little matter. I don't want my military doctor going around discussing my private things. You know our Pakistani people, they love to gossip.'

'He takes care of all my private things,' Prince Naif chuckled. 'And he never talks to anyone.' Then he turned towards the doctor and said, 'Take care of my brother's private things as if they were my own private things.' He rolled with laughter. General Zia forced a smile, got up and moved towards his office. The doctor didn't join in the joke and followed him sullenly.

After spending eight years looking after Prince Naif's libido nothing about these rulers surprised Dr Sarwari. They all spent too much time and energy keeping their cocks in shape. If they channelled some of this zeal towards their day jobs, the world would be a much better place, Dr Sarwari had thought in moments of despair. He had ordered the livers of so many houbara bustards to make aphrodisiacs for the Prince, he had rubbed so many ointments made from the Bengal tiger's testicles on the Prince's member that he himself had lost all appetite for sex. Even his colleagues in the Saudi medical establishment knew his status as the full-time caretaker of the royal member. After all, the Prince had his own heart specialist, skin specialist and even a plastic surgeon on the royal payroll. But what was dearest to the Prince's heart was his sexual health and Dr Sarwari was the chosen man for the job. The Royal Dick Doctor, they called him behind his back.

With this job description Dr Sarwari could not be faulted when he shut the door to General Zia's private office and asked: 'You wanna a bigger or you wanna a longer?'

General Zia, who had never heard the doctor speak, was baffled both by his mixture of Arabic and American accents and his strange question. He ignored his hand gestures.

Dr Sarwari was pleasantly surprised when General Zia explained his problem. He smiled for the first time.

General Zia was ready when the doctor suggested an on-the-spot probe. He had thought about it so much that he automatically turned his back to the doctor, unfastened his belt and slipped his trousers down. He could feel movement behind him, then a rubber-gloved hand on his buttocks.

'Birather, bend please.' General Zia still couldn't get over the man's American accent. He had always heard him speak Arabic with the Prince. He put his elbows on the table. 'More,' the doctor ordered. He put his right cheek on the table and tried to think of something to distract himself.

His head was between two flags. Pakistan's national flag, green and white with a thin right-facing crescent, on one side and on the other side, the flag of the Pakistan Army. He had almost made up his mind to reverse the crescent on the national flag after an Islamic scholar pointed out that it was a descending moon and not an ascending one, but then his advisers reminded him that the flag had been around for forty years and since nobody actually had any problem with the direction of the crescent, it was better to leave the flag alone.

He was relieved to feel that the doctor's probing finger was lubricated.

He looked at the army flag. Underneath the crossed swords was the famous slogan that the Founder of the Nation had given this country as its birthday present and motto: 'Faith. Unity. Discipline.' Suddenly, the slogan seemed not only banal and meaningless to him but too secular, non-committal, almost heretical. Faith? Which faith? Unity? Discipline? Do soldiers need that slogan? Aren't they supposed to be united and disciplined by the very nature of their calling? He felt the doctor's breath on his arse. The rubbered finger was replaced by a cold metallic tube which didn't hurt but caused some discomfort.

It also dawned on him that when the Founder came up with this slogan, he had civilians in mind, not the armed forces. This slogan, he told himself, had to go. His mind raced, searching for words that would reflect the true nature of his soldiers' mission. Allah had to be there. Jihad, very important. He knew it would please his friend Bill Casey. He couldn't decide on a third word but he knew it would come.

The doctor patted his buttock and said: 'You can get up please.' The General pulled up his underwear before turning round, making sure that the doctor didn't get a glimpse of his front. He still remembered his first question.

The doctor was grinning. 'You eat a sugaa?' The General shook his head in confusion.

'Yes. Yes. I have a sweet tooth.'

'Birather, that's why you so sweet.' The doctor patted his cheek with his gloved hand and General Zia blushed at the thought of where that hand had just been.

'You've worms, sir.' The doctor opened the palm of his left hand and showed him some tiny dead worms.

'Why does it itch so much, then?'

The doctor's grin broadened. 'They like prisoners. They worms. They eat sugaa, they get energy, they wanna out. They wanna find escape. The itch is like . . .' He tried to think of an expression, then made a shovelling movement with his hands. 'The itch is worms tunnelling. Making tunnels.'

General Zia nodded his head slowly. This was the second time in three days that he had been warned about tunnels. Here he was, worried about being trapped in a whale, while the enemy was eating away at his innards. A blasphemous thought occurred to him; what if there was an army of little Jonahs trapped in his stomach praying to get out?

'I'll cut down on sugar.'

'No cuttin sugaa.' The doctor took out bottle of Canderel. 'Sugaa finish. OK? No sugaa. Take this.'

The doctor shut his bag and General Zia held his face in both hands and kissed him on both his cheeks in the customary Arab fashion.

Then he realised his pants were still around his ankles.

Later over dinner, savouring the bitterness of bitter gourd, Bill Casey spoke like a ghost with the enlightenment of hindsight. 'Brother Zia.' He dabbed the corner of his mouth with his napkin to wipe off the drool. 'You think your folks are tryin' to kill ya? You should see those vultures at Capitol Hill. They have already killed me.'

CHAPTER 9

The first light of the day catches me dozing on my feet, my back against the wall, my toes clenched in my boots, my sweat-soaked khaki shirt open to my navel. The light is a long thin shaft coming through the tiny gap where the metal door is clamped against the bathroom wall. The shaft of light illuminates the ancient dust particles of the Lahore Fort prison; it highlights the bathroom wall in front of me, revealing bits of graffiti, something for me to do besides fantasising about impossible escape plans. When my car journey with Major Kiyani ended in the Fort, I expected a prison cell worthy of a trainee officer and an expert team of interrogators. What I got is this shithole and my own company.

The stench has invaded my pores and become a part of me. I am light-headed from lack of sleep, my lips are parched and my feet are swollen after standing all night. Walking half the night – three steps in one direction, two in the other – has obviously not given me the exercise I need. I think about taking off my boots. I bend down to do so, see the yellow muck on the floor closely and give up on the idea. I stretch my arms and concentrate on the reading material instead.

The scribbling on the walls is in three languages and the writers have used a variety of materials. I can read two of the languages, the third I have to guess. I can make out the etchings done with nails. The dried rust is probably blood, and I don't want to think what else they might have used.

There are hammers and sickles and date trees and fifteen varieties of breasts. Someone, who seems to have managed to bring in a ballpoint pen, has drawn a driveway, lined on both sides with apple trees, leading to a little house. My predecessors in this place had a lot to say, both personal and political.

I was lashed one hundred times and I liked it.
Pray for an easy end.
Asia is red with the blood of martyrs.
Asia is green and may Allah keep it this way.
Roses are red. Violets are blue. This country is khaki.
Screw the First Lady, not this nation.
Scream on the first lash. And don't faint because when they start again they will count from one.
Dear son, I did it for your future.
Major Kiyani is my bitch.
Lenin lives.
I love Nadia.
Lenin was a faggot.

A Persian couplet I can only vaguely decipher: *the lover, long tresses, snakes.* I think I get the picture.

127

I think about contributing my own two bits. Something like . . . 'On a very hot evening Under Officer Shigri had a flash of brilliance . . .'

Not enough space on the wall.

The silent drill conspiracy that Major Kiyani is trying to unearth was a fucked-up idea, which, like most fucked-up ideas, was conceived at the end of a very hot day in the Academy. We were taking potshots at a Bruce Lee poster in Bannon's room after a busy day on the parade square. All the heat that our bodies had accumulated during the drill rehearsal suddenly started to seep out, the starch of our uniforms stuck to our bodies like rough glue, sweat ran like lizards crawling over our flesh, our feet had suffocated and died in their shiny leather coffins. Bannon's room, with its over-efficient, noisy air conditioner, was the obvious hideout. Bannon had designed his room like a bunker; there was no bed, just a king-sized mattress on the ground, covered by a camouflaged canopy he had improvised with four bamboo sticks. On the floor, a little fat Buddha sat on a copy of *Stars and Stripes*. The Buddha had a secret chamber in his stomach where Bannon kept his supply of hashish. His uniforms hung neatly in the doorless cupboard. The only liberties he had taken with his designer bunker were the air conditioner and a life-size poster from *Game of Death*, which covered the entire inside of the door. The poster was a shot from the climax of the film, after

128

the last surviving villain, Kareem Abdul-Jabbar, had managed to get his paw on Bruce Lee's right ribcage, leaving four neat, parallel scratches. Bruce Lee's hands, in classic defensive posture, were spotlessly clean; his mouth was yet to bleed.

The official reason for our regular visit to Bannon's room was that we were working out the details of our silent drill display for the President's inspection. We needed to review the squad's progress, plot every single manoeuvre and work on our inner cadence.

But we really ended up there every day after the parade because Obaid loved to put his cheeks against the air conditioner's vent and I wanted to play with Bannon's Gung Ho Fairburn Sykes knife and listen to his stories of Operation Bloody Rice in Vietnam. He had done two tours of duty, and if he was in the right mood he could transport us to his night patrols and make us feel the movement of every single leaf on the Bloody Rice trail. He embellished his stories with a generous smattering of *Cha obo*, *Chao ong*, *Chao co*, probably the only Vietnamese words he knew. He called his slippers his Ho Chi Minhs. Obaid had his doubts.

'What was a drill instructor doing hunting down commies in a war?'

'Why don't you ask him?' I would say, and then go on to show off my own knowledge of the subject, culled from two classes on the history of the Vietnam War. 'It was war, Baby O, the biggest that

129

America fought. Everyone had to fight. Even the US Army priests and barbers were at the front.'

But today Bannon was in one of his dark, knife-throwing moods. It was difficult to get a word out of him if it wasn't about the pedigree of his Gung Ho. We lay under the camouflaged canopy. An unlit joint dangled from Bannon's mouth as he held his Gung Ho from its tip and contemplated its path towards Bruce Lee.

'Give me a target,' he said to no one in particular.

'Third rib from the top,' Obaid said without moving his cheek from the air conditioner's vents. Bannon held the handle of the knife to his lips for a moment. Then his wrist flicked, the knife circled in the air and ended up between Bruce Lee's third and fourth rib. 'Damn. The air conditioning,' he said. 'Gung Ho works best outdoors.' He suggested switching the air conditioning off and having another go. But Obaid wouldn't have any of that. Obaid went for Bruce Lee's right nipple and drew a blank, hitting the blue space above his right shoulder.

I removed the knife from the poster and walked backwards, keeping my eyes locked on Bruce Lee's right eye, my assigned target. When you do short-range targets it's usually your own eye that fails you, not the way you handle your weapon. The target has to exist in the cross hairs of your eyeballs. If the target doesn't live in your eye, you can keep your hands as steady as you want and you can hold your breath till you turn blue but there is no guarantee that you'll get the target. As the knife left my fingertips, I shut my eyes and only opened them when I heard Bannon going, 'Oh man, oh man.' I got up from the mattress, walked to the poster, removed the knife from the iris of Bruce Lee's right eye and threw it over my shoulder towards Bannon. I didn't have to look back to find out that he had caught it. Obaid shouted: 'Don't be a bloody show-off, Ali. It's only a circus trick.'

Bannon put the knife back in its leather sheath and lit his joint. 'In Danang we captured this gook who had killed nine of my men with a knife. The man was a fucking monkey. He hid in the trees; for all I know he swung from tree to tree like a fucking Chinky Tarzan. Nobody ever saw him. He got 'em all in the same fashion, during the patrol. Our guys would be out there with their M16 targeted at the bush, ready for an ambush, they would hear a branch move, they would look up and then swishhhh.' Bannon jabbed two fingers at his Adam's apple. A red rope was tightening in his eyes, his speech was slightly slurred. The air conditioner was refusing to exhale the thick hashish smoke in the room.

'I had some landmines planted around our bunker and put up a sign: "Ho Chi Minh sucks running dogs." To lure the enemy, you know; we did that all the time. But this gook never showed up.'

The joint was dead. Bannon lit it again and tried to remember where he was.

'So the point is, when we finally caught him, my boys wanted to make hamburger meat out of him. But I said we had to interrogate him, go by the book. It turned out he was a circus guy. You believe that? He'd travelled up to Taiwan throwing his daggers around his mama-pyjama girl. And then his eighty-year-old dad was killed working in his paddy field, just shot down in one of these raids. So this guy gave up his big-titty woman and circus tent. He didn't join the Viet Cong, which he would have been justified in doing. He just took to the jungles with his circus dagger.' He took a deep puff and exhaled a spiral. 'So there, Baby O, that's the point of my sorry-ass tale. You can throw a knife in a circus and you can have your big-titty women and you are a fucking freak show. You can have the same knife, polish it up with a bit of purpose and you are a man. A real man, not a fucking air-con soldier like you.'

I extended my hand towards Bannon. He mimed a question with his joint. 'Are you sure?'

I was very sure. Obaid looked at me with panicked eyes. Bannon handed me the joint and I took a proper puff and held it in my lungs till my eyes watered. It was between exhaling that sweet, acrid smoke and throwing up half an hour later that I got the fucked-up idea that landed me in this shithole.

CHAPTER 10

As he went through the newspapers the morning after broadcasting his special address to the nation, General Zia found himself cheering up. He spread the newspapers on the dining table one by one, till the gleaming mahogany surface was covered with his pictures and his words. He put his red pencil aside, savoured his tea and gave an approving nod to the duty waiter in the corner. The thing General Zia liked about his Information Minister was that although he was a devious bastard with a fake MBA who had made a lot of money ordering useless books that never arrived at the military libraries, he knew how to handle these newspaper editors. General Zia had tried to cultivate these editors himself and found out that they were the kind of intellectuals who prayed with him devoutly then rushed off to get drunk in the hotel rooms that his government provided them, with the booze that the Information Minister bought them. And the following morning their editorials were messy transcriptions of what General Zia had told them between their prayers and the boozing sessions.

This morning, however, was different. The nation's press had finally shown some spark. The editors had used their imagination while reporting his speech. Every newspaper had it as the banner headline. The message had gone out loud and clear. '*The Battle for Our Ideological Frontiers has begun.*' He was particularly pleased with the three-picture strip idea that the *Pakistan Times* had come up with to illustrate the main points from the extempore part of his speech. *First of all I am a Muslim* was the caption under a picture of him draped in a white cotton sheet with his head reclining on the black marbled wall of Khana Kaaba in Mecca. *Then I am a soldier of Islam* appeared under his official portrait, in which he was wearing his four-star General's uniform. *And then, as an elected head of the Muslim state, I am a servant of my people* was the caption for the third picture, which showed him in his presidential dress, looking dignified in a black sherwani and his reading glasses, not imposing but authoritative, not a military ruler but a president.

Heads of state, especially the heads of state of developing countries, seldom get the time to sit back and admire their own achievements. This was one of those rare moments when General Zia could recline in his chair with the newspaper in his lap, order another cup of tea and let the collective goodwill of his one hundred and thirty million subjects engulf his body and mind. With his red pencil he jotted a note in the margin of the paper to tell the Information Minister to nominate the editor of the *Pakistan Times* for a national literary award. He'd also tell the Information Minister that if you speak from your heart people *do* listen. He decided that from now on all his speeches would include a section starting with: '*My dear countrymen, now I want to say to you something from my heart.*' He imagined himself at public rallies flinging his written speech away, into the crowd, the papers flying above the heads of his audience. '*My fellow countrymen, I don't want to read from a written script, I am not a puppet who would parrot page after page of words written by some Western-educated bureaucrat. I speak from my heart . . .*' He brought his fist down on the dining table with such force that the teacup rattled, the *Pakistan Times* slipped off his lap and the red pencil rolled off the table. The duty waiter standing in the corner tensed up at first, then, noticing the ecstatic smile on the General's face, relaxed and decided not to pick up the paper and pencil from the floor.

On any other day, General Zia would have read the editorials, looked for negative comments, scanned the adverts for female models not properly covered, but he was so content over the coverage of his speech, his heart was so full of tenderness for the newspapers and journalists, that he didn't see the back page of the *Pakistan Times*. He missed the picture which showed him in full military regalia, golden-braided peaked cap on his head and a couple of dozen medals dangling from his chest. A silk sash with the emblems of all the armed forces crossed his torso diagonally, his hands entangled over his crotch as if trying to restrain one another, drool forming in the corner of his mouth, his eyes wide open and staring, like the eyes of a child who has wandered into a sweet shop to find its owner fast asleep.

The First Lady stayed away from newspapers. There were too many words she couldn't make sense of and too many pictures of her husband. She herself rarely appeared in the papers and if she did she was usually attending a children's festival or the Quran recitation competitions for women General Zia dispatched her to so she could represent the government and hand out prizes. The Information Minister sent her the clippings of these pictures and she usually hid them from General Zia because he always found fault with her appearance. If she wore make-up, he accused her of aping high-society Westernised women. If she wore no make-up, he said she looked like death, very unlike a first lady. He constantly lectured her that as the First Lady of an Islamic state, she should be a role model for other women. 'Look at what Mrs Ceauşescu has done for her country.'

The First Lady had never met Mrs Ceauşescu and her husband never bothered to explain who she was or what she did. She did take other visiting first ladies shopping, but it was no fun because the shopkeepers either refused to take money from her or quoted her prices so low that she couldn't even haggle. The bazaars were cleared of shoppers before her arrival and she felt as if she was on the set of a television soap opera. General Zia did encourage her from time to time to read newspapers to keep abreast of the political and social changes he was bringing about in the country, but she never bothered. 'These newspapers are full of what you said and what you did and who you met. And you are always here, lounging around the house. Don't I see enough of you that I shouldn't have to see you staring at me from every page of every single rag?'

With such indifference to the national press it couldn't be a coincidence that the First Lady found a copy of the *Pakistan Times* on her bedside table, carefully folded to reveal the picture on the back page, the picture that would destroy her faith in all men forever and result in the unceremonious sacking of the editor of the *Pakistan Times*.

The first thing that shocked the First Lady about the picture was the amount of flesh oozing out of the white woman's blouse. She immediately knew that the woman was wearing one of those new bras with wire construction that pushed the breasts up, making them seem bigger. Many of the other generals' wives wore these bras, but at least they had the decency to wear proper shirts that didn't show any flesh, only hinted at their enhanced shape. The woman in the picture was wearing a blouse cut so low that half her breasts were out, pushed up and pressed together so closely that the diamond on her necklace was resting on the cusp of her cleavage.

And then, there was her husband, the Man of Truth, the Man of Faith, the man who lectured women on piety on prime-time TV, the man who had fired judges and television newscasters who refused to wear a dupatta on their heads, the man who made sure that two pillows could not be shown together on an empty bed in a television drama, the man who made cinema owners blot out any bare legs or arms of actresses from the film posters; the same man was sitting there staring at these globes of white flesh with such single-mindedness that it seemed as if his own wife had been born without a pair.

The caption said innocuously: *The President being interviewed by the famous foreign correspondent Joanne Herring.*

Interview my foot, she thought. It seemed that it wasn't Ms Herring interviewing him, but General Zia interrogating her breasts. She put the paper aside, drank a glass of water, thought of their thirty-four years together, reminded herself of her five grown-up children, of their youngest daughter still to be married. For a moment she doubted what her eyes had just seen and picked up the paper again. There was no mistaking this. It was not the kind of thing where you can write a letter to the editor and demand a correction. General

Zia's eyes, normally crossed, the right one looking in one direction while the left one wandered away to take in something else, were for once focused in the same direction, on the same objects. The angle of his stare was so obvious that if she drew two lines with a pencil, they would connect the iris of his eyes straight to the two white spheres pushed up and pulled together.

She tried to remember what this woman was wearing last time she saw her. She remembered very clearly what her husband had looked like when he saw this woman last time.

The First Lady had started to suspect that her husband was up to something when he asked her to pack his old safari suit for their US visit. Her suspicions deepened when she was told that their first stop would not be Washington DC or New York but Lufkin, Texas, where they were to attend a charity ball. Jeddah, Bejing, Dubai, London, she could understand. These were regular stops for General Zia. But Lufkin? Safari suit? The old man was definitely up to something fishy, the First Lady had thought, checking his beige-coloured, polyester safari suit for any missing buttons.

General Zia had abolished all types of Western dress from his wardrobe except for military uniforms. He always wore a black sherwani for state occasions and, taking their cue from him, the bureaucrats had all started wearing minor variations of the same dress. The more adventurous ones experimented with cuts and colours, and occasionally their headgear, but basically stuck to what General Zia had started calling the National Dress. But like all men of principle, General Zia was always ready to make an exception for a higher cause. And if the cause was a fund-raiser for Afghan jihad, then no principle was sacred enough.

The charity ball in Lufkin was being hosted by Joanne Herring, prime-time news anchor on Lufkin Community Television and Pakistan's Honorary Ambassador to the United States; an appointment made after her four-hour-long, soul-searching interview with General Zia. Joanne was on a mission to rid the world of evil but she insisted on having fun while doing it.

And God, Lufkin could do with a bit of exotic fun.

Contrary to popular belief, oil millionaires in Lufkin have dull lives. Their political influence is marginal and only very few of them enjoy the wheeler-dealers' lifestyle that the media outside Lufkin likes to project. Their ten-thousand-dollar donation to their local Congressman gets them a letter signed by an aide in the White House. Those with deeper pockets can splash out one hundred thousand dollars and get invited to the annual prayer breakfast with Ronald Reagan in Washington DC where the President joins them for the prayer from the podium for fifteen minutes and then leaves them to their tepid porridge and coffee. So the arrival of a president – even if this was the President of Pakistan, a country they knew nothing about – and the fact that the man was not only a president but a four-star general, the chief of the largest Muslim army in the world and one of the seven men standing between the Soviet Red Army and the Free World, as their favourite news anchor reminded them every day, meant it was time to dispatch their tuxedos and ball gowns to the dry cleaner's.

Joanne had started using Pakistan's flag as the backdrop for her show in the run-up to the ball. The crème de la crème of the East Texan community and would-be supporters of the jihad against the Soviets were sent invitation cards carrying a picture of a dead Afghan child (caption: *Better dead than red*). Others showed a nameless Afghan mujahid in an old shawl with a rocket launcher on his shoulder (caption: *Your ten dollars can help him bring down a Russian Hind helicopter*). 'Now, don't that fry your tater? Ain't that the bargain of the century?' Joanne had followed her invitation with enthusiastic phonecalls, turning the small Texan town into a base camp for the Afghan mujahideen, fighting six thousand miles away.

The Holiday Inn in the city of Lufkin christened its fourth floor the Presidential Floor. Joanne had provided them with a Pakistani flag and an audio-tape of Quran recitation that was promptly forwarded to their meat supplier to be played as the slaughter started. The President would get his halal meat. The waiters were taught to say their salaam in Urdu.

Despite these efforts, when General Zia's convoy pulled into the porch of the Holiday Inn he was disappointed to see only a small office-like structure with a Pakistani flag flying over it. He installed the First Lady in the Presidential Suite. She complained about the size of the bedroom, the complimentary toiletries in the bathroom and really lost her cool when she asked hotel reception to connect her to the Army House and she was put through to the local Salvation Army store.

General Zia, meanwhile, changed into his safari suit with some difficulty. His stomach stuck out like a football and his safari shirt could barely contain it. He mumbled something about meeting an important Texan senator, picked up his briefcase and went to another room on the same floor, bearing a sign that said 'Presidential Office'. He did feel that the hotel was beneath his status. He himself was a humble man who needed only a cot and a prayer mat, but heads of state needed to stay in proper presidential hotels in order not to lose their sense of purpose. He needed to maintain the honour of his country, but he could hardly bring up this hotel business with Joanne after all she had done for his country and the Afghan cause.

He put his briefcase on the desk, picked up the hotel stationery pad and tried to calm his pounding heart by scribbling on the paper. His host, his comrade in struggle, Joanne, would be here shortly and just thinking about what she might be wearing, what she would smell like, made him nervous. A stream of perspiration ran down his spine. To distract himself, he tried to make notes for his speech at the charity ball:

1. Joke comparing Islamabad and Lufkin. (Half the size and twice as dead?)
2. Islam, Christianity . . . forces of good, communism evil (use the word godless).
3. America superpower but Texas the real superpower? And Lufkin soul of the real superpower? (Ask Joanne for a cowboy saying?)

Someone knocked on the door. He jumped from his seat and stood up in anticipation. Should he leave his desk, receive her at the door? Handshake? Hug? Kiss on the cheek?

General Zia knew how to greet men. No one who ever met him forgot his double handshake. Even cynical diplomats couldn't deny the genuine warmth of his hugs. Politicians got converted to his cause with his understanding hand on their knee and a friendly slap on their back. It had taken him some time to figure out how to deal with women, though, especially foreigners. He had invented, then perfected, his own style; when he reached a woman in a reception line, he put his right hand on his heart, and bent his head as a gesture of respect. The women who had done their homework kept their hands to themselves and nodded in appreciation. Those intent on testing the limits of his piety extended their hands, got a four-finger, limp handshake and a refusal to look into their eyes.

But Joanne was different. When she had come to interview him for the first time at the Army House, she had ignored his hand on his heart, his nodding head, even his attempt at a handshake and had kissed him on both his cheeks, forcing Brigadier TM to look in the other direction. He had realised at their first meeting that he was dealing with a special person, a person to whom he could not apply his social rules about women. Weren't there women warriors who had fought shoulder to shoulder with men in the first Muslim war? Wasn't she an ally in his jihad against the godless communists? Hadn't she promised to do more than the whole of the State Department? Couldn't she be considered an honorary man? A mujahid even? At this point his logic usually broke down as he remembered her golden, blow-dried hair, the heart-shaped diamond necklace that nestled between her breasts, her voluptuous red lips and the breathy whispers in his ears that made the most ordinary exchange seem like a secret plan.

Allah tests only those He really likes, he told himself for the umpteenth time and sat down on the seat with a very firm resolve. 'Yes, come in,' he said.

The door opened and a swirl of sandalwood perfume, peach-coloured silk and mauve lipstick came at him, cooing, 'Your Excellency. Welcome to the fine city of Lufkin.' General Zia stood up, still not sure whether he should leave the desk, still uncertain whether to kiss or hug or extend his hand from behind the safety of the desk. Then as Joanne lunged towards him, the self-control that had helped him survive three wars, one coup and two elections vanished. He left the table that was to be his defence against temptation and moved towards her with extended arms, unable to focus on her face or her features. In her embrace he noted with satisfaction that she wasn't wearing her high heels, which made her a head taller than he was. They were the same height without her heels. Her left breast pressed lightly against the strain of his safari suit and General Zia closed his eyes, his chin resting on the satin bra strap on her shoulder. For a moment the First Lady's face flashed in front of his eyes. He tried to think of other things: moments from his glorious career; his first handshake with Ronald Reagan; his speech at the UN; Khomeini telling him to take it easy. The dream ended abruptly as she wriggled out of his arms, held his face in her hands and planted a kiss on both his cheeks. 'Your Excellency, you need a trim.'

General Zia sucked his stomach in. She twirled his moustache gently with her fingers and said, 'Texans are big-hearted people, but when it comes to facial hair they are very small-minded. Now if you'll ask that handsome hulk outside your door to let my man in, we can take care of this.'

For the first time in his life, General Zia shouted an order at Brigadier TM. 'Let the man in, TM.'

Lufkin's only businessman without an invitation to the charity ball entered the room, an old black man with a barber's leather bag. '*Salaam alaikum,*' he said. 'You folks call it mooch, I know. I am gonna make this mooch sharp, Your Highness.' Before General Zia could say anything he had tucked a white towel around his neck and was clipping away at his moustache, still talking. 'You gonna meet old Ronnie? Can I give you an important message? Tell him he ain't no John Wayne. Stop tryin'. Lufkin is a fine ol' city but some folks is still racialist. They say there is a nigga in the woods when their kids don't eat. I tell them nigga has seen woods in Korea, nigga has seen woods in Nam. Now this nigga ain't in the woods, nigga is here and he got a razor on your neck, so be careful 'bout what you say.' He held a silver-framed mirror in front of him. General Zia's burly thick moustache had been trimmed to a thin line. It was sharp, all right. 'That's gonna make your lady's tater fry.'

It didn't make the First Lady's tater fry, in fact it barely got a sarcastic glance from her. 'I am just trying to please my hosts. All for a good cause,' General Zia had muttered as the First Lady switched channels on the television.

146

'Hostess, you mean,' she had said, settling on a rerun of *Dallas*.

The First Lady wasn't given to acts of rashness and her first impulse was to tear the newspaper apart, throw it away and try to forget the whole incident. He would see it and realise what a fool he was making of himself. At the age of sixty-three, with five titles before his name and a nation of one hundred and thirty million people to answer to, he was flying over floozies from Texas and then sitting there ogling their tits.

Then it suddenly occurred to her that there were thousands more out there looking at this picture: what might they be thinking? Nobody of course would be bothered about the famous foreign reporter, she guessed. She was a professional, she was an American, she could wear what she liked. If she had to wear push-up bras and low-cut dresses to get interviews with presidents, well, she was getting paid to do it. And as for him? She didn't really know what the masses thought of him, but he was surrounded by people who'd tell him that it was all a conspiracy on the part of the newspaper, that the picture had been doctored and the editor should be put on trial in a military court for publishing obscene material.

But even if they believed what they saw in the picture, what then? He is only a mere mortal like us, people would say. Under all that talk of piety and purdah, there is a red-blooded man who can't resist a bit of a peek. And then it occurred to her that there was another person, not in the picture, not named in the caption, who would be the real object of the nation's ridicule. She could hear the giggles in cabinet meetings: *We never knew the President likes them big and white.* She could hear the sniggers in the National Command bunker: *The old soldier is still homing in on the targets. Fine pair of anti-ballistics, sir.* And what about those high-society begums: *Poor man. Can you blame him? Have you seen his wife? She looks as if she just walked out of her village after spending the whole day in front of the stove.*

The First Lady felt as if the nation of one hundred and thirty million people was, at this moment, looking at this picture, pitying her, making fun of her. She heard howls of laughter going up from the beaches of the Arabian Sea to the peaks of the Himalayas.

'I'll gouge these eyes out,' she hissed, looking at the picture. 'I'll make mincemeat out of your old prick, you bastard.'

The duty waiter came running from the kitchen. 'I am going for a walk. Tell TM's men not to follow me,' the First Lady said, rolling the newspaper into a tight baton.

SENTIMENT DU FER

CHAPTER 11

The man blindfolding me seems like an expert at this kind of thing. The half-moon scar on his freshly shaved left cheek, his pencil-thin moustache and his neatly pressed shalwar qameez give him the air of a reformed hoodlum. His fingers are gentle and he makes a swift little knot at the back of my head. He holds my hand and leads me out. The blindfold is loose enough for me to open my eyes but it's tight enough that I can't catch any stray rays of light. I wonder if you are supposed to keep your eyes open or shut behind the blindfold. As we step out of the bathroom, I breathe in large gulps of air, hoping to rid my body of the bathroom stink, but I can still taste it at the back of my throat. Not even Obaid's collection of perfumes would be enough to kill this stench.

The corridor is wide, the ceiling is high and the floor under my boots is made of uneven stone slabs. The sound of our boots – which fall into a parade-like rhythm after the first few unsure steps – echoes in the corridor. We stop. He salutes. I just stand, half at attention, half at ease. I assume you are not supposed to salute someone you can't see. The room smells of rose air freshener and Dunhill smoke. Paper rustles, a cigarette lighter sparks, a file is thrown across the table.

'Do what you need to do, but I don't want any marks on him.' Major Kiyani's voice is hoarse, as if his throat is reluctant to deliver this particular order. The file is picked up.

'I am not a butcher like you guys,' an impatient voice whispers.

'Let's not be so touchy,' Major Kiyani says. A chair is dragged. 'I am talking to my man here.'

Don't listen to him, I tell myself. It's the same old good-cop, bad-cop bullshit. They are all sons of the same bitch.

Steps move around the room. The burning end of Major Kiyani's Dunhill is close to my face for an instant, then he is gone.

'Sit down please.' The voice addressing me belongs to the good cop but he is obviously not looking at me. I shuffle forward and stop.

'We need to remove that thing.'

I stay still. Are you supposed to remove your own bloody blindfold?

'Please uncover your eyes, Mr Shigri.'

The Army major sitting in front of me is wearing a Medical Corps insignia on the right shoulder of his khaki uniform; on a round, red velvet badge, two black snakes are curled around each other, mouths half open as if in a censored kiss. His long grey sideburns defy the military haircut regulations.

He is slowly turning the pages of a yellow-green file, the tip of his tongue under his teeth, as if he has just discovered that I am suffering from a rare condition he has never treated before.

'I don't work here,' he says, waving his hand to indicate the office.

The place has leather chairs, a green leather-topped table and a sofa with velvet covers. An official portrait of General Zia adorns the wall. The picture has been touched up so generously that his lips appear to be pink under his jet-black moustache. If Major Kiyani's uniform, with his nameplate, wasn't hanging on the wall, I would think we were sitting in the office of a bank manager.

I sit on the edge of the chair.

'We need to carry out a few tests. It's very simple. You have multiple-choice questions in the first one. Just tick the one you think is right without thinking too much. In the second part, I'll show you some pictures and you'll describe in a few words what you think those pictures mean to you.'

First my loyalty to my country was suspect, now they want to probe the dark corners of my brain to find out what is causing all the turmoil in the land.

'If you don't mind, sir, may I ask –'

'You can ask all you want, young man, but this is just a routine assessment. I have been sent from Islamabad and I am supposed to take back the results. I think it's better that you spend your time with me doing this rather than with the people who are trying so hard not to leave any marks on you.'

Like all good cops, he makes sense.

He pushes a stack of stapled papers towards me, puts a pencil on top and removes his wristwatch.

'There are no right or wrong answers in this,' he says, trying to reassure me. 'The only thing that matters is that you finish all sixty questions in twenty-five minutes. The trick is not to think.'

You can say that again. If I wasn't the thinking type I would still be marching up and down the parade square commanding some respect, not sitting here trying to pass loony tests.

I glance at the paper. The cover page just says 'MDRS P8039'. There is no hint of what is under that cover sheet.

'Ready?' he asks, giving me a faint, encouraging smile.

I nod my head.

'Go.' He places his watch on the table.

Q 1: Would you describe your present mental condition as
a. depressed
b. mildly depressed
c. happy
d. none of the above

My dad was found hanging from a ceiling fan. Baby O has disappeared with a whole bloody plane. I have spent the past two nights locked up

154

in a civilian shithole. ISI is investigating me for crimes that I have clearly not committed. I have just untied a blindfold from my own eyes with my own hands. What do you think?

There is no space to write, just little squares to tick.

Mildly depressed, it is then.

There are questions about my spiritual health – mildly spiritual; any suicidal thoughts – never; my sexual life – occasional wet dream. Belief in God?

I wish they had an option saying 'I wish'.

I tick the square that says 'firm believer'.

By the time it comes down to the questions about whether I'd rescue my best friend's kitten drowning in a river or tell myself that cats can swim, I have begun to enjoy the test, and my pencil ticks the squares with the flourish of someone celebrating their own sanity.

The good cop picks up his wristwatch from the table and gives me an appreciative smile. He wants me to do well.

There is that inevitable question about drugs. It doesn't give you the option to say 'only once'. It doesn't ask you if you enjoyed the experience.

Never, I tick.

Running back from Bannon's room, instead of following the Martyrs' Avenue I jumped over a hedge and started walking in the shrubs that surround the parade square. A lone firefly emerged from nowhere and hovered in front of me as if

155

leading the way. The hedge ran around the parade square like a perfectly formed wall with sharply cut edges. The grass under my boots was damp with early-evening dew. I was thinking hard, like you think when your blood absorbs Chitrali hashish and rushes to your head with urgent messages from beyond, clearing all doubts, transforming your whims into immaculate plans. The messages I was receiving were so loud and clear that I kicked the hedge just to make sure that it was all real. The hedge lit up as thousands of fireflies blinked from their slumber and launched a fated assault on the night. Bloody good, I said; time to wake up and spread the light.

According to the *Reader's Digest*'s special issue on the War on Drugs, no scientist has ever been able to map the effects of weed on the human mind. They shouldn't even keep the Chitrali hashish in the same room as their lab rats.

What I saw was this: a shadow flitting around the pole that flies the Pakistani flag on the dais at the edge of the parade square. The man climbed onto the dais, looked left and right then slowly unwrapped the flag from the pole where it had been hoisted down for the night.

What fluttered through my mind was the flag draped around Dad's coffin. I could hear the funeral prayers in my head, louder and louder. The coffin opened and through the crescent and star on the flag I saw Dad's face grimacing at me.

What is a Shigri to do?

I obeyed my orders. I went down on my elbows and knees and locked onto my target. Years of taking forbidden short cuts and climbing the walls of the Academy to watch late-night movies had prepared me for this moment. I stayed glued to the hedge and waited.

Some sick fucker was trying to steal our flag. Some fucker was trying to rob my dad's grave. I was thinking with the clarity that only Chitrali hashish could induce. I crawled on my knees and elbows, moving with the stealth of someone determined to save the country's honour and his father's medals. The fireflies swirled around my head. Wet foliage was finding its way into my boots and my uniform shirt, but my eyes were focused on the thief who was crouching on the dais now, struggling to untie the flag from the rope used to hoist it. He seemed in no hurry, but I quickened my crawl, determined to catch him red-handed. A thorn buried deep in the foliage lodged itself just behind my elbow. There was slight burning, followed by wetness on my sleeve. It didn't slow my crawl.

I jumped over the hedge as I closed in on the dais, and before the thief could see me I had pounced and pinned him to the ground.

'Why are you wrestling with an old man like me?' Uncle Starchy's voice was calm. He offered no resistance.

I felt like somebody had caught me poking the hole in my mattress. Never smoke that stuff again, was the promise I made myself.

'I thought somebody was messing with the flag,' I said, getting up.

'It's already messed up, I was taking it for a wash,' he said, searching the dais as if he had dropped something. His hand disappeared under his shirt, fumbled there for a moment, then came out holding a small, empty jute sack.

'You are being foolish, son. Where do you think you are going?' he said, looking around in panic.

For a moment I thought he was talking to me. I was feeling stupid, but I wasn't going anywhere, so I stood still and followed his gaze. He went down on his knees and put his face close to the dais and started moving around on his knees as if his foolish son was a worm.

Uncle Starchy had the slow grace of a lifelong drug addict. He moved with such agility and sense of purpose that I joined in the search without knowing what we were looking for. He peered down from the dais and spotted something on the little grass patch between the dais and the edge of the parade square; with the flag wrapped around his hand, he lunged at it. I saw it only for a fraction of a second as it wriggled, raised its jade-green head and its zebra stripes convulsed along its lengths. Then it curled itself into a spiral. Uncle had caught it by the tail and was stroking the back of its head with his forefinger as if caressing a rare jewel. The krait's head collapsed on itself and Uncle bundled it into the flag and held it with his two fingers, away from his body.

I would have thought I was still hallucinating if Uncle Starchy himself hadn't launched into an explanation. 'There is nothing pure in this country, not hashish, not heroin, not even chilli powder.'

I wondered what Uncle Starchy was on today.

'This is nature's nectar.' He waved the bundled flag in front of my eyes. The snake seemed to have gone to sleep. The crumpled moon and star on the flag was still.

'Uncle, you need to see a doctor.' I put my finger to my forehead and moved it in a circle. 'You've been drinking gasoline again.'

'That has a horrible smell and your tongue feels like a piece of dead meat. Disgusting.' He spat in disgust.

'And this?' I pointed towards the bundle in his hand. 'That looks like a sharp bugger. It could kill you.'

Uncle smiled a faint smile, felt the bundle tentatively with his hand, then gripped something with his two fingers. He pulled it up gently and I got a good look at the beautiful head on this little beast, his eyes two miniature emeralds, his mouth opened to reveal a gleamy, checkered pattern on the floor of his mouth; his forked tongue lashing out in angry little stabs.

Before I could realise what Uncle Starchy had in mind, he opened the buttons on his shirt, bared his shoulder and brought the krait's head within striking distance. Its tongue lapped into Uncle

Starchy's shoulder. He jerked his hand backwards, his head tilted left in slow motion and almost fell on his shoulder, his eyes closed and a whimper escaped his mouth. Then his eyes opened slowly. They were alert, like two soldiers starting their watch. His forehead, normally strewn with a network of wrinkles, was relaxed. Even his shadow seemed to have lengthened and ran the entire length of the parade square.

He tied a tight knot on the flag, stuffed it in the jute sack and, having secured his prisoner, looked at me as if expecting a review of his performance.

'It could kill you,' I said, sounding and feeling protective.

'Only if you're greedy,' he said, and then added as an afterthought, 'or if you inject it.'

'What?'

'It's a medicine if you take it pure. Mix it with metal and it becomes poison. You might feel as if you are drugged for a while, but in the end it will kill you. Try this. Put a drop on the point of a knife, scratch an elephant's skin with it and the elephant will drop dead. Elephant might dance first. Elephant might think he's got wings. Elephant might drag his feet. But elephant will drop dead in the end.'

The moon shone through a transparent cloud and Uncle's shadow shrunk to his own length as if he was being folded into a manageable size.

'How much for a shot?' I said, slipping my hand into my empty pocket, fully aware that Uncle Starchy never charged for his wares.

'Who do you think I am, sir? A drug pusher?' He was back to his usual mumbling self. The light in his eyes was already fading.

'I need to take care of some family business,' I said apologetically.

'He is drained now.' He patted his jute sack. 'It'll take him another week to produce what you need.'

On the seventh day I opened the stack of freshly starched uniforms that Uncle Starchy had deposited on my bed, and a finger-sized glass phial rolled out with a few drops of amber liquid sticking to its bottom.

I am offered tea, probably as a reward for completing the first test two minutes before the allotted twenty-five minutes. I hate tea, but the hot syrup singes the back of my throat and for a moment the smell that had lodged itself on my palate is burnt away.

The second test has no questions, just pictures. Not proper pictures but some crazy bugger's abstract version of life in which you can't tell whether it's an amoeba or a map of India's strategic defence capabilities.

Careful, I tell myself. I linger over my cup of tea. This is where they can really tell the loonies from borderline geniuses like me.

The first picture, I swear, is of a fox's severed head.

'Lake. Bermuda Triangle, maybe,' I say.

Every third month there is an article in *Reader's Digest* about aeroplanes disappearing over the

Bermuda Triangle. It has to be the sanest answer. I can see that the doctor is scribbling down my answers; in fact, he is writing down much more than I am saying.

There is a giant bat hanging upside down in the second picture.

'Bow tie.'

'Anything else come to your mind?' he asks.

'A pink-and-black bow tie. A very big bow tie.'

I am shown two penises attacking each other.

'Military boots,' I say. 'Military boots at ease.'

A man hunched in the middle of a mushroom cloud.

'A hurricane. Maybe an underwater submarine.'

Bloodthirsty witches are wrestling.

'Horseshoe.'

A pair of baby pigs stare at me.

'Yoda in the mirror.'

The last picture is as clear as the painter of these sick pictures could make them; a pair of testicles placed on a block of pink ice.

'Mangoes,' I say. 'Or some fruit. Maybe on ice.'

I sit and stare into the empty cup of tea while the doctor records his last observations feverishly on his notepad.

He is definitely in a hurry. He throws his pictures, papers, pencil in his briefcase, wishes me luck – 'Good luck, young man' – and is already standing at the door, adjusting his beret; another Medical Corps insignia, another pair of snakes with their tongues out.

'Sir, why were you sent –?'

'Remember, young man, our motto is *To do or die. Never ask . . .*'

'Sir. Medical Corps' motto is to *To serve humanity without* –'

'Look, young man, I have to catch a flight to Islamabad. They want the results back immediately. They are probably trying to find out if you know what you have been doing. Do you?'

'I haven't done anything.'

'That answer doesn't figure in this questionnaire so I can't really include it in my assessment. You can tell him that.'

He signals to the soldier who brought me from the bathroom and who has suddenly appeared in the doorway.

'Good luck. It seems you are from a good family.'

The soldier doesn't blindfold me. He walks me into a room that is trying very hard to look like a torture chamber. A barber's chair with rubber straps on its armrests is connected to amateurish-looking electrical devices. An assortment of canes, leather whips and scythes are arranged on a table along with a glass jar of chilli powder. Nylon ropes hang from a hook on a wall and a pair of old tyres is connected to the ceiling with metal chains, probably to hang the prisoners upside down. The only new item is a white Philips iron, unplugged. A torture chamber that doubles as a laundry room, I wonder. It all seems decorative, a bit like an abandoned theatre set. But then I look up at the ceiling, see splashes of dried blood and, looking around again, realise that all the paraphernalia is functional. I still can't figure out how the hell they managed to splash someone's blood onto the ceiling.

'Sir, please take off your uniform,' the soldier says respectfully.

I guess I am about to find out.

'Why?' I say, trying to muster up some officer-like dignity.

'I want to make sure there are no marks on your body.'

I take off my shirt, slowly. He takes it from me and puts it on a hanger. My boots are put aside. He folds my trousers carefully. I spread my hands, challenging him to come and do whatever it is that he needs to do. He points to my underwear.

I oblige.

He goes around me. I stand upright, hands folded at the back, not fiddling, not scratching. If he wants to see me naked, he'll not get the satisfaction of looking at a coy pansy.

I am waiting for the interrogation to start but he doesn't seem to have any questions.

'Sir, please stand in a corner and don't touch anything.' He plugs the iron into a socket before leaving the room.

Even professional torturers must procrastinate sometimes, I tell myself. Or maybe it's some kind of do-it-yourself torture system; you stand and stare at these instruments and imagine how your various body parts would respond to them. I try not to think about the amber light on the iron. Major Kiyani did say no marks.

He returns with the yellow-green file and a new-found interest in my family.

'Are you related to the late Colonel Shigri?'

I take a deep breath and nod.

'I came to his funeral. You probably don't remember me.'

I search his face for any clues to his intentions.

'I hope you'll forgive me, sir. I am only doing my duty.'

I nod my head again as if I have already forgiven him. He seems like someone who wants to help but doesn't want to be misunderstood.

'You know he built this place. On two weeks' notice. I was the construction supervisor.'

'I thought Mughals built this place.'

A torture chamber is not exactly the right place to discuss the achievements of your ancestors.

'No, sir, this extension, the offices, the barracks and all this stuff underground. He ordered the construction.'

Nice work, Dad.

The file in his hand is marked 'Confidential' and carries my air force number. I wonder what it says about me. About Obaid? About us?

'Did he order this as well? Did he use to . . . ?' I wave my hand towards the barber's chair and chains hanging from the ceiling.

'The Colonel was only doing his duty.' He shuts the file and clasps it to his chest under his folded arms. I knew Dad was running the logistics of guerrilla war in Afghanistan for General Zia. I knew he was liaising between the Americans who were funding the war and the ISI, which was responsible for distributing these funds to the mujahideen. But he never told me his duty involved building and managing facilities like this one.

'We are all doing our duty,' I whisper and lunge towards the table besides the barber's chair, where I pick up a scythe and hold it to my neck. The metal is cold but it doesn't seem that it can cut anything.

'Don't move. If you move you'll find lots of marks on my body.'

He unfolds his hands, still not sure what I want from him.

'Give me that file.'

He clutches the file with one hand and extends his arm towards me. 'Sir, don't be foolish.'

'For five minutes. Nobody will know.' The threat in my voice is overshadowed by the implicit reassurance.

He moves hesitantly towards me, clutching the file to his side. He probably has no experience of being blackmailed by naked prisoners.

'This is the least you can do after all my father did for you,' I urge him.

I have no idea what Dad might have done for him. But he did say he had attended the funeral.

'Five minutes.' He looks towards the door and scratches the half-moon scar on his cheek, which has suddenly turned red.

I nod energetically and extend my hand towards him, offering him the scythe as a sign of my peaceful intentions.

He takes the scythe with one hand and gives me the file. His hand trembles.

The preliminary report filed by Major Kiyani...

I flip over the cover page. The first report is my own statement. I turn the page and something falls out. I pick up a Polaroid picture from the floor. The picture is fuzzy; a mangled propeller, a smashed canopy, a wing ripped from the fuselage. It all adds up to a crashed MF17. The picture has a date at the bottom; it shows the day Obaid went AWOL. My eyes blur for a moment. I put the picture back in the file. Another form, another statement with Bannon's signature. 'Paper profile: Under Officer Shigri.' Words like *bright officer, personal loss, secretive behaviour* flash in front of my eyes before I hear footsteps approaching the room.

'Later,' says the soldier. He grabs the file from me and before I can anticipate his next move, lifts me up by my waist, shoves my head into the tyre and pulls a metal chain. I find myself hanging halfway between the floor and the ceiling.

Major Kiyani's voice is hoarse and he is not pleased to see me swinging calmly in the air, my torso balanced on the tyre.

'I said no marks.' Major Kiyani walks below me

in a circle. Dunhill smoke wafts into my nostrils and I inhale it eagerly. 'I didn't say, start a picnic here.'

Then he picks up the Philips iron and stands close to my head, his gelled hair and burly eyebrows level with my face. He brings the tip of the iron close to my left eyebrow. My eyes squeeze shut in panic. I smell burning hair and jerk my head backwards.

'Tarzan, people are asking about you. You better start talking before their goodwill runs out. It would take me less than a minute to iron the truth out of you but then you would never want to take your clothes off in front of anyone. I am sure even you can't live with that.'

Then he turns towards another soldier who has followed him into the room.

'Put some clothes on him and take him to the VIP room.'

CHAPTER 12

Clutching the rolled-up newspaper in both hands, the First Lady walked across the lawns of the Army House, ignoring the duty gardener who lifted his head from a rose bush and raised his soiled hand to his forehead to offer her salaam. As she approached the main gate of the Army House, the duty guards stepped out of their cabin, opened the gate and got ready to follow her. She waved the newspaper at the guards without looking up, signalling them to stay at their post. They saluted and returned to their cabin. The standard procedures for Security Code Red that the guards were following didn't say anything about the First Lady's movements.

She couldn't remember the last time she had walked through the gate. She always went out in a mini-convoy of two outriders, her own black Mercedes-Benz followed by an open-top jeep full of armed commandos. The road under her feet looked like an abandoned runway, neat and endless. She had never noticed the ancient trees that lined the road on both sides. With their white-washed trunks and branches laden with dozing

169

sparrows, they seemed like the backdrop for a ghost story. She was surprised when nobody stopped her at the entrance to the Camp Office adjacent to the Army House, where her husband was busy playing the President.

'Get in the bloody queue,' a voice shouted at her, and she found herself standing at the end of a long queue of women, all middle-aged or old, all covered in white dupattas. She could tell from their faces that they were poor but had made the effort to dress up for the occasion. Their cotton shalwar qameez suits were neat and pressed; some had dusted their cheeks and necks with talcum powder. She noticed at least two shades of red nail polish. The First Lady could see her husband at the other end of the queue; teeth flashing, moustache doing its little dance for the television camera, the middle parting in his oiled hair glinting under the sun. He was distributing white envelopes and as he handed over the envelopes he patted the women's heads as if they were not poor women getting some much needed cash but schoolchildren at a morning assembly receiving consolation prizes from their headmaster. The First Lady thought of barging forward and confronting him in front of the television crew. She thought of unfurling the newspaper in front of the camera and giving a speech, telling the world that this Man of Faith, the Man of Truth, this Friend of the Widows was nothing but a tit-ogler.

It was only a passing whim, because she realised not only that her speech would never make it to the nation's television screens, it would also start some ugly rumours in Islamabad which would circulate to the four corners of the country before the day ended: that the First Lady was a lunatic who felt jealous of the poor widows her husband was trying to help. She thought of opening the newspaper and showing the picture to the other women in the queue, but realised that they would think she was overreacting. 'What is wrong with a president talking to white women?' they'd ask. 'All presidents do that.'

She looked at the long line of women ahead of her, pulled her dupatta over her forehead tightly and decided to wait patiently in the queue, inching forward as the women in the queue moved towards their benefactor. Her hands kept rolling the newspaper into a tighter and tighter cone. The woman in front of the First Lady had been eyeing her suspiciously since she joined the queue. She looked at the First Lady's diamond ring, her gold earrings, her mother-of-pearl necklace and hissed. 'Did your husband leave you all this jewellery, or did you have to kill him to get it?'

With General Zia refusing to leave the Army House even for state functions because of Code Red, his Information Minister was running out of indoor ideas to keep his boss in the television news headlines. When General Zia ordered him to slot in some prime time for the President's Rehabilitation Programme for Widows, the Information Minister was reluctant at first. 'But we always do that during

Ramadan, sir,' the Information Minister had muttered apologetically. He was not sure where to get hold of so many widows at this time of the year.

'Is there a law in this country which prohibits me from helping poor people in the month of June?' General Zia shouted back at him. 'Has there been an economic survey that says our widows need help during Ramadan but not tomorrow morning?'

The Information Minister crossed his hands at his crotch and shook his head enthusiastically. 'It's a brilliant idea, sir. It would be a nice change for the news agenda. People are losing interest in all the talk about the Soviets going home and our Afghan mujahideen shooting at each other.'

'And make sure that the hundred-rupee notes are new. Those old women love the smell of fresh currency.'

The orders went out to the Ministry of Social Welfare to produce three hundred properly dressed widows for the ceremony. The cashiers at the State Bank clocked up overtime stuffing new one-hundred rupee notes into three hundred white envelopes. A press release was sent out announcing that the President would distribute alms to the deserving widows. The Information Minister drafted an additional note which would be released to the editors after the ceremony. It said that the President mingled with the widows and their courage brought tears to his eyes.

In the morning, a convoy of buses deposited two

hundred and forty-three women at the Army House guardroom. The officials at the Department of Social Affairs, despite their best efforts, had not been able to round up the required number of genuine widows and at the last moment had roped in some of their female staff, their friends and relatives.

A panicked major on guard duty called Brigadier TM and told him that there were hundreds of women waiting to get into the Camp Office. He had no means of body-searching them as there were no women police on duty and according to the Code Red standard operating procedures he couldn't let them in without a proper body search.

'Hold them there,' Brigadier TM said, abruptly, terminating his morning exercise regime of five hundred push-ups. He jumped into his jeep, buckling on his holster with one hand.

The women milled outside the gate of the Army House. Some of them who had attended these ceremonies before threatened the duty guards and said they would complain to the President. 'We are his guests, not some beggars off the road. *He* invited us.' The guards, getting more jittery by the moment, were relieved when Brigadier TM jumped out of his jeep and ordered the women to line up in three rows.

For Brigadier TM, an all-women gathering was a security nightmare even when he wasn't implementing Code Red. All those loose shalwar qameez dresses, all the flowing dupattas, the bags, the jewellery that sent the metal detectors wild and then the bloody burqas! How did you know they weren't carrying a rocket launcher beneath that tent? How did you even know they were women? Brigadier TM put his foot down straight away on the issue of widows in burqas. He sent for the Information Minister, who was supervising the camera crew on the lawns of the Camp Office. 'I know these burqas look good on television and I know the President likes them but our security level is red and I can't allow in any ninjas whose faces I can't see.'

The Information Minister, always reasonable when it came to dealing with men in uniform, promptly agreed and ordered the women in burqas to board the bus and leave. Their loud protests and at least one offer to take off the burqa were ignored. Then Brigadier TM turned his attention to the remaining women, now subdued after seeing what had happened to their sisters.

'You will not leave the queue,' Brigadier TM shouted at the top of his voice. 'Nobody will bend down to touch the President's feet. Nobody will try to hug him. If he puts his hand on your head, don't move abruptly. If anyone disobeys these instructions . . .' Brigadier TM put his hand on his holster and then stopped himself. It seemed a bit excessive to threaten a bunch of widows with his revolver. 'If any of you break these rules you'll never be invited to meet the President again.' Brigadier TM realised the lameness of his own threat as the rows began to dissolve and the widows started chattering, like students catching up after the summer vacation. He jumped into the jeep and sped away towards the marquee on the lawns of the Camp Office, where the camera crew was getting ready to film the ceremony. Brigadier TM saw a lone woman, with a newspaper in hand, walking towards the widows whom the guards were now trying to form into a queue. He thought of turning round and finding out why the hell she wasn't sticking with the other widows but then he noticed that General Zia was already talking to the Information Minister. He shouted at her before rushing towards the President.

'Get in the bloody queue.'

General Zia always felt a holy tingling in the marrow of his backbone when surrounded by people who were genuinely poor and needy. He could always tell the really desperate ones from the merely greedy. During the eleven years of his rule, he had handed out multimillion-dollar contracts for roads he knew would dissolve at the first hint of monsoon. He had sanctioned billion-rupee loans for factories he knew would produce nothing. He did these things because it was statecraft and he had to do it. He never got any pleasure out of it. But this ritual of handing over an envelope containing a couple of hundred rupees to a woman who didn't have a man to take care of her made him feel exalted. The gratitude on these women's faces was heartfelt, the blessings they showered over him were genuine. General Zia believed that

Allah couldn't ignore their pleas. He was sure their prayers were fast-tracked.

A television producer with an eye for detail walked up to the Information Minister and pointed to the banner that was to serve as the backdrop for the ceremony.

President's Rehabilitation Programme for Windows, it read.

The Information Minister knew from experience that a spelling error could ruin General Zia's day and his own career. General Zia photocopied the newspaper articles, even those praising him, and sent them back to the editors with a thank-you note and the typos circled in red. The Information Minister placed himself strategically in front of the banner and refused to budge during the entire ceremony. This was probably the first and the last time that the Information Minister was not seen in the official TV footage in his usual place and in his usual mood; he had always stood behind his boss with his neck straining above General Zia's shoulders and always grinned with such fervour that it seemed the nation's survival depended on his cheerful mood.

'Pray for Pakistan's prosperous future and my health,' General Zia said to a seventy-five-year-old widow, a shrivelled apple of a woman, a deserving veteran of these ceremonies and hence the first one in the queue. 'Pakistan is very prosperous,' she said, waving the envelope in his face. Then she pinched his cheeks with both her hands. 'And you are as healthy as a young ox. May Allah destroy all your enemies.'

General Zia's teeth flashed, his moustache did a little twist and he put his right hand on his heart and patted the old woman's shoulder with his left. 'I am what I am because of your prayers.'

General Zia, occupied for the last few days with the security alert triggered by Jonah's verse, felt at peace for the first time in ages. He looked at the long queue of women with their heads covered, with eyes full of hope, and realised they were his saviour angels, his last line of defence.

Brigadier TM stood out of frame and bristled at the way these women were disobeying his instructions. But the camera was rolling and Brigadier TM had enough television manners to stay out of the picture, control his anger and focus on the end of the queue where a catfight seemed to be in progress.

Most of the women in the queue knew why it was taking the President so long to hand out a few hundred rupees. The President was in a talkative mood, enquiring after the health of each woman, patiently listening to their long-winded answers and asking them to pray for his health. The one hour and thirty minutes scheduled for the ceremony were about to run out and more than half the women were still waiting in the queue. The Information Minister thought of stepping forward and asking the President if, with his permission, he could distribute the rest of the envelopes, but then he remembered the misspelt word he was covering and decided to stay put. Brigadier TM looked at his watch, looked at the President chattering away with the women, and decided that the President's schedule was not his problem.

The First Lady wasn't getting the sisterly support she had expected from the other women in the queue. 'Begums like her bring us a bad name,' the woman in front of the First Lady whispered to the woman ahead of her, making sure that the First Lady could hear. 'Look at all the gold this cow is wearing,' the woman said, raising her voice. 'Her husband probably died trying to keep her decked out in all that finery.'

The First Lady pulled her dupatta even further over her head. She tightened it across her chest in a belated attempt to hide her necklace.

Then she realised that to these women she must appear a fraud, a rich begum pretending to be a widow coming to feed off the official charity.

'My husband is not dead,' she said, raising her voice to the point where ten women in front of her could hear. The women turned round and looked at her. 'But I have left him. And here, you can have these.' She removed her earrings and unhooked her necklace and pressed them both into the reluctant hands of two women standing in front of her.

The whisper travelled along the queue that a woman at the back was distributing gold.

General Zia's right eye noticed the pandemonium at the back of the queue. With his left eye he

178

sought out the Information Minister. He wanted to find out what was happening, but the minister was standing in front of the backdrop as if guarding the last bunker on a front line under attack.

An incredibly young woman, barely out of her twenties, shunned the envelope extended towards her by Zia, and instead removed the dupatta from her head and unfurled it like a banner before the camera.

Free Blind Zainab, it read.

General Zia shuffled back, Brigadier TM rushed forward with his right hand ready to draw his gun. The television cameras cut to a close-up of the shouting woman.

'I am not a widow,' she was shouting over and over again. 'I don't want your money. I want you to immediately release that poor blind woman.'

'We have set up special schools for the blind people. I have started a special fund for the special people,' General Zia mumbled.

'I don't want your charity. I want justice for Zainab, blind Zainab. Is it her fault that she can't recognise her attackers?'

General Zia glanced back and his right eyebrow asked the Information Minister where the hell he had got this widow. The Information Minister stood his ground; imagining the camera was taking his close-up, his mouth broke into a grin. He shook his head, and composed a picture caption for tomorrow's papers: *The President sharing a light moment with the Information Minister.*

Brigadier TM could stand disorder at one end of the queue, but now there were women wagging fingers and shouting at both ends, those furthest from him cursing the last woman in the queue and this one right in front of him defying presidential protocol. He took out his revolver and moved towards the cameraman.

'Stop filming.'

'This is good, lively footage,' the cameraman said, his eye still glued to the camera. Then he felt something hard poking his ribs and switched off the camera.

Brigadier TM had the protesting woman removed and the ceremony started again, this time without the television camera. General Zia's movements became mechanical, he barely looked at the women when they stepped forward to receive their envelopes. He even ignored their blessings. If his enemies had infiltrated his saviour angels, he was thinking, how could he trust anyone?

By the time the last woman in the queue stepped forward to receive her envelope, General Zia was already turning towards his Information Minister. He wanted to give him a piece of his mind. General Zia extended the envelope towards the woman without looking at her; the woman held his hand and pressed a small metallic ring into it. He only turned to look when he heard the sound of glass breaking.

His wife was standing there striking her glass-bangled wrists against each other, something that women only did when they heard the news of their husband's death.

Later she would listen patiently as General Zia blamed his enemies in the press, pleaded national interest and invoked their thirty-eight years together. He would say everything the First Lady had thought he would. She would agree to continue to do her ceremonial duties as the First Lady, she would appear at the state ceremonies and she would entertain other first ladies, but only after kicking him out of their bedroom.

But here at this moment, she only said one thing before walking off. 'Add my name to that list of widows. You are dead for me.'

CHAPTER 13

The soldier escorting me back from the torture chamber unties my hands, doesn't bother to remove my blindfold, holds my neck down with one hand, puts his boot on my buttocks and shoves me into a room. I land face down, my tongue tastes sand. The door that shuts behind me is small. I am relieved to notice that I am not in the bathroom where I spent the night. I fumble with the rag covering my eyes, the knot is too tight. I yank it down and it hangs around my neck like a poor man's dog collar. My eyes blink and blink again but don't register anything. I open them wide, I narrow them. I don't see a thing. Have I gone completely blind? I stand still, scared to move my hands and feet, scared to find myself in a grave. I breathe, and the air smells of a duvet that has spent a night out in a monsoon, but it's better than last night's stench. Tentatively, I move my right hand, stretch out my arm. It doesn't touch anything. I stretch out my left hand; it flails in a vacuum. I stretch my arms to the front, to the back, I make a three-hundred-and-sixty-degree turn with my arms outstretched, they don't come in contact with anything. I keep my hand in front of me and walk, counting my steps. Ten steps and my hand scrapes a brick surface. I run my hand over the slim, flat bricks that the Mughals used to build this fort. Conclusion: I am still in the Fort. I am in a part of the Fort which is not an extension built by the army. I move left. Twelve steps and I run into another specimen of Mughal masonry. I knock on the wall, and as I should have known, there is only the dead sound of my knuckles against a historical monument.

I am not in a grave. I have ample space, I can breathe. I am in a luxury-sized dungeon. My eyes adjust to the dark, but they still can't see anything. The darkness just grows darker. It's the kind of darkness which is ancient, manufactured by the sadistic imagination of the Mughals. Those buggers may have lost their empire but they knew how to build dungeons. I go down on my knees and embark on a crawling tour of my abode. The sand is real sand, beneath it the floor, endless cold slabs of stone. Anyone planning to dig a tunnel here would need to hire a mining company. In this monument to sixteenth-century architectural values, the only concession to modern times is a plastic bucket in a corner that I butt my head against. It probably hasn't been used in a long time, but the stale smell that emanates from it makes it absolutely clear that I shouldn't expect any visits to a loo.

I sit with my back to the wall and shut my eyes,

hoping the darkness will get less dark, the way it does in a cinema. I open them again. This place is no cinema. I can't even muster any imaginary shadows.

Minutes pass, hours pass. How should I know how long I have been here? If I stay still I'll lose my eyesight or parts of my brains and probably the use of my limbs. I jump up in panic. On your feet, Mr Shigri, get busy. I command myself to run. I run on the spot for a while, my body warms up. I keep my mouth shut and concentrate on breathing through my nose. Not a good choice of exercise, as I realise I am breathing in sand from the floor which has begun to fly in the air. I stop. I put my hands behind my neck and sit on my toes and start doing frantic squats. I do five hundred and without a pause jump in the air and land with my hands on the sand, body parallel to the ground. One hundred push-ups; a thin film of perspiration is covering my body, and an inner glow brings a smile to my face. As I sit back with my back to the wall I think that Obaid could probably write an article about this, send it to *Reader's Digest* and fulfil his dream of getting one hundred dollars in the mail: 'Aerobics for Solitary Prisoners'.

I started my brief career as a swordsman by practising on a bed sheet. I hung the sheet over the curtain in my dorm and marked a circle roughly at the height where my target's face would be.

I stood with my back to the bed sheet and tried to pierce it from all possible angles, from above my shoulder, with my left hand, with backhand swipes. After one hour the sheet was in shreds and the circle more or less intact, mocking my swordsmanship.

The next day, as Obaid got ready to go out for the weekend, I pretended that I had a fever. Obaid came to my bed, put his hand on my forehead and nodded his head in mock concern. 'It's probably just a headache,' he said, pulling a face, disappointed at the prospect of having to watch *The Guns of Navarone* without me.

'I am not a city boy like you. I am from the mountains where only women get headaches,' I said, irritated at my own lie. Obaid was mystified. 'What do you know about women?' he taunted me, spraying his wrists with a sharp burst of Poison. 'You don't even remember what your mother looked like.' I pulled my bed sheet above my head and started to detach myself, bit by bit.

I locked the room as soon as he left and dressed up in uniform; boots, peaked cap, sword belt, scabbard, the whole works. From now on every rehearsal would be a full dress rehearsal. There was no point doing this by halves, it didn't make sense not to simulate the exact circumstances. I took out a white towel. Instead of a circle, this time I drew an oval shape with a pencil, then two small circles for eyes, an inverted seven for a nose. I took extra pleasure in drawing a broom of a moustache. I hung my creation over the curtain, put my right hand on the hilt of the sword and took five steps back. I came to attention, with my eyes fixed on the moustached face on the towel. I drew the sword and extended it towards the target. It flailed in the air inches away from the towel.

Five steps is the regulation distance between the parade commander and the guest of honour inspecting the parade and nobody can change that. I tried throwing the sword. It did pierce the chin but throwing the sword is not a possibility. You can't do that with a live target because if you miss, then you are left standing there empty-handed. Not that I could afford to miss. Not that I was going to be given a best-of-three-type chance.

I knew what the problem was. It wasn't the distance. It wasn't the fact that my target would be moving; the problem was the relationship between my hand as it wielded the sword and the sword itself. These were two different entities. Through practice I could improve my hand–eye coordination, I could make them work together better but sadly that wasn't enough. My arm and the sword needed to become one. The muscles in my tendon had to merge with the molecules that made up the sword. I needed to wield it like it was an extension of my arm. As Bannon had pointed out again and again in our knife-throwing sessions, I needed to work on my *sentiment du fer*.

It was time to look for the sentiment of steel within myself.

I took off my sword belt and lay down on the bed with my shoes on and stared and stared at the two small circles on the towel and did Total Detachment, an exercise of my own invention. It's a slow exercise and few have the mental stamina required to do it because it involves complete abandonment of your thoughts and total control of your muscles. I was able to master it during that holiday when Colonel Shigri sought forgiveness for his sins over the Quran during the day, then plotted his next foray into Afghanistan over Scotch in the evenings. I had a lot of time at my hands.

Starting with my scalp, Total Detachment works its way towards my toes. I contract, hold, and let go my muscles, knot by knot, while the rest of my body stays unaware; both anticipation and longing are counterproductive.

It's not in the muscles. The sentiment of steel is all in the head. The sword should feel your will through the tips of your fingers.

Obaid was surprised to find me in uniform on his return. I ignored his account of *The Guns of Navarone*, produced a black leather eyepatch cut out of my old drill boot and asked him to wear it. For once he didn't ask me any questions, nor did he make any show-off-Shigri jokes. He didn't say a word when I drew the curtains and switched all the lights off one by one.

He did speak up when he heard the buckle of my sword belt click. 'I hope you know what you are doing.' I switched the table lamp on, took out a bottle of white boot polish and dipped the tip of my sword in it. Obaid kept looking at me as if I was growing horns right in front of him but he had the good sense not to speak. 'OK, Baby O. You can move all you want but if you want to keep using both your eyes stay as still as you can. And yes I know what I am doing. Save your lecture for later.'

I flicked the table lamp off. I walked towards Obaid and stood very close to him, I could smell cardamom on his breath. That was his idea of good oral hygiene and he always carried a few green pods in his pocket. I marched backwards. One, two, three, four, five steps. I put my right hand on the sword hilt, held the scabbard straight and steady with my left. In the darkness the sword caught the moonlight filtering from the slit in a curtain and it glinted for a moment. That's how it would happen on the day, if there are no clouds, I thought. But what I thought was irrelevant. The command had communicated itself from my mind to the tendons in my forearm and the dead molecules in the sword metal were alive and my will was the tip of the sword that found the middle of the leather patch. I put the sword back in the scabbard and asked Obaid to turn on the light. When Obaid turned around after flicking the light switch, I saw the little white dot in the middle of the black eyepatch on his right eye. My shoulder muscles sagged with satisfaction. Obaid came and stood in front of me, flipped his eyepatch and extended his tongue, offering me the half-chewed cardamom shell: a green fly on the red velvety tip of his tongue. I took it and put it in my mouth, savouring its sweet smell. The bitter seeds had already been eaten by him.

He came forward and put his hands on my shoulders. I stiffened. He put his lips close to my ear and said, 'How can you be so sure?'

'It's in the blood,' I say, taking out a white hankie from my pocket to polish the tip of the sword. 'If you ever found your father swinging from a ceiling fan, you would know.'

'We know someone who can find out,' he said with his chin on my shoulder. I could feel the heat from his cheek.

'I don't trust him. And what am I going to say? "Officer Bannon, can you use your connections to shed light on the circumstances of the tragic demise of a certain Colonel Shigri who might or might not have worked for the CIA, and who might or might not have killed himself?"'

'You have to start somewhere.'

I wiped the tip of the sword vigorously one last time before putting it in the scabbard.

'I am not starting anything. I am looking for an ending here.'

He brought his lips to my ear again and whispered, 'Sometimes there is a blind spot right under your gaze.' His cardamom breath raged like the waves of a sweet sea in my ears.

★   ★   ★

I must have dozed off because when I wake up, the shock of being in the dark is new and someone is trying to prod the back of my head with what seems to be a brick. My initial reaction is that the pitch dark is trick-fucking my brains and I am inventing imaginary company. I close my eyes again and put the back of my head on the same spot on the wall and again it gets a little push from the brick. I turn around and trace the outline of the brick with my fingers. It is protruding half an inch from the wall. As I am tracing its outline, with a heart that desperately wants to believe in miracles, the brick moves again. It's being pushed from the other side. I put my hand on it and gently push it back. This time, it's pushed towards me more forcefully. The brick is now jutting halfway out from the wall. I hold onto it and gently ease it out of the wall, hoping for the cell to be flooded with light, with birdsong. Nothing happens. It's still as dark as the Mughals intended it to be. I squeeze my hand into the gap, my fingers touch another brick. I prod at it and the brick moves, I give it a little push, it disappears. Still not even a flicker of light. I can feel human breath held at the other end, then gently released. I hear a giggle, a well-formed, deliberate, throaty man's giggle.

The giggle stops and a whisper comes through the hole in the wall; a casual whisper as if we are two courtiers in the Court for the Commons in the Fort, waiting for Akbar the Great to arrive.

'Are you hurting?'

The voice asks me this as if enquiring about the temperature in my cell.

'No,' I say. I don't know why I sound so emphatic but I do. 'Not at all. Are you?'

The giggle returns. Some nut they put in here and forgot, I tell myself.

'Keep your brick safe. You will put it back when I tell you to. You can tell them anything about me but not about this.'

'Who are you?' I ask without bothering to put my face near the hole. My voice echoes in the dungeon and the darkness suddenly comes alive, a womb full of possibilities.

'Calm down,' he whispers back intensely. 'Speak in the hole.'

'What are you here for? What's your name?' I whisper, with half my face in the hole.

'I am not so stupid that I'd give you my name. This place is full of spies.'

I wait for him to say more. I shift my position and put my ear in the hole. I wait. He speaks after a long pause. 'But I can tell you why I am here.'

I keep quiet and wait for him to read me his charge sheet, but he stays quiet, perhaps needing encouragement from me.

'I'm listening,' I say.

'For killing General Zia,' he says.

Bloody civilians, I want to shout in his face. Major Kiyani has done it deliberately, thrown me into a king-sized grave and given me a crazy civilian for a neighbour and created a channel of communication. This is probably his idea of torture for people from good families.

'Really?' I say with the famous Shigri sneer. 'You didn't do a very good job of it. I spoke to him two days ago and he sounded very alive to me.'

For a civilian his response is very measured.

'So are you his personal guest? What did you do to deserve this honour?'

'I am from the armed forces. There's been a misunderstanding.'

I can tell he is impressed because he is quiet for a long time.

'You're not lying?' he says, his voice half-question, half-bewilderment.

'I am still in uniform,' I say, stating the fact but it sounds like an attempt to reassure myself.

'Put your face in front of the hole, I want to see you.'

I put my face in the hole and whisper excitedly. 'You got a light?' If he has got a light, he might have a cigarette as well.

I am stunned when the spit hits my eye, too stunned even to respond in kind. By the time I come up with 'What the fuck?', he has shoved the brick back in the hole and I am left rubbing my eye and feeling like an idiot, spat on by someone whose name I don't know, whose face I haven't seen.

What did I say? I get up in anger and start to pace up and down the room, my feet already know when to stop and turn. I try to remember my last words to him. All I told him was that I am still wearing my uniform. I thought civilians loved our uniforms. There are songs on the radio, and dramas on television and special editions of newspapers celebrating this uniform. There are hundreds of thousands of ladies out there waiting to hand their phone number to someone in uniform. My civilian neighbour is probably suffering from an extreme case of jealousy.

How the hell am I supposed to know about civilians or what they think? All I know about them is from television or newspapers. On Pakistan National Television they are always singing our praises. The only newspaper that we get in the Academy is the *Pakistan Times* which on any given day has a dozen pictures of General Zia, and the only civilians who figure in it are the ones lining up to pay their respects to him. They never tell you about the nutters who want to spit at you.

I hear the brick scrape against the other bricks. I hear the low whistle from the hole in the wall. I think of replacing my own brick in the wall and turning my loneliness into solitude, as Obaid used to say. But my neighbour is in a communicative mood. I put my ear on the side of the hole, making sure that no part of my face is in his line of attack.

'Are you going to apologise?' he whispers, obviously taunting me.

'For what?' I ask casually, without putting my face to the hole in the wall, without bothering to lower my voice.

'Shh. You'll get us killed,' he says furiously. 'You guys put me here.'

'Who are we guys?'

'The khakis. The army people.'

'But I am from the air force,' I say, trying to create a wedge between the nation's firmly united armed forces.

'What's the difference? You guys have wings? You guys have balls?'

I decide to ignore his jibes and try to have a proper conversation with him. I want to give him a chance to prove that he is not a complete civilian nutcase before I slam the brick in his face.

'How long have you been here?'

'Since two days before you people hanged Prime Minister Bhutto.'

I ignore his attempt to implicate me in crimes that I have clearly not committed. 'What did you do?'

'Have you heard of the All Pakistan Sweepers Union?' I can tell from the pride in his voice that he expects me to know it, but I don't, because I have no interest in the politics of this profession, if cleaning the gutters can be called a profession at all.

'Of course. The body that represents the janitors.'

'I am the Secretary General,' he says, as if that explains everything, from the Mughal architecture of this dungeon to his irrational hatred for his fellow countrymen in uniform.

'So what did you do? Not clean the gutters properly?'

He ignores my joke and says in a grave tone, 'They have charged me with plotting to kill General Zia.'

That makes two of us then, I should say, but I can't really trust this guy. What if he is one of those moles planted by Major Kiyani to gain my confidence? But Major Kiyani's men would not have either the imagination or the stomach to play the part of a sweepers' union member.

'Were you plotting to kill him? How were you going to do it?'

'Our central committee sent an invitation to General Zia to inaugurate National Cleanliness Week. I was opposed to inviting him because his *coup d'état* was a historic setback for the workers' struggle against the nationalist bourgeoisie. It's all on record. You can read my objections in the minutes of the meeting. The intelligence agencies infiltrated our union, our Maoist friends betrayed us and formed a parallel central committee and invited General Zia. Then his security people found a bomb in the gutter that he was supposed to sweep to inaugurate Cleanliness Week. Look at how the *fauji* minds work. I was the one opposed to inviting him. I didn't want him anywhere near our gutters and who was the first person your people arrested? Me.'

'So did you plant a bomb?' I ask.

'Every member of the Pakistan Sweepers' Union believes in political struggle,' he says grandly, closing the subject.

We both stay silent for a while and somehow the place seems even darker.

'Why would anyone want to kill him?' I ask. 'I think he's very popular. I have seen his picture on trucks and buses.'

'The problem with you khakis is that you have started believing your own nonsense.'

I don't answer him. I realise that he is a bloody civilian but of a kind that I haven't met before. He chuckles and starts to speak in a nostalgic tone. 'You know what they tried with our union before collaborating with the Maoists?'

'No,' I say, tired of pretending to know things that I don't have a clue about.

'They tried to infiltrate it with mullahs like they have done with every single trade union. They even tried to hijack Cleanliness Week with their slogan: *Cleanliness is half the faith.*' He starts to laugh.

'So what?' I really don't get the joke. That slogan is written on half the public lavatories in Pakistan, not that anyone cares, but then no one finds it funny either.

'All the sweepers are either Hindus or Christians. And you people thought you could send in your hired mullahs and break our union.'

The image of bearded ones trying to infiltrate the ranks of the nation's sweeping community. OK, not a very bright idea.

'But let me tell you something that I would never say in public,' he says in an intense low whisper. 'The Maoists are probably worse than the mullahs.'

196

'Look, I know you are the Secretary General and all, but do you really believe that Zia and his generals are sitting there worrying about how to break the power of the janitors? I'm sure you are far too intelligent to believe that.'

Maybe it's my patronising tone that sends him into a silence followed by an angry outburst.

'You are a part of the reactionary bourgeois establishment which has never understood the dialectics of our history. I came this close to bringing down the government.'

I wish I could see him. Suddenly he sounds old and cranky and full of ideas that I don't understand.

'We called a strike. Do you remember the 1979 strike by the All Pakistan Sweepers Union? Of course you wouldn't know. The sweepers in your cantonments are not allowed to join unions. And in three days the rubbish piles were mountain-high and all the gutters were clogged and your civilian bourgeois brothers had to carry their own rubbish to the dumps.'

I want to interrupt him and ask him how that is different from when the sweepers are not on strike, but I hear a scraping sound on my dungeon's door.

I am quite amazed at the speed and accuracy with which I replace the brick in the wall. I am ready to get out of this black hole. I am certain that Major Kiyani's little game has come to an end. He might be General Akhtar's personal pet but his leash can't be this long. I am looking forward to cleaning my teeth, getting into a fresh uniform and above all feeling the sun's rays piercing my eyes.

The only light I see is a tunnel of brightness that blinds me momentarily as the door opens slightly. The only thing I see is a hand pushing in a stainless-steel plate. Before I can get up, greet the person behind the door, receive or send a message, snatch his gun and take him hostage or beg him for a cigarette, the door is shut again and the room is dark and full of the smell of hot food.

You want freedom and they give you chicken korma.

CHAPTER 14

General Zia ul-Haq picked up the photo-copied clipping marked *New York Times* from the stack of his morning papers and sighed. There she was again: Blind Zainab, her head and face draped in a white dupatta, a cheap pair of plastic sunglasses covering her eyes. He knew it was her before he read the caption under her picture, even before he saw the headline: BLIND JUSTICE IN THE LAND OF THE PURE.

The mornings had become unbearable since the First Lady stopped serving him breakfast. With her at the table, he could at least vent his frustration over the day's headlines by shouting at her. These days, sitting alone at the twenty-four-seat dining table, he looked like a librarian from hell; he picked a paper, underlined the bad news, made circles around any good bits, jabbed at the pictures of the opposition leaders and flung the paper towards the duty waiter who lurked in a corner desperately hoping that at least some of the news was good.

What was wrong with the Western press? Why were they so obsessed with sex and women? This was the third story in the international press about Blind Zainab. A simple case of unlawful fornication had been turned into an international issue. Why? General Zia wondered. Maybe because the woman was blind, he thought, because she wasn't much to look at. Trust Americans to devote front-page space to fornicating blind women. Perverts.

General Zia remembered the *NYT* reporter who had interviewed him: all ballpen-chewing reverence about how he had never met such an erudite leader in the whole Muslim world. General Zia had talked to him for two hours, gifted him a small Persian carpet and walked him out to the porch after the interview. He did remember the reporter asking about the blind woman's case and he had given his standard reply. 'The matter is in the court. Would you ask the President of the United States about a criminal case being heard in a US court?'

He looked at the picture again. He had never quite believed that this woman was blind. Blind people don't get their photos published on the front pages of American papers. He adjusted his reading glasses, read the story carefully and realised it wasn't all bad. He was described as a *'smiling dictator', 'a man with impeccable manners', 'a man who told jokes about himself', 'a man who talked openly and frankly in fluent English but refused to discuss the blind woman's case'*. The relief didn't last long as he put the article aside and found another clipping from the *New York Times'* editorial page: a two-paragraph piece, again titled *'Blind*

Justice'. He knew that the negative editorials in US papers meant the owners of these papers were out to get you and they were probably doing it at the behest of their government in Washington. He underlined the words *barbaric, wily dictator, our government's fundamentalist friend who is relentlessly marching his country back in time.* With every word that he underlined, his blood pressure went up. His left eye twitched. He looked at the top of the editorial page and underlined the name Arthur Sulzberger. He picked up the phone and called his Information Minister, who had set up the interview and thus saved his job after the widows fiasco.

'What kind of name is Sulzberger?' he asked, dropping his customary greeting (How are you and how are the wife and kids?).

The Information Minister was a bit hazy. 'Sir, forgive my ignorance but I haven't heard the name.'

'Did I ask you whether you know this person? All I am asking is this: what kind of name is it? Is it Christian, Jewish, Hindu?'

'I am not sure, sir. It sounds German.'

'I know some newspapers call you Disinformation Minister, but you don't have to take that title so seriously. Find out and let me know before the evening prayers.' He slammed down the phone.

The Information Minister's first port of call was his own monitoring desk, which maintained files on all correspondents, editors and publishers. They had never heard the name. He called up a local reporter who had shown him his *NYT* card many times, but it turned out that this guy worked as a stringer for the *NYT*'s regional stringer and had never heard the name.

Reluctantly, very reluctantly, the Information Minister passed the request on to the information cell in the Inter Services Intelligence. He knew that it would be fed back to General Zia and he'd be asked why the country needed an Information Minister if the intelligence agencies had to do all his dirty work.

When the ISI told him politely in mid-afternoon that they had nothing on Arthur Sulzberger, his frustration resulted in the cancellation of publishing permits for two local film magazines. Then a flash of brilliance: the *New York Times* was in New York. He slapped his forehead and called up Pakistan's press attaché in New York, who didn't have an answer but was confident that he'd find out in half an hour as he had excellent contacts in the *NYT* newsroom. The press attaché called up a friendly Pakistani cab driver who he knew read every word in every paper and always alerted him to any stories about Pakistan.

'Sulzberger,' the cab driver shouted into his cab phone, jumping a Manhattan traffic light. 'Sulzberger . . . that Jew.'

The information travelled from his cab to the Pakistani consulate in New York, reached the Information Ministry in Islamabad over a secure teleprinter and five minutes before his deadline the Information Minister received a note marked '*Classified*'.

The owner of the *New York Times* was a Jew.

General Zia heard it with a sense of relief. He knew in his guts when he was right. He shouted at the Information Minister: 'What are you waiting for? Put out a press release and tell them all this fuss about that blind woman is Jewish propaganda. And next time we go to America invite Sulzberger for lunch. Take a large Persian carpet for him.'

At the end of such a hectic day at the office the Information Minister couldn't bring himself to tell the General that he had issued the press release about Jewish propaganda first thing in the morning. His office had standard operating procedures when it came to rebutting negative stories about General Zia. These were divided into two categories: Jewish and Hindu propaganda. And since the story had appeared in the *New York Times*, you couldn't really put it on the Hindu propaganda pile.

General Zia knew that Arnold Raphel wouldn't help, but called him up anyway. The ambassador had, of course, seen the interview.

'Some nice quotes,' he said, trying to cheer General Zia up.

'The editorial,' General Zia said, then paused. 'The editorial is very unfortunate. I don't mind personal insults, but somebody is trying to malign our friendship. Somebody is trying to undermine all the good work we have done together.'

'It's probably a bunch of liberal op-ed writers on a lean news day, Mr President. I wouldn't worry about it too much.'

'It could jeopardise our chances for the Nobel, you see. I was hoping we would receive it together.' There was a moment's silence at the other end. 'For liberating Afghanistan,' he added, and thought this Arnie chap wasn't very bright.

'We can discuss it at the party, Mr President, I hope you will be able to come.'

General Zia realised that a statement blaming the Jewish press and talking to the US ambassador would not solve the Blind Zainab problem when yet another group of women staged a protest in Islamabad the next day. 'All rich begums,' the Information Minister told him. 'More chauffeurs than protesters.'

When confronted with a legal dilemma like this, General Zia always picked up the phone and called ninety-year-old Qadi, his man in Mecca who had retired as a judge of the Saudi Sharia Court thirty years ago and since then had never missed a prayer in Khana Kaaba. The man practically lived in the House of God.

The phone call started, like it always did, with the General expressing his desire to die while on a pilgrimage to Mecca and to be buried at Qadi's feet. Qadi assured him that Allah would grant him his wish and enquired about the purpose of this phone call.

'With your blessings I have introduced the new laws in Pakistan and by the grace of Allah hundreds of sinners have already been convicted: we have two hundred thieves waiting for their hands to be amputated, thousands of drunkards have been lashed in public.'

'Allah may help you, Allah may help you,' Qadi kept muttering.

'We have just had a death-by-stoning sentence passed and I was calling about that.' General Zia didn't want to mention Zainab's name.

'Real test, my birather. A real test.' Ninety-year-old Qadi's voice was suddenly booming over the phone. 'Our rulers of this Saudi kingdom, may their rule last till the Judgement Day, they don't have courage for this. They like to make easy on everyone's eyes; chop, chop after Friday prayers and everyone goes home happy. They not only chop the head off the criminal, they kill the spirit of law. People just become spectators. Adultery is a crime against society and people must carry out the punishment themselves. You cannot pass the responsibility onto some hired executioner and think you have done Allah's work.'

'Yes, Qadi, I wanted your guidance on this matter: what happens if the accused says that she was forced to fornicate? How do we establish whether she is telling the truth? I mean, sometimes you can look at a woman's face and tell that she is a fornicator, but we need legal procedures to establish it.'

Qadi spoke as if he had thought about this for a long time. 'Women always make this excuse after they are caught fornicating, but we all know that rape is not easy to commit. The perpetrator will need at least four accomplices. There will have to be two men holding her by her arms, two pinning down her legs and then the fifth one between her legs, committing the act. So the answer is yes, a woman can be raped and it's a serious crime.'

'So the woman will be required to recognise all five culprits in the court?' Zia asked.

'Our law, you know, is not set in stone, it encourages us to use our common sense. So the two men who are holding her down by her arms, maybe the woman would not be able to recognise those two and the judge can make an exception.'

'And what if she didn't see any of the culprits? What if they were wearing masks?'

General Zia could tell the old man was suddenly angry.

'Why would a rapist wear a mask? Is he a bank robber? Bank robbers wear masks. Kidnappers wear masks. I have never heard of a rapist wearing a mask in my forty years as a judge.'

General Zia felt stupid as Qadi continued, this time in a cold, admonishing, teacher-like voice. 'Rapists like to see their own reflection in the woman's eyes. That is one reason they'd never wear masks,' said Qadi.

'And what if the woman in question was blind?' General Zia asked.

Qadi clearly didn't get General Zia's drift.

'Do you mean morally blind or someone who Allah has not given the physical powers to see?'

'Blind. A woman who can't see.'

'The law doesn't differentiate between those who can see and those who can't. Let's assume for the sake of legal argument that the rapist was blind in this case, would he be entitled to any special privilege? So the victim, blind or not, is entitled to the same scrutiny, same rights.'

'How will she recognise her rapists and the other people who held her down?'

'It can be done in two ways: if she is married, her husband will have to establish in the court that she is of good character and then we'll need four male Muslims of sound character who have witnessed the crime. And since rape is a very serious crime, circumstantial evidence wouldn't do. "We heard screams and we saw blood and we heard the man hitting her" is not enough evidence; witnesses will be required to have witnessed the actual penetration. And if the woman is not married she'll have to prove that she was a virgin before this horrible crime was committed.'

General Zia felt much better by dinner time. He had already passed Qadi's legal advice to his Chief Justice and was now composing a speech in his head that he would ask the First Lady to deliver at the annual charity bazaar of the All Pakistan Professional Women's Association. He tried to test some of the arguments on the First Lady after reminding her of her promise to carry out her state duties. She listened silently at first, but when he reached the part about the victim having to establish her virginity the First Lady interrupted him.

'Are you talking about Blind Zainab's case?'

'Well, yes, but basically we are trying to establish a legal precedent that will safeguard women's honour. All women's honour.'

'I don't know anything about the law and I'll make this speech if that's what the law says.' The First Lady pushed her plate away. 'But how is this woman supposed to prove that she is a virgin if a bunch of men banged her for three days and three nights?'

CHAPTER 15

I follow the chicken korma smell and crawl my way towards the door. I pick up the plate and put it back. It's hot. I suddenly feel very hungry. I sit down with my back against the door and start to eat. My world is reduced to the tender chicken flesh dripping with creamy curry. Even the bitter whole spices that get stuck in my teeth seem like portents of a prosperous, free future. I have only finished half my plate when the brick is pushed out. I take my plate to the hole and remove the brick.

'I wanted to check they have given you food because sometimes they like to starve the newcomers. You can share mine. Lentil soup garnished with gravel and fifty-fifty bread that is half flour and half sand. Your military chefs are very consistent. I have received the same food for nine years.'

I feel the guilt that the privileged prisoners must feel. I put my plate aside. 'No. They have given me food.'

We sit in silence for a while. The absence of any prospects of freedom in the near future hangs heavy in the air. Suddenly this plate of rich, hot food seems like the promise of a long sentence. I feel the walls of this dungeon closing in on me.

'Did your strike work then?' I am desperate for conversation about anything that is not the quality of food or the texture of darkness in this part of the Fort.

'The idea was that people faced with so much uncollected garbage would rise up in solidarity with us. But nobody even noticed. Our people get used to everything. Even the stench of their own garbage.'

'I am sure someone must have noticed. Otherwise you wouldn't be here.'

'Oh yes, you people noticed. After some intelligence analyst realised that mullahs couldn't infiltrate our ranks, they started cultivating our own Maoist faction.' His whisper suddenly gets animated. 'I wouldn't say it in public but Maoists really are worse than mullahs.'

I don't know why he is going on about Maoists, but I know he wants a reaction to his confession. But the only Mao I know is that Chinese guy with the cap and I have no clue what his people are doing in Pakistan, let alone in the sweepers' union.

'That is probably true,' I say thoughtfully. 'China has produced nothing worthwhile since Sun Tzu. Even the fighter jets they give us are flying coffins.'

Secretary General is clearly not interested in the quality of his motherland's air defences.

'I proved to them, with an empirical analysis of

our so-called peasants' movement, that our modes of production are determined by the petty bourgeoisie and not what they call feudal landlords, but these Maoists are very dogmatic. In Pakistan, you cannot have a peasants' revolution. Don't you agree?' He is begging me to agree.

'Yes,' I say. 'Of course. Pakistani peasants are happy, no one goes hungry here.'

'Is that what they teach you in the army? That our peasants are well fed and every night before going to sleep they dance their joyous dance around their bountiful crops. You people live on another planet. This is even worse than the Maoist propaganda.'

'They don't teach us anything like that,' I say, and it's true. 'Just because I wear a uniform, you think that I don't know anything about our people. I am from this country, I am also a son of the soil. I come from a peasant family.' That may not be accurate, but we did have an orchard in our backyard on Shigri Hill.

'Don't use your pseudo-feudal jargon with me. That is precisely the problem with our peasants. Maoists think that we live in an agrarian society. But look at our modes of production, look at the land ownership patterns. We live in a pre-agrarian, pre-feudal era. And these Maoists talk of a peasant revolution. It's the worst kind of bourgeois romanticism.'

I think about the interrogators who have had to deal with him. He probably taught them a thing or two. Secretary General is not finished with me yet. 'Have you seen a single peasant in this prison?'

'You are the only person I have met,' I say.

He is silent for a moment, probably suddenly realising that I am very new to this place, and that he doesn't know all that much about me. But his urge to conclude his argument overcomes the awkwardness of our exchange and he continues.

'There aren't any. Not real peasants. Not revolutionary peasants. The ones I have met are fighting *for* their feudal lords, not *against* them. They are fighting to preserve the status quo. They are fighting so that their feudal lords can keep them in their shackles. They are subverting the genuine class struggle of workers like me and you.'

I am relieved. I am finally in the fold. I am a worker and my struggle is genuine.

'According to our party manifesto, there is no difference between a sweeper and a soldier,' he says, I think just to underline the rules of our engagement. 'These are both forms of exploitative labour that the military-industrial complex thrives on.'

I have no problems being called a worker in a generic sense but I don't think I would make a very good sweeper.

'Were you a sweeper?' I ask him. 'I mean before becoming the Secretary General.'

'No,' he says, in an irritated voice. 'I was a mango farmer before I started organising the sweepers.'

'Secretary General, can I raise a point of dissent here? I suspect you oppose a peasants' revolution because you fear that first of all they'll take over your mango orchards,' I say in a triumphant tone, as if we were not in an underground prison but at a meeting of his central executive committee. I sigh deeply and imagine smoke-filled rooms, littered with overflowing ashtrays.

Secretary General is silent for a moment, then he clears his throat and speaks in an apologetic voice. 'I was a Maoist myself. I organised the mango orchard owners all over the country. I was the founding chairman. Within a year we had formed strategic alliances with mango farmers in India and Mexico. But our members were bourgeois at heart, every single one of them a class enemy. They would attend our study circles during the day and then go and throw mango parties for your generals at night. If only they had understood, we would have become the largest farmers' collective in the entire capitalist world. Imagine the blow to the capitalist economy.'

'Secretary General,' I address him formally, 'can I put another point of dissent on record? Do you really think you can bring the capitalist economy down by fixing mango prices?'

There is silence at the other end. I close my eyes and when I open them again the darkness seems tinged with fluorescent circles dancing in the dead air.

'I realised that. That's why I declassed myself and started organising the sweepers. But your army people are scared of even the poorest of the poor who clean your gutters.' At this he replaces the brick in the wall.

On the floor, face down, my left cheek on the cool sand, arms stretched out, palms upward, I am trying to clear my head of sweepers and Maoists and peasants and fluorescent circles. Secretary General seems too well read to have plotted anything, let alone a plan involving a bomb in a gutter. Will he believe me if I tell him about my plan? We can probably compare notes. We can probably learn from each other's failure, share tips about our interrogators. There is complete silence from his side. I guess it's my turn to make a peace move.

I take the leftover food and push the brick towards him. 'I have got some chicken here if you'd like it,' I whisper.

I can hear him sniff the plate. His hand enters the hole and he shoves the plate towards me, spilling the curry over my shirt. 'I don't eat collaborators' leftovers.' The brick is shoved in with a sense of finality.

I guess I am not going to be part of the revolution.

I take my shirt off and try to clean it, in the blackness, with the blindfold hanging around my neck. There is nothing more disgusting than a curry stain on your uniform shirt.

Someone cares enough about me to provide me with proper food but not enough to set me free or at least put me in a cell with a window.

Secretary General has read my thoughts. The brick scrapes and he speaks as if talking to himself. 'You know the most beautiful thing in this fort? Not the Palace of Mirrors or the Court for the Commoners. No. It's an underground cell with a window. They put me there for a month. You can actually see the sky. The window opens on to the lawns of the Fort. Sparrows sing there all day long. It was the happiest time of my life.'

A prisoner genuinely nostalgic for another prison; it will never happen to me.

'And what did you do to get such a privilege? Named your fellow sweepers in the conspiracy?'

'You have spent too much time on the parade square marching up and down to understand the complexity of the relationship between the oppressor and the oppressed.'

'Teach me.'

'They sent in their best man to interrogate me. Zia's right-hand man. Colonel Shigri. On the very first day he had electrical wires put on my privates, but after he couldn't break me, he became a friend. He moved me into a cell with the window. A very fine man. He must be a general by now.'

To think that the hands that cradled you also put electrical wires to someone's testicles is not a very appetising thought. A shudder of loathing runs through my body. My stomach feels bloated.

'They put me back in this dungeon after his transfer. He believed in dialogue. The only man in khaki I have had a decent conversation with. I wonder if he got his promotion or –'

'He is dead. He hanged himself.' I want Secretary General to shut up. He does for a few moments.

'He didn't seem like the kind of person –' Secretary General's voice comes out all broken.

'I know,' I say curtly. 'They made it seem like he hanged himself.'

'How do you know? They have brainwashed you into believing anything they want you to believe.' I don't like his dismissive tone.

'Just because I am wearing a uniform, just because they gave me chicken to eat, you seem to think I am a fool. You think I am just another idiot in uniform. Listen to me, Mr Secretary General, I don't need your lectures. There are certain things in life called facts, empirical realities I think you call them. I do not need to look at some little red book written by a Chink in a funny hat. I don't need any communist pamphlets to tell me what the facts of my life are. I can find them for myself.'

I slam the brick back in the wall and tell myself that it's over. I don't need lectures from a civilian nutter any more. I don't want one more loser telling me that Colonel Shigri changed his life.

Shirtless, I lie back on the floor. The sand and stone underneath my naked back feel good. I grab sand in both my hands and play the sand clock; I let it trickle out of my fists slowly, trying to coordinate the flow from both my hands. It is difficult, but I have time to practise.

There is a blind spot behind you, announced a red banner, one of the many dotting the flight line to mark the annual Flight Safety Week. *HIDDEN HAZARDS HURT*, screamed the giant orange letters on the tarmac. There was a bright new take-off line painted down the middle of the runway and new yellow markings for taxi routes. Even the rusting cut-out of the rooster on the windbag sported a new bronze crown.

'Our guest must be getting bored. Take him for a joyride on your next flight,' the Commandant suggested after unveiling a plaque carrying this year's motto for the flight safety campaign: *Safety is in the eye of the beholder.*

'Love to,' Bannon said. 'Show me some of that pilot shit you do.'

'Tomorrow,' I said. 'I'll arrange a picnic for you in the skies.'

It was time to run some safety checks on Colonel Shigri's past.

I placed an order with Uncle Starchy for one of his specials that evening. Uncle Starchy produced a crumpled cigarette from under his shirt: 'Smoke one every day and you'll never get a headache and your wife will never complain.' Uncle Starchy winked.

I straightened the cigarette and slipped it into the little pocket on the sleeve of my flight suit.

'Uncle, you know very well that I am not married. Hell, nobody is married here.'

'Preparation. Preparation,' he muttered before whipping his donkey gently and driving off with his bales of laundry.

Bannon turned up wearing an orange scarf, a flying jacket and a baseball cap with a bald eagle on it. He watched me closely as I carried out the pre-flight checks and prepared for take-off. Bannon seemed disappointed at the size of the cockpit, but he ran his hand over the canopy and said, 'Sweet little bird.' After harnessing his safety belt, he rummaged under his seat then looked puzzled.

'No parachutes?' he said.

'Don't worry,' I said. 'We won't need them.'

Safety . . . Here, There and in the Air another banner greeted us at the end of the runway as we took off and started climbing towards the training area.

Against the backdrop of a cloudless sky-blue sky, our twin-seater MF17 seemed not to move, as if hanging by invisible threads in an aviation museum. I checked with the air traffic control tower. It was one of those rare days when there is no head- or tailwind. Beneath us Pakistan was breathtakingly symmetrical, green squares of vegetation divided by flat rivers reflecting the gentle rays of sun.

'Want to see the Black and White Valley?'

Bannon sat tense in his seat as if not sure whether to trust my flying skills.

'Been in too many whirlybirds with my dead men. Too many memories,' he said, fidgeting with his safety harness.

'This ain't no chopper and I ain't dead,' I mimicked him in an attempt to cheer him up. He forced a nervous smile. 'Here. I have got your favourite.' I produced the joint from my pocket and held it towards Bannon. 'Climbing to ten thousand for manoeuvres,' I said into my mouthpiece, eased the stick backwards and trimmed the controls again. We were now rooted to our seats as the plane climbed steadily. The G meter read 1.5, gravity tugged softly at our cheeks.

Bannon sat there, unsure whether or not to light up. 'Go ahead, be my guest,' I said. 'Safety is in the eye of the beholder.' I took out a lighter, stretched out my left hand, flipped open the air vent on his side of the glass canopy and sparked the joint. The plane shuddered slightly, the vibration pattern changed, and the sound of the propeller slicing the air at 2100 revolutions per minute filtered through.

The Black and White mountain range appeared on our left. The Black Mountains were covered with lush green pine trees and thick shrubs, while the White Mountains formed a series of grey barren ridges. The altimeter read six thousand feet, the propeller pointed just above the horizon; a cow-shaped cloud nudged the tip of our right wing, dived below and disappeared. Bannon, in his nervousness, smoked more than half the joint in two long puffs. The cockpit was full of aircraft fuel and hash fumes. I held my breath. I was responsible for the safety of the ship. He extended the last bit of the joint towards me. 'The machine knows who is flying it,' I said, shaking my head. His eyes laughed a stoned laugh.

'Want some fun?' Without waiting for an answer I put the plane into a thirty-degree dive, trimmed my ailerons, gave some right rudder and yanked the stick to the right. Bannon tried to jump in his seat but the plane was pulling hard, the gravity pinned him down. The right wing kept rolling up and soon we were inverted, hanging from our safety harnesses. I decided to hold the plane there and pressed the intercom button.

'Who shafted Colonel Shigri?'

It's a great vantage position to see the world from; with your feet pointing at the sky, neck stretched and eyes staring at earth, just the way I used to hang upside down from the apple tree in our backyard on Shigri Hill.

'Fuck,' Bannon said, his voice sounding metallic on the intercom. 'Get my fanny back on the ground.'

I obliged. I eased the stick to the left and pushed the right rudder in; the plane completed a roll. I checked the altimeter. Six thousand feet. Exactly where we had started.

'Wasn't that a perfect roll?' I looked towards Bannon, my left hand working the trimmer. Bannon's face was yellow, and his forehead had broken into sweat. His burp filled the cockpit with the smell of Coca-Cola and half-digested omelette.

'Fury Two levelling off at six thousand.'

The tower babbled on for a few seconds.

'Roger,' I said, without listening.

Bannon was talking.

'Nothing to do with us. I heard stuff but that's all bullshit. You've got to look at the context and the context in this case was this.' He counted invisible money with the thumb and forefinger of both his hands. 'There was a lot of moolah going into Afghanistan. This whole jihad against communism was nothing but loads and loads of mazuma. The mujahideen just loved their greenbacks, you know. And yes we brought them mules from Argentina and ack-acks from Egypt and AK47s from China and stingers from Nevada but what really worked with them was the dollar. Not questioning their motives here, mind you. Your average muj is happy with a shawl on one shoulder and a rocket launcher on the other, he is the best guerrilla fighter we have got – God, I could have used some of them in Nam – but what I am saying here is that the leadership, the commanders with their villas in Dubai and their cousins trading in Hong Kong, I mean nobody could keep track of anything. Although money wasn't their basic motive, the muj just loved their dollars. But so did your brass and it's only natural that in a situation like this some of it went missing.' He was still holding the end of the joint in his hand. I took it and flicked it out of the air vent; it ballooned up before dancing away into the space.

'Spare me the analysis. Are you saying Colonel Shigri was one of those people who wanted your greenbacks?'

Dad's bank manager came to see me the day after his funeral and transferred his account to my name. Three hundred and twelve rupees in credit.

'Oh no. Not at all. Not remotely suggesting that.'

I yanked the stick to the left, and pushed in the right rudder to keep the plane from drifting. I wanted to have a good look at Bannon's face. He took a deep breath and peered out of the cockpit, surveying Black Valley where some enterprising bugger had cut down the pines on a mountainside and arranged whitewashed stones to read: *Mard-e-Momin, Mard-e-haq, Zia ul-Haq, Zia ul-Haq.*

'I'm all ears,' I said, banking away from the mountains. I was in no mood to give him an Urdu lesson or explain what the Man of Faith was doing on top of a Black Valley mountain.

'You know how much money was passing through Colonel Shigri's hands? Not putting a price on the hardware here, not counting the humanitarian aid. Just the moolah in Samsonites. Three hundred million dollars cash. Every quarter. And that is American taxpayers' money, not taking into consideration the Saudi royal dosh. So twenty-five mil goes missing – and I say this with my hand on my heart – that sounds like a big pile of greens but it was nothing. No one batted an eyelid at our end. Hey, you don't count pennies when you are fighting the single worst enemy since Hitler. But. But. Twenty-five mil is a lot of money for your folks. You knew your dad better than I did. I know he had his flash uniforms and rigid principles but the man liked his Scotch, he liked his female companions, so you never know.' I stared at him without blinking. 'Look, man, all I'm saying is this: I don't know and you don't know how much a hooker costs in Switzerland. But it sure don't cost twenty-five million US dollars.'

'Do I look like someone who has inherited twenty-five million dollars?'

He looked at me blankly, wondering why was I taking it all so personally. I rummaged in my pocket and produced a crumpled fifty-dollar bill. 'This is all I've got.' I threw the note in his lap where it lay like an unproven accusation.

I wondered if I should tell him that I helped Dad take care of that money. Bannon would have never believed me. I took a deep breath and pressed the radio button. 'Fury Two, beginning radio silence drill.'

I pushed the stick forward till it wouldn't go any further, threw in the full left rudder; the plane went into nose dive and its wings danced a 360-degree dance. The plane headed down, revolving on all three axes. The nose was chasing the tail, the wings were whirring like the blades of a blender; negative Gs were pulling our guts into our throats. The green squares of fields and shimmering straight canals were dancing and becoming bigger with every rotation. I glanced towards Bannon. His hands were flailing in the air, his face contorted with a suppressed scream.

Dad was screwing hookers in Geneva while I was waking up every day at five in the morning to justify his investment in my public-school education and spending my summer vacations inventing physical exercises for myself?

Bannon was a bullshit artist.

The altimeter read two thousand feet. I cut the throttle, yanked the full right rudder in, eased back the stick and the plane slowly curved upwards. The greens began to recede again. Bannon's voice was frightened, hoarse.

'Are you trying to kill an American?'

'I am just trying to talk,' I flicked the radio button on and gave the air traffic controller a call. 'Radio silence out. Spin recovery completed.'

Bannon began to speak in a measured tone, as if making a speech at his favourite aunt's funeral.

'He didn't have a case officer or anything. It was a loose arrangement. But we knew he was one of the good guys, and trust me, there weren't many of them. We were gutted. I wasn't involved then. I wasn't even on the South Asia desk, man, but I knew some guys who had worked with him and they were crying in their beers. It was a big loss. And not that people didn't raise a ruckus, but it was all about staying the course and moving on, all diplomatic bull.'

'So nobody bothered to find out?'

'No they didn't. Because they knew. The orders came from the top. They didn't want to rock the boat, so to speak. I mean it's no secret. Shit, sure you know. From the very top.' He waved to the black mountain with white stones. 'Mard-e-Haq.'

I was pleasantly surprised at his grasp of Urdu. I patted his shoulder and gave him an understanding nod.

'So what are you doing here now? What do you want from me?'

'Shit. I am only the Silent Drill instructor. You know the rules.'

I stayed quiet for a moment. 'It must have come up in meetings, memos. After all, he was your best man.' I moved the stick left and started preparing for landing.

'What were they going to say? Hey, stop the Cold War, our cross-eyed Mard-e-Haq is not fighting by the book? But trust me, man, this is all guesswork. Educated guesswork done by folks in Langley who loved your dad, but guesswork nonetheless. Nobody knew for sure. It was all very low-level stuff. I've got no clue who pulled the trigger.'

'I would have understood if it was the barrel of his gun in his mouth. He was that kind of a man. But it was his own bed sheet,' I said, before asking the tower for permission to land and informing the air traffic controller that I had an airsick passenger on board.

Secretary General's whispers are echoing in the cell. I can't decide if he is in a delirium or trying to entertain me. 'Comrade, I think I've gone blind. I can't see anything.' I rub my own eyes and don't see anything. But I know I am not blind. 'I swear I can't see anything. They brought food, they opened the door but I didn't see anything. Not a thing.'

'It's probably night-time, comrade,' I say, trying to suppress a yawn. Remember day and night? Night, day, then again night.

CHAPTER 16

After the Inter Services Intelligence's counter-espionage unit carried out its weekly sweep through the living quarters of the Army House for any bugs or jamming devices, Brigadier TM started an old-fashioned, hands-on inspection of the premises. He removed the hand-woven burgundy silk covers from the sofa cushions and ran his fingers along their velvet lining. He gave the matching drapes a good shake, combed his way through the brown silk tassels and looked suspiciously at the silver curtain hold-backs. The Persian rugs, plundered from the palaces of Afghan kings and presented to General Zia by Afghan mujahideen commanders, were removed one by one and TM's boots searched for any uneven surfaces on the grey synthetic underlay. The table lamps, shiny brass with silk cord switches, were turned on and off and on again.

Brigadier TM's mistrust of the ISI was based on a simple principle: the cops and thieves should be organised separately. His problem with the ISI was that everything was being done by the same people. After sweeping through the living quarters with their bug detectors and scanners and patting the seats of some random chairs they had simply signed a document saying no espionage devices were detected. Brigadier TM never knew whether to trust these signed documents. After all, potential presidential assassins don't go about their business signing affidavits as they close in on their target. Brigadier TM had done his staff and command course, and he understood why a country needed an intelligence service, why an armed service needed spies to spy on its own men and officers, and he could live with that. But there was another reason he didn't like these military intelligence types. Brigadier TM didn't like them because they didn't wear uniforms. It was hard enough to trust anyone who didn't wear a uniform, but how on earth could you trust someone *with a rank* who didn't wear a uniform? Brigadier TM considered ISI a menace on a par with the corrupt Pakistani police and lazy Saudi princes, but since his job was to watch and keep quiet, he never mentioned it in front of General Zia. Going through the trophy cabinet, he concluded that the sheer amount of stuff in the Army House was a security hazard. 'Who needs all these photos?' He stood in front of a wall covered with framed portraits of former generals who had ruled the country. Brigadier TM couldn't help noticing that they had progressively got fatter and that the medals on their chests had multiplied. He came to the end of the row of photographs and stood in front of a large portrait. In this oil painting, Muhammad Ali Jinnah, the Founder of Pakistan, was wearing a crisp Savile Row suit and was absorbed in studying a document. With a monocle in his left eye and his intense gaze, Jinnah looked like a tortured eighteenth-century chemist on the verge of a new discovery.

Brigadier TM looked at the Founder's portrait with admiration; he didn't mind civilians if they were properly dressed and behaved like civilians. 'Look at this guy.' He took a step towards the portrait. 'He was a civilian and he wore civilian clothes and he said civilian things, but at heart he was a soldier.' TM didn't mind saluting this guy, out of sheer patriotism, the kind of patriotism that only a decorated soldier can feel; he took a step backwards and saluted. As his foot landed on the carpet, his hand made an arc in the air and his open palm reached his eyebrow, the frame tilted. It tilted ever so slightly, but Brigadier TM's alert eyes noticed the tilt and he suddenly looked around. He felt embarrassed and shy, like a child who has disturbed an immaculate ikebana arrangement at a rich cousin's house. Brigadier TM moved forward, held the frame by its corners with both his hands, took a step back to see if it was level and then with a shudder let the frame go. His right hand reached for his holster and stopped. The Founder had winked at him from behind his monocle. He could swear he had seen his left eye move.

'I have done that myself sometimes.'

When TM heard General Zia's voice, he turned round and saluted, this time less aggressively, shifting his feet slightly to cover the frame so that Zia couldn't see the tilt in it.

Without his uniform and presidential paraphernalia, General Zia seemed to have shrunk. His silk gown floated about him. His moustache, always waxed and twirled, drooped over his upper lip. He was sucking it nervously. His hair, always oiled and parted down the middle, was in a state of disarray, like a parade squad on tea break.

'He was the only true leader we have ever had,' General Zia said and stopped as if expecting Brigadier TM to correct him.

Brigadier TM was still in shock. He didn't believe in superstitions. He didn't believe in co-incidences. He knew that if your gun was oiled and safety catch unlocked, it would shoot. He knew if your wind-speed calculations were accurate and you knew how to control your descent, your parachute would land you where you wanted to land. He knew if you mentioned a prisoner's daughter's name after keeping him awake for three days, he would talk. Brigadier TM had no experience of monocle-wearing dead men in gilt-edged frames blinking back to his salutes.

'This portrait is not security-cleared, sir. General Akhtar should not have violated Code Red.'

'Dear son, I can live with the rumours in the American rags but do I have to be scared of pictures gifted to me by my own intelligence chief? Is General Akhtar under suspicion now? Are you saying I am not safe even in my own drawing room?' General Zia paused for a moment, then added, 'Or do you not like the man in the picture?'

'He was a civilian, sir, but he got us this country.'

General Zia thrust his hands in the pockets of his gown to hide his irritation; Brigadier TM had no sense of history. 'Well, if you compare him to that *banya* Gandhi, or that fornicator Nehru, yes, of course he was a great leader. But since then there have been others who in their own humble way . . .' General Zia looked at TM's blank face, realised that he wasn't going to get any compliments from him and decided to change the subject.

'Son, I feel like a prisoner in this house. These ISI people are stupid. They know how to fight the Russians, by jingo they've got their spies spread across half the world, but they can't figure out who is trying to assassinate their own President.'

One thing that Brigadier TM never did was snitch on his brothers in uniform, even if they chose not to wear their uniforms. He also tried to change the topic, came up with a proposal and immediately regretted it.

'Why don't you go for an Umra, sir?'

General Zia went to Mecca at least ten times a year and Brigadier TM had to accompany him. He knew General Zia felt very safe there, but he also knew that General Zia behaved like a twelve-year-old having a bad birthday. He threw tantrums, he cried, he smashed his head against the black marble wall of the Khana Kaaba, he sprinted around it as if he was in some kind of competitive run, not on a pilgrimage.

'Do you think Jinnah would go on a pilgrimage under these circumstances?'

Brigadier TM felt the Founder's eye blink at the back of his head. He wanted to point out that Jinnah had never gone on a pilgrimage to Mecca. He wanted to say that even if he had found the time to get away for some spiritual replenishment, the Founder would have probably headed for a pub in west London. TM stood at attention, ignoring Zia's question. He wriggled his toes in his boots; he wasn't sure if his head was getting the blood circulation it needed.

'Did Jinnah ever have to make these decisions?' General Zia made a last desperate attempt to educate Brigadier TM about the vestiges of history. 'Did Jinnah ever have to fight the Russians in the morning and convince the Americans in the evening that it is a fight still worth fighting? Was he ever a prisoner in his own Army House?'

'Yes, sir.' Brigadier TM shouted and brought his heels together.

'I think I need to be in the country.'

Brigadier TM felt relieved. He didn't want to go to Mecca. He didn't want to be in that empty, black marble room again.

★　★　★

232

Brigadier TM felt alive when there was action or at least the promise of it. You are twenty thousand feet above the ground, free-falling, you adjust your posture, you let your body ride the air currents, you dive, you lose a thousand feet, you do a somersault, you spread your arms and legs, you pull your ripcord and suddenly the world is real, a patch of concrete in front of the presidential dais, or thick bush behind the enemy lines.

He had felt the same sense of anticipation as he walked behind General Zia and entered the Khana Kaaba's compound on his first visit. He was offered a white robe, one like the ones everyone else was wearing, but he took one look at the Saudi policemen escorting them and refused. He was in the House of God but that didn't mean that he should forget his duty. They asked General Zia if they should let his security chief in, dressed in his battle fatigues, but Zia was crying violently and nodding his head constantly. The Saudi police couldn't really tell if he approved or not. General Zia snivelled and buried his head in his white robe and started to pray loudly as they walked towards the black room at the centre of the compound. Brigadier TM looked around for any potential threats. The worshippers were few and scattered and prone; in their various states of worship they looked like logs thrown about randomly. The light was stage bright but cool. Brigadier TM liked well-lit places. The centre of his attention was the black marble, low-ceilinged cubicle draped in black silk.

He didn't expect any security risks here. The room had been there for more than fourteen hundred years but he had to take precautions as he knew it was being opened specially for General Zia. The rest of the pilgrims had to make do with touching its outer walls and kissing the gold-embroidered black silk that adorned its walls.

He had ordered a file on the place from the ISI when he did his routine risk assessment and they had sent him a photocopied page from a high-school Islamic Studies book.

It was the exact spot where Abraham had tried to slaughter his son, where Mohammed had smashed idols and declared that all non-Muslims who laid down their arms would be safe.

The only people carrying arms tonight were Saudi security people. Brigadier TM wondered if they even knew how to use them. The place hummed with respect and prayers and he took his hand off his holster. His gaze became that of a tourist, fleeting, slightly curious and not suspicious. He noted with interest that most of the worshippers were black but there were people from other nations. He saw a white woman sitting in a corner reciting the Quran. He couldn't suppress his smile when he saw an old Chinese man holding his rosary with one hand and a walking stick with the other and dragging his feet around the black cubicle.

Brigadier TM thought that maybe after his retirement he would come here as a pilgrim and see if he could feel what others felt.

Their hosts, Saudi princes in gold-bordered silk kaffiyehs, led the way. He had lost count of how many princes there were in this kingdom.

As they approached the black marble cubicle in the centre, Brigadier TM moved in front of the posse, having suddenly realised that, after all, they were entering the unknown. The door opened and nothing happened. There was nobody ambushing them. There was nobody welcoming them either.

The room was empty.

There were no flashes of divine light, no thunder, the walls of the room were black and without a single inscription. And if it hadn't been for General Zia's choked voice seeking forgiveness, it would have been a quiet room full of stale air. Allah's house was a dark, empty room. Brigadier TM shrugged his shoulders, stood at the door and kept an eye on the pilgrims going around the Khana Kaaba.

Brigadier TM felt the Founder's eye blink at the back of his head again. General Zia realised that TM was not in the mood for small talk. He wrapped his nightgown tightly around himself and left the room muttering something, of which Brigadier TM could only make out 'get some sleep'. What General Zia was saying was, 'Who can get any sleep on a bitch of a night like this?'

Brigadier TM walked towards the frame, trying to avoid eye contact with the Founder. His hands slipped into both his pockets and came out wrapped in white handkerchiefs. He held the frame by its edges and removed it from the nail from which it hung. He held the frame in front of his chest, carried it to the sofa and placed it carefully with the Founder facing down. He pulled his trouser leg up with his right hand and produced a dagger from a leather sheath clipped above his ankle. He removed the hooks one by one, inserted the tip of the dagger under the cardboard, lifted it and tossed it aside. A thick green velvety cloth covered the back of the portrait. His fingers traced the area where he thought the Founder's face was. Behind the Founder's monocle-covered eye his fingers found a hard round object. He took his dagger again, cut a neat hole around it and picked out a grey metal disc slightly thicker but not bigger than a fifty-paisa coin. He picked it up with his handkerchief-covered hand and held it away from his body as if it was about to explode.

As Brigadier TM was still examining both the sides of the disc, trying to decide whether it was some artistic contraption that the painter of the portrait had used or a lethal device set to blow him away, the metal surface parted from the middle, like the curtains on a miniature theatre, and a concave little lens blinked at him. The metal curtains immediately shut again.

Brigadier TM closed his palm around the spy camera and tried to crush it until his knuckles hurt.

Remote-controlled bombs, reinforced bullets, daggers thrown from a distance, the glint from a marksman's rifle, shoulder-held surface-to-air missiles, bodyguards with grudges and itchy fingers: Brigadier TM could handle it all without his heart beating a beat faster. But this sneaky little camera made him so angry that he forgot his duty for a moment; instead of calling in the forensic experts and trying to track down the camera feed, he walked towards General Zia's bedroom. He hesitated outside the door of his bedroom for a moment, took three deep breaths to compose himself and then knocked.

First Lady opened the door, installed herself in the middle of the frame and looked at him with mocking eyes, as if he was a child who had knocked on his mother's bedroom door after wetting his bed.

'What is it now?' she asked. 'Does he have a midnight appointment with a foreign lady correspondent? Or is India about to attack us again?'

Brigadier TM really didn't know how to answer back to a woman.

He opened his palm and showed it to the First Lady.

She gave him a withering look. 'Your boss doesn't live here any more.' Then she turned and shouted along the corridor. 'Look, Zia, your friend has got a present for you.'

CHAPTER 17

'Do you like mangoes?' Secretary General's whisper is barely audible. His breathing is heavy. It seems he is in pain. The bastards haven't given him any food either. How much time has passed? Can't be more than three days. I crawl towards the hole in the wall, knocking down little sand pyramids I have been building to mark the days. Not that I know when the day starts or when it ends. There hasn't been a single knock on the door. There hasn't been a single sound from anywhere. 'I don't like mangoes,' I say. 'Not worth the effort. We had apple trees in our backyard on Shigri Hill. I like apples. Pick them, rub them against your pants and eat them. No hassles.'

Secretary General is quiet for a long time as if collecting my words from the floor and trying to make a sentence out of them.

'You related?'

'Yes.'

'Brother?'

'Worse.'

He stays quiet, then his fists hit the wall. Thrice.

'You thought you could do it all by yourself? You have no sense of history. You should have joined hands with your fellow soldiers. Comrades-in-arms.'

If only Secretary General knew.

'I was his only son.'

As I walked from the parade square towards my dorm I could feel the asphalt surface of the road melting under my boots. In the distance the road evaporated into mirage after vaporous mirage, each of them disappearing as I came closer. Bannon and Obaid were still on the parade square, doing yet another session of extra drill. There was no point going to my dorm. I headed straight for the comfort of Bannon's bunker. The air conditioner was on and my sweat-soaked shirt turned stiff within minutes. I took it off and sat there in my white vest looking around for something to take my mind off the drill commands still reverberating in my head. I lay down on the floor with my head on the mattress and put my boots next to the air-conditioner vent. I rummaged under the mattress and as expected found a brown envelope with the July issue in it. Thai beauty Diana Lang and Yasser Arafat shared the cover: *Lang Shots* and *Arafat's Guns and Poses*, said the cover of *Playboy*'s World Special issue.

I decided to save Yasser Arafat's interview for later and opened the centrefold. The door opened and Bannon walked in, fanning himself with his peaked cap. 'I give up. Your friend isn't going to make it.'

He ignored my hand which was struggling simultaneously to stuff the magazine into the envelope and push the envelope under the mattress. Little streams of sweat were running down Bannon's white crocodile face, his hair stuck to his scalp and he was whispering to himself, 'Two weeks before the President's inspection and I got people who can't even lockstep.'

I brought my feet down from the air-conditioning vents and asked Bannon what he was talking about.

'Baby O ain't going to stay in the Drill Squad. As soon as the parade begins, he starts to sweat like a whore in church. He just hasn't got the aptitude.'

'Obaid may not be a natural on the square but he is very keen,' I said. 'I have never seen anybody as motivated as he is. He stands there in our dorm at night simulating his moves.'

'He might have made a good kamikaze but he is just not cut out for going through the whole damn drill.'

'He is very emotional about it. Surely you can . . .'

I let the sentence hang in the chilled air. Surely he would know what I meant. We just couldn't let Obaid down.

'It's for his own good,' he muttered. 'You tell him to turn right and he goes left. You ask him to throw the rifle and he just stands there. And this is with my verbal commands. Imagine the

240

mayhem when we are in the silent zone. We were doing our rifle spirals today and his every throw came at my head. He'll kill someone or get killed. You try and put some sense into his head. He'll make a fine officer but no way is he rehearsing with us. I have to go and fill out my final report.'

Bannon left the room without looking back, without promising anything.

I was still contemplating whether I should find out what Yasser Arafat was doing in a magazine full of oriental girls with heart-shaped pubic hair when the door opened and Obaid walked in, kicked the door shut behind him, leaned against the Bruce Lee poster and stared at me as if I was the sole reason for his lack of hand–eye coordination.

His khaki uniform was marked with patches of sweat, his blue scarf tightly wrapped around his right hand and there was a bruise on his right cheek. His normally serene eyes were swirling pools of anger.

The reasons for his regular thrashing on the square were obvious to me. You could score top marks in war history, you could simulate your drill movements all night long, but when the silent zone kicked in, you couldn't look in your manuals to find out what to do and how to do it. Obaid did all my studying for me. He drew my navigation maps, he took care of my inability to concentrate on any textbook for more than two paragraphs and he prepared notes for me. Despite the lack of an academic bone in my body, or maybe because of it, I was soaring ahead in the drill department, already commanding the squad, whereas he still loitered in the reserve pool. Anyone who could sit down and read a book outside the classroom for ten minutes straight would never make a good officer let alone a coherent pair of military boots on the parade square. And Bannon did have a point: one wrong step, a single wrong note from silent cadence, could wreck the elegant routine we had devised for the President's inspection. It could also destroy the sword manoeuvre that I had prepared for the President.

I thought of distracting Obaid with Yasser Arafat's pictures, but I looked at his contorted face and gave up on the idea. He opened and closed his fists. There was a fury in his eyes that I had never seen before. I moved towards him to put my hand on his shoulder. He recoiled and turned round, put his hands on his face and started to bang his head against the wall.

'It will be all right,' I said and felt like one of those doctors who tell you to live life to its fullest after informing you that you have only six weeks to live. He was still for a moment, then he sprang from his position and hurled himself towards Bannon's bed, bringing down the bamboos hoisting the camouflaged canopy over the mattress. All the books he read hadn't taught him the basic military rule: you manage your anger by kicking ass, not by rearranging the furniture in your room. He picked up the pillow and threw it at the wall.

Disappointed by the lack of impact, he picked up the ceramic Buddha. I lunged forward and stopped him. 'Not the Buddha,' I said, taking it from his hands. His fingers were warm on Buddha's air-conditioned ceramic face. He looked around for something else to throw. The air conditioner's cold air had dried up some of the sweat patches on his shirt. As I moved closer to calm him down, I picked up the cardamom on his breath and the musky smell of his drying sweat.

'Let's talk it through,' I said. That's what he normally said in such situations.

'You are trying to keep me out.'

'Look, Baby O . . .' I fumbled for words and tried to fill the silence by moving my hand from his shoulder to the back of his neck. His hair bristled under my palm, his neck was still warm despite the chill in the room. I felt angry at my own lack of empathy and it came out.

'Look, it's not a picnic that I am not taking you on. It's for your own good, Baby O.'

He ignored my patronising tone. 'There is a much simpler way,' he said. 'What is this place full of? Aeroplanes? What do we need to do? Take a plane and go for the –'

'We are not having that discussion again,' I cut him off. For a man in uniform his ideas about soldiering were naive. He considered himself some kind of character from *Jonathan Livingstone Seagull*, the latest addition to the pile of books on his bedside table, and talked about aeroplanes as

243

if they were not million-dollar fighting machines but some kind of vehicle for his spiritual quest.

'*The wind was a whisper in his face and the ocean stood still beneath him . . .*' he said with his eyes closed. 'I could do it all by myself.' He patted my cheek.

'You can hardly land that bloody thing. Forget it.'

'Who needs to land?' He produced a navigation map with coordinates drawn and a red circle around the Army House. 'Twenty-three minutes, if there is no head- or tailwind.'

I snatched the map from him, flung it over my shoulder and stared into his eyes. He stared back unblinking. I thought of telling him about Uncle Starchy's nectar but immediately decided against it.

'Colonel Shigri didn't kill himself and I am not about to,' I said. Then put my mouth to his ear and shouted at strength 5: 'Is that clear?'

Screw my inner cadence, I thought.

'Is that clear?' I shouted again.

He pressed his ear over my mouth, leaned into me, and put his hand on my waist.

'If you want to do it here, you've got to have me in the squad. You need a back-up.'

I removed his hand, took a step back. 'Listen, stick to your Rilke or whatever you're reading these days. What are you going to do? Hey, look, this is my sword, here comes the General, look, I am taking a swipe.' I did a limp-wristed mime with an imaginary sword. 'Oops, sorry, I missed. Can I have another go?'

I think I killed him with those words.

I didn't see his fist coming at my guts, and as I doubled over, his knee hit my ribs and sent me reeling onto Bannon's bed, face down. I found myself sprawled on the heap of bamboos and the camouflaged canopy. The surprise of being hit by Baby O was so overwhelming that I didn't feel any pain. The Bruce Lee poster blurred for a moment. Obaid came and stood over me and looked down as if he had never seen me before. My boot caught him between his shins and he fell beside me.

I rubbed my lower ribcage and sighed. Obaid propped himself up on one elbow and watched me closely. He sat up suddenly as if he had made up his mind about something. Planting both his knees around my hips, he started to pull my vest out of my trousers. He gently rubbed my lower ribcage with both his hands, all the time looking into my eyes. I didn't like him watching my reactions so I closed my eyes, my hips raised themselves involuntarily and my starched khaki trousers suddenly felt very tight. I hoped Bannon would take his time filling out that report.

He moved my vest upwards, the chilled air sent shivers through my chest and my nipples turned shamelessly erect and purple; my belt was unhooked. I sucked my stomach in and held my breath as his hand wandered into my pants. He didn't hold me, just let the back of his hand rest against my cock as if it was a chance encounter. I was scared of the lips that were gently brushing their way towards my chest. I was scared of being kissed.

I breathed in the smell of jasmine oil from his hair and sank back into the mattress; a bamboo crunched under me and I tried to get up in a fit of panic. His hand in my pants pinned me down. His lips travelled along the outline of my jaw, his fingertips made tiny, airy circles on the tip of my cock. I groaned and my hips began to move but he pressed me down with his knee. His lips traced my ribcage and kept travelling downward. I did some hard thinking with my eyes shut. There is a stream near my house on Shigri Hill; I found myself standing in it during the winter, testing my first erection against the ice-cold water. My body leapt up and my cock touched the tip of his nose and he laughed.

There was more surprise for me as he wriggled out of his pants and took my hand to his cock. I found myself tracing a curve, not just a slight curve, but the semicircle of a new moon. His cock was bent like a bow and his erection arched towards his navel. He sighed and lay down beside me. His eyes were shut and a gentle smile was spreading around his lips, a smile so serene, so full yet gentle, that he seemed to have retreated into his world where the wind whispered in his face and the ocean beneath him was still.

I didn't dare speak for a long time. The air conditioner turned off at some point and the only sound in the room was that of two scared boys breathing.

246

'No. No,' he whispered in the end, cupping me in his hands in a futile attempt at not leaving any traces on the bed. 'Not on the sheets.'

He spoke with his face staring up at the ceiling. 'You wouldn't do anything stupid.'

'And you will not do anything fucked up,' I said.

'I wouldn't,' he said.

In the morning he was gone.

CHAPTER 18

Even if Zainab wasn't blind she would not have been able to read her own interview in the newspaper because she was illiterate. Her news came from smells, birds, textures of the wind. And this morning she could feel the bad news in the air. She could hear the sound of impatient birds in the wind, she could feel migration and long lonely nights marching towards her.

She held her breath for a moment, ignoring the portents that floated in the air, and tried to concentrate on the job at hand.

Zainab stood pressed against the iron bars of her cell, breaking little crumbs from a piece of bread and throwing them to a group of sparrows who descended on the jail every morning. Like many blind people, she could count the number of birds by listening to the fluttering of their wings. There were probably fifteen of them. They were picking playfully at the crumbs, their hunger already satiated because there was enough food for them in the jail. Every morning there were a number of women with pieces of leftover bread, their hands stretching out of the iron bars trying to entice the same set of sparrows, hoping to see them peck at the crumbs, and with some luck to get them to pick the food from the palms of their hands. This morning though, the sparrows were more interested in playing with each other.

Zainab didn't feel like the other inmates on death row; they prayed, they cried, they obsessively followed the progress of their petitions for mercy, and after their last appeal was denied, they turned their attention to the afterlife and started seeking forgiveness all over again. Zainab had committed no crime and she was comfortable in her cell – called the black cell because it accommodated death-row prisoners – and she lived in it as if it was her home. She had woken up this morning, cleaned her cell, massaged her pregnant cell mate's feet and put oil in her own hair. After feeding the birds she would visit other cells, which were not black cells, and massage the feet of two other pregnant prisoners. 'Why would anyone want to kill a poor blind woman?' was her recurring answer to all the excitement that her lawyer and other women's groups outside the jail were creating about her death sentence. Even the jailer respected her for her politeness, the way she helped other prisoners and taught their children to recite the Quran. Zainab was the jail superintendent's favourite prisoner and it was she who had given her the pair of sunglasses that so infuriated General Zia. 'They will protect you against the sun.' Zainab had accepted them with a smile without complaining, without showing any self-pity, without pointing out that sunlight couldn't enter the dead white pools that were her eyes. Behind the plastic sunglasses her eyes were all white. She had been born without corneas. There was the obvious talk of bad omens when she arrived in this world but her face was so luminous and her other faculties so intact that she had been accepted as an unfortunate child and she had made the most of her circumstances. Even now that she had become the first woman to be sentenced to death by stoning under new laws, she had shown a puzzled fortitude that baffled women activists who were fighting her case in the courts and on the streets. 'Stoning?' she had asked after she was sentenced. 'Like they do to the Devil in Mecca during haj? They have been doing it to him for centuries and they haven't been able to kill him. How are they going to kill a healthy woman like me?'

After wearing the sunglasses for a few days Zainab had started liking them; they helped her with the headaches she got after standing in the sunlight for too long. And the other prisoners' children always giggled when she took them off to show them her milk-white eyes.

Zainab heard a pair of wings flapping, heavier than the wings of the sparrows. She heard her sparrows flutter in a panic but they didn't fly away. Some hovered in the air, others moved away from her. Her hand stopped throwing the crumbs for a moment, feeling protective towards her sparrows, not wanting to give to the crow what was theirs. Then she remembered a crow from her childhood who had kept her company on many a dark day. Another bad omen, the villagers had said, but it was good company for her and she would always save some bread for him. Could it be the same crow? Her hands started to break the jail bread and throw it out again. What if the crow was really hungry? All the prisoners and even some of the jail staff, she knew, fed these sparrows.

She heard the jailer's footsteps coming towards her. She could tell from the way she walked that the jailer was bringing bad news. She tried to ignore the guilt in the approaching footsteps and continued to feed the bird. She could tell that the crow had taken over the area. The sparrows had flown away except for two who were still skirting around the circle claimed by the crow, rushing in to pick on a piece when the crow's back was turned and dashing back to a safe distance. She could feel on her fingertips that their wings were poised for escape. She could also tell that it was more of a game they were playing, to see, if one distracted the crow, how close the other one could get.

The jailer's shadow blocked the sunlight. Zainab could tell from the smell of the jailer's sweat that she was in trouble. She was breathing heavily, shifting her weight on her feet, pretending that she wasn't there.

The news was definitely bad.

What bad news could you bring to a prisoner condemned to death? She had no hopes about the clemency appeal that her lawyer had filed on her behalf. The other prisoners in her cell had discussed it. They knew that although the General had changed his mind many times over many things, one thing he never did was miss a chance to turn down the mercy plea in a death-sentence case. Something to do with someone called Bhutto who was the ruler before Zia. Zainab knew that Bhutto was hanged and not stoned to death. She didn't really know what his crime was either. Zainab wasn't really expecting her sentence to be commuted, so maybe the jailer had received her black warrants and was worried about how to arrange a stoning. Zainab felt bad for the jailer; why did such a nice, competent woman have to go through such trials?

She heard the crow flap its wings urgently, but instead of flying away it settled down again, probably having chased the last sparrow away.

'Zainab, your picture has been published in a newspaper,' the jailer said. Zainab knew the jailer was avoiding the subject by telling her about the newspaper instead of giving her the news about her black warrant. 'You look good in the picture with your sunglasses.'

Zainab threw the last bit of bread, hoping to hit the crow on its head. She missed.

'They are going to transfer you to another prison. Because of that picture and the interview you gave.'

Zainab remembered the interview. Her lawyer had read out a few questions to her and she had repeated the same story that she had told at the district court, at the High Court, in the appeal against her death sentence, the same story she had told her fellow prisoners, over and over again without adding or omitting anything despite her lawyer's best efforts.

'Your picture was printed in America. Apparently the orders have come from the very top to take you to a place where you can't give interviews.'

Zainab didn't know much about interviews or places from where you could or could not give interviews, she had only told them what had happened.

'It was dark but they had torches. There were three of them. There might have been another one outside the door. They smelled of car petrol, their hands were soft so they weren't peasants. They tied my hands, they hit me when I asked them to let me go in their mothers', sisters' names. They were animals.'

'But I like it here,' she told the jailer. 'My cell mate is due to give birth in two weeks. I have other friends here. I want to live here.'

Then she thought about what she had just said. 'I want to die here.'

'The orders have come from the President,' the jailer said, using a tone that she had never used with Zainab before, making it clear that it was final, even more final than her death sentence.

Zainab also smelled fear in her voice and wondered whether the jailer would be punished as well.

And that thought, her having to leave her friends behind, and the idea that the jailer who gave her the sunglasses might be punished, overwhelmed Zainab for an instant and she did something that she had never done before. Blind Zainab who had listened in silence when a lecherous judge sentenced her to death, she who had not given her tormentors the satisfaction of a scream, she who had spent her life thanking God and forgiving His men for what they did to her: Zainab screamed and Zainab cursed.

'May worms eat the innards of the person who is taking me away from my home. May his children not see his face in death.'

The jailer felt relieved. She was irritated by Zainab's reckless fortitude. She didn't want her to go quietly.

It is a well-known fact that curses are the last resort of frustrated mothers and useless weapons for people who do not even have the courage or vocabulary to come up with proper invective for their enemies. It is also a well-known fact that most curses don't work. The only way they can work is if a crow hears a curse from someone who has fed him to a full stomach and then carries it to the person who has been cursed. Crows, notoriously gluttonous, never feel as if their stomachs are full. They are also wayward creatures, their movement can never be predicted. They never bother carrying anything anywhere. Zainab didn't even notice when the crow, having checked the ground for any leftover bits of bread, flapped its wings languidly and took off. When he was high above the jail, from where he could see other groups of sparrows doing their silly dance in front of the prisoners, he felt a western current in the air above him. He flew up, stopped flapping his wings and two days later crossed the border into India where the wheat season starts early and the electric poles are safer.

Zainab packed her two pairs of clothes and waited for her own journey to begin. She was hand-cuffed and put in the back of a jeep. She noticed that there were no guards with her. Where was a handcuffed blind woman going to go? She prayed for an easy birth for her cell mate and forgot all about whom she had cursed and why.

The crow tucked his wings under his body and let the current carry him.

Crows may not have a conscience but their memory lasts for ninety years.

It was after the jeep carrying her stopped and didn't move and nobody came to tell her to get off that Zainab thought she had arrived at the place she was being carried to. She took her clothes bundle, moved aside the canvas curtain and got off the jeep. She smelled a lot of smoke and a lot of men and for a moment she thought they had sent her to a men's jail. She heard a passing siren and she kept walking, hoping to be led to a cell to live the rest of her life. The people who surrounded her were impatient. In jails people know how to stay still. After walking a few yards and avoiding stepping on anyone's feet, she held the arm of a man who seemed still and patient and asked: 'Where am I supposed to live?'

The man pressed a soggy two-rupee note in her hand and told her to wait like everyone else.

'I am not a beggar,' she said, but the man had already walked off.

A hand gripped her arm firmly. 'Where do you think you are going, old woman? We are taking you to the Fort. The press won't be able to bother you there.'

CHAPTER 19

I wake up to my neighbour's desperate whispers echoing in my cell. 'Comrade. Comrade.' My fists are clenched and sand sticks to my sweaty palms. 'Comrade.'

It takes me a moment to orient myself, another to recognise the source of these whispers. By the time I rub my palms against the back of my trousers and move towards the hole in the wall I am thinking that it seems I have been accepted back into the struggle.

'Yes, comrade,' I say with the flourish of a veteran communist.

His voice is raspy and full of excitement.

'Can you smell a woman?' he says.

'I can smell them from a mile away, Comrade Secretary General. Specially if they smell nice.'

'No,' he whispers agitatedly. 'Can you smell a woman here?'

I take a deep breath and smell the stench of my own teeth, which haven't been brushed for I don't know how many days.

'Did you smell it? She is close, very close.'

'As close as your revolution?'

'This is not the time to make jokes. We need to stick together. I think it might be the cell next to yours.'

'This is the Fort. What could a woman possibly do to end up here?'

'You don't know these people. They are capable of anything. She is definitely in the cell next to you. Talk to her.'

'I am in no mood for female company, Secretary General. I don't like women on an empty stomach. You talk to her.'

'The bourgeoisie protect their own even in prison. Why couldn't they have put her in the cell beside mine? You get chicken to eat and a woman as a neighbour and what do I get? An army deserter as a neighbour and stinking food.'

'I am not a deserter,' I explain. 'I am still in uniform.' There is the silence of two hungry men in the dark.

'You know what you could do, comrade . . .' His whisper is suddenly full of genuine longing and his breathing is heavy.

'I am with you, comrade,' I say.

'You can find the brick in the wall with her cell. You can talk to her. You can ask her to put her tit in the hole and then you can touch it.'

'And what makes you think she'll do it?'

'Tell her you are in the army.'

I hear steps in the corridor; they stop in front of my dungeon. I put the brick in the hole and sit down with my back against the wall.

There is a knock on the door. Who knocks on a prisoner's door? They probably want to see whether I am dead or alive. I try to stand up without making any sound. My knees tremble, I put a hand on the wall for support, try to moisten my chapped lips with my tongue and say in a faint but firm voice: 'Yes.'

The door opens with a creak, the light is dull and faded and the sharp smell of home-made jasmine perfume overwhelms me. The man wielding a pair of handcuffs is not wearing a uniform but I can tell from his civilian hairstyle that he is one of Major Kiyani's men. No point asking him what his orders are. After starving me in this black hole for eternity they have decided to formally arrest me. Life is not about to get better. I wish Secretary General could see me in handcuffs. He would be proud. The soldier takes his time with my blindfold, adjusting it over my eyebrows and nose, blocking out any stray rays of light, making sure I can breathe. Even from behind my blindfold I feel a surge of bright white sunlight as I am led up the stairs and into the cloister between the Court for the Commons and the Palace of Mirrors. The air in the Fort smells of grass, freshly cut and watered. I wish I could scratch the back of my neck.

The jeep goes through a crowded bazaar. I smell cakes and cow dung and raw mangoes. I hear the hawkers hawking and traffic police constables whistling at buses and buses honking back, a duet that is melody to my ears after days and nights of the dungeon's silence. The jeep comes out on a leafy avenue, the air is full of floating pollen, the traffic is orderly, the cars sound new and stop at traffic signals. The trees along the road smell like sun-burnt eucalyptus. The jeep stops at a place smelling of metal polish and army boots. A gate opens and the jeep moves forward slowly. In the distance I can hear the rumble of an aircraft preparing to take off. And then the very familiar smell of aircraft fuel, and the sound of idling propellers.

They want to fly me back to the Academy with honour because they have found no evidence against me.

Or they want to throw me out of the plane because they have found no evidence and don't need it.

I read in *Reader's Digest* that in some Latin American country that is what the army was doing: taking prisoners up in a plane and then throwing them from an altitude of twenty thousand feet, over the sea. Handcuffed.

I flex my arms as a hand grips my shoulder and leads me up a ladder. Anyone trying to throw me off this plane would come with me. I am not going alone.

I can tell as soon as I step off the ladder and into the plane that I am in a Hercules C130. Why do they need a whole C130 to transport a single person? A C130 is like a huge flying truck, it can take twenty thousand kilograms, the combined weight of an armoured jeep and a tank, and still have space left for their crews. Its backdoor ramp is like the gate of a town house, a vehicle can pass through it, dozens of paratroopers can jump. Or somebody can be thrown out. The man holding my shoulder asks me to sit in a webbed seat, fastens my nylon seat belt, asks me if I'd prefer my hands behind me or in front. In front, of course, you moron. My hands are free for a moment. No time for heroics.

I smell the animals before I hear their muffled bleating and the sound of their tiny, nervous feet on the metal floor of the cabin. They smell like freshly bathed goats but their bleating sounds oddly strangled. I wriggle in my seat and want to announce that I am on the wrong flight. The back gate creaks shut, the propellers pick up speed and suddenly the cabin is full of the pungent smell of animal piss. As the aircraft's nose lifts off the runway, the smell becomes even stronger. The animals are obviously not used to flying.

Distracted by the din of the aircraft and stench of the animals, I jump from my seat when a hand tousles my hair and a rasping voice says, 'You shouldn't have done it, sir.'

'What?' I say, genuinely baffled.

'Whatever you did. They wouldn't put handcuffs on you if you hadn't done anything.'

Fuck off, I want to say. I stay silent.

'Do you want me to remove your blindfold?'

'Are you sure?' I say, suddenly very courteous.

'They didn't say anything about you. And we are airborne, what can you possibly see?'

261

He tries to move the blindfold above my eyes and his fat fingers linger on my cheeks more than they push the cloth. I bend my head offering him the knot at the back of my head. His attempts to untie the knot are exaggerated. His fingers are straying onto my neck, my shoulders. Then he puts his teeth on the knot and I can feel his slobbering lips at the back of my neck, inches below where he should be directing his efforts. He comes closer and I can feel his cock poking my shoulder. For a moment I think of bringing my handcuffed hands up and strangling his cock with the chain between my handcuffs.

You might be going to your death, but there is always someone else there pursuing their own agenda.

I am adjusting my hands for the right angle of attack when his teeth get into the knot in the right place; one hard jab of his cock in my armpit and my blindfold is off.

He is sweating after all the hard work. His load-master's overalls are olive green and oil-stained and they rise like a little tent over his crotch. *Fayyaz*, his nameplate shamelessly announces. I stare at his face without blinking as if remembering his pathetic features. He shuffles back to his seat across the cabin.

Between us on the floor are nine mountain lambs in various stages of misery, shivering under their tight little woolly curls. Their hind legs are tied with rope so that they can't move. Some are sprawled

262

on the floor of the cabin, others are on their knees. One of them has thrown up and is struggling to breathe with his face on the floor, others are huddling together. Under their meshed muzzles, their faces are perplexed question marks.

Since when did the Pakistan Air Force start dealing in livestock? I want to ask Fayyaz, but he is only a fat horny loadmaster.

'Where are they going?' I ask.

'Same place we are going,' he says with a coy smile.

'Which is where?'

'I am not allowed to tell you,' he says, looking at the lambs as if they might hear the destination and not like it.

'Have you ever been to the Lahore Fort?' I ask him casually.

'No. But I have seen it on TV.' He is puzzled.

'No, Loadmaster Fayyaz.' I chew his name before spitting it out. 'There is another fort under that fort they show on the television. It's for the collaborators, the likes of you.' I start looking at the lambs again.

'They are going for the party,' he says with his hands folded in his lap. It seems he has got a handle on his runaway lust. 'They can get the finest goat meat in Islamabad, but they want Afghani lambs. I doubt whether these will survive till the fourth of July.'

'The Americans are having a party?'

'It's their Independence Day. We have been

bringing food from all over the country for the past week. It must be a big party.'

I close my eyes and wonder whether Bannon is going.

The lambs have just begun to get used to the din of the aircraft and the fluctuating cabin pressure when the aircraft starts to descend steeply. They retch and bleat under their muzzles. The one with his face on the floor gets up and raises his front legs in an attempted capriole but stumbles and falls into his own piss.

'I need to put your blindfold back on,' the loadmaster says, in a voice full of expectations. I beckon him towards me with my cuffed hands and give him a murderous look. He is a man of the world. He gets the message and puts my blindfold back without touching a single hair on my body.

The back door opens as soon as the aircraft comes to a standstill. I can hear the lambs sliding down the ramp, their first and last flight probably already a nightmare in the past. Another hand on my shoulder and I am led down a ladder. The air outside smells of hot concrete, burning landing gear and evaporating air fuel. It's heavenly compared to the smell inside the cabin. A short walk, then a wait under the sun. The jeep I am thrown into smells of rose air freshener and Dunhills. I don't think I have been brought here for the party.

CHAPTER 20

Geneeral Akhtar's devotion to his boss
General Zia was not the ordinary devotion that a three-star general shows
towards a four-star general. Their mutual depend-
ence wasn't that of two soldiers who can rely on
each other to get a piggyback to the base if injured
in the battle. Theirs was a bond between two dogs
stranded on a glacier, each sizing up the other,
trying to decide if he should wait for his comrade
to die before eating him or do away with the niceties
and try to make a meal out of him immediately.

But there was a difference between the two:
General Zia with his five titles, addresses to the
UN and Nobel Prize hopes was satiated. General
Akhtar, always playing second fiddle to his boss,
was starving, and when he looked around the
frozen landscape, all he saw was General Zia –
fattened, chubby-cheeked and marinating in his
own paranoia. Publicly, General Akhtar denied any
ambition; he encouraged journalists to describe
him as a silent soldier, happy to command his
ghost armies in secret wars. But when he stood in
front of the mirror in his office day after day and

counted the three stars on his shoulder, he couldn't deny to himself that he had become a shadow of General Zia. His own career had followed General Zia's ambitions like a faithful puppy.

If General Zia wanted to become an elected president, General Akhtar not only had to ensure that ballot boxes were stuffed in time but was also expected to orchestrate spontaneous celebrations all over the country after the votes were counted. If General Zia announced a National Cleanliness Week, General Akhtar had to make sure that the gutters were disinfected and security-checked before the President could show up to get his picture taken. On good days General Akhtar felt like a royal executioner during the day, and a court food-taster in the evening. On bad days he just felt like a long-suffering housewife always clearing up after her messy husband. He had started to get impatient. The title of 'second most powerful man in the land', which he had enjoyed in the beginning, had started to sound like an insult. How could you be second most powerful when your boss was *all*-powerful?

The puppy had grown up and felt constantly starved.

General Akhtar had learned to put the puppy on a leash and take him for short walks, because he knew he couldn't let him run wild. Not yet.

It was on one of these puppy-on-the-leash walks that he was walking along the corridor of his headquarters, minutes after his camera feed from the Army House abruptly disappeared. He ran his operations from a four-storey, nondescript office block. There was no signboard outside the building to identify it, no postal address for this enterprise; even the white Corollas entering and leaving the car park had no number plates. But still every cab driver in town somehow knew about the occupants of this building and the nature of their business. General Akhtar was walking on a frayed grey carpet, his ears taking in the familiar night-shift sounds; most of the staff had already left for the day but he could hear the muffled voices from behind the closed doors. His night-shift handlers were talking to his operators in distant, unsuspecting countries; Ethiopia, Nepal, Colombia. There was one consolation for General Akhtar: he might be the second most powerful man in a Third World country but the intelligence agency he ran was worthy of a superpower.

Since no women worked in the office block, the toilets were marked 'Officers and Men'. General Akhtar passed the toilets and entered an unmarked room at the end of the corridor. More than a dozen telephone operators watched wall-mounted audio-tapes connected to telephone monitors; the tapes started to roll as soon as the subject under surveillance picked up the phone. It wasn't just the usual set of politicians, diplomats and journalists whose phones were tapped; many of General Akhtar's closest colleagues would have been surprised to find out that their every phone call, their every verbal indiscretion was recorded here.

The operators working in the monitoring room had strict orders to continue their normal functions regardless of the rank of their visitor. A dozen heads wearing headphones nodded silently as General Akhtar entered the room.

He tapped the shoulder of the first operator in the row, who seemed completely absorbed in the task at hand. The operator removed his headphones and looked at General Akhtar with a mixture of respect and excitement. During his eleven months at the agency, he had never been addressed by General Akhtar. The operator felt his life was about to change.

General Akhtar took the headphones from his hands and put them on his own ears. He heard the moans of a man obviously in the middle of pleasuring himself as a woman on the other end urged him on in a motherly voice. General Akhtar gave the operator a disgusted look; the operator avoided eye contact with him and said, 'The Minister of Information, sir.' The operator felt apologetic, even though he was only doing his duty.

'I don't need to know,' General Akhtar said, removing the headphones. 'Come to my office. With one of these.' He pointed to the little black box that connected the phone line to the tape recorder. 'Bring a new one. The ones Chuck Coogan sent us.' General Akhtar walked off to a chorus of nodding heads.

The operator gave his colleagues a triumphant look, strangled the Information Minister's sighs and started preparing his toolbox for his first ever visit to General Akhtar's office. He felt like a man who had been personally selected by the second most powerful man in the country to do a very important job in his personal office. As he shut his toolbox and straightened his shirt, the operator felt like the third most powerful man in the country.

General Akhtar's office looked like that of any other senior bureaucrat at the pinnacle of his power; a large desk with five telephones and a national flag, a framed picture of him and Bill Casey laughing as General Akhtar presented the CIA chief with the casing of the first Stinger that had brought down a Russian Hind. In one corner stood a small television and video player. On the wall behind his chair was an official portrait of General Zia, from the time when his moustache was still struggling to find a shape and his cheeks were sunken. General Akhtar removed the picture carefully and punched in the combination for the safe behind it, took out a tape and put it in the video player. The picture was black and white and grainy and he could not see General Zia's face, but he knew his hand gestures well and the voice was unmistakable. The other voice was slightly muffled and the speaker wasn't in the frame.

'Son, you are the only person in this country I can really trust.'

General Akhtar grimaced. He had heard the same thing over and over again for the past two months, minus the word 'son' of course.

269

'Sir, your security is my job and this is the kind of job where I can't take orders from anyone else. Not from General Akhtar, not from the First Lady and sometimes not even from you.'

Suddenly Brigadier TM's head filled the screen. 'Sir, all these changes, without my security clearance.'

A hand appeared in the picture and handed General Zia a piece of paper. General Zia looked at the paper through his glasses, put it in his pocket and got up. The other figure entered the frame, they both met in the centre of the screen and General Zia spread his arms. General Akhtar moved forward in his chair and tried to listen to their voices, which because of their embrace had become even more muffled. He heard sobbing. General Zia's body was shaking. He moved a step back and put both his hands on Brigadier TM's. 'Son, you don't have to take orders from anyone, not even from me.'

There was a knock on the door. General Akhtar pushed the stop button on the video recorder and asked the operator to come in. Then the General stood up and paced the room as the operator got busy with one of the five phones on his table.

General Akhtar stood in front of the mirror and looked at his face and upper body. He was three years older than General Zia but physically in much better shape. Unlike General Zia, who hated the outdoors and had gone all puffy in the cheeks, General Akhtar still managed a weekly game of golf and an occasional field trip to the army divisions posted at the border. The golf gave him the chance to get some exercise and catch up with the US Ambassador on matters of national security.

General Akhtar's hair was thinning from the sides but his barber did a good job of mixing his crew cut with a clever camouflage for his expanding bald patch. He had stood here many times, in front of this mirror, put a fourth star on his shoulder and struck a pose for the cover of *Newsweek*. He had rehearsed his acceptance speech for the Nobel Peace Prize. 'All the wars I have fought, all the liberty that the people of the region enjoy, the cold war that has turned into warm, glowing peace . . .'

'Would you like me to activate the monitor, sir?' the operator asked him. The operator had shown no curiosity, had resisted the temptation to snoop around and had behaved like a professional spy. Never ask why, just who, where and when. The operator was pleased with himself.

General Akhtar gave out a phone number without turning away from the mirror and watched the operator's face closely. He noticed a shadow cross the operator's face as he finished writing down the number. His hands, which had been moving with such professional concentration before, shook as he fed the number into the little black box. General Akhtar wondered what the operator would make of it. He was sure that he would not say anything, not that anyone would listen to a telephone operator, but he looked hard in the mirror at the operator's reflection. The operator was now back to his professional self and busy putting away his instruments in his toolbox.

He was thinking of getting out of this office and then finishing the remaining two hours of his shift before starting his part-time job as a signboard painter at a cinema. He was thinking that even if he was given a full-time job at the agency he would continue painting over the weekend. The operator was not thinking at all about the fact that the second most powerful man in the country had just ordered him to put a tap on the telephone line of the most powerful man in the country.

Many of General Akhtar's fellow generals described him as cold, calculating, even a cruel man. But in reality, General Akhtar's cruelty was always a second thought, almost incidental to his job. He didn't like his job because he could listen to people's most intimate conversations or get people killed. He didn't feel any real sense of power when he picked up his phone and gave his agents a list of people who were becoming a threat to national security. But when he did pick up the phone, he liked his agency to respond like a properly oiled weapon. He would have liked it if these situations never arose, but when they needed to be dealt with, he wanted it to be done efficiently. He didn't like the stories about bullets stuck in the chamber or targets disappearing at the last moment.

When the operator reached the door and put his hand on the handle, General Akhtar said: 'Thank you.'

The operator hesitated for a moment, looked back and smiled, and that's when General Akhtar realised that he didn't know his name.

'What is your name, operator?'

The operator, who had rehearsed the answer in his mind for the whole eleven months that he had worked here, replied with a flourish, almost sure that he was taking a step further in his life; hoping to be appointed the senior operator, hoping to be embraced by the organisation, elevated to an officer rank, maybe given one of the old Corollas that the officers discarded every year when the new models arrived.

'Same as yours. Akhtar, sir. But with an E. Akhter Masih.'

General Akhtar wasn't impressed. There are probably a million Akhtars in this country, he thought, and two million Masihs. And this smart-ass can't keep his mouth shut about as ordinary a coincidence as that. Could he be expected to keep his mouth shut at all? Could he be expected to forget the numbers, the names, the transcripts of the phone calls that he handled all day? Was it wise to hire a Christian when everybody knows they love to gossip? The only other Christians who worked in General Akhtar's agency were sweepers. Must be a reason, he thought.

'Do you know what Akhtar means?'

'Yes, sir, a star. A very bright star.'

'You are quite intelligent for an operator. But remember some of the stars that you see at night are not really stars. They died millions of years ago but they were so far away that their light is beginning to reach us only now.'

There was a certain spring in Operator Akhter's footsteps as he walked to the bus stop after work that day. He was aware of being alive. The fume-filled air was fragrant in his lungs, his ears were alive to the chirping of the birds, the bus horns were love tunes in the air, waiting to be plucked and put to words. Not only did he share a name with his boss, his inherent intelligence had also been recognised; 'quite intelligent for an operator', 'quite intelligent for an operator', General Akhtar's words echoed through his head. Those who thought that the General was arrogant had obviously not been worthy of his attention, Operator Akhter thought.

It can be said that Operator Akhter was a bit careless – careless like people are who have just heard the good news they have been waiting for all their lives. It also must be said that Operator Akhter wasn't intoxicated, nor was he reckless. He stepped onto the road like a person whose luck had just turned. It can be said that he didn't look left or right; it was almost as if he expected the traffic to part for him. These are facts and cannot be denied. But the car that came at Operator Akhter was determined, and when it locked onto its target it didn't hesitate; it didn't want to punish him for his bad pedestrian-crossing manners, it didn't want to break his legs or leave him a cripple as a punishment for feeling optimistic. No, the driver of this car was very clear-headed and far too determined for a casual roadkill. Before the life went out of his eyes, after his broken ribs punctured his lungs and his heart frantically pumped blood in a last futile attempt to keep him alive, Operator Akhter was surprised to see, the last surprise of his life, that the white Corolla that crushed him had no number plate.

General Akhtar picked up the receiver on the new phone that Operator Akhter had connected, called General Zia and offered to resign from his post as the Chief of Intelligence.

'I should not have trusted that Christian, sir.'

'Who was it?'

'The painter, sir, who made that portrait. Akhter Masih.'

'Has he told you who was behind this?'

'No, sir, he had a car accident.'

General Zia sighed.

'You are the only man in this country I can still trust.'

'It's an honour, sir.'

'There was this message from Shigri's son . . .'

'No need to call back, sir. We already have him. I'll bring his statement with me, sir. It was a little sting and we have got much more than we were expecting. He is only the tip of this iceberg, sir . . .'

'Do talk to him personally. Give him my salaam.'

'There is another urgent matter, sir. The National Day Parade.'

'How am I supposed to go to the parade under Code Red?'

'Sir, there is not a single country in the world that doesn't have a national day.'

'Can't we have a national day without the National Day Parade?' General Zia liked his own idea and got very excited. 'We'll just have a national day here in the Army House. Let's call some widows. No, maybe we should designate this national day as National Orphans' Day. Get some children here, set up some rides.'

'Sir, people want a military parade on National Day. They want to see tanks and they want to wave at fighter planes flying past –'

'But the security protocol –'

'Sir, we can have the National Day Parade on any day that you choose to have it. We can record it and broadcast it on National Day.'

In that moment General Zia realised why he had never been able to get rid of Akhtar. He was always one step ahead of the enemy even when the enemy was invisible.

General Akhtar rightly interpreted that moment of silence as presidential consent to go ahead with the arrangements for the National Day Parade.

'Convey my gratitude to Brigadier TM, sir, for discovering that stupid camera. I'd recommend him for a promotion, but I know you want him by your side. He is the only true hero this country has got.'

CHAPTER 21

'Are you ready?' Major Kiyani's voice asks from the front seat. I nod my head without saying a word. He comes to the back of the jeep, the door opens. I take a deep breath and move towards the door; my head spins with the effort but I put my other foot forward and find the ground beneath my feet solid, welcoming. Major Kiyani unties the knot on my blindfold. We are in a car park full of white Corollas, most of them without number plates. The only exception is a black Mercedes with three bronze stars on the numberless plate and a flag covered in a little plastic sheath. Office buildings surround us on all sides, fading yellow and dotted with iron-barred gates that lead to staircases. Beyond the antennae and satellite dishes sprouting from its roof I can see Islamabad's fog-covered mountains.

We are not meeting General Zia.

Major Kiyani walks in front of me without looking back and enters one of the gates. I hear the hum of the electronic machines behind closed doors. At the end of the corridor is another gate. A soldier in uniform salutes Major Kiyani, opens the door and salutes again. Major Kiyani doesn't bother to respond. I look towards the soldier and nod my head. Major Kiyani walks into the first room on the right and comes out with a black gym bag, which he passes to me. We stop in front of a white door that says 'Officers Only'. I step in and smell the sweet smell of disinfectant and hear the sound of running water. Major Kiyani stays in the doorway and says: 'Get cleaned up, you are going to have lunch with a VIP.' I hear him walking away. I look into the gym bag and find a bar of soap, a razor, toothbrush, a fresh uniform and a bottle of perfume: Poison.

Who am I having lunch with that they want me to be perfumed?

Is one of Dad's friends coming to bail me out?

I catch my reflection in the bathroom mirror and see a phantom. My eyes are two shallow red pools, my face is dried cactus, my uniform shirt has curry stains on it.

A wave of self-pity rises from the pit of my stomach. I try to suppress it by telling myself: All right, I look like someone who lives in dirty bathrooms and Mughal dungeons. But at least I get an occasional lunch invitation.

My movements are slow. I turn on the tap and put the tip of my forefinger in the water. I look in the mirror. The person who stares at me is still a stranger. They probably cleaned up Obaid's cupboard, sealed his books and clothes in a trunk and put it in storage. They sent me this bottle of perfume so that I don't forget why I am here. I wonder how they explained it to Obaid's father. I wonder if he thinks his son is a martyr. My eyes burn.

I quickly splash water first on my eyes, then on my face. I pull my shirt out of my trousers, take off my shoes and stand in front of the mirror, naked to my waist. I look around for any windows. There is an extractor fan, but the opening is too small and probably opens into a room full of armed guards.

We'll have lunch, then.

Major Kiyani shouts from outside: 'You don't want to keep the General waiting, do you?'

I am in a dining room, a proper bloody dining room with white tablecloths, white china and a jug of orange juice. Gleaming brass dish covers can't contain the aromas wafting through the room. The prisoner, it seems, has died and gone straight to heaven.

Major Kiyani stands in the doorway, puffing on his Dunhill, fidgeting with the gold ring on his middle finger. The food waiting on the table seems to be the least of his worries. I can barely wait for those covers to be lifted. Even the onion rings lying in the salad dish are making my heart beat faster. Major Kiyani looks out into the corridor and moves out a few steps. I raid the orange juice jug and pour myself a glass. My mouth, raw with the past few nights' horrible flavours, stings, but my throat welcomes it and I empty the glass in one long swig. The footsteps in the corridor come closer. Heels click. Major Kiyani's laughter is subdued, nervous. General Akhtar enters the room followed by Major Kiyani and a turbaned waiter in white uniform. I stand up and bring my heels together, suddenly feeling like the host at this lunch. General Akhtar sits at the head of the table. Major Kiyani sits on the edge of his chair. I am not sure what to do. 'Sit down, son.' General Akhtar gives me a benevolent smile as if he is the only man in this world who understands me. His actions speak otherwise. I want to eat. He wants to talk.

'I have seen your file,' he says, rearranging his knife and fork on his plate. 'You've got your father's sharp brain but it's quite obvious that this boy, this friend of yours . . .' He looks towards Major Kiyani who says, 'Obaid, sir. Obaid-ul-llah . . .'

'Yes, this Obaid chap was not very clever. I won't ask you where he was trying to fly off to because you have already told Major Kiyani that you don't know. But I'll just say that this Obaid chap probably read too many books and obviously did not understand most of them. I am sure you could have come up with a better idea.'

I look up at him for the first time and my appetite begins to disappear.

General Akhtar is decked up like a sacrificial cow, all golden braid and shiny medals. I am certain that he hasn't gone to so much trouble just for his meeting with me. He is dressed to go to the party.

Two men in uniform meeting over lunch: one all dressed up for the fourth of July bash, the other one on short leave from a Mughal dungeon.

Why eat before a party? I think. And he reads my thoughts. He is not the head of intelligence for nothing.

'I always eat before going to a party, you don't know what you'll get there. And today I've got two. We're also holding the parade today for National Day,' he says, lifting one of the brass dishes. He picks up a quail from a pile of roasted little birds and pushes the dish towards me.

I put a little bird on my plate and stare at it for a long time as if hoping it will grow its wings back and fly away, but it lies there in its crisp brown skin, blackened at its joints.

'Look at me when I am talking to you,' General Akhtar says, staring at his plate. Then he lifts his head and gives me a fatherly smile as if the only thing he is concerned about is my table manners.

I look up and see a balding head and pale thin lips that have probably never uttered a word he really meant.

I hold my fork with one hand, and sneak my other hand under the table and squeeze my balls. I need the pain to remind myself of the context of this roast-bird feast.

The bird looks even tinier at the end of his retired boxer's hand. A whole piece of breast goes into his mouth and he pulls out a bunch of cleaned bones from his thin lips. He smiles a yellow smile and dabs the corner of his thin lips with a starched white napkin.

'It's not easy for me.' He picks up another dish cover and starts chewing on a slice of cucumber. 'There is friendship and there is loyalty to one's country. If you are not loyal to your father can you be loyal to a friend? See, we are both in the same boat.'

I am surprised at the rate at which this brotherhood is expanding.

I am also surprised that Dad used to call him General Chimp. Because the man is, clearly, a reptile. Evolution took a wrong turn and this man ended up a mammal instead of growing scales and claws.

'I hope you are keeping him somewhere comfortable,' he says to Major Kiyani, who puts down his knife and fork and mumbles into his napkin. Something about the number of available rooms in the Fort.

'You put him in that shithole?' He looks at Major Kiyani with complaining eyes. 'Do you even know who he is?' Major Kiyani puts his napkin back and looks up with a twinkle in his eyes.

'Did you ever work with Colonel Shigri?'

'No, sir, never had the pleasure. I did investigate the circumstances of the Colonel's tragic demise. I think I helped out the young man here with the paperwork.'

'He was a man of principles. He lived his life by his principles and he died by his principles.'

The General's sense of humour is not really helping my appetite. 'But, my son,' he turns towards me, 'what is evident here is that you have kept your dignity. Even in these difficult times you have held your head high.' He picks up an invisible breadcrumb from his lap. 'And that, my dear son, comes from blood, from being of a good family. Your dad would have been proud, my son.'

Why the hell does he keep calling me 'my son'? Even my own dad never called me 'my son'.

'As you realise, it's very difficult for me. On the one hand, there is my late friend's son who has already seen enough tragedy in his life. On the other hand, there's the security of the country, which is my responsibility.' He spreads his arms, pointing his knife and fork towards his chest, underlining the enormity of the task.

'What would you do in my position?'

I would stop stuffing my face with tiny birds while deciding someone's fate, I want to say.

'I don't know what you know, sir,' I say obliquely, throwing in a truckload of humility. 'And I obviously don't have the experience you've had.' I can see he wants to hear more so I throw in a punchline picked up from Secretary General's perpetual grouse against me and my uniform. 'That's why you are where you are and I am where I am.' I don't say what the comrade always says after that: we are both going blind and we will die without touching a woman ever again.

'I'll tell you a story that might explain my

dilemma,' says General Akhtar, 'a true story. I was your age, a lieutenant in the Indian Army, must have been a couple of months before the partition. I was ordered to accompany a train full of Hindus going to Amritsar and I was told to make sure that it got there safe and sound.

'You must have heard about the trains from the Indian Punjab arriving in Lahore carrying Muslims. Full of cut-up bodies. All those stories about unborn children being carved out from their mothers' wombs and their heads being put on spears were true. I didn't see any myself, but I knew they were all true. But orders were orders, and I set off with the train, telling my platoon that every single passenger on the train was my responsibility.

'As soon as we left Lahore we encountered groups of people with machetes and sticks and bottles of kerosene trying to block the train, seeking their revenge. I kept sending them off with a wink. I told them that the security was the army's responsibility. Our new country would need these trains. Let's not destroy them. I kept talking to the passengers, reassuring them that I would get them to Amritsar. We were travelling at a snail's pace. I was trying my best to keep the attackers at bay. But at some point the military training just took over. I knew what my new country wanted from me. I called my subedar major and told him that we would stop the train for the night prayers. I would go about two hundred yards from the train to pray. And I would come back after offering my prayer.

"Do you know how long the night prayer is?" I asked him. I didn't listen to his answer. "That's all the time you have," I said.

'You see, it was difficult but logical. I didn't disobey the orders that I was given and what needed to be done was done with minimum fuss. I didn't want any unborn children speared under my watch. But I also didn't want to stand on the sidelines pretending to be a professional. History makes these great sweeps and unpleasant things happen. At least my conscience is clear.'

I have quietly pushed my plate away, the bird intact except for one half-chewed leg.

'My dear son, I'll do anything in my power to get you out of this but what can I do for someone who is messing around with our national security? Do you even know where this friend of yours . . .' He looks towards Major Kiyani who interjects. 'Obaid, sir, Obaid-ul-llah.'

'Yes, do you even know where he was headed?'

'I don't know sir, I don't know.'

'Well, we both know where he was going, but I am sure you had nothing to do with it. Now don't disappoint me, do what is necessary.'

I want to know how they found out. I also want to know how far he managed to go. How did they get him? Surface-to-air missile? A sidewinder from a chasing aeroplane? Did he make a last call to the control tower? Any messages on the black box?

Baby O has left nothing except a bottle of perfume for me.

'You don't have to do anything. Major Kiyani here will write the statement on your behalf. Sign it and I'll take care of everything else. That's General Akhtar's promise to you. You can go back to the Academy and carry on your dad's mission.'

What does he know about my dad's mission?

I take the napkin from my lap and put my feet firmly on the ground.

'Sir, your people may not always be telling you the truth. I'll carry out your orders but forget my case for a moment, there is this guy in the cell next to mine, the sweepers' representative, who has been there for nine years. Everyone has forgotten about him, he has never been charged.'

General Akhtar looks towards Major Kiyani. 'This is the height of inefficiency. You are still holding that stupid sweeper revolutionary. I think you should let him go.' He picks up his cap, gives me that 'my dear son, I did what you asked me to, now go be a good boy' look and leaves the room.

I get up from my chair, give Major Kiyani a triumphant look and salute General Akhtar's back.

CHAPTER 22

The military band struck up 'Wake up the Guardians of our Frontiers' – a tune that General Zia would have hummed along to on another occasion, but now he looked anxiously towards an approaching column of tanks. He was inspecting the National Day Parade from the presidential dais and the red velvet rope around it suddenly seemed an inadequate defence against the obscenely long barrels of the M41 Walker Bulldogs. He tried not to think about the late Egyptian President, Anwar Sadat, who had been slain standing at a dais like this, inspecting a parade like this, accepting a salute from a column of tanks like this.

General Zia shared the dais with General Akhtar who, with his passionate arguments about sending the right signals to the nation, had convinced General Zia to attend this parade, but now General Akhtar himself seemed bored by the proceedings. This was the first time General Zia had stepped outside the Army House since the morning he had stumbled on Jonah's prayer. The parade was being held under Code Red and even an uninvited bird trying to invade the airspace above it would find itself the target of a sharpshooter. Zia had gone through the lists of invitees himself, taking out all unfamiliar names. Then Brigadier TM had crossed out all the names of people who in the distant past might have been related to someone who might have said something negative about General Zia's moustache or his foreign policy. There were no crowds to mingle with after the parade. General Zia wanted it to end even before it began. The parade seemed like a serene blur of gold braid, starched khaki uniforms and row after row of shiny oxford shoes. He felt exposed without Brigadier TM at his side; there was no one to keep the crowds away, no one to come between him and an assassin's bullet. His anxiety was captured in all its sweaty detail by the television cameras recording the parade for Pakistan National Television. In stark contrast, General Akhtar's face betrayed no emotion, only the quiet pride of a silent soldier.

The cameras showed the approaching column of tanks. The television commentator, handpicked by the Information Minister for his flair in describing military hardware in metaphors borrowed from Urdu ghazals, said, 'These are the tanks. The moving castles of steel that put the fear of Allah in the heart of our enemies.' As the moving tanks started to turn their barrels towards the dais to salute him, Anwar Sadat's bullet-ridden torso flashed in front of General Zia's eyes. He looked towards General Akhtar, whose eyes were fixed on

288

the horizon. General Zia didn't understand what General Akhtar was looking at, because the sky was a spotless blue and the air display was still hours away. For a moment, General Zia suspected that Akhtar was more interested in posing for the TV cameras, trying to look like a visionary.

General Zia was familiar with the routine of the parade and knew that Brigadier TM would land in the white circle right in front of the dais with his team of paratroopers after the march past. He wished he could fast-forward this parade and have Brigadier TM at his side. The tanks crawled past the dais with their barrels lowered. General Zia took the salute with one eye on the approaching Rani howitzers that were lowering their barrels towards the dais. He didn't feel threatened by the artillery guns. They seemed like giant toys and he knew there was no ammunition on board. 'The President, himself a veteran of the armoured corps, appreciates the tough life that the tank commanders lead,' the commentator said as the screen showed the General offering a sombre salute with a limp hand. 'It's the life of a lonely hawk who never makes a nest. The President salutes their courage.'

General Zia glanced towards General Akhtar again. He was beginning to wonder why he was avoiding eye contact.

General Zia began to feel better as the trucks carrying eighteen-foot-long ballistic missiles started to roll past. They were huge but they were also harmless in this context. Nobody would launch a ballistic missile at a target twenty feet away. Asleep on their launchers these missiles looked like giant models prepared by a school hobby club. It had been General Zia's idea to name these missiles after Mughal kings and birds of prey. He noted with some pride that the names he had given them were written in giant letters in Urdu and English: Falcon 5 and Ghauri 2. His heart suddenly jumped as the military band started to play the infantry's marching tune and the soldiers began to march past on foot, their naked bayonets pointed towards the sky. The infantry squadrons were followed by the very exuberant commando formations; instead of marching they ran, raising their knees to chest level and stomping with their heels on the ground. Instead of saluting, the commandos extended their right hands and waved their rifles as they passed the dais. 'These brave men crave martyrdom like lovers crave the arms of their beloved,' the television commentator said in a voice choked with emotion.

General Zia began to breathe easy as the military band finally shut up and the civilian floats came into view. Not a gun in sight on these ones. The first float represented rural life: men harvesting and pulling in their nets brimming with paper fish, women churning milk in fluorescent clay pots under the huge banners of Pepsi, sponsor of the floats. Another float passed by carrying drummers and Sufi singers in white robes and orange turbans. General Zia noticed that their movements were stilted and that they seemed to be lip-syncing to recorded music. He used the noise to lean towards General Akhtar and ask in a furious whisper: 'What is wrong with them?'

General Akhtar turned his head in slow motion, looked at him with a winner's smile and whispered back calmly in his ear: 'They are all our boys in civvies. Why take a risk?'

'And the women?'

'Sweepers from General Headquarters. Highest security clearance.'

General Zia smiled and waved his hand to the men and women on the float who were now performing a strange mixture of military drill and harvesting dance.

Pakistan National Television showed a close-up of the two smiling Generals and the commentator raised his voice to convey the festive mood.' The President is visibly pleased by the colourful vitality of our peasant culture. General Akhtar is delighted to see the sons and the daughters of this soil sharing their joy with the defenders of this nation. And now our Lionhearts in full colour . . .'

The cameras showed four T-Bird jets flying in a diamond formation, leaving behind streaks of pink, green, orange and yellow smoke on the blue horizon, like a child drawing his first rainbow. Their noses dipped as they flew past the dais making a colourful four-lane highway in the sky. They turned, executed a perfect lazy eight, a few loops; General Zia waved at them, the handful of civilian spectators waved their flags and the T-Birds flew away wagging their tails. General Zia heard the familiar rumble of a Hercules C130 approaching, an olive-green whale, floating slowly towards the parade. General Zia loved this part of the ceremony. Watching the paratroopers tumble out of the back door of a C130 had always been pure pleasure for General Zia and he couldn't take his eyes away. The paratroopers fell out of the rear of the plane as if someone had flung a handful of jasmine buds against the blue sky; they fell for a few seconds, getting bigger and bigger, and any moment now they would blossom into large green-and-white silken canopies and then float down gracefully towards the parade square, their leader Brigadier TM landing in the one-metre-wide white circle right in front of the dais. General Zia had always found the experience purifying, better than golf, better than addressing the nation.

General Zia knew something was wrong when both his eyes remained focused on one of the buds from C130 which had still not blossomed, while the others were popping open and beginning to float. This one was still in free fall, hurtling towards the parade square, becoming bigger and bigger and bigger.

Brigadier TM, like many veteran paratroopers, tended to delay opening his parachute. He liked to wait a few seconds before pulling at his ripcord, enjoying the free fall that precedes the opening of the parachute's canopy. He liked to feel his lungs bursting with air, the struggle to exhale, the momentary loss of control over his arms and legs. For a man who was beyond human weaknesses, one could say that this was his one vice: giving in to gravity to get a bit of a head rush for a few seconds. But Brigadier TM was also a professional who calculated risks and then eliminated them. While strapping up his parachute before embarking on this mission, he had noticed that the belt around his torso dug into his flesh. Brigadier TM was furious with himself. 'Damn it, I am sitting around the Army House all day doing nothing. I am getting fat. I must do something about this.' Standing in the back door of the C130 moments before the jump, Brigadier TM looked down at the parade square, tiny formations of men in khaki and a small crowd of flag-waving civilians. Like a true professional, Brigadier TM resisted the temptation to ride the crisp air some more, formulated a weight-loss plan in his mind and pulled at his ripcord early. His body prepared itself for the upward jerk that would come as his canopy sprang open and filled with air. Nothing happened.

General Zia felt beads of perspiration running along his spine, and his itch seemed to be returning. He clenched his fists and looked towards General Akhtar. General Akhtar wasn't looking up at the paratroopers. His eyes were searching the floats, which had been parked behind the artillery and armoured columns. In his head General Akhtar was silently rehearsing his eulogy for Brigadier TM;

trying to choose between '*The finest man ever to jump from a plane*' and '*The bravest man to walk this sacred soil*'.

Brigadier TM took a firm grip on his ripcord and pulled again. It seemed the ripcord had cut all its ties to the parachute, had lost its memory. As Brigadier TM spread his arms and legs outwards to steady his fall, he realised something that might have come as a relief under different circumstances: he hadn't put on weight. He was carrying someone else's parachute.

General Zia saw the man tumbling out of the sky towards him and thought that maybe he had misinterpreted the verse from the Quran. Maybe Jonah and his whale had nothing to do with it. Maybe this was how it was going to end: a man falling from the sky would crush him to bits in front of television cameras. He looked around for something to hide under. The marquee had been removed at the last minute, as the Information Minister wanted vista shots from a helicopter. 'Look up,' he whispered furiously to General Akhtar, who was looking down at his shoes, having reached the conclusion that he shouldn't mention the words *jump* and *plane* in his eulogy. Not in good taste. He pretended not to listen to General Zia's gibberish and offered his strong-jawed profile to the TV cameras.

The crowd, transfixed by the man falling past the floating parachutes, arms and legs stretched parallel to the ground and heading for the presidential dais, started to wave their flags and cheer, thinking that this was the finale of the performance.

Even before he pulled the emergency cord on his parachute, Brigadier TM knew that it wouldn't function. What really surprised him was that the hook that was supposed to activate his emergency parachute didn't even budge. It stuck to his lower ribcage like a needy child. If the circumstances hadn't been what they were, Brigadier TM would have raised his hands in front of his eyes and given them a taunting smile. The hands that could crack a neck with one blow, the hands that had once hunted a wild goat and skinned it without using a knife, were failing before a stubborn two-centimetre hook that could release the emergency parachute and save his life.

His lungs were bursting with air, his arms were feeling numb and he was trying to ignore the parade square with its colourful flags and stupid, noisy civilians. He put his thumb in the emergency parachute's ripcord ring again, got a firm grip on his lower ribcage with his four fingers, screamed the loudest scream of his life, managing to exhale all the air out of his lungs – and pulled.

General Zia took a step back. He still hadn't realised that the falling man coming at him was Brigadier TM. He shuffled back, trying to duck behind General Akhtar, who stood his ground, still not looking up. General Akhtar didn't have to think any further about what to say in his eulogy. Brigadier TM wrote it himself as his body crashed into the white circle right in front of the dais.

'*A professional who didn't miss his target even in death.*'

The paramedics who removed his smashed body from the white circle noticed that there was a big gash on Brigadier TM's left lower ribcage. Then they saw his clenched right hand firmly holding onto a metal ring, a piece of khaki cloth ripped from his shirt and three of his own ribs.

CHAPTER 23

We are drinking tea and discussing national security on the lawns of the Fort when the prisoners start to emerge from the passage that leads to the underground cells. A long line of shabby men with shaved heads, handcuffed, shackled and strung along a chain, shuffle out of the stairwell as Major Kiyani dissects the external and internal security threats facing the nation. He takes a handful of roasted almonds from a bowl and throws them into his open mouth one by one, between ticking off his strategic challenges. I glance towards the prisoners out of the corner of my eye because it would be impolite to turn round and look. I don't want Major Kiyani to think that I don't care about national security.

The military establishment that runs the Fort has been at my service since my meeting with General Akhtar. I left a blindfolded prisoner. I have returned like a forgiven prince: statement signed and submitted, name cleared, honour restored, glory promised. If I am to believe Major Kiyani, we are just waiting for some paperwork before I am sent back to the Academy. My experience tells me that I shouldn't believe him but it's fun to watch him fawn over me, making sure that I am fed properly, that I stay in the best room at the Fort. He is a changed man. We are celebrating the beginning of this new relationship. Politeness and mutual respect are the order of the day.

'Hindus are cowards by nature and it's understandable that they would stab us in the back, but we have learned to deal with that nation of lentil eaters. For every bomb blast that kills a few people in Karachi, we will hit back with a dozen blasts in Delhi, Bombay, Bangalore, you name it. If they use Taiwanese timers, we'll send them remote-controlled RDX beauties.' Major Kiyani chews his almonds properly before throwing another one into his mouth. His aim is very good. 'So they are not the threat. It's the enemy within, our own Muslim brothers who call themselves Pakistanis but speak *their* language: they are the real threat. We have got to learn to deal with them.'

Under the late-afternoon sun the Fort looks like a very old king taking a siesta. The shadows of the crumbling arches of the Court for the Commons stretch across the lawns, the sunflowers are in full bloom and stand tall with their heads bent like turbaned courtiers waiting for their turn at court. In the underground interrogation centre someone is probably being thrashed with such abandon that the ceiling is getting a fresh splattering of blood. We are sitting in lawn chairs, in front of a table laden with fine china crockery and the best afternoon snacks that Lahore has to offer.

Life can take a good turn if you are from a good family and if your meeting with General Akhtar has gone well.

'Anybody can catch a thief or a killer or a traitor,' Major Kiyani says, munching on a chicken patty. 'But what is satisfying about my job is that I have to stay one step ahead of them.' I nod politely and nibble at my Nice biscuit.

A Dunhill is offered and accepted with a restrained officer-like smile.

The prisoners circle the marble fountain outside the Palace of Mirrors, their shaved heads bobbing up and down behind the manicured hedges covered in purple bougainvillea.

They haven't been brought out to have tea with us.

They look like betrayed promises; broken and then put back together from memory, obscure names crossed out of habeas corpus petitions, forgotten faces that will never make it to Amnesty International's hall of fame, dungeon-dwellers brought out for their daily half-hour in the sun. The prisoners start to form a line with their backs towards us. Their clothes are tattered, their bodies a patchwork of improvised bandages and festering wounds. I realise that the 'no marks' rule is applied selectively in the Fort.

The tea cosy in front of me has an air force insignia on it, a simple, elegant design: a soaring eagle with a Persian couplet underneath it: *Be it the land or the rivers, it's all under our wings.*

'There are many ways of serving one's country,' Major Kiyani waxes philosophical, 'but only one way to secure it. Only one.' I put the cup on the saucer, move forward in my chair and listen. I am his attentive disciple.

'Eliminate the risk. Tackle the enemy before it can strike. Starve it of the very oxygen it breathes.' He takes a very deep puff on his Dunhill.

I pick up my cup and drink again. Major Kiyani might be a good tea-party host but he is no Sun Tzu.

'Let's say you caught somebody who wasn't really a threat to national security. We are all human, we all make mistakes. Let's say we got someone who we thought was going to blow up the Army House. Now, if after the interrogation it turns out that no, he really wasn't going to do it, that we were wrong, what would you do? You would let him go, obviously. But in all honesty would you call it a mistake? No. It's risk elimination, one less bugger to worry about.'

My eyes keep glancing towards the prisoners who are shuffling their feet and swaying like a Greek tragedy chorus that has forgotten its lines. Their shackles chime like the bells of cows returning home in the evening.

Major Kiyani's hand disappears under his qameez. He pulls out his pistol and places it between the plate of biscuits and a bowl of cashew nuts. The pistol's ivory handle looks like a dead rat.

'Have you been inside the Palace of Mirrors?'

'No,' I say. 'But I have seen it on TV.'

'It's right there.' He points to the hall with arches and a cupola on top. 'You should have a look before you go. Do you know how many mirrors are there in this palace?'

I dip my Nice biscuit in lukewarm tea and shake my head.

'Thousands. You look up and you see your face staring at you from thousands of mirrors. But these mirrors are not reflecting your face. They are reflecting the reflections of your face. You might have one enemy with a thousand faces. Do you get my point?'

I don't really. I want to go and have a look at the prisoners. To look for a secretary general. 'Interesting concept,' I say.

'Intelligence work is a bit like that. Sorting out the faces from their reflections. And then reflections of the reflections.'

'And them.' I point towards the prisoners and take my first proper look at them. 'Have you sorted them as yet?'

'They were all security risks, all of them. Neutralised now but still classified as risks.' The prisoners are standing in a straight row, their backs towards us.

In their tattered rags, they don't seem like a risk to anyone except their own health and hygiene.

But I don't say that. I nod at Major Kiyani appreciatively. Why start an argument when you are sitting

301

on a lush green lawn, the sun is going down and you are smoking your first cigarette after a century?

'This has been an interesting case.' Specks of chicken patty shine in Major Kiyani's moustache. He looks at me appreciatively like a scientist would look at a monkey after inserting electrodes in its brain. 'I have learned a lot from you.'

The air of mutual respect that surrounds this ceremony demands that I return the compliment. I nod like a monkey with electrodes in its brain.

'You didn't forget your friends even when you were . . .' Major Kiyani's hand dives in the air. He has the decency not to name the places where he kept me. 'But at the same time you were not sentimental. What is gone is gone, let's cut our losses, move on. I think General Akhtar was impressed. You played your cards right. Lose one friend, save another. Simple arithmetic. General Akhtar likes scenarios where everything adds up in the end.'

The prisoners now seem to be following some inaudible commands or perhaps they just know their routine. They shuffle left and they shuffle right, then sit down on their haunches. I hear groans.

If they have been brought out for exercise, they are not getting much. If they are expected to put on a show for me, I am not entertained.

'You always learn something.' Major Kiyani licks a glacé cherry off the top of a jam tart. 'In my line of work you always learn something. The day you stop learning, you're finished.' A bird's shadow crosses the lawn between us and the prisoners.

Is Secretary General among them? Probably all packed up, ready to go home and start the struggle all over again. It would be nice to say goodbye to him. I would like to see his face before they release him.

'Turn round,' Major Kiyani shouts. Then he looks towards me, his brown eyes howling with laughter over some joke that he doesn't want to share with me. 'Let's see if you recognise anyone.'

I am relieved that Major Kiyani hasn't sidestepped the issue. My goodwill towards him blooms like the sunflowers. I pick up another Nice biscuit. I made a deal with General Akhtar – I sign the statement and they let Secretary General go – and that deal is about to be honoured. That's the good thing about men in uniform. They keep their word.

I am expecting to see a man in a Mao cap. It goes against Secretary General's current political belief system, but my recently released prisoner's instincts tell me that I should look for a Mao cap.

I scan the faces, glazed eyes and sheep-sheared heads. There are no Mao caps. There are no caps at all. There is a woman in a white dupatta at the one end of the row. I don't know what they have done with her. Her eyes are all white. No corneas.

My eyes get stuck on a head with a glowing red patch in the shape of a triangle. Some weird skin infection, I think.

No, the fuckers ironed his head.

The head moves up, the eyes look at me blankly, a tongue caresses the parched, broken lips.

Under the ironed eyebrows, his long eyelashes have been spared.

Baby O closes his eyes.

Major Kiyani extends a plate of patties towards me. I push it aside and try to get up. Major Kiyani grabs me by my shoulder and pins me down in my chair, his eyes mean business now.

'I am very curious about one thing that you didn't mention in your statement,' he says. 'Why did he try to use your call sign?'

When someone dies, you are free to make up any old story about them. You can't betray the dead. If they come back from the dead and catch you betraying them, then you are trapped.

It suddenly seems as if Obaid has cheated on me by being alive. *I signed the fucking statement because you were dead. I cut a bloody deal because you were supposed to have been blown to bits because of your own stupidity. Now you are standing there asking for explanations. Couldn't you have stayed dead?*

Suddenly, I want to strangle Baby O with my own hands.

I pat Major Kiyani's shoulder. I look into his eyes. I try to harness the tea-party camaraderie that we have both been fostering.

'Major Kiyani, only a professional like you can appreciate this,' I say, trying to keep my voice from choking, covering up the surprise that you get when you see someone who you thought had taken a hit from a surface-to-air missile. Also the bigger surprise: your own desire to see them dead. 'It could only have been a case of professional jealousy.'

Baby O opens his eyes and puts his hand above his missing eyebrows to block the sun that must be piercing his eyes. His hand is covered in a bloodstained bandage.

'Which one of you is Colonel Shigri's son?'

If it hadn't been Secretary General's voice, I would have ignored it. If it hadn't been his hand-cuffed hands raised in air, as if he were trying to raise a point of order in his central committee meeting, I wouldn't have recognised him. I always imagined him to be old and shrivelled and bald, with thick reading glasses. He is much younger than his distinguished career would suggest. A tiny but milk-white shock in his short hair, a village tattooist's idea of an arrow piercing an apple of a heart adorning the left side of his hairless chest. He has the physique of a peasant and a bright open face as if the years of living in dark dungeons have given it a strange glow. His eyes are flitting between me and Major Kiyani. Trust Secretary General to confuse me with Major Kiyani. His eyes scan the table brimming with food and then our faces. It seems he is trying to decide which one is the teapot and which one the cup. A cloud's shadow travels across the lawn. My eyes squint. Major Kiyani reaches for his pistol. Before the shot rings out, I hear Major Kiyani's booming voice.

'I am, comrade. I am Colonel Shigri's son.'

CHAPTER 24

The three-member team of marines stationed at the gate of the ambassador's residence was having a hard time matching their guests with the guest list. They were expecting the usual tuxedos from the diplomatic corps and gold-braided khakis from the Pakistan Army, but instead they were ushering in a steady stream of flowing turbans, tribal gowns and embroidered shalwar qameez suits. If this was a fancy-dress party, the ambassador had forgotten to tell the men guarding his main gate. The invitation did say something about a Kabul–Texas themed barbecue, but it seemed the guests had decided to ignore the Texas part and gone all native for the evening.

The floodlight that hung on the tree above the marines' guardhouse – a wooden cottage decked in red, white and blue bunting for the evening – was so powerful that the usually noisy house sparrows who occupied the surrounding trees in the evenings had either shut up or flown away. The monsoon had decided to bypass Islamabad this year and the light breeze carried only dust and dead pollen.

The marines, commanded by twenty-two-year-old

Corporal Bob Lessard and helped by a steady supply of beer and hot dogs sneaked out by their colleague on catering duty, managed to remain cheerful in the face of an endless stream of guests who didn't look anything like their names on the guest list.

The local CIA chief, Chuck Coogan, one of the first guests to arrive, sported a karakul cap and an embroidered leather holster hung from his left shoulder. The US Cultural Attaché came wearing an Afghan burqa, one of those flowing shuttlecocks that she had tucked halfway over her head to reveal the plunging neckline of her shimmering turquoise dress.

The marines had started their celebrations early. They took turns going into the guardhouse to take swigs from bottles of Coors that were chilling in the cooler as Corporal Lessard crossed off another name on his clipboard and greeted the ambassador's guests with a forced smile. He welcomed a hippie couple draped in identical Afghan kilims which smelled as if they had been used to pack raw hashish.

'Freedom Medicine?' he asked.

'Basic health for Afghan refugees,' said the blonde girl with neon-coloured beads in her hair. 'For the muj injured in the guerrilla war,' said the blond goateed boy in a low voice, as if sharing a closely guarded secret with Corporal Lessard. He let them in, covering his nose with his clipboard. He welcomed Texan nurses wearing glass bangles up to their elbows and a military accountant from

307

Ohio showing off his Red Army medal, most probably taken off the uniform of a dead Soviet soldier by the muj and sold to a junk shop.

Corporal Lessard's patience ran out when a University of Nebraska professor turned up wearing a marine uniform. 'Where do you think you are going, buddy?' Corporal Lessard demanded. The professor told him in hushed tones that his Adult Literacy Consultancy was actually a programme to train the Afghan mujahideen to shoot and edit video footage of their guerrilla attacks. 'Some of these guys have real talent.'

'And this?' Corporal Lessard fingered the shoulder epaulette on the professor's crisp camouflage uniform.

'Well, we are at war. Ain't we?' The professor shrugged and tucked both his thumbs into his belt.

Corporal Lessard had little patience for soldiers behaving like civilians and none whatsoever for civilians pretending to be soldiers, but he found himself powerless in this situation. This evening he was nothing but a glorified usher. He'd had no say in deciding the guest list, let alone the dress code, but he wasn't going to let this joker get away with this.

'Welcome to the front line,' he said, handing his clipboard to the professor. 'Here you go. Consider yourself on active duty now.' Corporal Lessard retreated into the guardhouse, positioned himself on a stool from where he could keep an eye on the professor and joined the beer pot contest with his staff.

Beyond the guardhouse, the guests could choose between two huge catering tents. In the first one the central spread was a salad the size of a small farm, red cabbage and blueberries, giant ham sandwiches with blueberry chutney, all arranged in the shape of an American flag. Before a row of gas-powered grills, marines stood in their shorts and baseball caps, barbecuing hot dogs, quarter-pounders and piles of corn on the cob. Pakistani waiters in bolo ties and cowboy hats roamed with jugs of punch and paper glasses, dodging children who had already started hot-dog fights, and offering drinks to the few people who had bothered to venture into this tent. A long queue was forming outside the adjacent tent, where eight whole lambs skewered on long iron bars were roasting on an open fire. An Afghan chef was at hand to reassure everyone that he had slaughtered the lambs himself and that everything in the tent was halal.

The ambassador's wife had been feeling sick to her stomach ever since seeing the Afghan chef put an inch-thick iron rod through the first of eight baby lambs that morning. It was Nancy Raphel herself who had come up with the Kabul–Texas theme, but she was already regretting the idea because most of the guests were turning up in all kinds of variations on traditional Afghani clothes and suddenly her own understated mustard silk shalwar qameez seemed ridiculous. The sight of so many Americans decked out like Afghan warlords repulsed her. She was glad that her own husband had stuck to his standard evening wear, a double-breasted blue blazer and tan trousers.

She had planned an evening of culturally sensitive barbecue; what she got was a row of small carcasses slowly rotating on iron skewers, her guests queuing up with their Stars and Stripes paper plates, pretending they were guests at some tribal feast. Under such stressful circumstances Nancy almost collapsed with the sense of relief when her husband took a call from the Army House and told her that President Zia ul-Haq would not be turning up. She excused herself to the wife of the French Ambassador, dressed like an Uzbek bride, and retreated to her bedroom to calm her nerves.

The marines at the guardhouse could afford to party while on active duty not because it was the Fourth of July but because the security for the premises was being managed by a contingent of the Pakistan Army. Five hundred metres before the guardhouse, on the tree-lined road that led to the ambassador's residence, the guests were required to stop at a makeshift barrier set up by Brigade 101. The troops, under the watchful command of a subedar major, greeted the guests with their bomb scanners and metal detectors. They slipped their scanners under the cars, asked their non-white guests to open the boots of their cars and finally waved them towards the guardhouse where an increasingly cheerful group of marines welcomed them. The army contingent had set up their own searchlights to illuminate the road. Here, too, the trees were awash with light so intense that the birds' nests on the trees lining the road lay abandoned. A catering van sent by the district administration delivered their dinner early and the Subedar Major was livid when he discovered that the samovar which came in the van was empty. 'How are my men going to stay awake without tea?' he shouted at the civilian van driver, who shrugged and drove off without replying.

Embassy functions were usually select affairs, but watching the guests arrive from the guardhouse, Corparal Lessard thought that the ambassador seemed to have invited everyone who had ever put a bandage on an injured Afghan mujahid and every Afghan commander who had taken a potshot at a Russian soldier. Corporal Lessard relieved the professor of his duty when he saw the first guest in a suit, a lanky man with a flowing beard. 'OBL,' the bearded man said, and raised his hand as if he wasn't identifying himself to a party usher, but greeting an invisible crowd.

Corporal Lessard went through the list and looked at the man again.

'Of Laden and Co. Constructions.' The man

patted his beard impatiently and Corporal Lessard ushered him in with a smile and an exaggerated wave of his hand. Taking his turn at the beer pot, Corporal Lessard told a joke. 'What does a towel-head wear to disguise himself?' Then choking on his own beer, he blurted: 'A suit.'

The ambassador had reasons to be inclusive. A year into his job, Arnold Raphel was feeling increasingly isolated as dozens of American agencies ran their own little jihads against the Soviets along the Pakistan–Afghanistan border. There were those avenging Vietnam and there were those doing God's work and then there were charities with names so obscure and missions so far-fetched that he had a hard time keeping track of them. Now that the last Soviet soldiers were about to leave Afghanistan and the mujahideen were laying siege to Kabul, some Americans were tearing at each other's throats to claim credit, others were just lingering, reluctant to go home, hoping for another front to open. Just last week he had received a démarche about a group of teachers from the University of Minnesota who were writing the new Islamic books for Afghanistan and sending them to Central Asia. He investigated and was told to keep his hands off as it was yet another branch of yet another covert programme. Every American he met in Islamabad claimed to be from 'the other agency'.

He was certain that if he wanted to bring this

chaos under control, he first needed to bring them all under one roof and make a symbolic gesture so it became clear that there was one boss and it was him. And what better way to do it than throw a party? What better time to do it than the Fourth of July? He was hoping that this would be a farewell party where American nuts would be able to meet the Afghan commanders who had done the actual fighting, get their pictures taken, and then everybody would go home so that he could get on with the delicate business of implementing US foreign policy. Arnie had not prepared a speech but he had a few lines ready that he would weave into the big conversation that he wanted to have with his American guests: *'victory is a bigger challenge than defeat'*, *'answered prayers can be more troublesome than the sad echoes of unanswered prayers'*.

He wanted it to be a 'job well done, now push off to wherever you came from' kind of party.

Standing with the ambassador and feeling disgusted at the sight of respectable men gnawing at bones was General Akhtar. He also felt out of place and overdressed. He had turned up in his full ceremonial uniform, with gold braid and shiny brass medals, and now he found himself surrounded by small groups of white men dressed in loose shalwar qameez and the most astonishing variety of head-gear he had seen since his last visit to Peshawar's Storytellers' Bazaar. General Akhtar knew before everyone else that General Zia would not turn up for the party. 'He is not feeling too well, you know,' he told Arnold Raphel, looking closely for any reaction. 'Brigadier TM's loss is a big setback. He was like a son to General Zia. One of my best officers.' When Arnold Raphel offered indifferent condolences, it only strengthened General Akhtar's resolve to square things with the Americans one last time. He had won them their war against communism. Now he wanted his share of the spoils. He picked up a strawberry from the shortcake on his plate and said to Arnold Raphel, 'Mrs Raphel has done a splendid job with the arrangements. Behind every great man . . .'

OBL found himself talking to a journalist who was nursing a beer in a paper cup and wondering what he should file for his newspaper now that General Zia hadn't turned up. 'I am OBL,' he told the journalist and waited for any signs of recognition. The journalist, a veteran of diplomatic parties and used to meeting obscure government functionaries from far-flung countries with bizarre motives, pulled out his notepad and said, 'So what's the story?'

Out in the guardhouse, the University of Nebraska professor, now fully accepted as an honorary marine for the evening, raised his bottle and proposed a toast to the warrior spirit of the Afghans, then paused for a minute.

'What about our Pakistani hosts?'

'What about them?' Corporal Lessard asked.

'The guys on the trucks out there. Our first line of defence. What are they doing?'

'They are doing their duty. Just like us.'

'No, they are doing *our* duty,' the professor said. 'They are keeping the enemy at bay. They are guarding us while we enjoy this feast, this feast to celebrate our freedom. We must share our bounty with them.'

Corporal Lessard looked around the already crammed guardhouse. 'There are about two hundred of them. They wouldn't fit in.'

'Then we must take our bounty to them.'

Corporal Lessard, drunk on Coors and patriotism and the love that one feels for one's fellow human beings on days like this, volunteered to take a tray of food to the Pakistani troops. He thought of throwing in a couple of beers but he had been taught in his cultural sensitivity course not to offer alcohol to the locals unless you had an ulterior motive or the locals absolutely insisted. Corporal Lessard covered a stainless-steel tray with aluminium foil, hoisted it over his head and started walking towards the Pakistani troops. He walked in the middle of the road. The tree branches on both sides of the road hissed like snakes in his drunken vision. The road seemed endless.

OBL and the journalist found each other equally dull. The journalist listened with a smirk on his face when OBL claimed that his bulldozers and concrete mixers had been instrumental in defeating the Soviets in Afghanistan. 'My editor thinks that it's his pen that forced the Red Army to withdraw, and he can't even compose a sentence,' the journalist said with a straight face. OBL gave up on the journalist when he offered to pose for a photograph and the journalist said, 'I don't have a camera and even if I did I wouldn't be allowed to carry it into a diplomatic party.'

'That is very unprofessional of you,' OBL muttered, scanning various groups of guests enjoying themselves. He spotted General Akhtar in the middle of the lawn surrounded by a number of Americans wearing Afghan caps. He walked up and stood behind them, hoping that the circle would part to welcome him. He skulked for a few minutes, trying to catch General Akhtar's eye. To OBL's horror General Akhtar saw him and showed no signs of recognition, but the local CIA chief followed General Akhtar's gaze, moved right-wards, making space for him in the circle and said, 'Nice suit, OBL.'

General Akhtar's eyes lit up. 'We would have never won this war without our Saudi friends. How's business, brother?' General Akhtar asked, holding him by his hand. OBL smiled and said, 'Allah has been very kind. There is no business like the construction business in times of war.'

Arnold Raphel talked to a group of Afghan elders and kept looking sideways at his wife who had reappeared wearing khaki pants and a plain black T-shirt, replacing the loose ethnic thing she was wearing at the start of the party. On the one hand he was relieved that General Zia hadn't turned up, but on the other hand as a diplomat, as a professional, he felt slighted. He knew it wasn't an official state occasion, but General Zia had never missed any invitation from his office. Arnold Raphel knew that General Zia had gone completely bonkers since his security chief's death, but surely the General knew that a Fourth of July party at the American Ambassador's residence was as safe a place as you could find in this very dangerous country. 'Brother Zia is not coming. He is not feeling well,' he told the bearded Afghan covered in a rainbow-coloured shawl. The Afghan elder pretended he already knew but didn't care. 'This is the best lamb I have eaten since the war started. So tender. It seems you plucked him out of his mother's womb.'

A wave of nausea started in the pit of Nancy's stomach and rushed upwards. She put a hand over her mouth, mumbled something and ran towards her bedroom.

OBL soaked up the atmosphere, laughing politely at the light-hearted banter between the Americans and General Akhtar. He felt that warm glow that comes from being at the centre of a party. Then suddenly the CIA chief put his hand on General Akhtar's shoulder, turned towards OBL and said,

'Nice meeting you, OBL. Good work, keep it up.' The others followed them and in an instant the party deserted him. He noticed a man in a navy-blue blazer talking to some of his Afghan acquaintances. The man seemed important. OBL slowly started drifting towards that circle.

The party moved down to the den, a large basement hall with leather sofas, a forty-four-inch television screen and a bar; a blatant exercise in suburban nostalgia. Arnold had arranged for some of his American staff to see the recording of the Redskins versus Tampa Bay Buccaneers in the previous week's NFL play-off. The den was full of cigar smoke and noisy Americans. Instead of beer, which seemed to be the drink of choice upstairs, here people were serving themselves whiskeys. The Saudi Ambassador sat on a divan with a wad of fifty-dollar bills in front of him taking bets on the game. Somebody had forgotten to explain to him that the game was eight days old and that the Redskins had trampled the Buccaneers.

A tall American wearing a kaftan and a flyer's orange scarf around his neck handed General Akhtar a glass half full of bourbon. General Akhtar felt the urge to throw the whiskey at the stranger's face but then looked around, didn't see any familiar faces except the Americans and the Saudi Ambassador, who himself seemed too sloshed to care. General Akhtar decided to hold on to his drink. The noise in the den, the veteran spymaster in General Akhtar concluded, was the perfect backdrop for sounding out Coogan. Not even the most sophisticated bug would pick out any distinguishable sounds in the incomprehensible chorus that was going up: 'Lock him up, Jack, lock him up. Feed them dirt, Jack, feed them dirt.' General Akhtar raised his glass like everyone else but only sniffed his drink. It stank like an old wound.

Corporal Lessard was challenged by the Subedar Major from the back of the truck where the Pakistani soldiers were relaxing after security checking the last guests. The Subedar Major aimed his Kalashnikov at Corporal Lessard's forehead and ordered him to halt.

The marine raised his tray above his head, the aluminium foil covering it reflecting the searchlight held by one of the soldiers on the truck. 'I brought some chow. For you brave men.'

The Subedar Major lowered his rifle and climbed down from the truck. Two rows of soldiers peered down at the swaying American trying to balance the tray on his head.

The Subedar Major and the marine squared off in a circle of light marked by the searchlight.

'Hot dogs,' Corporal Lessard said, pushing the tray towards the Subedar Major.

General Akhtar shifted his glass from his right hand to his left and cleared his throat. Then on second thoughts he brought his hand up and mimed

General Zia's moustache, a universal sign used in Islamabad's drawing rooms when people didn't want to say the dreaded name. General Akhtar's right thumb and forefinger twirled invisible hair on his upper lip: '. . . has been having dreams,' General Akhtar said, looking into Coogan's eyes.

Coogan, his heart running with the quarterback who had just set off for a fifty-six-yard dash, smiled and said, 'He is a visionary. Always has been. They don't change. I am sure TM's free fall didn't help. By the way, nice line, Akhtar: *A professional who didn't miss his target even in his death.* If your boss had half your sense of humour, this Pakiland of yours would be a much livelier place.' Coogan winked and turned towards the TV.

General Akhtar felt a bit nervous. He had played these games long enough to know that he was not going to get a written contract to topple General Zia. Hell, he wasn't even likely to get a verbal assurance. But surely they knew him and trusted him well enough to give him a nod. 'He won't stop the war until you give him the peace prize.' General Akhtar decided to press his case. He had looked around and realised nobody was remotely interested in their conversation.

'What prize?' Coogan shouted above the chorus. 'Lock him up, Jack, lock him up.'

'Nobel Peace Prize. For liberating Afghanistan.'

'That is a Swedish thing. We don't do that kind of thing. And you don't know those snooty Swedes. They would never give it to anybody with . . .'

Coogan mimed General Zia's moustache and turned towards the television again, laughing.

General Akhtar could feel an utter lack of interest on Coogan's part in the matter at hand. He had won his war and he wanted to celebrate. General Akhtar knew what a short attention span the Americans had. He knew that in the subtle art of spycraft this non-commitment was also a kind of commitment. But General Akhtar wanted a sign clearer than that. He suddenly smelled the acrid smell of hashish in the room and looked around in panic. Nobody else seemed to be bothered. They were still busy urging Jack to lock them up and feed them dirt. General Akhtar noticed that the man who had poured him a drink was standing behind Coogan puffing on a joint. 'Meet Lieutenant Bannon,' Coogan winked at General Akhtar. 'He has been teaching your boys the silent drill. Our main man.'

General Akhtar turned round and gave him a faint yellow smile.

'I am aware of all the good work he has been doing. I think his boys are ready for the real thing,' General Akhtar said, looking at the joint in Bannon's hand.

OBL found himself strolling on the empty lawns amid discarded paper plates, half-eaten hot dogs and chewed-up bones. He suddenly remembered that he had not as yet eaten. He went towards the tent from where he had smelled the lamb's fat burning.

Inside the Kabul tent the Afghan chef minutely inspected the leftover of his culinary creation. Eight skeletons hung over the smouldering ashes of the barbecue fire. He was hoping to take some home for his family but even his small knife couldn't salvage any bits of meat from the bones. 'God,' he muttered, packing his carving knives, 'these Americans eat like pigs.'

Coogan's attention was divided between the misery that the Redskins were going through and this General who had been sitting there with his glass in his hands for ages without taking a sip. Coogan raised his glass to General Akhtar's, one eye fixed on the Redskins' quarterback who was demolishing the Buccaneers' defence and the other winking at the General. Coogan shouted, 'Go get him.'

General Akhtar knew he had his answer. He didn't want to let this moment go. He raised his glass and clinked it with Coogan's again. 'By jingo. Let's get him.' He took a generous sip from his glass and suddenly the liquid didn't smell as horrible as it had a second ago. It was bitter but it didn't taste as bad as all his life he had thought it would.

The Subedar Major looked at the tray, looked at the marine's face and understood.

'Tea? Have some?' the Subedar Major asked.

'Tea?' Corporal Lessard repeated. 'Don't go all English on me. Here. Chow. Eat.'

The marine removed the aluminium foil from

the tray, took a hot dog out and started chomping away.

The Subedar Major smiled an understanding smile. 'Dog? Halal?'

Corporal Lessard was running out of patience. 'No. No dog meat. Beef.' He mooed and mimed a knife slicing a cow's neck.

'Halal?' the Subedar Major asked again.

A house sparrow blundered into the floodlight and shrieked as if trying to bridge the communication gap between the two. Corporal Lessard felt homesick.

'It's a piece of fucking meat in a piece of fucking bread. If we can't agree on that what the hell am I doing here?' He flung the tray on the ground and started running back towards the guardhouse.

Nancy Raphel buried her head in her pillow and waited for her husband to come to bed. 'We should stick to our cocktail menu in future,' she said before falling asleep.

General Akhtar was greeted by a very disturbed major as he walked out of the gate of the ambassador's residence.

'General Zia has gone missing,' the major whispered in his ear. 'There is no trace of him anywhere.'

CHAPTER 25

The night in the dungeon is long. In my dream, an army of Maos marches the funeral march carrying their Mao caps in their hands like beggars' bowls. Their lips are sewn with crimson thread.

The brick in the wall scrapes.

Secretary General's ghost is already at work, I tell myself. 'Get some rest,' I shout. The brick moves again. I am not scared of ghosts; I have seen enough of them in my life. They all come back to me as if I run an orphanage for them.

I pull out the brick, put my face in the hole and shout at strength 5, 'Get some sleep, Secretary General, get some sleep. Revolution can wait till the morning.'

A hand traces the contours of my face. The fingers are soft, a woman's fingers. She passes me a crunched-up envelope. 'I found it in my cell,' she says. 'It's not mine. I can't read. I thought maybe it's for you. Can you read?'

I shove the envelope into my pocket. 'Nobody can read around here,' I say, trying to terminate the conversation. 'This place is pitch dark. We are all bloody blind here.'

A moment's silence. 'This seems like a message from the dead man. Keep it. I think someone is about to start a journey. It's not going to be me. You should keep yourself ready.'

CHAPTER 26

Geneeral Zia decided to borrow his gardener's bicycle in order to get out of the Army House without his bodyguards, but he needed a shawl first. He needed the shawl not because it was cold but because he wanted to disguise himself. The decision to venture out of the Army House was prompted by a verse from the Quran. To go out disguised as a common man was his friend Ceauşescu's idea.

The plan was a happy marriage between the divine and the devious.

He had returned from Brigadier TM's funeral and locked himself in his study, refusing to attend to even the bare minimum government work that he had been doing since ordering Code Red. He flicked through the thick file that General Akhtar had sent him on the ongoing investigation into the accident. The summary had congratulated General Akhtar for ensuring that Brigadier TM's sad demise wasn't broadcast live on TV. It would have been a big setback for the nation's trust in the professionalism of the army.

General Zia cried and prayed non-stop in an

attempt to stop himself from doing the inevitable, but like a relapsing junkie, he found his hands reaching for a volume of the Quran covered in green velvet. He kissed its spine thrice and opened it with trembling hands.

His knees shook with excitement when the book revealed not Jonah's prayer as he had been dreading but a simple, more practical verse. *'Go forth into the world, ye believers . . .'*

His tears dissolved into a knowing smile. Even the itch in his rectum felt like a call to action; he rubbed his bottom on the edge of the chair. In his relief, he remembered the advice Nicolae Ceauşescu had given him at a bilateral meeting on the sidelines of the summit for the Non-Aligned Movement. It was one of those meetings where heads of states have nothing to discuss and which interpreters try to prolong with an elaborate, flowery translation of the pleasantries. The two leaders came from countries so far apart and so different that Ceauşescu couldn't even talk to General Zia about boosting bilateral trade as trade between Romania and Pakistan was non-existent. And General Zia couldn't ask for his support on the Kashmir issue because Ceauşescu wasn't likely to know where Kashmir was, let alone what the issues were. There was one fact General Zia knew about the man that did interest him though: Ceauşescu had been in power for twenty-four years, and unlike other rulers of his longevity and reputation who couldn't get an invitation from any decent country, Ceauşescu had been welcomed by Secretary General Brezhnev and by President Nixon and had just been knighted by the Queen of Great Britain.

And here he was at the Non-Aligned Movement's meeting when his country wasn't even a member. Observer status they had given him, but clearly the man knew how to align himself.

General Zia was genuinely impressed and intrigued by anyone who had managed to stay in office for longer than he had. He had asked a number of veterans of the world stage what their secret was but nobody had ever given him the advice he could use in Pakistan. Fidel Castro had told him to stay true to his mission and drink lots of water with his rum. Kim Il-Sung advised him not to watch depressing films. Reagan had patted Nancy's shoulder and said, 'Nice birthday cards.' King Abdul Aziz of Saudi Arabia was more forthright than most: 'How would I know? Ask my doctor.'

With Ceauşescu, General Zia had the comfort of being a total stranger so he could afford to be direct.

The meeting had taken place in a small conference room on the forty-third floor of the Manila Hilton. The interpreter, a plump, twenty-six-year-old woman in a shoulder-padded suit, was shocked when General Zia cut the pleasantries short and said he wanted to use their scheduled ten minutes to learn about statecraft from His

Highness. Ceauşescu's Dracula smile widened, he put a hand on the interpreter's thigh and mumbled: '*Noi voi tot learn de la each alt.*'

General Zia imagined that Ceauşescu was saying that we should all drink a pint of fresh blood every day.

'We must all learn from each other,' the interpreter interpreted.

'How have you managed to stay in office for such a long time?'

'*Cum have tu conducere la spre stay în serviciu pentru such un timp îndelungat?*' the interpreter asked Ceauşescu, placing a leather folder on her lap.

Ceauşescu spoke for about two minutes, jabbing his fingers, opening and closing the palms of his hands and finally reaching for the interpreter's thigh. He found himself patting the leather folder.

'Believe only ten per cent of what your intelligence agencies tell you about public opinion. The key is that they should either love you or fear you; your decline starts the day they become indifferent to you.'

'How do I know if they are becoming indifferent?'

'Find out first-hand. Surprise them, go out to restaurants, show up at sports matches. Do you have football? Go to football matches, take a walk at night. Listen to what people have to say and then believe only ten per cent of what they say because when they are with you they will also lie. But after they have met you they are bound to love you and they will tell other people who will also love you.'

General Zia nodded eagerly while Ceauşescu spoke, and then invited him to be the chief guest at the National Day Parade, knowing full well that he would never come. He was getting up to leave when Ceauşescu shouted something to the interpreter. General Zia came back towards the interpreter, who had now opened her folder and spread it on her lap.

'Before you go to football matches, make sure that your team wins.'

General Zia tried to go to some of these public gatherings, but as soon as he left the VIP area and mingled with the people he would realise that he was amid a hired crowd; their flag-waving and slogans well rehearsed. Many of them just stiffened when he walked by and he could tell that they were soldiers in civvies. Sometimes they seemed scared of him, but then he would look at Brigadier TM by his side, using his elbows to keep the crowd at bay and he would immediately know that it wasn't him they were scared of, they just didn't want to be noticed by Brigadier TM. He went to some cricket matches and found out that people were more interested in the game and didn't seem too bothered about loving him or fearing him.

There was only one thing left to do now that Brigadier TM wasn't on his side; put Comrade Ceauşescu's advice to the test. To go out of the Army House without his bodyguards.

Instead of retiring to his study after his night prayers, he went to the bedroom where the First

Lady was sitting on a chair reading a story to their youngest daughter. He kissed his daughter's head, sat down and waited for the First Lady to finish the story. His heart was beating fast at the prospect of the impending adventure. He looked at his wife and daughter as if he was departing for a far-off battle from which he might or might not return.

'Can I borrow a shawl?'

'Which one?'

He was hoping she would ask him why he needed it. He was hoping he would be able to tell at least one person before embarking on his mission but all she asked was, which one?

'The older the better,' the General said trying to sound mysterious. She went to the dressing room and brought him an old maroon shawl with a thin embroidered border. She still didn't ask him why he needed it.

Feeling a bit let down even before the beginning of his adventure, General Zia hugged his daughter again and started to go out.

'Don't get that shawl dirty,' said the First Lady. 'It's my mother's.'

General Zia paused for a moment and thought maybe he should confide in her after all, but she picked up her book again and asked without looking at him. 'Was it Caliph Omar who used to go out at night disguised as a common man to see if his subjects lived in peace?'

General Zia nodded his head. The First Lady really had a sense of history, he thought.

He wouldn't mind being remembered as Caliph Omar the Second.

'Was he the one who said that even if a dog sleeps hungry on the banks of Euphrates, he'll never find salvation?'

'Yes,' General Zia said. His moustache did a little dance.

'He should see our Islamic republic now. Randy dogs are running this country.'

General Zia's heart sank, his moustache drooped but he muttered the verse that had exhorted him to go forth into the world and with renewed determination stormed out of the room.

He asked his gardener if he could borrow his bicycle, and the gardener handed it to him without asking why he needed it. When he stepped out of his living quarters the two commandos posted at the door saluted and started to follow him. He told them to wait for him at their post. 'I am going to exercise my legs.'

Then he wrapped the shawl tightly around his head and face, leaving his eyes and forehead uncovered. He climbed onto the bicycle and began to pedal. The bicycle was unsteady for the first few metres, it went left and it went right, but he found his balance and pedalled slowly, keeping to one side of the road.

As his bicycle approached the gate of the Army House, he started to have second thoughts. Maybe I should turn back. Maybe I should inform Brigadier TM and he can send some of his men in civvies who can follow me around. Then Brigadier TM's flag-draped coffin flashed in front of his eyes and his bicycle wobbled. General Zia was still undecided when his bicycle arrived at the sentry post at the gate of the Army House and the gate opened. He slowed down, looked left and right, hoping someone would recognise him and ask him what the hell he thought he was doing. As his mind raced for an appropriate excuse, a voice shouted from the sentry box.

'Don't feel like going home, old man? Scared of your woman?' He looked towards the sentry box, but didn't see anyone. His feet pushed the pedals hard. The gate came down behind him. The thought that his disguise was working reinvigorated him. The doubts cleared, he lifted his bottom from the bicycle seat and pedalled harder, his eyes moistening with the effort and with emotion. He waited at the red light at the crossroads which led to Constitution Avenue, even though there was not a single vehicle in sight. The light stayed red for a long time and showed no sign of turning green. He looked left and right and then left again and turned on to Constitution Avenue.

The avenue was completely deserted, not a soul, not a vehicle. An eight-lane road, it had not really been designed for traffic, which was thin in this part of town even during the day, but to accommodate the heavy artillery and tanks for the annual National Day Parade. The avenue, still wet from an afternoon shower, glistened yellow under the street lights. The hills surrounding it stood silent and sombre; General Zia rode slowly. His legs, unused to this movement, were beginning to ache. He first rode straight along the side of the road, then moved to the middle and started to zigzag. If someone saw him from the hills they would see an old man wrapped in a shawl, wobbling on his bike. They would have to conclude that the old man was probably very tired after working hard all day at the Army House.

When he had covered about half a mile without seeing a single person, a strange feeling began to set in: what if he was ruling a country without any inhabitants? What if it was a ghost country? What if there was really nobody out there? What if all the statistics from the census that said one hundred and thirty million people lived in the country, fifty-two per cent women, forty-eight per cent men, ninety-eight per cent Muslim, was all simply the work of his overefficient bureaucrats? What if everybody had migrated somewhere else and he was ruling a country where nobody lived except his army, his bureaucrats and his body-guards? He was breathing hard and feeling quite amused at the bizarre conspiracy theories one can harbour if one is a commoner on a bicycle, when a bush on the roadside moved and a voice shouted at him: 'Come here, old man. Riding around without a headlight? Do you think this road belongs to your father? Isn't there enough lawless-ness in this country?'

General Zia put his heels on the road instead of applying the brakes and his bicycle came to a shaky halt. A figure emerged from behind the bush, a man wrapped in an old brown shawl. Under the shawl General Zia could make out his policeman's beret.

'Get off that bike, uncle. Where do you think you're going without a headlight?'

The police constable held the handlebars of the General's bike as if he was about to pedal away. General Zia got off the bike, stumbling because of the shawl wrapped tightly around him. His head was buzzing with excitement at his first encounter with one of his own subjects, without any security cordons separating them, without any guns pointed at the person he was talking to.

Standing on the footpath along Constitution Avenue, under the watchful eyes of a tired old police constable, General Zia realised the true meaning of what the old Dracula had told him. General Zia realised that Ceauşescu's advice contained a metaphor that he hadn't understood before this adventure. What is democracy? What is its essence? You draw strength from your people and you become even stronger and that is exactly what General Zia was doing at this moment. Watched over by the silent hills surrounding Islamabad, a very ancient ritual was taking place: a ruler and his subject were face to face without any bureaucrat to complicate their relationship, without any gunmen to pollute their encounter.

For a moment the fear of death evaporated into the cold smog and General Zia felt as strong and invincible as the mountains surrounding them.

'Hold your ears,' said the policeman, taking a cigarette from behind his ear and producing a lighter from under his shawl. When he lit the cigarette the air suddenly smelled of kerosene fumes. General Zia tried to balance the bike on the pavement but the policeman gave it a kick and it went hurtling down the footpath and then lay flat.

General Zia took his hands out of the shawl and held his ears. It was a lesson in good governance but it was proving to be fun as well. He was already composing a speech in his head: *All the wisdom I need to run this country I learned from a lone police constable doing his duty on an empty road in the middle of the night in Islamabad . . .*

'Not like that.' The policeman shook his head in disappointment. 'Cock. Be a cock. A rooster.'

General Zia thought that the time had come to introduce himself but the constable didn't give him the opportunity to reveal his face; he held his shawl-covered head with one hand and shoved it down.

'Don't pretend that you don't know how to be a cock.'

General Zia knew how to be a cock, but last time he had done it was more than half a century ago in school, and the thought that there were people out here still dishing out that childish punishment bewildered him. His back was refusing to bend but the constable held his head down till it almost touched his knees; General Zia reluctantly put both his hands through his legs and tried to reach for his ears. His back was a block of concrete refusing to bend, his legs shook under the weight of his body and he felt he was going to collapse and roll over. He tried to look up as soon as the constable removed his hand from his head. The constable replaced it with a foot on his neck. General Zia spoke with his head down.

'I am General Zia ul-Haq.'

The smoke hit the constable in his throat and he burst into a coughing fit which turned into laughter.

'Isn't one General Zia enough for this poor nation? Do we need crazies like you running around in the middle of the night pretending to be him?'

General Zia wriggled his face in the shawl, hoping that the constable would get a glimpse of his face.

'Your Highness,' the constable said, 'you must be a very busy man. You must be in a hurry to get back to the Army House to run this country. Tell me a joke and I'll let you go. Have you ever met such a generous policeman in your life? Come on, tell us a joke about General Zia.'

This was easy, General Zia thought. He had entertained many journalists by telling jokes about himself.

He cleared his throat and started. 'Why doesn't the First Lady let General Zia into her bedroom?'

'Oh shut up,' the constable said. 'Everyone knows

that one. And it's not even a joke. It's probably true. Just say General Zia is a one-eyed faggot thrice and I'll let you go.'

General Zia had not heard this one before. Indian propaganda, he thought, fluttering his eyelashes just to double-check; his left eye saw the mud-covered canvas shoes of the policeman, his right eye followed a baby frog crossing Constitution Avenue. But his back was killing him, he wanted his spine straight. He whispered in a low voice: 'General Zia is a . . .'

He heard the sound of sirens starting in the distance, the same sirens that the outriders in his presidential convoy used. For a moment he wondered if someone else had occupied the Army House while he was here, talking to this perverted constable?

'I can tell that your heart is not in it. I try it on everyone I stop on this road and I swear that nobody has ever disappointed me. It's the only punishment they seem to like.'

The constable kicked him on his backside and General Zia went reeling, face forward, his spine snapping back straight and sending waves of pain through his body. The constable dragged him behind the bush.

'The real one-eyed one is on his way. Let me deal with him first. Then we'll have a long chat,' said the constable, removing his shawl and flinging it over General Zia.

The constable stood at attention on the roadside

and saluted as the convoy sped by with its flashing lights and wailing sirens. It was smaller than the normal presidential convoy. One black Mercedes followed by two open-topped jeeps, carrying teams of alert commandos with their guns pointed at the roadside. As the constable returned to start negotiating with General Zia the terms of his release, he heard the convoy reversing at full speed; the sirens sobbed and went qsuiet like a screaming child suddenly falling to sleep. Before the constable had time to realise what was happening, the commandos were upon him with their Kalashnikovs and searchlights. An old man in a shalwar qameez who was still sitting in the jeep pointed to the bicycle and said in a calm voice, 'That is the bicycle he took.'

For the short journey back to the Army House General Zia sat in the back seat of the Mercedes and pretended that General Akhtar wasn't there. He wound the shawl around himself tightly and sat with his head down like someone who has just woken up from a very bad dream.

But in his heart he knew what he had to do. General Akhtar with all his spies and wire-taps had never told him what one hundred and thirty million people really thought of him. He had not even told him ten per cent of the truth. He didn't look at General Akhtar but could tell from the smell in the car that he had been knocking down whiskeys at the American Ambassador's party. What next? Pig meat? His own brother's flesh?

He spoke for the first time when getting out of the car. 'Let that policeman go,' he said, very certain that nobody would believe the constable's bizarre story. 'He was only doing his duty.'

General Zia went straight to his study, sent for his stenographer and dictated two appointment letters. Then he picked up the phone and called a lieutenant general in charge of the military operations. After long apologies for waking him up in the middle of the night, he asked the Lieutenant General to relieve General Akhtar of his duties.

'I would like you to take charge now. I want you personally to go through all the files on all the suspects. I want you to visit every single interrogation centre General Akhtar is running and I want you to report back directly to me.'

As General Beg set out to take charge from General Akhtar, General Zia made the last telephone call of the night.

'Yes, sir.' General Akhtar was awake and expecting a thank-you call from General Zia.

'Thank you, Akhtar,' General Zia said. 'I have no words to show my gratitude. This is not the first time you have saved my life.'

'I was doing my duty, sir.'

'I have decided to promote you. Four stars.'

General Akhtar didn't believe what he was hearing. Would General Zia relinquish his post as the Chief of the Army? Was General Zia retiring and moving to Mecca? General Akhtar didn't have to wait long to find out. 'I have appointed you the

Chairman of the Joint Chiefs of Staff Committee. In a way, I have appointed you my boss . . .'

General Akhtar tried to intervene in a pleading voice. 'Sir, my work at the agency is not finished yet. The Americans are talking to the Soviets behind our back . . .'

A life of glorified bureaucratic tedium flashed in front of his eyes. He would have three adjutants, one each from the air force, navy and army, but no power over any of the three institutions. He would have his own flagged convoy but nowhere to go, except the inauguration of yet another extension to some housing scheme for army officers. He would stand at the head of every reception line ever organised for every second-rate dignitary visiting from every Third World country. Instead of running his intelligence agency he would be sitting at the head of an outfit as ceremonial as the crown of a fighting cock.

'This is life, Akhtar, the work will go on. I have asked General Beg to take charge for now.'

'I would like to request a proper handover . . .' General Akhtar made a last attempt to hold on to his safe houses, his tapes, his network of spies. Everything that gave him his powers was being taken away from him and he was being put behind a cage – a golden cage, but a cage nonetheless.

'You have earned it, Akhtar,' General Zia said. 'You have really earned the fourth star.'

CHAPTER 27

The Fort gates fly open, the jeep carrying us sails through the security cordons, salutes are offered and accepted. It's only when the driver asks my permission to turn on the radio that the facts of my new life begin to sink in: there are no blindfolds, no handcuffs, we are free and we have a week's leave pass before reporting back to the Academy. If this was the ending of *Where Eagles Dare* we would be reclining in our seats, lighting up cigars and chuckling over some predictable Nazi joke. But we are quiet; a pair of failed assassins, forgiven by the very person we set out to get. Petty deserters, a couple of kids admonished and sent home; not even worthy of being considered a threat to national security.

Our faces press against the windows of the jeep, looking out for the next milestone, examining the smoke coming out of the exhaust of overheated rickshaws, looking for objects to recognise. We are looking at the world like children on their first visit to the countryside; the khaki-covered seat between us stretches like the long list of our collective delusions.

'Are you hurting?' My attempt at starting a conversation is weak but spontaneous. I look out as I speak. A giant billboard featuring General Zia's picture bids us a safe journey.

'No, are you?' The jeeps smells of disinfectant and Burnol, the anti-burn ointment they put on Obaid's head.

The morning of our release the Fort had woken up in a fit of activity. A team of gardeners ran around with sprinklers, armed commandos were taking positions on the rooftop of the Palace of Mirrors. A three-star convoy came to a screeching halt on the main boulevard between the sprawling lawns.

Our saviour wears Ray-Bans and doesn't take them off as we are hauled before him. Major Kiyani and his reformed hoodlums are nowhere in sight.

General Beg talks like a man whom destiny has chosen to do makeovers. Everything about him is shiny, new, unruffled; his impatient hands scream new beginnings.

'My plane is waiting,' he says to a colonel who seems to be the new man in charge of the place, and who also seems to have more medals on his chest than brain cells. 'This place has been mismanaged badly,' General Beg says, which is not supposed to be an explanation directed at us but a general declaration about the state of the nation. 'You.' He points his finger at the Colonel's chest. General Beg has obviously seen too many baseball-coach-turns-nasty movies. 'You are going to clear it up. Do up the whole place. Get an architect to redesign it. Call in an interior decorator if you need to. This place needs a bit of atmosphere. At least open some parts of this thing to tourists. Why do you need the whole bloody Fort to run an investigation centre?' The Colonel takes notes like an apprentice secretary in desperate need of a permanent job. General Beg turns towards us.

'You guys are our future. You deserve better. You guys ended up here because of a bunch of inefficient idiots. All sorted now, all sorted. What a waste of time. I have to visit three cantonments today. I have my own plane waiting at the airport but still there are only so many hours in a day. Chief sends his good wishes. I'll have those files closed. Go back and work hard. Tomorrow's battles are won in today's drill practice. The country needs you.'

Just like that. The country suddenly needs us.

The driver of our jeep is a soldier in uniform and wants to know our destination. I know I can trust him. 'Where would you like to go today, sir?' he asks as the three-star convoy departs in a blaze of wailing sirens and commandos rushing down from the roofs. General Beg, it seems, doesn't want to stay away from his plane for too long.

There are no signs of the underground jails, the dark dungeons, the blood-splattered ceilings, the poetry in the stinking bathrooms. There is only the smell of freshly watered grass and history turning a new page.

'Out of here,' I say.

Obaid is slumped against the glass of his window. His nostrils twitch and he chews on his broken lips; he obviously doesn't like the Burnol smell that hangs heavy in the jeep. I rummage through my bag and offer him his bottle of Poison. He takes it with a wry smile and rolls it around in his hands as if it's not his favourite perfume bottle but a tennis ball that I have produced to distract him from our current situation.

We are like a couple who can't remember why they got together in the first place.

'Bannon,' he mumbles. 'Do you think they caught him?'

'Are you crazy?' I sneer at him and then control myself. I don't know why I feel I should sound polite and courteous and understanding. A newspaper hawker waves a paper at us, another picture of General Zia stares at me. 'Diplomatic immunity. They'd never touch him.'

'Do you think he is still at the Academy? After all this?'

'There is always some other job for an American. I wouldn't worry about him.'

'It was his idea,' Obaid says, as if we are returning from an abandoned picnic on a rainy day and blaming the weatherman.

'It was a fucked-up idea.' My irritation at his slow, measured sentences gets the better of me. I put my forehead on the glass window and stare at a group of people hanging on the back of a bus. A teenager offers me a mock salute, the man hanging beside him clutches at his crotch and offers to screw my mother. I don't know why Pakistanis are so passionate about men in uniform.

One of the fat Indian sisters is singing one of her sad love songs on the jeep cassette player.

'I like that song,' I shout at the driver. 'Can you turn it up?' The driver obliges.

'We are alive,' says Obaid. I turn round and look at his head covered in yellow paste. He is not in a state where I would want to start a discussion about what it means to be alive.

'So is General Zia,' I say.

But Secretary General is dead.

'That man who asked about your father, who was he? Did you know him?' Obaid's curiosity is casual. He's asking me if I had an OK time in the jail, if the food was decent, if I had interesting people to talk to.

'Have you heard of the All Pakistan Sweepers Union?'

Obaid stares at me as if I have learned to speak Greek during my short time in the prison. 'He was the Secretary General. We were neighbours. And he probably died thinking I killed him. He probably died thinking I was a bloody spy put in the dungeon by the army.'

'Why didn't he recognise you then? If you were his neighbour, I mean.'

'It's a long story. It doesn't matter now.' I reach across the seat and take his hand in mine.

'Good,' says Obaid, his lips giving the first hint of a smile. 'Don't go all sensitive on me. That's not the Shigri I know. Or did they manage to change you in a few days?'

I don't want to narrate my life-changing experience when I still don't know how and why has he come back from the dead.

'How far did you get?'

'Never took off.'

'Bastards,' I say.

'They were there. Before I could even get onto the runway.'

'Major Kiyani?' I ask and immediately feel stupid. 'Has to be him. How do you think he found out?'

'I thought about it. I knew you would think it was Bannon who told them, but why would he? He was the one who gave me the idea. And he is only a drill instructor.'

'He is quite an ideas man, isn't he? Specially for a drill instructor.'

Baby O believes life is a series of sweet coincidences. Like the poetry he reads, where random sentiments and metaphors walk hand in hand into the sunset while cause and consequence die a slow death on the pavement, like newborn bastard twins. I wish I could show him the world with Colonel Shigri's dead bulging eyes.

347

'Look, Ali.' When Obaid uses my first name, he is usually about to give me a lecture on the meaning of life, but there is none of the intensity that used to make his lectures such a joy to ignore. His voice comes out of an empty shell. 'I tried to do it because I didn't want to see you sticking your sword into him and then getting gunned down by his bodyguards in front of my eyes. I was scared. I wanted to do something.'

'You did it to save my ass? You just thought you would take off in a stolen plane, head for the Army House and they would all simply sit and monitor your progress? Do you even have any idea how many ack-ack guns there are around that bloody place? They probably shoot down stray crows over there.' I squeeze his hand to emphasise my point.

Obaid shudders. A whimper escapes his lips and I realise he is in pain. The buggers obviously didn't keep him in a VIP cell.

'You are still not listening to me, Shigri. I am not a kamikaze. You have all these expectations of your friends. You think I was going to do it for you? Sorry, I was just providing a diversion. I used your call sign, so that you couldn't carry out your silly plan. A sword, for God's sake. A sword?'

I squeeze his hand again. He whimpers loudly. The bandage slips. His thumb is covered in dried blood and the nail is gone.

Obaid wants to continue his explanation even though I have lost all my appetite for facts.

'I wasn't going anywhere. I was only interested in saving your life and so was Bannon.'

'I should have warned you about that double-dealing Yankee. I can't believe you trusted that dopehead instead of me.'

'It was a decent enough plan. Take off in an unauthorised plane, cause a security alert and the President's inspection is called off. And then at least I could talk to you. I would at least have the time to drill sense into your head.'

Thanks a bloody lot. Somebody's simple plan ruins your life's work and you are supposed to show gratitude.

'There is another way of looking at it, Baby O. You snitched on a friend, you almost got killed and you did it all to save General Zia's life.'

'No. Yours.' He closes his eyes. I think of telling him about Uncle Starchy's nectar, about the poetic patterns in my plan; maybe I should spell out the meaning of *sentiment du fer* for him, but one look at him and I know I shouldn't.

I take out the envelope that the blind woman gave me and start fanning his head. I don't know how it feels but if your skin has been burnt off with a Philips iron, it must hurt.

'Thank you for saving my life.'

'Do you think my hair will grow back?' asks Obaid.

The other fat Indian sister starts singing a new song. Something about a conversation going on for so long that it has become a rumour in the night. The envelope is addressed to the All Pakistan

349

Mango Farmers Cooperative. Probably Secretary General's last sermon to his lapsed fellow travellers.

'So what did you write in your state . . . ?' We both blurt out the same question at the same time, in the same words. Our questions collide in mid-air and the answer lies wriggling on the jeep floor like an insect trying to take off after breaking a wing.

What do you do when your only mission in life has failed?

You go back to where it all began.

'Have you ever been to Shigri Hill?' I tap the driver's shoulder. 'No? Take the next exit. I'll give you the directions. Stop if you see a post office. I need to mail a letter.' I turn towards Obaid. 'Asha or Lata?'

'Lata,' he says. 'The older one, the sad one.'

Let's take you home, Baby O.

CHAPTER 28

Shigri Hill is cloaked in mist. We shiver as the jeep deposits us at the beginning of the narrow pathway that leads up to the house. It's July and the plains have turned into God's frying pan but the air on the hill is thin and chilly. As Colonel Shigri used to say, it still carries an occasional message from Siberia. Shigri Hill might be a part of Pakistan but its climate has always been renegade; it's never shared the meteorological destiny of the plains. The Himalyan peaks surrounding the hill are covered in snow. K2 lords it over the mountains like a sullen white-haired matriarch. Grey transparent clouds float below in the valley. Overgrown almond trees rub shoulders with us as we make our way up to the house. Obaid is huffing with the effort of walking the steep climb to the house. 'Why didn't you people build a road here?' he asks, leaning against the slender trunk of an almond tree to catch his breath. 'Never had the time,' I say, holding his hand and moving on.

We take a sharp turn out of the almond tree grove and there it is, a wooden cottage with the pretensions of a summer palace, a house that nobody lives in. Sloping roofs perched on wooden arches, a long wooden balcony running along the side facing the valley. The lime-green paint has peeled itself over again and again during decades of neglect and now has settled into ghostly patches of turquoise. The house sits on the top of the mountain and from a distance it looks as if somebody stuck a doll's house on a ridge and forgot to play with it. Look at it up close and it seems sad and majestic at the same time, poised there in seclusion as if looking down on the world with contempt.

Obaid, who has never been to a hill station in his life, punches a passing cloud and breaks into a grin when his hand turns slightly moist.

The Burnol on his head has dried up and the burnt side of his scalp appears cobalt blue through the cracks. I wonder if it's the healing process or the beginning of an infection. Inside, the house is a glorious mess as if kids have had a non-stop party. Carpets are rolled up and thrown about, floorboards have been lifted and put back clumsily. We walk through heaps of clothes pulled out of cupboards and dumped in the corridors.

Those buggers didn't leave this place alone even after its occupants did. The only thing I am sure about is that they didn't find what they were looking for.

The main living room has a wall-to-wall glass window covered in drapes. I open the curtains and I can feel Obaid catching his breath at what he sees beyond the glass. The window opens on the ridge and the mountain falls away steeply. We are standing on the edge of the deep bowl of a lush green valley through which runs a silver snake of a river.

'Who built this place?'

'I don't know, my grandfather's father perhaps. It has always been here.'

'It's a shame that you're not interested in your family history,' says Obaid, then probably remembers my family history and doesn't wait for an answer. 'It's out of this world.' He stands with his nose to the glass.

We sit in front of the fireplace and look at the stars outside the windows. They hang low and burn bright. The mountains sleep like giants who have lost their way.

'The night is different here,' says Obaid.

'I know. It's very quiet. No traffic.'

'No. It arrives suddenly. Then it travels at a slow pace. It's like a boat that moves across the valley. Listen, you can hear it move, you can hear it row. The gentle splash of water . . .'

'That's the river below in the valley. It doesn't sleep at night. But I am sleepy,' I say.

The day arrives like somebody giving you a friendly thump on the shoulder. The sun is a mirror playing hide-and-seek with the snow-covered peaks; one moment a silver disc ablaze in its own white fire, the next moment veiled in a dark wisp of cloud.

Obaid stands in front of the window, contemplating a cloud that is gently nudging at the glass.

'Can I let it in? Can I?' Obaid asks me as if borrowing my favourite toy.

'Go ahead.'

He struggles with the window latches. By the time he slides the door open the cloud has dissolved into a puff, leaving behind a fine mist.

'What should we cook today?' Obaid shouts from the kitchen. It wouldn't have occurred to me but Obaid had bought a month's worth of groceries on our way here.

Colonel Shigri stays out of my dreams. Obaid doesn't ask me about his last night in the house. He doesn't ask me where and how I found him. I think he knows.

The study is unlocked but I stay away from it. Obaid wants to see the pictures. They are all there on the wall, all mixed up, out of order, as if Colonel Shigri's career progressed at random: General Akhtar and Colonel Shigri surrounded by Afghan mujahideen commanders with shawls and rocket launchers draped around their shoulders; Colonel Shigri with his bearded ISI officers in civvies holding the bits from the wreckage of a Soviet helicopter like trophies; Colonel Shigri with Bill Casey's arm around his shoulder, looking over the Khyber Pass. Then the earlier pictures: his fellow officers are thin, moustaches clipped, medals scarce and not a beard in sight.

'A comrade in uniform is potentially the deadweight that you'll have to carry one day.' Colonel Shigri had sipped slowly at his whisky, twelve hours before he was found hanging from the ceiling fan. He had returned from another of his duty trips with a coffin-sized Samsonite and was teaching me Pakistan's military history through its falling fitness standards. 'You owe it to your fellow soldiers to stay fit, to keep your weight down because one day you'll take a hit in battle and somebody will have to carry you on his back. That's what one soldier owes to another; the dignity of being carried back to one's own bunker even if near-dead. Hell, even if dead.' His voice rose and then he went quiet for a moment. 'But look at them now, look at their bloated bodies. Do you know why they let them-selves go?'

I stared at him. I stared at the suitcase and wondered what he had brought home this time.

'Because they know they are not going to be fighting battles any more. No, sir, they are drawing-room soldiers, sitting on their comfy sofas and getting fat. That is the first thing they think of – that they will never have to be in a battle again. But they also know in their heart of hearts that even if they were to end up in a battle, even if they got hit, nobody is going to carry them back to their bunkers. Do you understand?'

I didn't. 'Why wouldn't anyone carry them back?'

'Because they are too goddam fat to carry.'

I had carried Obaid on my back during our jungle survival course after a mock ambush. He dug his heels into my thighs, his arms around my neck kept getting tighter. I flung him down to the ground when he nibbled at my earlobe.

'Cadet Obaid. The first rule of survival is that you shall not screw your saviour.'

'Not even if it feels so good?' he had asked with his eyes half closed.

On our last night in the house Obaid discovers a half-empty bottle of Black Label in the kitchen. I stare at him. I don't tell him that I found the bottle in his study the morning the Colonel was found hanging from the ceiling fan.

We drink it with large quantities of water. 'It's very bitter,' says Obaid, pulling a face. 'Can I put some sugar in it?'

'That would be disgusting.'

He takes a sip, makes a face as if somebody has punched him in the stomach.

He likes it after the second glass. 'It doesn't taste that bad, actually,' he says. 'It's like drinking liquid fire.'

One more drink and there are tears in his eyes and truth on his drunk lips.

'I gave them your name. I told them about you. I told them you were practising with the sword.'

I take his hand into my hands. 'I would have done the same thing.'

I don't tell him that I *did* do the same thing.

'Why did they let you go then?' he mumbles.

'The same reason they let you go.'

Stars start to go out one by one as if God has decided to close His parlour for the night.

'They were never interested in what we were going to do and why. They just wanted our names on their files,' says Obaid, insightful like only a first-time drunk can be. 'We were General Akhtar's suspects, General Beg will find his own.'

'What if they actually liked my plan?' I say, draining the last dregs from the bottle. 'What if they just wanted to see if I could carry it out?'

'Are you saying that the people who are supposed to protect him are trying to kill him? Are they setting free people like us? Are you drunk? The army itself?'

'Who else can do it, Baby O? Do you think these bloody civilians can do it?'

Colonel Shigri had kept talking even after his sixth drink. I had tried to interrupt him in the middle of a long story about his latest trip behind the enemy lines in Afghanistan. He had asked me to start a fire in the living room but seemed to have forgotten about it. 'We don't have any ice.'

'Water would do,' he said and continued. 'There are people out there fighting the fight and there are people sitting here in Islamabad counting their money. People in uniform.' He paused for a moment and, through his bloodshot and blurry eyes, tried to focus on my face.

'You must think I am drunk.'

I looked at the glass in his hand and moved my

head in a half-hearted denial. How do you talk to someone who has only known you through your public-school report cards and suddenly wants to tell you their life story over a bottle of whisky?

He tried to hold my gaze, but his eyes were already drooping with the burden of honesty.

For the first and the last time in his life he talked to me about his day job.

'I had gone to pick up one of my officers, who'd lost a leg planting anti-personnel mines. Then I get this message that I should forget the officer and bring this thing back. This thing.' He pointed to the suitcase as if he had been ordered to carry a dead pig. 'Blast your way back, they told me.'

I think he noticed some interest in my eyes.

'I didn't kill anyone.' He looked at me and then laughed a slurred laugh. 'I mean this time. You know it's my job,' he shrugged. 'The thing about these Afghans is that they are not in it for the killing. They fight but they want to make sure that they are alive after the fighting is over. They are not in the business of killing. They are in the business of fighting. Americans are in it for winning. And us?'

He realised that he was going off on a tangent and mumbled something under his breath which sounded like 'pimps and prostitutes'.

'How is the fire, young man?' He was suddenly practical. Drunk practical. As if I had taken him for a drunkard and was trying to fool him.

'Let's go then, young man. Let's do our duty.'

358

He picked up his bottle of whisky and poured some into his glass with a tremulous hand. It sloshed, swirled and gurgled in the glass. At the door he turned back and said, 'Can you get my suitcase?'

By the time I dragged the suitcase to the living room, he was already sweating. The fire wasn't such a good idea. The sky was clear and our floating companions, the clouds, had gone back to Siberia or wherever they came from. Even the river down in the valley was silent.

Why do rivers decide to shut up on certain nights?

I dragged the suitcase into the middle of the room and fussed over the fire. The wood was dry, the weather was clear, we didn't need the bloody fire.

'I have saved a few lives in my time. Or I think I have. This whole bloody Afghan thing. I have done more than five hundred trips. All deniable missions. And now I end up with this.' He looked at the fire appreciatively. I looked at the suitcase.

My cheeks were glowing. The room was oven-hot.

'I took three days dragging this back,' he said, his voice full of remorse.

He stood up with his glass poised in front of his chest. He raised his glass to me and did a 360-degree turn. He seemed to be at a party that had gone on for too long but he was determined to get the last dance in.

'Open the suitcase,' he said.

Out of a very clear night sky a grey cloud, its edges bruised orange like a healing wound, appeared at the window as if Colonel Shigri had called in a witness.

I opened the suitcase. It was full of money. Dollars.

'This was my mission. To retrieve this money from someone who was dead. And I buried my man there and brought this here. Do I look like an accountant? Do I pimp my men for this?'

I looked at him. We held each other's gaze. I think for a moment he realised that he was talking to his son.

'Into the fire,' he said.

If I hadn't been so sleepy I might have tried to reason with him. I might have told him that whatever his ethics of war, the money wasn't his to burn. Instead I obliged. And soon started taking pleasure in watching hundreds of little dead American presidents, White Houses and *In God We Trust*s crumpling and turning into stashes of ash. I used both my hands and threw wads after wads of dollars into the fireplace. Soon the room was full of green smoke and twenty-five million dollars' worth of ash. I peeled off a bill from the last pile and slipped it into my pocket. Just to confirm in the morning that it wasn't a dream.

'Go to sleep, young man. I'll keep watch. I have asked them to come and collect their pimp money.' I looked at him and laughed. His face was covered with the soot flying around the room. He looked like a badly madeup black slave in a Bollywood film.

'Wash your face before you go to sleep,' he said. Those were his last words to me.

The rain rattles the window.

'Has the monsoon started?' Obaid asks, distracted by the sudden lashing of rain on the window.

'Monsoon is for you people in the plains. Here it's just rain. It comes and goes.'

THE MANGO PARTY

CHAPTER 29

The first of the monsoon winds caught the crow gorging on mustard flowers in a sea of exploding yellows in eastern Punjab, just on the wrong side of the Pakistani border. The crow had spent a good summer, grown fat and survived a number of ambushes by gangs of Brahminy kites which looked like eagles but behaved like vultures, ruled this area unchallenged in the summer and, despite their exalted name, showed no interest in the abundant vegetation, preying instead on common crows like this visitor from across the border. The crow obviously credited his own cunning for his survival but the curse that he carried was saving him for a purpose, for a death more dramatic than being eaten alive by a bunch of greedy kites with no respect for dietary rules.

One hundred and thirty miles away from the mustard field, in Cell 4 of the Lahore Fort, Blind Zainab folded her prayer mat and heard the rustle of a snake. It was a small snake, probably the size of her middle finger, but Zainab's ears instantly recognised its barely audible scurrying. She stood still for a second, then took off her slipper and

365

waited for the snake to move again. Keeping in mind a childhood superstition, she moved only when she was sure she could target it precisely. She brought the slipper down swiftly and, in three targeted strokes, killed it. Slipper still in hand, she stood still and her nostrils caught a whiff of the pummelled flesh. The dead snake's blood vapours floated in the dungeon air. Her headache returned with a vengeance, two invisible hammers beating at her temples with excruciating monotony. She reclined against the wall of her cell, threw her slipper away and cursed in a low voice. She cursed the man who had put her in this dark well, where she had nobody to talk to and was forced to kill invisible creatures to survive. 'May your blood turn to poison. May the worms eat your innards.' Blind Zainab pressed her temples with the palms of both her hands. Her whispered words travelled through the ancient air vents of the Fort and escaped into the tropical depression that had started over the Arabian Sea and was headed towards the western border.

The monsoon currents induced a certain restlessness in the crow and he took off, flying into the wind. The air was pregnant with moisture. The crow flew one whole day without stopping and didn't feel thirsty even once. He spent the night at a border checkpoint between India and Pakistan picking at a clay pot full of rice pudding that the soldiers had left outside in the open to cool down. The pot lay in a basket hanging from a washing line; he slept on the washing line with his beak stuck in the pudding. The next day the crow found himself flying over a barren patch, the monsoon wind turned out to be an empty promise. His mouth was parched. He flew slowly, looking for any signs of vegetation. The crow landed near an abandoned, dried-up well where he picked at a dead sparrow's rotting carcass. His lunch almost killed him. Dying of thirst and stomach pain, he took off on a tangent and followed the direction of the wind until he saw lights flickering in the distance and columns of smoke rising on the horizon. He tucked his left wing and then his right wing under his body by turns and flew like an injured but determined soldier. In the morning he reached his destination. The lights had disappeared and the sunrise brought with it the wonderful smell of rotting mangoes. He swooped over an orchard, then spotted a skittish little boy rushing out of a small mud hut with a catapult in his hand. Before the crow could take any evasive action, a pebble hit his tail, and he flew up to stay out of the boy's range. His restlessness was over. His crow instincts and his crow's fate combined to tell him that he must find a way to stay in this orchard.

The crow's fate was intertwined with that of one of the two big aluminium birds being put through the last maintenance checks in the hangar of the VIP Movement Squadron of the Pakistan Air Force, five hundred miles away. The engines had been tested, the fatigue profiles had been declared healthy, the backup systems checked for any malfunction. Both the C130 Hercules aircraft were healthy and superfit to fly. According to the standard presidential security procedures, however, the aircraft for General Zia's journey to attend a tank demonstration in Garrison 5, Bahawalpur, would not be chosen until a few hours before the flight. A fibreglass VIP pod, twelve feet long, was being put through a very strict hygiene regime by Warrant Officer Fayyaz personally. From the outside the pod looked like one of those shiny capsules that NASA launches into space. From the inside it looked like the compact office of a gangster. Warrant Officer Fayyaz dusted the beige leather sofas with its nova suede headrests and vacuumed the fluffy white carpet. He polished the empty aluminium bar and put a copy of the Quran in the drinks cabinet. It was mandatory for all vehicles and flights carrying the General to have a copy. Not that he recited it during his journeys. He believed that it added another invisible protect-ive layer to his elaborate security cordon. Now all Warrant Officer Fayyaz had to do was to put new air freshener in the air-conditioning duct and the pod would be ready. For security reasons the pod would not be fitted into one of the two planes till six hours before take-off. Only when this pod had been fitted into one of the two aircraft would it become the presidential plane. At this point it would automatically acquire the call sign Pak One.

Warrant Officer Fayyaz had a lot of time on his hands, enough to do a second round of dusting and polishing before he went to pick up the new air freshener from VIP Movement Squadron's supply officer, Major Kiyani.

The crow circled above the orchard, out of the range of the catapult, until the boy spotted a red-nosed parakeet and started to prepare an ambush. The crow swooped down and settled on the top branch of the tallest mango tree, hiding in the blackish-green branches, and picked at his first mango. As the smell had promised, the mango was overripe and dripping with sweet, sweet juices.

When I get the summons from the Commandant's office I am busy teaching a pair of my Silent Drill Squad members how to be an Indian; it involves completing a three-hundred-and-sixty-degree turn with their feet and head on the floor and their hands in the air. I caught them whispering during the silent drill practice and now I am administering a lesson on the virtues of silence. They are groaning like a bunch of pansies. Probably the Coke bottle tops that I put under their heads are causing some discomfort. If they thought I would come back tender-hearted from my tribulations, they have definitely revised their opinions by now. Bannon or no Bannon, the rules of the drill can't change. If they thought a few days in a jail could turn a soldier into a saint then they should try spending a week in the Fort. Only civilians learn their lessons behind bars, soldiers just soldier on. I put my half-smoked cigarette in the mouth of the one making the most noise, his hands flail in the air and his groans become louder as the smoke enters his nostrils. 'Learn some manners,' I tell him and start marching towards the Commandant's office.

The Commandant had accepted us back into the fold as if we were his errant sons. He walked into our dorm on the night we arrived from Shigri Hill and looked at us pensively from the doorway. Obaid and I stood to attention by our bedsides. 'I don't like it when my boys are taken away from me,' he said in a subdued voice, dripping with fatherly concern. As if we were not two just-out-of-the-dungeon prisoners but a pair of delinquents who had arrived home after lights-out time. 'As far as I am concerned and as far as the Academy is concerned you were away on a jungle survival course. Which is probably not very far from the truth.'

I have always found his Sandhurst brand of sentimentality sickening, but his words came out unclipped and unrehearsed as if he meant what he was saying. I didn't feel the usual nausea when he said things like putting it all behind us and drawing a line under the whole episode. He turned to go back and asked in a whisper, 'Is that clear?' We both shouted back at strength 5: YES, SIR.

He was startled out of his depression for a moment, smiled a proud smile and walked away.

'There goes another general wanting to play your daddy,' Obaid said bitterly, falling back on his bed.

'Jail has made you a cynic, Baby O. We are all one big family.'

'Yes,' he said, yawning and covering his face with a book. 'Big family. Big house. Nice dungeons.'

What could the Commandant possibly want from me now? A report on the progress of the Silent Drill Squad? Another lecture about jail being the university of life? Has someone from the squad been complaining about my new-found love for Coke bottle tops? I adjust my beret, straighten my collar, enter his office and offer an enthusiastic salute.

His reading glasses are on the tip of his nose and his two-fingered salute is even more cheerful than mine. There is a have-I-got-good-news vibe in his office. Has he got his third star? But he is beaming at *me*. I seem to be the source of his soaring spirits. He is making circles in the air with a paper in his hand and looking at me with eyes that say 'Guess what?'

'You must have made quite an impression on the big guys,' he says, a bit puzzled by whatever the paper has to say.

'"Silent Drill Squad is invited to perform after the tank demo at Garrison 5, Bahawalpur, on 17 August,"' he reads from the paper and looks up at me, expecting me to dance with joy.

What do I run? An elite drill squad or a touring bloody circus? Am I expected to go from cantonment to cantonment entertaining the troops? Where is Garrison 5 anyway?

'It's an honour, sir.'

'You don't know the half of it, young man. The President himself will be there, along with the US Ambassador. And if the Chief is going to be there, then you can expect all the top brass. You are right, young man. This is an honour and a half.'

I feel like the guy left for dead under a heap of bodies, who hears someone calling out his name. What are the chances of the rope snapping before your neck does? How many assassins get to have a second go?

'It's all because of your leadership, sir.'

He shrugs his shoulders and I immediately know that *he* hasn't been invited.

With that I realise for the first time that buried under the slick greying hair, privately tailored uniform and naked ambition, there is a man who believes that I have been wronged. He is on an epic guilt trip. Good to have suckers like him on my side but the only thing that is depressing about his ramrod posture, his shuffle towards me and the hands he places on my shoulders is that he means every word of what he is saying. He is proud of me. He wants me to go places where he himself would have liked to go.

I look over his shoulder towards the trophy cabinet. The bronze man has moved to the right.

His place is occupied by a paratrooper's statue. The parachute's canopy is a silver foil, the silver-threaded harnesses are attached to the torso of a man who is holding his ripcords and is looking up into the canopy. The temperature in the room suddenly drops as I read the inscription on the gleaming black wooden block on which the statue is mounted: *Brigadier TM Memorial Trophy for Paratroopers.*

'Go, get them, young man.' The Commandant's hands on my shoulders seem heavy and his voice reminds me of Colonel Shigri's whisky-soaked sermon. Once I am out of his office, I offer 2nd OIC an exaggerated salute and start running towards my dorm.

I know the phial is there, in my uniform maintenance kit, secure between the tube of brass shine and the boot polish, an innocuous-looking glass bottle. I know it's there because I have thought of throwing it away a number of times but haven't been able to do so. I know it's there because I look at it every morning. I need to go back and see it again, hold it in my hand and dip the tip of my sword in it. 'It ages very well.' I remember Uncle Starchy's low whisper. 'It becomes smoother, it spreads slower. But a poor man like me can't really afford to keep it for long.' I'll find out how well it has aged. I'll find out what hue it takes on the tip of my sword. I'll find out if the sentiment in my steel is still alive or dead.

Accidents in silent drill are rare but not unheard of.

CHAPTER 30

Genral Akhtar was scribbling on a paper with the intensity of a man who is absolutely sure about what he wants to say but can't get the tone right. His eyes kept glancing towards the green telephone, which he had placed right in front of him, in the middle of a small orchard of table flags representing his myriad responsibilities to the army, navy, air force and various paramilitary regiments. As the head of the Inter Services Intelligence he had never had to wait for a phone call, especially for information as trivial as this. But now, as the Chairman of the Joint Chiefs of Staff Committee, he presided over strategic reviews and inaugurated one army officers' housing project after another. Sometimes he found out about General Zia's movements from the newspapers. This irritated him, but he had learned to cultivate a studied lack of interest in intelligence matters: 'I am happy to serve my country in whatever capacity my Chief wants me to,' he said every time he happened to be around General Zia. The information he was waiting for was easy to get: there were two planes and only one VIP pod. All he wanted to know was which one of the two planes the fibreglass structure was going into, which one of the two planes would become Pak One. He tried not to think about it. He tried to concentrate on the last sentence of his address.

The speech was going to be simple. He would keep it short and punchy. He would not go into long-winded formalities like General Zia did – 'my brothers, and sisters and uncles and aunts'. His message would be short. In a mere ten lines, which would last no more than a minute and a half, he would change the course of history. 'My fellow countrymen. Our dear President's plane had an unfortunate accident in mid-air soon after taking off from an airfield in Bahawalpur . . .'

He read the sentence again. It did not seem very believable to him. There was something about it that didn't ring true. He should probably explain what had happened. A mechanical failure? He couldn't possibly say sabotage but he could hint at it. He crossed out the words *'had an unfortunate accident'* and replaced it with *'exploded'*. This sounds punchier, he thought. He added another sentence in the margin. '*We are surrounded by enemies who want to derail the country from the path of prosperity . . .*' He decided to stick with the *unfortunate accident* after all but added: '*The reasons for this tragic plane crash are not known. An inquiry has been ordered and the culprits, if any, will be brought to swift justice according to the law of this land.*'

375

He picked up the phone absent-mindedly. It was still working. He thought long and hard about the closing line of his speech. He needed something that would tie it all up, something original, something uplifting. There had been too much God-mongering under General Zia and he felt the Americans might like a nice secular gesture, something that would sound scholarly, reassuring and quotable. He was still divided between '*we as a front-line state against the rising tide of communism*' and '*we as a front-line state against the flood of communism*' when the phone rang. Without any preliminaries Major Kiyani read him a weather report. 'Two low-pressure zones that were gathering in the south are headed northwards. Delta One is definitely going to overtake Delta Two.' Instead of putting the phone down, General Akhtar pressed his forefinger on the cradle and went through a mental checklist, a list he had been through so many times that he felt that he could not be objective about it any more. He decided to go through it backwards.

9. Address to the nation: almost ready.
8. Black sherwani for the address to the nation: pressed and tried.
7. US reaction: predictable. Call Arnold Raphel and reassure him.
6. Where should I be when the news breaks: inaugurating the new Officers' Club in General Headquarters.
5. If Shigri boy has a go: problem solved

before take-off. If Shigri boy loses his marbles: the plan goes ahead.

4. The air freshener doesn't work: nothing happens.

3. The air freshener works: no survivors. NO AUTOPSIES.

2. Does he deserve to die? He has become an existential threat to the country.

1. Am I ready for the responsibility that Allah is about to bestow upon me?

General Akhtar shook his head slowly and dialled the number. Without any greetings he read out the weather report, then gave a pause and before replacing the receiver said in loud and clear voice. 'Lavender.'

He suddenly felt sleepy. He told himself that he would decide the last sentence of his speech in the morning. Maybe something would be revealed to him in his dreams. He looked into his wardrobe before going to bed and took a long look at the black sherwani in which he would appear before the nation tomorrow. His hope about figuring out the last sentence of his speech in his dreams turned out to be false. He slept the sleep of someone who knows he will wake up a king.

What woke him up was the red phone at his bedside, a call from General Zia. 'Brother Akhtar. Forgive me for bothering you so early but I am taking the most important decision of my life today and I want you to be here at my side. Join me on Pak One.'

The C130 carrying my Silent Drill Squad smells of animal piss and leaking aircraft fuel. My boys are sitting on the nylon-webbed seats facing each other with their legs stretched to preserve the starched creases of their uniforms. They are carrying their peaked caps in plastic bags to keep the golden-threaded air force insignia shiny. Obaid's head has been buried in a slim book since take-off. I glance at the cover; a bawdy illustration of a fat woman, part of the title is covered by Obaid's hand. '. . . *of a Death Foretold*' is all I can read.

'What is it?' I grab the book from him, go to the first page and read the first sentence.

'So does Nasr really die?'

'I think so.'

'It says so right here in the first sentence. Why keep reading it when you already know that the hero is going to die.'

'To see how he dies. What were his last words. That kind of thing.'

'You are a pervert, comrade.' I throw the book back at him.

'How about a rehearsal?' I shout above the din of the aeroplane.

My squad looks at me with weary eyes, Obaid curses under his breath. They line up sluggishly in the middle of the cabin. I can see their hearts are not in it. The smelly cabin of an aeroplane that has recently been used to transport sick animals, cruising at thirty thousand feet, is not the best setting for our elegant drill routine. But then the pursuit of perfection can't wait for the ideal environment.

We are in the middle of a rifle salute when the aeroplane hits turbulence. I stand and watch their reactions. Despite a sudden drop in altitude, followed by regular shuddering of the aircraft, my boys manage to hold onto their rifles and their positions. I bring the hilt of my sword to my lips, the tip of the sword is tinged a steel blue with Uncle Starchy's nectar. I put the sword back in the velvet-lined scabbard and watch them. The aeroplane goes into a thirty-degree turn and I am suddenly skidding towards my squad, trying to maintain my balance. Obaid puts his arm around my waist to steady me. The loadmaster shouts from the back of the plane. 'Sit down, please. Sit down. We are coming in for landing.'

The aeroplane starts to descend. My inner cadence tells me that my mission starts now. My poison-tipped sword tells me that it's ready.

An unmarked white Toyota Corolla started its journey from Rawalpindi with the intention of covering the 530-mile distance to Bahawalpur in five hours and thirty minutes. Those who encountered the car and its maniacal driver along the route were almost certain that the driver would not survive the next ten miles. The car ran over stray dogs and broke up cowherds making their way to the rubbish dumps in the suburbs. It zoomed through crowded city junctions, threatened and overtook the most macho of truck drivers. It didn't stop for children waiting at zebra crossings, it honked its horn at slow horsecarts, it swerved and dodged public transport buses, it threatened to run through railway crossings, it ran down footpaths when it couldn't find its way ahead on jammed roads, it was pursued in a futile chase by a road-tax inspector, it was sworn at by labourers repairing the roads, it stopped for re-fuelling at a petrol station and then took off without paying. The driver of the car was obviously in a hurry. Many of the people who saw the car whizz past were sure that the man driving it was suicidal. They were wrong.

Far from being suicidal, Major Kiyani was on a mission to save lives.

He had personally supervised the last dusting of the VIP pod and inserted the lavender air freshener in the air-conditioning duct. He was there when the pod was lifted by a crane, rolled into the C130's fuselage through its back ramp and fastened to the floor of the cabin by the air force technicians. He had to leave the VIP area and retreat to his office as General Zia's entourage started to arrive; in his new job he didn't have the security clearance to be around the red carpet.

It wasn't until Pak One had taken off from

Rawalpindi's military airport for Bahawalpur that Major Kiyani put his feet on the table, lit a Dunhill and casually glanced at the passenger list that had been left on his table before Pak One's take-off. His feet came off the table when he saw General Akhtar's name just below General Zia's. Like most veteran intelligence operators he believed that one should know only what one needs to know. Surely General Akhtar knew when to board Pak One and when to get off it; General Akhtar always knew the bigger picture. After eighteen names, starting with senior military ranks, he saw the first civilian name. Mr Arnold Raphel, the US Ambassador. He stood up from his seat. Why was the US Ambassador travelling on Pak One and not on his own Cessna?

Fear was Major Kiyani's stock-in-trade. He knew how to ration it to others and he knew how to guard against it. But the kind of fear he felt now was different. He sat down again. He lit another cigarette and then realised one was already smouldering in the ashtray. Was there anything that he had not understood about General Akhtar's instructions?

It took him another eight minutes and three Dunhills to realise that his options were limited. There were no phone calls he could make without bringing his own name onto the records forever, there were no security alerts he could issue without implicating himself. The only thing he could do was to be there physically before Pak

One took off for its return flight. He needed to get there and talk to General Zia before he stepped on that plane again. If General Akhtar was trying to play games with Pak One, it was a matter of internal security. But if General Akhtar was planning to bring down a plane with the US Ambassador on board then, surely, it was a threat to the nation's very survival and it was his duty to stop it from happening. Major Kiyani felt he was the only man standing between a peaceful August day and the beginning of the Third World War. He looked at the passenger list again and wondered who else was on the plane. Everybody, he thought, or maybe nobody.

The time to make educated guesses was long gone.

A quick look at the commercial flights schedule ruled out the possibility of catching a plane to a nearby city. He thought about making a few calls and getting an air force plane but that would require authorisation from a general and there was no way they would let him land at Bahawalpur. He picked up the keys to his Corolla and was barging towards the door when he looked at his watch. He realised that he would have to wear his uniform. No civilian could do that long a drive without being stopped a dozen times along the way. Then there was the problem of negotiating General Zia's security cordon. It couldn't be done without the uniform. He took out a uniform from the stationery cupboard. It was pressed and starched but covered in a thick layer of dust. He couldn't remember when he had last worn it. His khaki trousers were too stiff and impossibly tight around his waist. He left the zip button on his trousers open and covered this arrangement with his khaki shirt. He took out the dust-covered Oxford shoes from the cupboard but then realised that he was running out of time and nobody was going to see his feet in the car anyway. He decided to stick to his open-toed Peshawari slippers. He didn't forget to pick up his holster. He had one last look at himself in the mirror and was pleased to notice that despite the awkward fit of the uniform, despite the fact that his hair covered his ears, despite his Peshawari slippers, nobody could mistake him for anyone other than an army major in a hurry.

CHAPTER 31

General Zia was searching the sand dunes through his binoculars, waiting for the tank demonstration to start, when he saw the shadow of a bird moving across the shimmering expanse of sand. He raised his binoculars and searched for the bird, but the horizon was endlessly blank and blue except for the sun, a blazing silver disc lower than any celestial object should be. General Zia stood under a desert-camouflage tent flanked on one side by US Ambassador Arnold Raphel and on the other by the Vice Chief of the Army Staff, General Beg, with his new three-star general's epaulettes and tinted sunglasses. General Akhtar was standing a little further away, his binoculars still hanging around his neck, fidgeting with the mahogany baton that he had started to carry since his promotion. Behind them stood a row of two-star generals, Armoured Corps Formation commanders and battery-powered pedestal fans that were causing a mini-sandstorm without providing any relief from the August humidity. At least the tent did protect them against the sun, which beat down on the exercise area marked with red flags, turning it into a glimmering, still sea of sand. Holding to their eyes the leather-encased binoculars provided by the tank manufacturers, the generals saw the khaki barrel of an M1 Abram appear from behind a sand dune. The tank, General Zia noted with interest, had already been painted in the dull green colours of the Pakistan Army. Is it a free sample, he wondered, or has one of my eager generals in Defence Procurement already written the cheque?

The M1 Abram lowered its barrel to salute the General and kept it there as a mark of respect for the recitation from the Quran. The Armoured Corps' Religious Officer chose the General's favourite verse for these occasions: '*Hold Fast the Rope of Allah and Keep Your Horses Ready*'.

Lowering his binoculars, General Zia listened to the recitation with his eyes shut and tried to calculate the percentage of kickbacks. As soon as the recitation was over he turned to confer with General Beg about the mode of payment for these tanks. He saw his own distorted face in General Beg's sunglasses. General Zia couldn't remember Beg ever wearing these glasses before he appointed him his deputy and practically gave him the operational command of the army. When General Zia had gone to congratulate him on his first day in his new office, General Beg received him sporting these sunglasses even though it was a cloudy day in Islamabad; further proof, if proof was needed, that power corrupts. General Zia hated General

Beg's sunglasses but still hadn't found a way to broach the subject. It was probably a violation of the uniform code. What was worse, it made him look Western and vulgar, more like a Hollywood general than the Commander-in-Chief of the army of an Islamic republic. And General Zia couldn't look into his eyes.

General Akhtar saw them whispering to each other intensely and his resolve strengthened. As soon as the demonstration was over he would make an excuse and dash back to Islamabad in his own Cessna. General Zia seemed to have forgotten that he had invited his Chairman of the Joint Chiefs of Staff Committee. He didn't seem to remember that he wanted to consult 'Brother Akhtar' on the most important decision of his life. If this was a test, he had passed. Now he needed to be close to General Headquarters, close to the National Television Station, close to his black sherwani. He would need to address the nation in less than two hours. This unscheduled trip had added another layer of depth to his plan. Now nobody could say that he had deliberately stayed behind in Islamabad. They would say he was just lucky because he didn't stay for lunch at the garrison mess. In order to distract himself from the proceedings, he silently started to rehearse his address to the nation.

Listening to General Beg's long-winded reply about the payment for the tanks, General Zia made a mental note that after the tank trial he would settle this sunglasses business once and for all. General Beg was still going on about the direct link between the proposed tank deal and US military aid – all of it falling within the procurement objectives set in the US–Pakistan defence pact – when the first shot rang out.

General Zia terminated his conversation mid-sentence, put the binoculars to his eyes and searched the horizon. All he could see was a wall of sand. He tried to readjust his binoculars and as the sand began to settle he saw a red banner, the size of a single bed sheet, with a giant hammer and sickle painted on it, fluttering intact over a remote-controlled target-practice vehicle, like a golf cart carrying an advertising banner. The M1 Abram obviously couldn't see very well. He looked at Arnold Raphel who, with binoculars glued to his eyes, was still searching the horizon optimistically. General Zia wanted to make a joke about the tank being a communist sympathiser but the ambassador didn't look his way. Other target-practice vehicles started descending the sand dune, bearing other targets: a dummy Indian MiG fighter jet, a gun battery made out of wood and painted a garish pink, a cardboard bunker complete with dummy soldiers.

The M1 Abram's cannon fired nine more shells and managed to miss every single target. The tank turned towards the observers' tent, and lowered its barrel again, slowly, as if tired from all the effort. All the generals saluted, the ambassador put his right hand on his heart. The M1 Abram turned back and trundled up the sand dune. The remote-controlled target vehicles, with their dummy targets still intact, started to line up at the base of the sand dune. A gust of desert wind rose from behind the dune, a swirling column of sand danced its way towards the observers' tent, everybody about-faced and waited for it to pass. As they turned round, shaking the sand off their caps and flicking it off their uniforms, General Zia noticed that the red banner had come loose from its platform on the vehicle and was fluttering away, over the sand dune. Arnold Raphel spoke for the first time. 'Well, we got that one. Even if it wasn't our firepower but this anti-communist desert force.'

There was forced laughter followed by a moment of silence during which everyone heard the faint but unmistakable howling of the desert winds. General Beg took his sunglasses off with an exaggerated gesture. 'There is another trial left, sir,' he said, giving a dramatic pause. 'Lunch. And then the finest mangoes of the season.' He gestured towards an army truck full of wooden crates. 'A gift from All Pakistan Mango Farmers Cooperative. And for today's lunch, our host is the most respected Chairman of the Joint Chiefs of Staff Committee, General Akhtar.'

CHAPTER 32

The Martyrs' Boulevard dividing the freshly whitewashed garrison mess and the foot-ball-field-size lawns in front of it, is full of screaming sirens and Kalashnikov-carrying commandos jumping in and out of open-topped jeeps. Every general with more than two stars on his shoulders is escorted by his own set of bodyguards and heralded by his personal siren song, as if the occasion were not a lunch in their own dining hall but a gladiatorial parade where the one with the most ferocious bodyguards and the shrillest siren will win. The Garrison Commander's idea of a warm welcome seems to involve whitewashing everything in sight that doesn't move. The pebbled footpath on the lawns in front of the mess is white-washed, the wooden benches are painted white, the electricity and telephone polls are gleaming white, even the trunk of the lone keekar tree under which I have lined up my Silent Drill Squad is covered in a dull rustic white.

In this opera of wailing sirens and glinting Kalashnikovs, nobody seems to be bothered about a bunch of cadets at the edge of the boulevard.

My boys are slouching on their G3 rifles, trying to scratch their sweat-soaked bodies under starched khaki uniforms without being noticed. The Garrison Commander came to me soon after we disembarked from the truck, the enormity of the occasion seeming to overwhelm him. 'I know it's not a good time but General Akhtar asked for it,' he had said, gesturing towards my boys. 'Can you keep it short?' I gave him an understanding smile and said, 'Don't worry, sir. We won't be keeping him for long.'

The only person who is really pleased to see us is the bandmaster at the head of the military band formation, three rows of overdressed men lined up in the middle of the manicured lawn in front of the mess. After eyeing me for a while he marches up to me with his silver-crested stick, trailing a tartan doublet behind him, a fake red feather quivering in his beret. His face falls in disbelief when I tell him that we don't need the band to accompany us.

'How are you going to march without a beat?'

'Our drill is silent. It doesn't require music. And anyway, we are not going to march.'

'You can do it silently but your boys will need our drums to keep the timing. It'll add beauty to the drill.' Despite his feathers, tartan doublet and bonnet his face is absolutely dry. Not a single drop of sweat. I wonder how he manages that.

I shake my head. 'Just a rifle salute. With no commands,' I say, trying to reassure him. 'The President will take the salute. Meanwhile your men can rest.' He looks closely at my white-gloved hand upon my scabbard. He looks beyond me towards my boys who are wriggling their toes in their boots in an attempt to keep their blood circulation going, and shakes his head. He looks at me resentfully, as if I have made the whole silent drill thing up to put him out of business, then marches back and raises his stick in the air to signal to his band to start playing. They are probably the only lot more miserable than us, with their tartan shoulder drapes, fur-covered bagpipes and polished brass drums, so shiny you can't look at them without squinting. But they play on, defying the sun, despite the comings and goings of jittery commandos jumping in and out of the jeeps with their guns pointed at the empty horizon; they play on as if the whitewashed garrison mess with its whitewashed pebbles was the most appreciative audience they have ever found.

The hilt of my sword burns through my white glove. A fine layer of sand has settled on my shoes. I inspect the squad one last time. The boys are alert despite the sweat seeping from under their peaked caps and running down their cheeks. The wooden grips of their G3 rifles are probably melding into the flesh of their hands. We are under the shade of the keekar tree, but its whitewashed trunk doesn't change the fact that there are more thorns on it than leaves. Its shadow weaves a network of dried branches over a concrete floor marked with white lines for our drill movements.

Obaid winks upwards. I look to see if he is pointing at any approaching clouds. Nothing. All I can see is a crow perched on a branch dozing off with its beak tucked under its wings.

Inside the garrison mess the lunch awaits. The brigadiers and the generals have lined up in front of the mess entrance and their commandos have taken up positions on the roof of the surrounding buildings. The bandmaster is getting impatient with his men, his stick dances in the air, apparently asking them to play the same tune over and over again. He throws the stick in the air, catches it and gives me a triumphant look.

General Zia, it seems, is on his way.

I hear the wailing of the sirens before I see the two men on white Yamahas. They are wearing white helmets and ride parallel to each other. General Zia's convoy is probably behind them but all I can see is spiral after dancing spiral of sand; the storm seems to be chasing these motorcyclists. Oblivious to the whirlwinds that follow in their wake, they drive right up to the entrance of the garrison mess and execute a perfect split, both driving off in opposite directions, their sirens strangled in the middle of a high note.

The convoy of jeeps emerges slowly from the sand that is coming towards us in angry waves. First to arrive are open-topped jeeps with blaring sirens. The howling of the wind and the sirens compete with each other, the sirens dying down as the jeeps reach the entrance of the garrison mess. They deliver their gunmen and move to the car park. Behind the jeeps come two convertible black limousines; the commandos in them belong to a different breed. Wearing battle fatigues and crimson berets, they are not just sitting there cradling their guns; their Uzis are pointing outside, targeting us, the band, the swirling columns of sand. Behind them come three black Mercedes with tinted windows: the first one is flying a US and a Pakistani flag, the second one has a flag that carries the logos of all three armed forces and the third one a Pakistani flag on one side and the Chief of the Army's on the other. Through the tinted glass of the third Mercedes I catch a glimpse of big white teeth, a jet-black moustache and a hand that is waving to columns of sand dancing on the concrete. A matter of habit maybe, I tell myself, clutching the hilt of my sword. Suddenly it doesn't feel hot. Hell, it doesn't even feel like metal. It seems like an extension of my own hand. My own blood is flowing into the metal blade.

There is a moment of confusion at the entrance to the garrison mess. A white-turbaned waiter opens the door and for a second I suspect that the sandstorm might have convinced the General to cancel the drill, but the door closes again. I see a batch of commandos rushing towards us, followed by the three generals.

I have no business with the sidekicks.

The bandmaster's stick goes up in the air and the band starts to play a film song: *the weather has got other ideas today, the weather has got something else in its heart.* You have got to hand it to the bandmaster, I tell myself, the man knows his seasonal tunes. General Zia also seems to appreciate his taste in music. Instead of marching towards my squad, General Zia turns towards the band. The bandmaster's stick does frantic somersaults in the air before coming down and bringing the music to a stop.

General Zia pats the bandmaster on the shoulder while the other two stand back. His hands play an imaginary bagpipe, the bandmaster grins as if he has found the bagpipe player he always wanted on his team, the feather in his beret quivers with excitement, like the crown of a rooster who has just won the village beauty contest.

They are walking towards me now. General Beg, with his *Top Gun* Ray-Bans, on Zia's right side and General Akhtar two steps behind them. General Akhtar hits his baton on his leg with every step that he takes. He looks through me, betraying no recollection of our meeting over a dish of roasted quails. All I see of General Zia is a blur of big white teeth and a moustache so black that it looks fake. The hilt of my sword goes to my lips for the first salute and my squad comes to attention in unison. General Zia stands exactly five steps away from me, out of the reach of my sword. It's the regulation distance between the parade commander and the guy inspecting the parade. He returns me a limp-handed salute and then, violating all parade decorum, leans back and whispers so that the other two generals can hear him. 'When a son continues his father's good work, I become certain that Allah hasn't lost all hope in us sinners.'

'Permission to start the drill, sir?' I shout at strength 5. And suddenly, as if in respect for our drill display, the storm subsides; the wind quiets down to an occasional hiss, the sand particles, fine and scattered, are still flying in the air. In that moment, between me asking for permission and him nodding in approval, I take my first proper look at him. Instead of General Zia, he looks like his impersonator. He is much shorter than he appears on television, fatter than he seems in his official portraits. It looks like he is wearing a borrowed uniform. Everything from his peaked cap to the crossed sash across his chest is slightly ill-fitting, strangling his upper torso. There is a prominent grey mark on his forehead, probably the result of his five daily prayers. His sunken eyes are sending out mixed messages, one looking at me benevolently, the other looking beyond me at my squad with suspicion. There is a stillness about him as if he had all the time in the world for me. He opens his mouth and all I can think is that those teeth are not real.

'Please,' he says. 'In the name of Allah.'

I take one, two steps back, execute an about turn and as my right foot lands on the concrete, my squad comes to attention. Good start. My sword flashes in the air and finds its home in the scabbard. The hilt touches the mouth of the scabbard; my squad splits in two, marches ten steps in opposite directions and comes to a halt. I am in the middle of two rows when they turn round and march nine steps and stop. The file leaders on both sides extend their arms and throw the G3 rifles at me. My anticipating hands grab the rifles with a practised ease. I rotate them like spinning tops for exactly thirty turns and they go back to the safe and secure grip of the file leaders. The whole squad throws its rifles up in the air, with their bayonets pointing towards the sky, and catches them behind their shoulders.

I pull out my sword for the final inspection. My head is cleared of all distractions; I see everything with the dead bulging eyes of Colonel Shigri. I march towards General Zia with the sword parallel to my upper body. Halt. My squad divides itself into two files behind me. My sword hilt goes to my lips and comes down outwards. My arm is parallel to my body, the tip of my sword pointing to the ground between our feet. General Zia salutes. 'Silent Squad. Ready for inspection, sir.'

His left foot is hesitant but my left foot has already taken the first step for a slow march and he has no choice but to follow. Here we are at last, shoulder to shoulder, my sword stretched in front, his arms at his sides, slow-marching in step, about to enter the silent zone. Forty-five years of military service and he still doesn't have any control over his movements. If it weren't for my nimble footwork we'd be out of step. The Silent Squad is split in two files facing each other, eyeballs locked, rifles at the ready. I see his head jerk back involuntarily as the first set of rifles make a loop across our path. But now that he is in the middle of the tunnel formed by flying rifles he has no option but to move in step with me.

The most heavily protected man in the country is in a circle of whirling bayonets and inches away from the hungry, poisoned tip of my sword.

He has realised that in order to go through this he needs to keep looking ahead but he can't seem to help himself; I can feel his one eye glancing towards me. It's a genuine miracle that my boys haven't mistimed their throws and pierced our faces with their bayonets. The last pair is ready with their rifles poised when I wink at the boy on my left. I would never know but I can guess that exactly at the same moment General Zia's roving right eye makes contact with the boy standing on our right. They both miss a beat, the same bloody beat, and then throw their rifles. The bayonets flash through the air as the rifles complete half a circle and instead of gliding across each other clash in mid-air, making a momentary X as if posing to be photographed for a rifle regiment's badge. Shigri to the rescue then: my boot kicks General Zia in his shins, and as he stumbles backwards my left hand breaks his fall and my right hand goes to work; nothing spectacular, nothing that anyone would notice, just a gentle nudge with the tip of my sword on the back of his flailing hand, drawing a single drop of blood. It couldn't have hurt more than a mosquito bite. The reaction from the spectators – rushing jackboots, cocked rifles, commandos striking poses and the duty doctor shouting instructions at paramedics – is exaggerated, but not unexpected.

'If Allah wants to protect someone, nobody can harm them,' he says after the duty doctor has cleaned up the drop of blood and declared his wound a minor scratch. I try not to look at the commandos posted on the mess rooftop and shake my head in agreement. He produces a pocket watch out of his uniform shirt pocket and looks towards General Akhtar, who, it seems, is not reacting very well to the heat. Monster-shaped sweat patches are beginning to appear on his uniform. 'What do you think, Akhtar, shouldn't we pray before lunch?' He puts his arm around my shoulder and starts walking towards the mess without looking at General Akhtar. I notice that General Akhtar wants to say something. His mouth opens but no words come out and he follows us, almost dragging his feet. The American Ambassador steps forward. 'What a coincidence, Mr President. I have to attend prayers too. There is a church five miles from here and an orphanage that I am supposed to visit . . .'

'Oh. Of course. But you are coming back with

us. I am not leaving you in this desert. And since Brother Akhtar is here, let's finalise this tank business on our flight back.'

'I'll be here before take-off,' says Arnold Raphel. As he walks off towards the car park, a familiar face greets him. Bannon is wearing a suit and gives me a formal nod and waves his hand as if he remembers my face but has forgotten my name. I am glad he didn't show up during the drill. I needed my concentration. A team of commandos rushes off to accompany them.

A waiter wearing a white turban opens the door of the mess and ushers us into a world where the air is sand-free and chilled, where large glass cabinets hold tank models and tennis trophies, where the white walls are covered with paintings of turbaned horsemen chasing spotted deer. The garrison commander leads us towards a big white hall, muttering apologies that the new garrison mosque is still under construction. General Akhtar falls in step with me. I try to quicken my pace, hoping to avoid the inevitable arm around my shoulder. He puts his arm around my shoulder. 'That was very well done.' He sounds disappointed. Then he leans towards my ear and whispers, 'I told them to let you go, you know it was a mistake. By the way, you really know how to control that sword. It could have gone anywhere. Your father never knew when to stop.'

'It all comes with practice.' I give a pause and then say loudly, 'Sir.'

He takes his arm off my shoulder abruptly as if he doesn't want to be seen with me any more. Obaid might have told them about my sword practice but nobody in the whole world knows about Uncle Starchy's nectar.

My eyes track General Zia's feet for any signs. He is walking straight and steady as if his blood has never tasted the tip of my sword.

'Smooth and slow.' I remind myself of Uncle Starchy's promise.

We sit down in front of a water pipe fitted with a series of stainless-steel taps for our ablutions. My memory of how to do it is vague, so I glance around and do what everybody else is doing. Hands first, then water in the mouth thrice, left nostril, right nostril, splash water over the back of my ears. I keep glancing at General Zia. There is something mechanical about his movements. He takes water in his one cupped hand, pours it into the other, then lets it go before rubbing both his hands on his face. He is not actually using the water. I have a feeling that he is not even doing his ablutions, just miming them. By the time I finish, I have water splashes all over my uniform. The zeal of the occasional worshipper, I suppose.

During the prayer I am again glancing left and right to take my cue whether to go down on my knees or raise my hands to my ears. It seems a bit like cheating at the exam, but I hope the examiner here is more understanding. General Beg seems to think so because he has got his *Top Gun*

Ray-Bans on. What kind of person doesn't want God to look him in the eye while praying? Then I pull my thoughts together and start reciting the only prayer I know. The prayer I said at Colonel Shigri's funeral, the prayer for the dead.

CHAPTER 33

General Akhtar salutes with extra care, making sure that his palm is straight, his eyes level, his spine stretched, every muscle in his body throbbing with respect. That Shigri boy lost his marbles in the end but the plane General Zia is about to board has enough VX gas on it to wipe out a village.

General Zia is a dead man and dead men in uniform deserve respect.

Under any other circumstances General Akhtar would have walked with him, right up to the plane, waited for General Zia to climb up the stairs and for the aircraft door to shut before walking back on the red carpet. But the two hundred yards of red carpet that stretches between them and the plane is the distance he is determined not to cover. He has already changed his estimated time of arrival in Islamabad twice and now he needs to leave, right now, even at the risk of appearing abrupt, rude or disrespectful. He, after all, has a country to run.

General Zia, instead of returning his salute, moves forward and put his arms around General Akhtar's waist.

'Brother Akhtar, I want to tell you a story. I called you because I wanted to share this memory with you. When I was in high school my parents couldn't afford a bicycle for me. I had to get a ride from a boy in my neighbourhood. And look at us now.' He moves his arm in a half-circle, pointing at the C130 and the two small Cessna planes parked on the tarmac. 'We all travel in our own planes, even when we are going to the same place.'

'Allah has been kind to you,' General Akhtar says, forcing a smile. 'And you have been kind to me. To us.' He looks towards General Beg whose eyes are fixed on the horizon where a small air force fighter has just taken off on a reconnaissance sortie. The plane's mission is to search the surroundings for any natural hazards and act as a bogey target in case anyone in the area wants to take a pot shot at Pak One.

Five miles from where the generals stand, the crow hears the roar of an aeroplane approaching. Startled out of its full-stomached slumber, the crow flutters its wings in panic, then gets distracted by a mango rotting on the branch above him and decides to continue his nap for a little longer.

General Zia doesn't notice that General Akhtar is squirming in his grip, straining to get away. He continues his reminiscence. 'People always talk about the past, the good old days. Yes, those were good times, but even then there was nothing like a free ride. Every week my bicycle-owning neighbour would take me to a mango orchard near our school and wait outside while I climbed the boundary wall, went in and came back with stolen mangoes. I hope Allah has forgiven a child's indiscretions. Look at me now, brothers. Allah has brought me to a point where I have my own ride and my own mangoes gifted by my own people. So let's have a mango party on Pak One. Let's bring back the good old days.'

General Beg smiles for the first time. 'I am one of those unfortunate people whom Allah has not given the taste buds to enjoy the heavenly taste of mangoes. I am even allergic to the smell. But I hope you enjoy the party. There are twenty crates of them, you can take some for the First Lady as well.' He salutes and turns round to go.

'General Beg.' General Zia tries to muster up an authority that seems to be deserting him. General Beg turns back, his face patient and respectful, but his eyes hidden behind the mercury coating on his glasses. General Zia rubs his left eye and says, 'Something has got into my eye. Can I borrow your sunglasses?' General Zia has his eyes fixed on General Beg's face, waiting for the sunglasses to come off, waiting to get a good look into his eyes. He remembers the intelligence profile he had ordered before giving Beg his promotion. There was something about his taste for expensive perfumes, BMWs and Bertrand Russell. There was nothing about any allergies, nothing about mangoes and absolutely nothing about sunglasses.

Both of General Beg's hands move in unison. His left hand removes the sunglasses and offers them to General Zia, while his right hand goes into his shirt pocket, produces an identical pair and puts them on. In the moment that his eyes are naked, General Zia discovers what he already knows: General Beg is hiding something from him.

It is General Zia's right eye that reaches the verdict. His left eye is wandering beyond Beg, beyond the sword-wielding Shigri boy trying to suppress his grin (like father like son, General Zia thinks, no sense of occasion). In the distance the mirage of a man is running on the tarmac. The man is in uniform and he is charging towards them recklessly, breaking the security cordons, ignoring the commandos' shouts to halt, ignoring their cocked Kalashnikovs, oblivious to the confused snipers' itching forefingers. They would have shot him if he wasn't wearing his major's uniform and if he hadn't held his hands in the air to show his peaceful intentions. General Akhtar recognises him before anybody else and raises his hand to signal to the snipers to hold their fire. The snipers keep his legs and face in their cross hairs and wait for the mad Major to make any rash moves.

General Akhtar's relief is that of a man perched

on the gallows, the rope already around his neck and a black mask about to come down on his face, the hangman adjusting the lever while saying hangman's prayer; the man with the noose around his neck looks at the world one last time and sees a messenger on horseback in the distance, galloping towards the scene, flailing his hands in the air.

General Akhtar is relieved to see Major Kiyani.

General Akhtar isn't sure what message Major Kiyani might have brought, but he is relieved anyway. Just at the moment when he is about to give up praying for divine intervention, his own man has come to the rescue.

General Zia, still stunned at General Beg's smooth manoeuvre, still holding the sunglasses in his hand, gives only a casual look at the Major who has slowed down now and is approaching them like a marathon runner on his last lap. It is only when he stops a few feet away from them and salutes and General Zia, instead of hearing a solid thud of the military boot, hears the plopping sound of a Peshawari chappal striking the concrete that he looks at the Major's feet and says, 'Bloody hell, Major, why are you running around in your slippers?'

That would prove to be General Zia's last lucid thought, his last utterance that would make any sense to his fellow travellers on Pak One.

CHAPTER 34

You might have seen me on television after the crash. The clip is short and everything in it is sun-bleached and faded. It was pulled after the first few news bulletins because it seemed to be having an adverse impact on the nation's morale. You can't see it in the clip, but we are walking towards Pak One, which is parked behind the cameraman's back, still connected to generators and an auxiliary fuel pump, still surrounded by a group of alert commandos. Heat loops around its wings and fuel vapours are rising in whirlpools of white smoke. It looks like a beached whale, grey and alive, contemplating how to drag itself back to the sea. You can see General Zia's flashing white teeth in the clip but you can tell immediately that he is not smiling. If you watch closely you can probably tell that he is in some discomfort. He is walking the walk of a constipated man. General Akhtar's lips are pinched, and even though the sun has boiled everything into submission and drained all colour out of the surroundings you can see that his usually pale skin has turned a wet yellow. He is dragging his feet.

407

General Beg is inscrutable behind his sunglasses, but when he salutes and departs, his pace is brisk. He walks like someone who knows where he is going and why. You can see me only for a few seconds behind them, my head rising above their shoulders, and if you look really closely you can see that I am the only one with a smile on his face, probably the only one looking forward to the journey. My squad has already flown back on another C130 with their packed lunch of roast chicken and soft buns. I have been invited onto Pak One for a mango party. I hate mangoes but I'll eat a few if I can see Colonel Shigri's killer foaming at the mouth and gasping for his last breath.

The clip also doesn't show that when I salute General Zia and start walking towards Pak One, my smile vanishes. I know I am saluting a dead man but that doesn't change anything. If you are in uniform you salute; that is all there is to it.

CHAPTER 35

The telephone logs kept at Langley's Ops Room would later reveal that the early shift on the South Asia Desk logged one hundred and twelve calls in an attempt to locate the US Ambassador to Pakistan, Arnold Raphel. The search for Arnold Raphel was triggered by a tip-off that the local CIA chief received from a major in the Pakistan Army; there are too many mangoes on Pak One and the air conditioning might not work. Chuck Coogan did not have the patience or the time to work with culture-specific codes. He informed Langley and when the duty analyst told him that they had intercepted a message from a Pakistani general about Pak One and mangoes, Chuck got worried. 'Let's keep the ambassador off that plane.' Chuck Coogan made a mental note to include a paragraph about the breakdown of the chain of command in the Pakistan Army in his monthly debrief and started working the phone.

The calls were routed through the South-East Asia Bureau in Hong Kong, through the Islamabad Embassy and finally through the liaison office in Peshawar. In a last desperate attempt, a communication satellite was ordered to change its orbit to get a bearing on his satellite phone receiver. The logbook wouldn't mention the reason for this urgency. The logbook wouldn't say that Arnold Raphel had decided to visit an orphanage associated with a local church in an attempt to not get stuck with General Zia, to avoid the embarrassing post-mortem on the M1 Abram's performance.

The satellite receiver, a clunky silver contraption cased in a hard plastic box, is switched off and stashed under the back seat of the ambassador's black Mercedes. The Mercedes is parked in the brick-lined courtyard of a Catholic church under construction. The scaffolding has been covered with white plastic sheets for the ambassador's visit, the emblem of the Carmelite sisters, with its three stars and a silver cross, hangs limp from the mast on the roof of the church. Behind the Mercedes, the commandos from the Pakistan Army are stretching their limbs in the open-topped jeeps, cooling down under the scarce shade of date trees and listening to the strains of music coming through the church door.

Arnold Raphel is inside the low-ceilinged hall, sitting on the front bench surrounded by barefoot nuns, listening to the strangest choir of his life. There is a man on the harmonium and a twelve-year-old boy sits besides him playing the tabla. *'In the school of the crucified one, in the school of the*

410

crucified one,' sings the man playing the harmonium, and a choir of well-scrubbed children wearing khaki shorts and white half-sleeved shirts stretch their arms out and tilt their heads towards the right to mime the crucified one. The ceiling fan, the iced Coke, the sound of proper American English in this remote desert village, lulls Arnold Raphel, a strange calm descends on him and for a few moments he forgets about the awful tank trial and about his impending return journey with General Zia. This is not the kind of church he occasionally visited in a Washington DC suburb. There is incense on the altar, and the nuns smile at him extravagantly. A plump Jesus painted on a backdrop in various shades of gold and pink, with a marigold garland around his neck, looks down on the congregation with his kohl-lined eyes. '*You don't pay any fees, you don't pay any fees.*' Arnold Raphel bends forward to hear the nun's whisper who is translating the hymn for him. '*You don't pay any fees, in the school of the crucified one.*' His eyes are transfixed by the nun's bare feet. There are rows and rows of delicate crosses on both her feet, tattooed with henna. A smile plays on Arnold Raphel's face and he decides to stay on till the end of the service. General Zia can have his own goddam mango party on Pak One, he thinks, I should go back on my own Cessna. '*You have to pay with your head, you have to pay with your head, on the chopping board.*' The orphans cut their throats with imaginary swords and the chorus sings on.

'In the school of the crucified one. In the school of the crucified one.'

The chief communication officer in Langley throws his hands up in the air and reports that the ambassador is probably having a very long siesta. 'Pak One has got clearance to taxi. It is taking off within minutes,' reports the communication satellite picking up the air traffic control's calls from the garrison. The duty analyst at the South Asia Desk looks at all the calls logged in his register, starting with the first call made by a general with the unlikely name of Beg who had pleaded that the US Ambassador shouldn't join the mango party on Pak One and decides that there is no need to pursue the matter any further.

Trust these Pakistani generals to get excited about a goddam smelly fruit, he tells his colleagues, clocking off his shift.

CHAPTER 36

Major Kiyani looks down at his slippers and for a moment forgets why he isn't wearing his military boots. His head feels dizzy as if he has just come off a roller coaster. He sucks in air with the lust of a dying fish. Throughout the entire five-hundred-and-thirty-mile drive he has rehearsed one sentence: 'It's a matter of life and death, sir, it's a matter of life and death, sir.' He looks around. Arnold Raphel is nowhere in sight. There is not a single American on the tarmac. General Akhtar looks at him with pleading eyes, imploring him to say God knows what. Major Kiyani suddenly feels that he should salute, walk back to his car, drive back to his office, at a reasonable speed this time, and resume his duties. But he can feel the snipers' guns pointed at the back of his head and two pairs of very curious eyes inspecting his face, waiting for an explanation. A matter of life and death, sir, he says quietly once again to himself, but then between gulping a few more cubic feet of oxygen blurts: 'It's a matter of national security, sir.'

A dark shadow falls across General Akhtar's

tense, yellow face. He wants to shoot Major Kiyani in the head, board his Cessna and fly back to Islamabad. He expects his men to take decisive action, to cover his flanks in battle, to provide him an exit when he needs one, not behave like pansies discussing national security.

He sucks in his thin lips and holds on to his baton tightly. Suddenly Major Kiyani seems to him not the rescuer on horseback waving the irrefutable proof of his innocence, but the Angel of Death himself.

General Zia's eyes light up, he punches the air with his clinched fist and shouts: 'By jingo, let's suck the national security. We've got twenty crates. General Akhtar, here my brother, my comrade, we are going to have a feast on the plane.' He puts one arm around General Akhtar's waist, the other around Major Kiyani's and starts walking towards Pak One.

General Zia is feeling safe surrounded by these two professionals but his mind is racing ahead. A jumble of images and words and forgotten tastes are coming back to him. He wishes he could speak as fast as his mind is working but he can't arrange his words properly. By jingo, he thinks, we will get rid of that bastard with sunglasses; we'll hang him by the barrel of Abram One and fire the gun. We'll see how Abram One misses that one. He laughs out loud at that thought. 'We'll buy those tanks. We need those tanks,' he says to Arnold Raphel and then realises that the ambassador isn't at his side.

'Where is Brother Raphel?' he shouts. General Akhtar sees his opportunity and squirms in General Zia's grip. 'I'll go and look for him.' General Zia tightens his arm around General Akhtar's waist, looks into his eyes and says in a spurned lover's voice. 'You don't want to suck national security with me? You can slice it with a knife and eat it like those city begums. You can have it anyway you want, brother. We have got twenty crates of the finest national security gifted by our own people.'

General Zia approaches the red carpet and a dozen generals line up to salute him. As their hands reach their eyebrows, General Zia winces and instead of returning their salute inspects their faces. General Zia wonders what they are thinking. He wants to ask them about their wives and children, to start a conversation to get an insight into his commanders' thinking but he ends up issuing an invitation that sounds like an order. 'The party is on the plane.' He points his finger at Pak One. 'All aboard, gentlemen. All aboard. By jingo, let's get this party started.'

It is at this point, taking his first step on the red carpet and chaperoning a dozen confused generals towards Pak One that General Zia feels the first pang of an intense, dry pain in his lower abdomen.

The army of tapeworms, sensing a sudden surge in his blood circulation, begins to wake from their slumber. The tapeworms feel ravenous. A tapeworm's average age is seven years and it spends its entire life searching for and consuming food. The life cycle of this generation begins on a very lucky note. Climbing up from his rectum, they attack the liver first. They find it healthy and clean, the liver of a man who has not touched a drop of alcohol in twenty years and has quit smoking nine years earlier. His innards taste like the innards of a man who has had food tasters taste every morsel that he ate for an entire decade. Having worked through his liver, the army starts to make a tunnel in his oesophagus and keeps moving up and up.

Their seven-year life cycle would be cut down to twenty minutes, but while they were alive, they would eat well.

CHAPTER 37

Pak One is a palace compared to the C130 that flew us here. It's got air conditioning. The floor smells of lemony disinfectants. We are sitting behind the VIP pod, in proper seats with armrests. There is even a waiter in a white turban offering us iced Coca-Cola in plastic glasses. This is the good life, I tell myself. I am poking Obaid in his ribs with my elbow, trying to point towards the cargo lift that's depositing a stack of crates through the plane's ramp. Obaid has got his nose buried in the book. He doesn't even glance towards me. Warrant Officer Fayyaz's bald head appears from behind the stack of wooden crates. Elaborate messages have been stencilled in blue ink on the crates. '*The mangoes that we present you are not just seasonal fruits, they are tokens of our love, a sign of our devotion.*' All Pakistan Mango Farmers Cooperative is stencilled in bold letters on all the crates. Secretary General's fellow travellers are still playing their double game. Warrant Officer Fayyaz secures the crates to the floor of the plane with a plastic belt and gives the belt a forceful shake to see if it is secure. It is.

As the ramp door on the aircraft comes up and creaks shut, the cabin is suddenly full of the overwhelming smell of mangoes. One mango's smell is nice, the smell of a tonne of them can induce nausea. Fayyaz looks through me as if he had never tried to molest me. Major Kiyani is standing with his back reclined against the VIP pod as if he expects to be invited in at any time. He seems straitjacketed in a uniform a size too small. I give Obaid another nudge in the ribs. 'Look at his feet.' Obaid glances at him impatiently. 'He is wearing slippers. So? At least he has started wearing a uniform. One thing at a time.' He buries his nose in his book again. Major Kiyani comes towards me and stares at my face as if he has suddenly remembered that he has seen me somewhere but doesn't quite know what to say to me. I vacate my seat. 'Sir, why don't you sit here?' He almost falls into the seat as if his knees have refused to carry his weight. Warrant Officer Fayyaz shouts from behind the mango crates. 'I'll have to offload you, Under Officer. We are not allowed to carry standing passengers on Pak One.' I have half a mind to squash his head with a mango crate, but two bearded commandos manning the C130 door are already looking at me suspiciously. 'Let's go, Obaid,' I say, moving towards the door without looking at him, feeling as if I have been ejected from my ringside seat at General Zia's deathbed. From the door I look back and Obaid waves his book towards me and

418

at the same time mouths what to me sounds like: 'I am about to finish.'

I give him a scornful look, nod towards Major Kiyani who has slumped in his chair with his eyes closed, tip my peaked cap to the commandos on the door and shout, 'Enjoy your VVIP flight.'

'Brother Raphel, you have not had lunch with us,' General Zia says in a complaining voice and takes Arnold Raphel's hand in both his hands and starts walking towards Pak One. 'I know you were taking a siesta with Jesus and Mary.' General Zia puts an arm around his waist and lowers his voice to a whisper. 'Now we must put our heads together and suck national security.' Arnold Raphel, still reeling from his spiritual encounter with the Carmelite sisters and their singing orphans, thinks General Zia is cracking a joke.

Arnold Raphel looks towards his Cessna, his mind races through a list of excuses, but by the time he reaches something starting with Nancy, General Zia's arm is around his waist and he is marching him up the ladder into Pak One.

General Akhtar buries his face in his hands and looks down through his fingers at the fluffy white carpet on the floor of the VIP pod. He notices a thin streak of blood crawling towards him. He traces it to its source and sees that General Zia's shiny oxfords are oozing blackish red blood. He panics and looks at his own shoes. They are spotless.

Suddenly a ray of hope, faint but a ray of hope nonetheless, penetrates the doom engulfing his soul. Maybe the Shigri boy has inflicted an inner wound and Zia is bleeding to death. Maybe the plane will get to Islamabad safely. Maybe he'll have to rewrite his speech, just changing the lines about *an unfortunate accident* to *President's sudden demise*. Would he be ready to take over the country if the plane makes it to Islamabad? General Akhtar suddenly remembers a long-forgotten prayer from his childhood and starts to mutter it. Then halfway through his prayer, he changes his mind and lunges towards the VIP pod's door. 'Major Kiyani, tell the crew to keep the air conditoning off, the President is not feeling too well.'

'By jingo, I am dandy,' General Zia protests, then looks down at the puddle of blood around his shoes on the carpet, but like a junkie in denial, he refuses to make a connection between the grinding pain in his abdomen, the fluid trickling down his pants and the streak of blackish-red blood on the carpet. He decides he needs to change the subject. He wants to take the conversation to a higher level so that nobody would notice the blood on the floor. He knows that the only person he can rely on is Arnold Raphel.

The C130's doors secured, the pilot move his throttles forward and the four propellers start picking up speed. General Zia looks towards Arnold Raphel and says to him in a pleading voice, 'We'll buy those tanks. What a sensitive machine have you built. But first, tell me how will history remember me.' The voices in the VIP pod are being drowned out by the din of the aeroplane. Arnold Raphel thinks General Zia is asking him about the target sensors on the Abram One tank. Arnold Raphel, Carmelite orphans' hymns still ringing in his head, loses his cool for a moment and gives the first and the last undiplomatic statement of his life. 'No, Mr President, they are as useless as tits on a boar.'

General Zia can't believe what Arnold Raphel just said: the world would remember him as a bit of a bore.

In a moment of panic General Zia feels that he must rectify this historical misconception. There is no way he was going to go down in the textbooks as the President who ruled this country of one hundred and thirty million people for eleven years, laid the foundations of the first modern Islamic state, brought about the end of communism but was a bit of a bore. He must tell them a joke, he decides. Hundreds of hilarious one-liners that he has tested in his cabinet meetings run through his mind and blur into one endless cosmic joke. He rehearses one in his head. He knows that jokes are all about timing. 'What did the seventy houris say when they were told that they would spend the eternity with General Zia in paradise?' He can't remember the houris' exact words. There was something about being condemned to hell for eternity but it's dangerous to tell a joke if you can't get your punchline right. Then a flash of genius. He must tell a family joke. He wants to be remembered as a witty man. But he also wants to be remembered as a family man.

'Because the First Lady thinks he is too busy screwing the nation,' he says jumping in his seat. It is only when nobody around him laughs that he realises he has blurted out the punchline and now can't remember the rest of the joke. He yearns for a moment of lucidity, a flash of clarity that would cut through the muddle that is his mind. He looks around at the wretched faces, and realises that he will not remember this joke. Ever.

He turns to General Akhtar in an attempt to preserve his legacy and keep the conversation going. 'How do you think, Brother Akhtar, history will remember me?' General Akhtar is pale as death. His thin lips are muttering all the prayers he can remember, his heart has long stopped beating and his underpants are soaked in cold sweat. Most people faced with certain death can probably say a thing or two they have always wanted to say, but not General Akhtar. A lifetime of military discipline and his natural instinct for sucking up to his superiors overcome the fear of death and with shivering hands and quivering lips General Akhtar tells the last lie of his life. 'As a good Muslim and a great leader,' he says, then takes out a crisp white handkerchief from his pocket and covers his nose.

★   ★   ★

As I watch them gather on the red carpet near the ladder up to the C130, I begin to wonder if I should have trusted Uncle Starchy's folksy pharmacology. General Zia is still standing on his feet with his one arm around General Akhtar's waist. They look like lovers who don't want to let go of each other. Maybe I should have thrust the blade in the back of his neck when I had him at the tip of my sword. Too late now. I am already strapped in a seat in General Beg's plane. He offered me a lift after I was offloaded from Pak One. Our Cessna – his Cessna – waits on the tarmac for Pak One to take off. Protocol demands that Pak One should leave the runway first.

'Good to see you, young man.' He waves his peaked cap at me. He opens a fat book with a fat man on its cover and starts flicking through the pages. *Iacocca: An Autobiography* reads the title. 'Lots of work to do.' He nods towards the pilot.

What's with books and soldiers? I wonder. The whole bloody army is turning into pansy intellectuals.

I look out of the window as the American Ambassador walks up to General Zia; double handshakes, hugs as if the General is not meeting the ambassador after two hours but has found his long-lost sibling. General Zia's grin widens, his teeth flash and his other arm wraps itself around the ambassador's waist. Bannon is in his suit, standing behind them, puffing nervously on a cigarette. There is an air of important men sharing a joke, spreading goodwill. It's only when they start climbing the stairs that I realise that General Zia is dragging his feet. He is almost hanging onto the shoulders of the two men flanking him. 'The elephant will dance, the elephant will drag his feet, the elephant will drop dead.' Uncle Starchy had given me a step-by-step guide to the effects of his nectar.

If I hadn't been sitting on that plane I would have flung my peaked cap in the air and shouted three cheers for Uncle Starchy.

General Beg notices the grin on my face and wants to take the credit. 'You have come a long way, my boy. From that horrible Fortress to my plane; imagine the journey. Managing an army is not very different from managing a corporation.' He caresses fat Iacocca's face. 'Treat your people well, kill the competition and motivate, motivate, motivate.' He pauses for a moment, savouring his own eloquence. 'My plane will take us to Islamabad.' He turns towards the pilot. 'My plane could drop you at the Academy but I think it's better that you take a jeep from there. I have to attend to some important business in Islamabad. I need to be in Islamabad.' He taps the pilot's shoulder. 'When will my plane reach Islamabad?'

If Uncle Starchy's nectar works as he promised, by tonight this man will become the chief of what *Reader's Digest* has described as the largest and the most professional Muslim army in the entire world, and with some creative interpretation of the constitution, may even be the President of the country.

Pity the nation.

Pak One begins to taxi and General Zia puts both his thumbs in his safety belt and surveys his companions. His pain has subsided for the moment. He is satisfied by what he sees. He has got them all here. All his top generals are here except the one with the sunglasses who got away. His heart skips a beat when he remembers the look in General Beg's eyes. Shifty bastard, must be taught a lesson. Maybe I should make him an ambassador to Moscow and see how he wears his sunglasses there. He takes another look around and reassures himself that everyone who matters is here, even Brother Akhtar who seems to be sweating yellow sweat. And most important of all, Arnold Raphel and the CIA type who hangs around with the ambassador. Who in their right mind would think of killing the US Ambassador? Good, he thinks. All my friends are here. I have got them all. There is strength in numbers. If someone wants to kill me, he must be here too. We will all go down together.

But why would anyone want to kill me? All I am doing is having a little mango party on the plane. Is that a sin? No. It's not a sin. Did Allah ever forbid us from sucking national security? No. But let's say a prayer anyway. He starts to recite Jonah's prayer but does not recognise the words

425

that come out: '*My dear countrymen, you are cursed, you have worms . . .*' He has practised the prayer every night. A prayer and you are absolved. One moment you are in a whale's belly, in the depth of darkness, and the next moment you are thrown into the world, alive. Like being born again. He tries again; he opens his mouth and a guttural noise comes out. He looks around in panic and wonders if they can tell that he has forgotten all his prayers. He wants to shout and correct them because he has not forgotten any prayers, he remembers them all; it's just this terrible pain in his guts that is wiping out his memory. He thinks maybe he should pray for the others. Allah likes it when you pray for the others. In fact, it is better than praying for yourself. He surveys the faces in the VIP pod and lifts his hands to pray for them.

'Motherfuckers,' he shouts.

They all look at him as if he is an irritating child and the only way to deal with him is to ignore him.

Pak One lines up in the middle of the runway and the propellers begin to pick up speed. The pilots, already beginning to sweat and fanning themselves with their folded maps, go through the final checks. The air traffic controller respectfully gives clearance for take off. Outside the VIP pod, in the back of the plane, Major Kiyani opens another button on his trousers and starts to breathe easy. It's all going to be OK, he tells himself. General Akhtar always has a plan B and plan C.

He has carried out his orders. The air conditioning will not be turned on. 'General Akhtar's orders,' he has told the pilots. He is already feeling better. General Akhtar knows how this world works. General Akhtar also knows at what temperature the world works best. Warrant Officer Fayyaz sits down with the cadet absorbed in reading a book and rubs his thigh with his own; the cadet doesn't even notice.

Inside the VIP pod General Akhtar shifts in his seat and tells himself that all his life he has waited for this moment and even now, if he can find a good enough excuse to get off the plane, he can fulfil his destiny. The man who has spent a decade creating epic lies and having a nation of one hundred and thirty million people believe them, the man who has waged epic psychological battles against countries much bigger, the man who credits himself for bringing the Kremlin down on its knees, is stuck for an idea. He knows the air conditioning is off but does anyone really know how an air freshener works?

He thinks hard, raises his hand in the air and says, 'I need to go to the loo.' And Bannon, of all people, a lowly lieutenant, puts his hand on his thigh and says, 'General, maybe you should wait for this bird to take off.'

Ambassador Raphel thinks that he'll put in a request for transfer to a South American country and start a family.

★   ★   ★

One and a half miles away, in a sleepy mango orchard, perched behind the dust-covered dark green leaves, the crow flutters its wings and starts flying towards the roaring noise generated by the four fifteen-hundred horsepower engines of Pak One which is leaving the runway, never to touch down again.

Our Cessna starts to taxi towards the runway as soon as the presidential plane gets airborne. The climb is steep for an aircraft of this size. Pak One seems to struggle against gravity but its four engines roar and it lifts off, like a whale going up for air. It climbs sluggishly but clears the runway and turns right, still climbing.

Our own take-off is noisy but smooth. The Cessna leaves the runway lightly and takes to the air as if it were its natural habitat. General Beg is absorbed in reading his book with his Ray-Bans perched on the tip of his nose. The pilot notices that I am plugging my ears with my fingers and passes me a set of headphones and forgets to unplug them. I can listen in on his conversation with the tower as well as the tower's calls to Pak One.

'Pak One setting course for Islamabad.'

'Roger,' the air traffic controller says.

'Clearing runway. Turning right.'

'*Allah hafiz*. Happy landings.'

So absorbed am I in their inane exchange that I get a real jolt when our Cessna drops suddenly.

It recovers quickly and starts climbing again. General Beg's hands are in the air. 'A bloody crow. It came at my plane. Did you see it? Can you imagine there are crows flying around when we have cleared the whole area of all possible hazards. Crows in the Code Red Zone. Whoever heard of that? It's thanks to my pilot here that we are still alive.' The pilot gives us a thumbs-up sign without looking back.

'Bird shooters,' says General Beg as if the apple has just fallen on his head. 'This is what this place needs: bird shooters.' He starts scribbling in a file and misses one of the rarest manoeuvres in the history of aviation.

Pak One's nose dips, it goes into a steep dive, then the nose rises up and the plane starts to climb again. Like an airborne roller coaster, Pak One is treading an invisible wave in the hot August air. Up and down and then up again.

The phenomenon is called phugoid.

Flying sluggishly, the crow surfs the hot air currents. Having eaten his own weight in mangoes, the crow can barely move his wings. His beak droops, his eyes half close, his wings flap in slow motion. The crow is wondering why he has left his sanctuary in the mango orchard. He thinks of turning back and spending the rest of the day in the orchard. He tucks his right wing under his body and goes into a lazy circle to turn back. Suddenly the crow finds himself somersaulting through the air, hurtling towards a giant metal whale that is sucking in all the air in the world. The crow has a very lucky escape when he dips below the propeller that is slicing air at a speed of fifteen hundred revolutions per minute. But that will prove to be his last stroke of luck. The crow hurtles through the engine, spins with the intake cycle and is sucked into a side duct; his tiny shriek is drowned out by the roar of the engine.

A pilot on a routine C130 flight would not even give a second glance to a crow in its path and carry on flying. A pilot flying Pak One would try to steer clear of it. When you are flying the President (and the US ambassador) you try to stay away from any hazards even when the risk ratio might be that of an ant and an elephant squaring up to each other. Sweating profusely, the pilot curses the inherent stupidity of the army generals and puts the aircraft into a shallow dive. He knows he has not avoided the bird hit, when the pressure needle monitoring his port engine suddenly dips and the air conditioning is switched on automatically. A refreshing puff of cold air send shivers through his sweat-soaked spine. A whiff of lavender makes him forget his orders to keep the air conditioning off.

General Zia feels the plane going into a dive, unhooks his safety belt and stands up. He is suddenly clear in his head that the time has come to show the buggers who is in charge around here. Eleven years, he thinks. Can you rule Allah's people for eleven years if Allah is not on your side?

General Zia stands firm, hands on his hips, like a commander on a turbulent sea. His audience slide in their seats and find themselves pinned against each other like people in a nasty turn on a roller coaster.

General Zia flings his right arm backwards and then brings it up slowly, like a baseball pitcher explaining his action to a bunch of children. He raises a fist and out of this fist comes his index finger. 'This plane, by the will of Allah, will go up.' He brings his index finger up as if pulling the nose of the plane up with his fingertip. They all watch, first in relief and then in horror, as the plane actually starts to go up again. They slide backwards. Arnold Raphel's head is on General Akhtar's shoulder for a moment. He excuses himself and tightens his safety belt.

General Zia sits down, slaps his thighs with both his hands and looks around, expecting applause.

General Akhtar changes his mind and thinks maybe all his life without knowing it he has been serving a saint, a miracle maker. He looks at General Zia with reverence and thinks maybe he should confess to what he has done and General Zia will be able to undo it. Turn the VX gas in the air-freshener tube back into lavender vapours. Then he stops himself and thinks if General Zia really was a saint, he would know that the plane's pilots are dead by now. VX gas takes two minutes to paralyse, another minute to kill. If you are flying Pak One you can't really do much in that one minute. If General Zia is really a saint, maybe he can bring the pilots back from the dead.

The air-conditioning ducts hiss into life.

General Akhtar was hoping death to announce itself with a whiff of lavender but what he smells is a dead bird's smell.

He is still thinking about how to articulate this problem when the plane's nose dips and it goes down into another dive.

The back door of the VIP pod opens. Loadmaster Fayyaz asks, 'Shall I serve the mangoes, sir?'

'What a vulgar word? What the hell is phugoid?' General Beg is suddenly very curious.

'It's just what an aeroplane does when its controls are neutral. The plane will start going down. But when it goes down beyond a certain angle, its internal axis will correct itself and the plane will start going up again. Then it will go down again. But before that it will go up. Until somebody takes the controls again.'

'How do you know all this?'

'I studied it in my Aerodynamics class.'

'Why are the controls neutral? Why is nobody flying this bloody plane?' he asks me.

Why?

'Pak One. Come in, Pak One. Pak One.' The air traffic controller's voice is on the verge of tears.

Bannon's voice comes over the headphones. 'Jesus, fucking Christ. These zoomies are sleeping. No. They are dead. The pilots are dead. We are all fucking dead.' He chokes on his last sentence and the only sound that comes over the headphones is electrical static.

General Zia's eyes are ablaze at his own miraculous powers. 'I'll teach the buggers. Look, it will go up again. Look. Here it goes. Look.' He raises his index finger in the air. The plane keeps going down.

Some of the passengers in the VIP pod are sprawled on the carpet now. General Akhtar keeps sitting in his seat. Keeps his safety belt on. Waiting for another miracle.

General Zia raises both his index fingers in the air like an amateur bhangra dancer and shouts: 'Now tell me who is trying to kill me? You think you can kill me? Look who is dying now.'

Tapeworms are eating through General Zia's heart now. The krait's poison has dulled his pain but he can feel his innards being torn apart. He inhales the cold air-conditioned air in an attempt to hold on to life. He breathes in VX gas.

If they are all trying to kill General Zia, who is trying to kill them?

Before I turn to God, I scream at General Beg, 'Sir, please do something. The plane is going down. The pilots are dead. Did you hear that?'

General Beg throws his hands in the air. 'What can I do? Who is the aerodynamics expert around here?'

He removes his Ray-Bans and looks out of the window. He doesn't seem very worried.

God, I don't want to be one of those people who turn to You only when their ass is on the line. I don't promise anything. It's not the time to make rash commitments but if You can save one person on that plane let it be Obaid. Please God, let it be Obaid. If there is a parachute on that plane, give it to him. If there are any miracles left in Your power let them happen now. And then we'll talk. I'll always talk to You. I'll always listen to You.

I open my eyes and see Pak's One's tail whiplashing out of a giant ball of orange fire.

First, there is the thunder of seventy-eight tonnes of metal and fuel and cargo propelled by four 4300 horsepower engines colliding, skidding, against the hot desert sand, titanium joints pulling at each other, resisting and then letting go; fuel tanks, full to capacity, boil over at impact and then burst. The desert receives a shower of metal and flesh and sundry objects. It lasts no more than four minutes. Medals go flying like a handful of gold coins flung from the sky, military boots shining on the outside and blood dripping from severed feet, peaked caps hurled through the air like Frisbees. The plane coughs out its secrets: wallets with children's smiling pictures, half-finished letters to

434

mistresses, flight manuals with emergency procedures marked in red, golden uniform buttons with crossed swords insignias, a red sash with the army, navy and air force logos sails through the air, a hand clenched into a fist, bottles of mineral water still intact, fine china crockery with presidential crests, titanium plates still bubbling away at the edges, dead altimeters, gyroscopes still pointing towards Islamabad, a pair of Peshawari slippers, an oil-stained overall with its nameplate still intact; a part of the landing gear rolls and comes to halt against a headless torso in a navy-blue blazer.

Three minutes later the desert receives another shower: twenty thousand litres of A-grade aviation fuel splashes in the air, combusts itself and comes back to the desert. It's a monsoon from hell.

And the flesh; all kinds of flesh: brown melting into white, ligaments, cartilages, flesh ripped from bones, parched flesh, charred flesh; body parts strewn around like discarded dishes at a cannibals' feast.

The charred pages of a slim book, a hand gripping the spine, a thumb with a half-grown nail inserted firmly into the last page.

When Pakistan National Television abruptly interrupts an early-evening soap opera and starts to play a recitation from the Quran, the First Lady waits for a few minutes. This is usually a preamble to breaking news. But the mullah doing the recitation has chosen the longest surah from the Quran and the First Lady knows that he will go on for a couple of hours. The First Lady curses the Information Minister and decides to do some house chores. Her first stop is her husband's bedroom. She picks up the glass of milk from the side table, then puts it back when she notices a black spot on the bed sheet. She looks at it closely and curls her nose at the spot of blood. 'Poor man is sick.' The First Lady feels a pang of guilt which turns into anger and then utter hopelessness. 'He is getting old. He should retire on health grounds if nothing else.' But she has known him for too long to harbour any hopes of a serene retirement life. The First Lady picks up the new issue of *Reader's Digest* from the side table. There is a cover story about how to put your life back together after your husband has cheated on you. Marriage therapy? she wonders.

Not for me, she thinks, throwing the blood-stained sheet into the laundry basket.

Our Cessna circles the ball of orange fire. My eyes scan the horizon for a parachute, then the desert for a lonely figure walking away from the fire and smoke. The sky is clear blue and the desert around the ball of fire and flying debris is empty and indifferent; no one is walking out of this inferno. The pilot doesn't have to wait long for his instructions. 'It doesn't look good. There is no point landing here.' General Beg has made up his mind. 'We need to get back to Islamabad.'

He ignores my head banging at the back of his seat. 'No, we cannot keep going in circles and have one more look. No, young man, we are not dropping you off here. There is nothing to look for. Come on, chin up. Behave like a soldier. We have a country to run.'

The last phase of Code Red kicks into action and the desert is assaulted by emergency vehicles of every possible size and description. Trucks full of ordinary soldiers with mission unknown, armoured cars with machine guns cocked, ambulances with oxygen cylinders at the ready, commandos in open-topped jeeps, fire engines with red helmets hanging out the doors, buses full of aircraft technicians as if Pak One has suffered a minor mechanical failure. Barricades are set up, emergency communication systems start crackling with eager voices, miles of red tape are strung around the scene of the crash.

A catering van pulls up as if the dead might feel hungry and ask for an afternoon snack.

A soldier wearing a white mask walks through the rubble carefully, trying to avoid trampling the body parts, picking his way through the pieces of smouldering metal and documents stamped secret, his eyes searching for a sign that would confirm what people in Islamabad want him to confirm. He wonders why anyone would need a confirmation from a scene as hopeless as this. But Pakistan National Television will keep playing the recitation from Quran, the flag will stay at full mast, the rumours will spread across the country but not be confirmed until the evidence is found. The First Lady will not be informed until they have definite proof.

The soldier trips on a decapitated head with glistening hair parted in the middle and finds what he was looking for.

A strange way to get killed, he thinks. It seems like he died many times over. A face broken off just above the nose, moustache half burnt but still twirled, lips and chin melted away to reveal a set of shiny white teeth, frozen in an eternal mocking grin.

As he bends down to pick up his piece of evidence, he notices a copy of the Quran, open in the middle and intact. Not a scratch on it, not a lick of fire or smoke. Before he kisses the Quran and closes it carefully he reads the verse on the page that is open in front of him and tries to recall a half-remembered story about an ancient prophet.

لَا إِلَـٰهَ إِلَّا أَنتَ سُبْحَـٰنَكَ إِنِّى كُنتُ مِنَ ٱلظَّـٰلِمِينَ

ACKNOWLEDGEMENTS

Books, people, places that have inspired and helped during the writing of this alleged novel. They are in no way responsible for the contents of this book, though.

Sargodha. *Fateh*. Patricia Duncker. Andrew Cowan. Patricia. Richard Holmes. Anne. Masood. Mirza. Sam. Abbas and Barry. Norwich. Gordon House. Michèle Roberts. Arif. Arif. Sara Wajid. Nick. Emily. Diana. Anu. Asad Mohammed Khan. *The Bear Trap*. Lyceum. Bajwa. *Charlie Wilson's War*. *Ghost Wars*. Abdullah Hussain. Anne. Shafi. Raja. Elissa. Dr Manzur Ejaz. *Aaj*. Victoria Shepherd. *The Feast of the Goat*. Laura. *Newsline*. Minnie Singh. *Chronicle of a Death Foretold*.

Ann Gagliardi and Clare Alexander, the best readers one could ask for.